The Superintendent's Daughter

Also by Marjorie Eccles

The Superintendent's Daughter

A Gil Mayo Mystery

Marjorie Eccles

THOMAS DUNNE BOOKS
St. Martin's Minotaur
New York

THOMAS DUNNE BOOKS.
An imprint of St. Martin's Press.

THE SUPERINTENDENT'S DAUGHTER. Copyright © 1999 by Marjorie
Eccles. All rights reserved. Printed in the United States of
America. No part of this book may be used or reproduced in
any manner whatsoever without written permission except in
the case of brief quotations embodied in critical articles or
reviews. For information, address St. Martin's Press, 175 Fifth
Avenue, New York, N.Y. 10010.

www.minotaurbooks.com

ISBN 0-312-25338-9

First published in Great Britain by Constable & Company
Limited

First U.S. Edition: December 2000

10 9 8 7 6 5 4 3 2 1

1

Orbury House 14th April

Hi, Jools!

Well, you suggested it, so I'm taking you at your word! I'm going to write down everything that's happened since we last met and send it on to you. On second thoughts, perhaps not <u>quite</u> everything. Everyone has to have secrets, even you and I, and there's a part of me I can't share with anyone. That's for my diary, or what I call my diary for want of a better name – a lovely thick, leatherbound book which Max gave me when he knew that I'd once had ambitions to become a writer. He said if I recorded all my thoughts and ideas, it would become a habit I could make use of.

Remember how I told Miss Thomas when we were leaving school that's what I wanted to be – a writer, or maybe a journalist? (Which wasn't neccesarily the same thing, as my dad remarked cynically!) And how Tank Engine only raised her eyebrows and commented in that put-down way she had, 'Then you'll have to aquire a great deal more application, Kathryn, not to mention improving your grammar and learning how to spell!' and steamed off, chugging away on her thick legs. I don't believe she was right, except perhaps about the application! My spelling's not as bad as all that, and I think imagination counts for much more – which I've plenty of – and being able to comunicate. Most people wouldn't recognise a perfectly grammatical sentence if it jumped up and bit them anyway, and I've never had any trouble letting people know exactly what I mean, have I?

Old Tank would be delighted to know that five years later she's been proved right. I haven't made it as a writer so I don't suppose I shall now. I really did try for a while, and I'm sure I could have done it if I'd had more time. But I hadn't realised it was such hard labour and there's always been something else to do, you know how it is, like helping Mum make up the floral arrangements in the shop, delivering them, visiting Dad . . . and in between, having a good time, I have to say! All of which seems so trivial, now that I've discovered what it means to make a real comittment.

What comittment is this? I hear you say. Well, it's something so big and wonderful and amazing I can hardly believe it myself. I can't tell you yet because it's on hold, for the moment, with the terrible trouble that Dad's in, though I'm longing to tell him, so that he can share my happiness . . .

Sorry – that isn't precisley true, and I've promised myself that every word I write to you will be a faithful record of my feelings. The truth is, I don't really want to tell anyone at all yet, I want to hug it to myself a bit longer, but especially not Dad, because I'm afraid that deep down he wouldn't see it as we do, he'd be angry and upset, and I can't do that to him. Everything would be spoiled, for all of us, and that would be so sad. So I shall really really try to keep our secret. You'll be the first to know about it, after I've found a way to tell him, I swear it.

I've plenty to do here at Orbury, what with one thing and another, but all the same, there are times when I'm at a loose end. When I'm free, with nothing to do, mixed-up thoughts start churning around in my head and even when I'm busy, they stop me keeping my mind on what I'm doing, which could be dangerous for Dad. Yesterday Dunston – she's the bossy nurse from the agency – bawled me out for forgetting to record his medication on the chart, which she needn't have done, because I blamed myself quite enough, thank you!

When he was in hospital, I stared for hours at the clipboard on the bottom of the bed, watching the temperature graph, wishing I knew what the medical things they'd written about him meant. Conolly, Hugh, it said at the top. (He'd be glad to know they'd missed out the Evelyn, given him for his father, a name he's always found embarrassing, wouldn't any man?) Religion, C of E. (Last known attendence, my christening, I might add!) Date of birth, 29.5.1950. (In County Cork, Ireland, though he left when he was three and has never been back.) Date of admission. Details of medication, pulse rate, all the other intimate details.

Not much to sum up my father, the man Mum chucked out after just one affair too many, but who I dearly love. It doesn't take any account of what he's really like, a lovely man in spite of everything.

I dare say Mum's right, he wasn't a good husband, but he looked after me – and Jamie, of course – better than some fathers who are there all the time. He's always kept in close touch with us – and with Mum for that matter – though she keeps him at arm's length, as if she's frightened she'll weaken if she lets him get too near.

I don't want to dwell on what Dad's suffering, through no fault of his own. When I think of how he enjoyed life, what fun he was to be with, it makes me feel depressed and angry, which I don't want him to see. He notices too much as it is. We talk when he's feeling up to it, he watches television until he falls asleep, sometimes I read to him and even though he's in so much pain for a lot of the time, we manage to laugh together, as we always used to, before Terri.

She *would* be called Terri, with an i, wouldn't she? Anyhow, that's how I think of it, before Terri. The happy times we used to have before he went completely bananas and actually married her, the last of his 'floozies' as Mum called them. He won't talk about her, and why should he? I wouldn't want to if it was me. She was driving the Ferrari after that party they'd been to. She was the lucky one, as usual, killed outright. Whereas Dad – well, the car was a write-off after she drove it into that oncoming oil tanker and he broke his pelvis and both legs, among other things.

He was in the Intensive Care unit of Lavenstock General for a while where they took him after the accident, but they fixed him up eventually. He should have been OK, broken bones mend, even vital organs can be repaired, but during those tests they always do in hospital, they discovered he also had cancer, and that it was very advanced. I've thought since that he must have known something was wrong before that, but was scared to go and see a doctor and have it confirmed. There was nothing more they could do for him by keeping him in at that stage, so he wasn't justified in occupying a bed that was needed for someone else. They were very kind and put it tactfully but that was what it amounted to.

I didn't want him to be transfered to another hospital, and niether did he, not even a private one, and the thought of a hospice was dire, but he refused to go back to that penthouse flat where he and Terri had lived. The flat's big enough, but I suppose it held too many memories and anyway, all those naff furnishings she stuffed the place with made it a totally unsuitable place for nursing a sick man in. Of course, it was left to Max to think of the obvious solution. It was just so generous of him to make the offer. A typical Max gesture, we both agreed.

Max Fisher is Dad's business partner and closest friend. He's brilliant. To me, as well as Dad. He lives here in Orbury House, which

7

is a big Georgian house in extensive grounds which he and Dad bought in a grotty condition and did up as offices when their business began to get off the ground. Max didn't need to be careful about the money, seeing how rich he is, but Dad did. Fisher-Conolly Security Systems is what the company is called, and after a shaky start, it took off like an Exoset missile. Max lives in the part of the house which isn't offices. Even that's far too big for one person living alone, but knowing Max, I should think he gains some sort of tax consession from the arrangement! Dad's room and mine are in a sort of wing, and Max is careful not to overdo his daily visits, but when I need a break, when it all gets too much for me, I can go to his part of the house and listen to him playing his piano or relax with a swim in the indoor pool he's had installed. Best of all is when we just sit quietly and read, or talk. It's amazing how he can open my mind to other possibilities, as he has done so often since I came to live here ... like how my life can take any direction I want it to, in the same way as he's always controlled his own life. He has a very forceful personality and can make you believe anything's possible. The other day, I picked up the Times crossword which he'd nearly finished. He says doing crosswords will help my spelling. In one across, four words, he'd written 'candle to the sun', which he said was a quotation. 'That's me,' I remarked jokingly. 'What's you?' he said. 'Candle to the sun – me and you.' He was quite sharp, for him, when he realised what I meant. 'Don't say things like that, Kat! Those sort of anallergies have a way of coming back at you. Too near the sun and you're liable to get your wings singed.'

Dad of course protested when Max first suggested that he should come here, the usual things about not being a burden, and invading his privacy and so on, but Max just waved them aside. Dad also argued a bit when I insisted on moving in here as well, to help look after him. But when I reminded him that I wasn't expecting to take over the nursing, and I should be here mostly just for the company, that he'd be doing _me_ a favour in letting me stay with him, he eventually gave in. In fact I do quite a lot for him, the non-technical stuff that is, and look after him during the day if Dunston's not here. It's what I want to do, and it means the nursing bills are less, which seems to comfort him.

'Well, you don't make money by giving it away,' my mother used to say sarcastically, which wasn't fair because nobody is more openhanded than Dad, unless it's Max. But she was mostly refering to his insistance on her taking out of Orlando's only the percentage according

8

to profits that they'd agreed on when he bought the shop and let her run it. Like a lot of self-made people, he's careful with what he has, though he's never been tight-fisted with me. Just the opposite! Look at the Sierra Cosworth he bought me for my eighteenth. It's still going strong after four years, still the envy of all our friends (the male element especially!) They all think I'm spoilt. I remember even you said so at the time, though I know you understand that money for its own sake hasn't ever meant all that much to me. I can take it or leave it. If that sounds improbable in view of how people seem to see me ... well, that's how it is!

All this about me – but I haven't forgotten that letter of yours. Wow! And I thought I had problems! I'm sorry I haven't mentioned it before, but I've thought about it for two days and I'm still amazed. I don't know what to say to you. I can see why you haven't written to me for so long. You're in a state, I can tell, which also amazes me. I never knew anyone in my life so together as you used to be. Even physics exams, though you were worse at physics than me, didn't freak you out. I want to try and help, though as you know, I'm not one for giving advise, being so scatty I'm usually the one who needs it! Anyway, I don't really think you need me to tell you what to do. Reading between the lines, I think you've already decided, and for what it's worth, my opinion is that it's the only possible thing to do. Nobody, but nobody, needs hassle like that. Especially you.

Old friends are the best friends, Dad says. Like he and Max have known each other for yonks, even before they were at UCL together. When he has the energy to talk, it's mostly about his time at university and the friends he made there. I think that was the happiest time of his life. He was free to do as he wanted, and I gather that didn't include much work!

'Over twenty-five years ago now, Kat,' he said the other day. 'The Me generation they're calling us now. But you can't imagine the freedom we felt!' He added something I imagine must be a quotation, something about being young, and to be alive was very heaven. And then he laughed. 'See, Kat, my time at university wasn't all wasted. I'm not entirely the money-making phillistine your mother imagines!' He's right. He's a very surprising person, my father.

Most of his time there must have been wasted, though, because he only achieved a third class degree, which he says is worse than useless, and then married Mum immediately after he left. I suppose there could be bigger disasters, but off-hand I can't think of any!! They mix about as well as oil and water. She says she was taken in by his good looks and his promises, when all he wanted was sex, though he says he did love her. I can see her point. Men often confuse sex with love, and Dad's never been one to hide the fact that he finds women attractive – and vice versa. He's good looking, sure, I know you'll agree with that. A big man, but so gentle with it, and I'm sure it's that which women like even more. And from photographs I've seen, Mum must have been quite sexy when she was young. All those short tennis skirts with frilly knickers!

She was really good at tennis, still is. She could have gone proffessional if she hadn't married Dad. Women used to do that, didn't they? Amazingly, some of them still do – get married and tied up with a bunch of kids, I mean, wave goodbye to their freedom without a thought, even the ones who were set on careers. I met Sharon Fairbrother last week, the one who used to get A plus for everything. You should have seen her! Two toddlers in a twin pushchair and another just about to put in an appearance on the scene, by the looks of her. Her ankles were all swolen and her hair was a complete mess! Catch me!

I mean, look at Mum. First there was me, then Jamie. And Dad even then having his bits on the side, if she's to be beleived. Then the divorce and years of skimping and scraping, taking whatever job she could get that would enable her to look after me and Jamie as well. Dad hadn't made his money then.

But later, when he did, he bought Orlando's and made her the offer of running it for him. Mum accepted. 'Somebody in my position can't afford to be too proud,' she said, with that bitter little smile that's become a permanent feature now. It wasn't an offer to be sneezed at, though, and it shows that Dad still had some good feelings towards her. Because he didn't just go out and buy a flower shop out of the blue, did he? He'd looked around and thought about it and seen it as a way he could help her without her losing face. There's that nice flat over the shop, and the more sucessfull the shop has become, the more money she's been able to take from the profits. I think at one time she became a little bit greedy and kept nagging him for a bigger share, because its sucess was down to her and she knew that however much she was entitled to, it stood to reason he was getting more. Plus, he was coiling it in in other directions. By then Fisher-Conolly Security

10

Systems were being installed all over the country. That makes it sound as though he's a millionare, which he never would have been. Whatever he makes, he spends. He never holds on to money long enough for it to have the chance to stick to his fingers.

I've just read back what I've written and it looks OK to me, my spelling I mean. Tank Engine used to say I should use a dictionary and check, but that only works if you know which word is wrong. In which case you wouldn't need a dictionary, would you?

Your idea of getting me to write everything down was brilliant. I don't know why I didn't think of it myself. It's very good therepy. I feel better already, in fact I could go on, but I want to get this in the post to you. I feel sort of lost without you to talk to, like we used to for half the night. Maybe I should ring you, but I don't think I'd better, it may put you in an awkward position. And it would be taking advantage of Max. America's a long way off and when we start talking, we never know when to stop, as Mum will vouch!!

I'm looking forward to hearing what you've decided to do. I bet I'm right.

Luv,

2

Lightning flashed, thunder rumbled. Rain streamed down the windows, pounded on to the flat roof of the Lavenstock Division Police Headquarters, continuing the torrential downpours of the previous two weeks. ' "Records show that it is likely to have been the wettest June this century, possibly since records began. The prospects for Wimbledon fortnight are not good," ' Detective Superintendent Gil Mayo read out of the *Guardian*.

His temper not improved by blinding statements of the obvious, he threw down the offending paper. 'Wimbledon – so what? What about Saturday's fête?'

His inspector, Abigail Moon, didn't think it prudent to point out, even jokingly, that the *Guardian* was hardly likely to be unduly concerned with the fate of a fête in a small Black Country town, however important it was to Lavenstock.

Mayo loosened his tie. The air-conditioning was on the blink yet again. Intermittent clanking noises throughout the day, along with blasts of hot air, had so far brought forth no result, and with the windows closed against the rain, the tropical plant house at the Botanical Gardens had nothing on the offices here. 'Is somebody going to tell those repairmen to turn that damn system off altogether, or do I have to do it myself?' he demanded.

'They can't,' Abigail said. 'They have to leave it on to test it.'

'They need to test it to know hot air's coming out instead of cold?'

Abigail sighed, murmured something non-committal and made a tactical withdrawal. When Mayo was in this mood – unusual but not entirely unheard-of – there was no reasoning with him, although she'd every sympathy with him this time. He had a meeting due this afternoon, sticky enough without these sort of problems. And the fête on Saturday had already built up into a big headache.

Fanning her face, she went back to her own office, the faulty air-conditioning making it marginally hotter than her boss's upstairs, though she hadn't mentioned that to him, either. Flaming June! The first day of Wimbledon. People expecting cloudless skies, temperatures in the eighties, a scorching sun that would grill the spectators at the Centre court to a crisp, burn the grass off and melt the ice-cream. No chance.

More importantly for Lavenstock, the town was currently acting host to a delegation from its twin town in France, and a big outdoor event was scheduled for Saturday: a pipe-and-drum parade led by the Ajax-Stennet Component Company band, barbecues, street theatre, a funfair, a British cheese and wine stall ... the lot. A big influx of young French people had accompanied the delegation, staying with families as part of the exchange ritual, and every available police officer had been mustered, including CID, to be posted on the look-out for troublemakers, lager louts, drug-pushers and so on. A wet and miserable day would double everyone's grief.

It was a shame, really. A concerted effort had meant that the town ought to have looked at its very best. Shopkeepers had co-operated and suitably dressed their windows in English rural fashion, and anything unsightly had been carted away. The Parks Department had laboured mightily with the municipal gardens, bringing the geraniums and French marigolds to the point where you needed sun-glasses to look at them, the central flowerbed in the Town Hall square had been planted with a red, white and blue *tricolore* in lobelia, alyssum and busy lizzies. And now – the foreign visitors were resignedly clearing the shops and the market stalls out of plastic macs and umbrellas, envying the stolidity of their British counterparts, who were in fact, Abigail suspected, more comfortable with this kind of thing and were settling down to make the best of it ... Pity about the tennis, of course (especially as we had a chance of winning for the first time in forty years), and what about the ladies' hats at Ascot? It could be a disaster for the coming Test Match, too, but it was great for the gardens.

'Damn the gardens!' Mayo grumbled, sweating.

Possibly the only person in the whole of Lavenstock police station who was comfortable today was the suspect being inter-rogated in Interview Room 3, and that was only because, in the face of logic, you somehow didn't expect anyone with a black skin to mind the heat. At any rate, Dustin Small was acting cool, in more senses than one – he'd already been questioned for an hour on the subject of a batch of electrical goods stolen from a warehouse and their eventual appearance at various car-boot sales, and it wasn't bothering him any. He tipped his chair on to its two back legs, completely at ease, which was more than DC Keith Farrar was, his immaculate image somewhat tarnished by the sweat that had made his blond, blow-dried hair limp as wet string, and was making unsightly damp patches under the arms of his Armani-style shirt.

'Come on, Dustin, names! You're wasting everybody's time. Tell us who the others were and let's get this over with. *We* know you're in it up to the neck, *you* know, so do us all a favour.'

13

'If you say so,' replied Dustin negligently, in broadest Black Country. 'But you'll have to prove it, mate, won'tcha?' He leaned further back. He'd have put his feet up on the table, only he knew from past experience that DC Fah-rah wasn't such a mug as he looked.

Farrar, unwilling to let a suspect – especially a scrote like Small – see he was rattled, decided to terminate the interview. After which, he escorted Dustin back to his cell. Being downstairs, on the north side, it was unarguably the coolest place in the building. 'Any chance of a cuppa?' asked Dustin, settling himself on the bed for a relaxing siesta, his hands linked behind his head.

Farrar gave him a disgusted look and toiled back through the sweltering corridors, picking up a cold drink for himself from the dispenser on the way. Praise be, still working! He took it back to the CID room, where Jenny Platt was desultorily writing a report. Her face glowed with the heat and her curls stuck damply to her forehead, but she still looked crisp and newly ironed in a sleeveless white blouse and cotton skirt.

'That Dustin!' Farrar said, sinking down on to his chair. 'God give me strength.'

The day wore on.

Upstairs, Mayo saw the last of his visitors out and sat down to get his thoughts in order before clearing his desk and heading for home. The serial clunks and groans of the day still punctuated his reflections. A fan had been brought into his office, but all it did was blow his papers about and stir the hot air, recently made more intolerable by the cigarette smoke from Peggy Lowden's little black cigars. His office was usually a no-go area for smokers and Ms Lowden knew this as well as anyone, but she was a member of the local Police Authority, as well as being chairman of the Community Relations Committee, and had taken advantage of the fact that today's meeting had been about Saturday's arrangements and consequently touchy, from his point of view.

The telephone rang: on the other end was Alex, refreshing as a draught of cool water. His irritation dissolved like Alka Seltzer.

'Gil, any chance of you not being late tonight?' A simple question, without any hint of criticism. As an ex-police officer herself, Alex Jones was constantly aware of the possibility of being overtaken by events.

'Do my best, love. But why tonight, in particular?'

'Something rather special's cooking.'

'In that case, I'll do better than try. In fact, I'm on my way now, this minute.'

'My, I must be improving!'

'Like good wine, all the time.'

They both knew he wasn't referring to her cooking, which was never going to be anything more than in the middling class, despite well-intentioned efforts to improve. He was smiling at the lilt in her voice as he put down the receiver. It was good that she was back on course, after a year of personal trauma. Not being a woman, he'd no idea how it could possibly feel to lose the frail life taking form within your body, but he knew, by God he knew, how a man felt to see the woman he loved suffering. He wished sadly that he could have helped her more, but he always doubted his own abilities when it came to expressing sympathy, or to initiating affection. Unless he could demonstrate either in practical terms he was rudderless. He could only hope and believe that Alex had understood.

It was still throwing it down as he joined the traffic queue in the overburdened one-way system, and he was forced to crawl along with his windows steaming up. As he wound the nearside one down, the smells of gassy exhaust fumes and hot metal and the stink of malt and hops from the brewery rolled in. What a summer! When you might reasonably expect to go home and enjoy a bottle of cold white wine and a light meal under the trees in the garden. Or perhaps not. The lawn would be sending out mute reproaches that it needed mowing – again. After all this rain, it was growing faster than the British economy, and neither was good news.

Grass-cutting on a regular basis was now a fact of life for Mayo, a mega sacrifice, seeing how little he liked gardening, that he knew virtually nothing about it and didn't want to know any more. It had originally come about in answer to a silent cry for help from his elderly landlady, who owned the house where he and Alex occupied the top flat. Miss Vickers had been head-mistress of the girls' school before her retirement and had decided ideas about order and discipline. An untidy garden distressed her almost as much as a split infinitive or a sentence ending with a preposition. But her brother, who usually tended it, had suffered a stroke. Mayo had come across her one evening in spring struggling valiantly with the hopelessly entangled garden hose. Though he'd occasionally pushed the lawn mower around to help the old couple ever since he came to live in the flat, given time and opportunity, he'd been mortified that he hadn't thought of volunteering further assistance now. Hence the sackcloth and ashes, the regular chore.

'It's all getting too much for me, Gil,' Freda Vickers had admitted, after he'd got the hose wound tidily back on its reel and they were sitting with a cup of so-called coffee in her kitchen. She was without doubt the world's worst coffee maker, but she meant it kindly and he'd learned to let it cool so that he could get it down without actually letting it touch his taste buds. 'Not only the garden, but the house as well. That's why I've never relet the first floor after the Brownlows left. It's the responsibility of it all, more than anything, and Gerald, when he comes out of hospital, isn't going to be able to do much. We're seriously thinking of buying one of those new bungalows they've built out towards Over Kennet.' She sipped reflectively. 'Of course, we'd have to sell this house. I think it'll go quickly – we shan't be greedy about the price.' Before he could stop her, she'd topped his coffee up with more scalding, milky mixture, so weak he felt he ought to be saying the last rites over it. 'It was such a lovely house before it was split up,' she added with apparent inconsequentiality.

He'd reported the conversation to Alex and, the seed having been sown, it didn't take long before the idea of buying the house when Freda Vickers put it on the market began to take root in Alex's mind.

'It's too big,' he objected.

'If you mean it'll give us more room to spread out, not to mention breathe, OK, it's big. I'd prefer to say generously proportioned, myself. It has such a lovely feel to it. You'll be

16

able to have a study, and up here will be spot on for my painting.'

And empty bedrooms, which there was no chance of filling. Except by one of those children who had mysteriously taken to appearing for short stays. Like the widowed WPC Lawson's little boy when she had enforced overtime. Like other children who were taken out by Alex for the day, looked after for the weekend – and no shortage of them in these days of one-parent families.

But Alex was already deep in love with the idea of the house and anything that could bring the sparkle back to her eyes he could become in love with, too. He hadn't seen her so animated for months.

'What do I need a study for, for God's sake?' he grumbled, tokenly.

'Somewhere to keep all your clocks together,' she suggested with magnificent timing, as they all began to chime, strike or bong the hour, beginning with the longcase that took up most of the tiny hallway and ending with the silvery chime of the porcelain mantel clock. Nicer for everyone, was the subtext, as she waited for the dissonance to die down so that she could continue. 'We can even have visitors – occasionally. '

There was a great deal more in this vein, which might have alarmed Mayo, had he not also been starting to feel enthusiastic, despite himself. He'd never noticed the limitations of the flat when he'd lived there alone, or before that, with his daughter Julie, but he'd begun to see its inadequacies since Alex had come to share with him. He had, from time to time, made desultory inquiries into buying something better, but the prices had frightened the life out of him and he'd been in no rush to make his mind up to move. He was a man whose native Yorkshire caution had accustomed him to taking a considered view. But before he knew where he was, the Vickers had gone, he'd signed on the dotted line and work had begun on the ground floor they'd vacated. The house had always been kept in excellent structural order but, said Alex, it needed a revamp as far as fittings and decorations were concerned. He knew when he was beaten and resigned himself to seeing more of her sister about the place than he cared to. Unavoidable, this, since Lois would be as eager to get her teeth into this one as Alex. In partnership, they ran Interiors, a home designers' business that was the *dernier cri* as far as Lavenstock was concerned, but altogether too rich for Mayo's digestion.

The old lady had begged one favour of them before she left: that she would be allowed to leave behind the ancient, motheaten grey cat she called Moses. 'He's too old to settle in a new place – and really, he almost lives with you already.'

'Or tries to,' Mayo said.

So Moses's Machiavellian campaign to be accepted into the Mayo household had paid off at last, aided and abetted by Alex, who wasn't above letting him into the flat when Mayo wasn't there, and sometimes when he was. The damned cat now claimed what he'd always known to be his rightful place on the hearthrug, where he reigned supreme, his smugly slitted eyes resting unblinkingly on an outwitted Mayo, for years the unreciprocating object of his feline affections.

Mayo let himself in through the front door into the smell of new paint, nearly falling over a pile of decorators' paint pots, planks and dust sheets. That meant the kitchen was in the latter stages of being finished, but he wouldn't spoil Alex's pleasure by inspecting the work before she could take him on a conducted tour. He'd grumbled at first that he could see this decorating lark spinning out into the winter, but Alex had shown that she'd no intention of letting the workforce get away with any such thing. Co-ordinating plumbers, decorators and builders with a mixture of joking and coercion was second nature to her now and under her supervision the work was going briskly ahead with, he had to admit, as little fuss as you could expect. Meanwhile, they were continuing to live in the upstairs flat, in unaccustomed chaos, or as much chaos as Alex was capable of allowing, which was to say it was slightly untidy, with samples of wallpaper, furnishing fabrics and paint charts scattered on one or two surfaces.

He was brought to a halt by the sound of voices behind the closed door of the sitting-room as he arrived at the top of the stairs. Female voices and laughter. He swore. Alex hadn't said anything about visitors so someone must have dropped in since

18

she'd telephoned him. He deeply hoped it wasn't her sister. Lois was strong medicine, to be taken in measured doses.

He heard the laughter again and some sixth sense told him, even before he opened the door, who it was in the room with Alex. Before he had time to argue with himself that it was unlikely in the extreme, he had the door opened and there she was: his energetic and decisive mother.

Mayo took most things in his stride, but he was very much taken aback to see her. Her visits were usually planned affairs, by reason of the distance between Lavenstock and her home in Yorkshire, involving a half-way stop with Mayo's sister.

He stepped inside the door amid the flurry of greetings, and the deafening welcome of Bert, the raucous fourth member of the family. He cuffed the side of his cage with a rolled-up newspaper to shut him up. That parrot was getting above himself since Alex had started letting him out of his cage sometimes, in order to enlarge his limited view of life.

In the ensuing quiet, he kissed his mother and said sternly, 'You've never driven down the motorway in this weather!' Though it was sometimes hard to credit it, she was, after all, in her late seventies and although she insisted she was perfectly capable of driving herself back and forth, and ably and regularly demonstrated the fact, it wasn't without some addition to the grey hairs of her children.

'No, I came by train, seeing Prue's in Singapore or somewhere equally ridiculous, so that I couldn't make my usual half-way stop.'

Frances Mayo didn't share her daughter's taste for travel, she refused to be brainwashed into being part of that growing, affluent army of globe-trotting pensioners who were never at home. Her idea of a good holiday was a grand drop of sea air and a good blow once a year at Scarborough.

'Well, I'm glad to see you're learning sense.' He smiled at her.

'Actually, I found it very convenient, and a lot less tiring. Maybe it does make sense for such a long journey – my car has rather a lot of miles on the clock,' she replied, as if the train journey was her own idea and not what he'd been advising for years.

Mayo exchanged glances with Alex above her head, raising

his eyebrows. He didn't quite like to ask Frances what she was doing here at all, but he couldn't help wondering. She was in no hurry to enlighten him.

It came at last. 'Well, Giles,' she said, after they'd finished eating and cleared away, and she'd refused coffee but accepted a cup of tea before departing for the Saracen's, where she'd reserved her usual room. 'What's all this about Julie?'

'Julie?'

'I saw you looking for a letter when you came in.'

She never missed a thing. Never had – skimped homework, torn trousers, illicit cigarette stubs when he was fourteen and had thought it macho to experiment with smoking. And it was true, his eyes had gone straight to the pretty little china toast rack on the mantelpiece. They didn't go in much for toast racks, he and Alex, but it was useful for slotting newly arrived mail into. There was still no letter with a foreign stamp. There hadn't been one for nearly a month now, which was unusual. Julie had always written more or less regularly, and if it hadn't been for the last scribbled postcard, Mayo would have been getting seriously worried, since he had no point of contact with her at the moment. She'd departed from her last known address in America and would let him know when she had another, she wrote. He'd been uneasy with this. He still had a tendency to monitor her life, but Alex had reminded him that Julie was a grown woman, after all, with the right to come and go as she pleased, the right to make her own mistakes.

'I had a very strange phone call from her the other day,' his mother went on.

So that was it. Julie and her grandmother had always been close, distance being no bar. Frances was an ex-junior school teacher, and lived alone in her grey stone house in the small Yorkshire town on the Pennine slopes where she'd taught for so many years, a respected and active figure in the community. She was an unflappable and sensible woman, with a gleam of humour in her eye, and it had always been her grandmother to whom Julie had turned when she needed advice or support after her mother had died. Far from resenting this, Mayo had been glad of it, realising that fathers had their limitations when it came to adolescent girls. It was no surprise that Julie had contacted her grandmother now, but he could only hope it didn't mean she was in trouble. 'She rang from Texas?' he asked.

'So she implied.'

'Implied?'

'Well, somehow I wasn't sure. She asked after Bert,' she added, as if this explained why.

Hearing his name, the parrot – parakeet, to be correct – handsome in his blue, black and crimson livery, who'd been sulking after the outrage on his cage, his beady eyes hooded, began a sideways parade back and forth along his perch, setting up a low-key chuntering, his prelude to the ear-splitting squawks which indicated he was about to upstage everyone else.

'She asked *you* about Bert?'

'That's what I meant about it being a strange call. How should *I* be expected to know anything about his state of health, for goodness' sake? She wasn't really concentrating, didn't have her mind on who she was talking to – saying the first thing that came into her head, I imagine. I had the impression she was wanting to tell me something, but couldn't quite bring herself to do it.'

Julie's attitude had obviously disturbed her much more than she was admitting. What else would have brought her down here on the spur of the moment, when she could quite easily have telephoned? Missing the annual Wakes Fair, no less, the most important date in Steynton's calendar.

'Shut up, Bert, for God's sake give us a break,' Mayo pleaded, as the mutterings from the cage by the window escalated. To no avail. But Moses slowly rose and jumped lithely as a kitten on to a bookcase adjacent to the cage. Reaching out a grey velvet paw, he pushed it through the bars and swung it, giving Bert the feline equivalent of a sharp clout round the ear, so astonishing the parrot that he was immediately rendered mute.

'Did you see that?' Mayo demanded into the blessed silence, his respect for Moses going up several notches, aware for the first time that there might after all be advantages to having the animal in permanent residence.

'He won't do it again if he's any sense, Bert's a bird to bear grudges. He'll have his revenge,' Alex said with a laugh. 'More tea, Frances? I shouldn't worry, you know, first thing Julie always does is ask after Bert, it's automatic. He is her parrot, after all.'

'Not so's you'd notice,' said Mayo, who'd had the bird wished on him as a temporary expedient which had turned permanent, pretty much as the cat had been. He had a feeling, sometimes, that women saw him as a pushover.

'Maybe,' Frances murmured. 'One thing she did say, however. She said she might be back in England soon – but you know, I had a distinct feeling that she might well be here already.'

Mayo gave his mother a sharp glance. 'Then why hasn't she let us know?'

'Oh, you know what young women are.'

Which was precisely why he wasn't reassured. But, if her grandmother was right, Julie was acting very much out of character – though she'd surprised him before now. She'd been all set for a career in catering and then suddenly had dropped out of college and begun wandering all over the globe – well, France, Australia, and latterly Texas, where she'd been helping to run a seafood restaurant on the waterfront at Galveston on the Bay of Mexico.

'Itchy feet. I've got itchy feet, Dad, that's all,' she'd said, when he'd asked her if he was ever going to see her for more than a few days at a time, between continents. But in her last letter she'd written – a phrase or two that had made his heart sing – 'I think I've had enough . . . Maybe it won't be long now before I'm home.'

3

The rain had stopped by the time Maggie Vye left her shared office in the Houses of Parliament and took a taxi home from Westminster. Thankfully shutting the door of her small flat behind her, she threw down her briefcase, kicked off her shoes and loosened the waistband of her skirt – God, that was better! – opened the french windows to the narrow strip behind the house that one day she was going to make attractive with pots and climbers and trellising. When she had time. Up to now, she'd only got as far as picking up a white plastic table and a couple of chairs from Homebase. Life as a backbencher in the Commons tended to preclude such trivial activities as shopping around for garden furniture.

A glance at the paper as she went to pour her evening gin and tonic revealed nothing surprising in the headlines: a leading Conservative had been forced to resign his place on the Privy Council after certain financial shenanigans had come to light. Rain had interrupted play at Wimbledon throughout the day. Prospects for the Test Match were not good. Abandoning the paper, she took her drink outside. The garden smelt sweet, the sour London earth had been cleansed by the soft, warm showers, and traffic fumes absorbed in the rain-soaked air. The fragrance of the exquisite peach-coloured rose that had draped itself over the fence from her neighbour's garden into hers was delicious. A blackbird sang its heart out. She could allow herself a few minutes to savour this best part of her day before making a sandwich and settling down to the enormous pile of work she'd brought home with her, a normal occurrence on the evenings when she wasn't required to be at the House. Far from minding this, she actually looked forward to it, being a self-confessed workaholic, and she always functioned more easily at home than amongst the continual interruptions at Westminster.

Home was a garden flat at the back of a tall, narrow, yellow London brick house in a busy street. The strip of garden with a scruffy apology for a lawn had high surrounding fences and got little sunlight. The four-roomed apartment, including kitchen and bathroom, was dark, too, and cramped. It wasn't a particularly attractive place to live at all, she thought, if we're being honest (and Maggie was nearly always honest, even with herself) but it was all she could afford at the moment, London prices being what they were. And it was hers, wonderfully hers, to live alone in, to work or rest, to eat or not, exactly as she wished.

As the honourable member for her home town of Lavenstock, she'd served several gruelling years as an opposition back-bencher, having been elected by a fairly narrow majority in a by-election caused by the forced resignation of a Conservative cabinet minister, then the sitting member for Lavenstock, over allegations of sleaze. Playing on the voters' disillusionment with their hitherto very popular representative, Maggie had defeated the next candidate the Conservatives had thrown into the ring by taking the high moral line, a squeaky clean stance she'd been at pains to maintain. Since then she'd worked untiringly, and she'd been returned at the general election with a greatly increased majority, not entirely due in her case, she hoped, to the landslide towards Labour. She had recently been asked to serve on a select committee on the environment in Tony Blair's new government and was tipped for possible high office in the not too distant future. It had been hinted that she might have gone further already had she been prepared to be more compromising.

She became aware that the telephone was ringing and, reluctantly putting aside her drink, she went indoors to answer it.

'You are coming up on Thursday, aren't you, Maggie dear?'

'Of course I am, Rollo. Don't I always?'

'Just that I wanted to make a suggestion or two about your speech. At the fête, you know.'

'Yes, Rollo, I do know.' She was presenting the prizes, for God's sake! But Maggie was careful not to allow her asperity to escape down the line. Rollo Forbes was a good party agent, a good man, a loyal friend. He sometimes drove her mad with his pernickety ways, his constant stream of soft, meaningless endearments, but she'd known him for years and he'd helped nurse her through a difficult campaign and continued to support her and look after her interests in the constituency. Unlike most of her male colleagues, Maggie didn't have a spouse at her side and she was unceasingly grateful to Rollo for his support, and she did try, very hard, not to be impatient with him for his constant checking up. Belt and braces, plus string, that was Rollo. What need was there, for instance, for him to check that she'd be in Lavenstock for her surgery, she thought, looking at her watch, running her hand impatiently through her mop of thick hair (once blonde, now ashy), she'd been there from Thursday to Sunday whenever she possibly could, ever since she'd won her seat. Nothing less than an earthquake would have stopped her. Personal ambition was as important to Maggie Vye

24

as it was to every other politician at Westminster, but she also possessed that rather rarer quality: integrity, and a belief that the reason she'd been elected was to serve her constituents. Besides, she couldn't afford to allow her guard to drop, aware that there was still a strong Conservative allegiance in the constituency and support might easily swing the other way.

'I thought you'd like to know I've solved the problem of that fund-raising affair next month,' Rollo announced, sounding pleased. 'Something's turned up. We've found another host, another venue.'

'Such as who, where?' Maggie had her own ideas about salmon, strawberry and champagne lunches, even at fifteen pounds a pop. Nothing wrong with champagne and strawberries, except that such dos weren't much in her line and that sort of garden party image was apt to give out the wrong signals to some Labour supporters, the old guard in particular. She hadn't been wholly distressed when the event, at one of the bigger houses in the area, had been cancelled. Other people had felt differently, however, and there had been some bitter things said about obligations when the hosts had suddenly and unforgivably cancelled, in favour of an anniversary trip to the Bahamas.

But now, Rollo went on, Max Fisher had volunteered to step in. Max! Ye gods. She made what she hoped were appreciative noises. When everything, including the food, which was sure to be delicious, was being provided by Max, who was in addition throwing open the grounds of his home – and in case of inclement weather, the house itself – it was difficult to voice her reservations without seeming ungracious. There weren't many places like Orbury House available at the drop of a hat – and for free – for that sort of function.

'Good of him to step in at such short notice.'

'I gather he'd have offered before, if it hadn't been that his business partner – Hugh Conolly, the one who had the accident, and then cancer, you know – was still alive. He could hardly have thrown a party while his friend was dying in the same house.'

'Hardly.'

Maggie hadn't seen Hugh Conolly for years. She'd been shocked and upset when she'd heard that he'd died, it hardly

25

seemed possible. All men are mortal ... but Hugh had always seemed more alive than most, in those long-ago days when they'd known each other. A golden lad. Brilliant, but erratic. Unhurried, good-humoured. But since then, their lives had followed very different paths and they'd lost touch. She hadn't even been to his funeral. *Sic transit* ...

'Did you – er – get my letter?' Rollo asked suddenly.

'What letter?'

'I thought it better to write, rather than ring. I sent it first class, you should have had it yesterday.'

'Hang on.' With her free hand, Maggie sifted through the pile of personal mail lying on the telephone table, as yet unopened. 'Yes, it's here. You might as well have saved yourself a first class stamp, it's only arrived today. Wait a minute, until I open it.'

'No, don't read it now!' he intervened quickly. 'It's something I don't want to discuss on the telephone, that's why I wrote. But I did want to give you the chance to think about it before we meet again, angel.'

She got rid of him as quickly as she could and put down the receiver, feeling exasperated. Typical Rollo! She could hardly wait to open his letter and satisfy her curiosity as to why whatever was too delicate to discuss over the telephone couldn't wait until the weekend. But when she'd read the letter through, she almost wished she hadn't. Her enthusiasm for the rest of her evening's work was completely destroyed.

Clouds had gathered and now the rain started again, a real downpour, plunging the garden outside into impenetrable gloom. She took off her glasses and massaged the beginnings of a headache, staring at her reflection mirrored in the darkened window, for once seeing herself as others saw her. An ordinary woman, built on sturdy lines, with an alert, intelligent, animated face, too impatient and busy to bother with the tiresome, irrelevant business of clothes and make-up. Chain store suits bought off the peg when she'd half an hour to spare, a quick haircut when necessary, and that was it. She sighed. It had been borne in on her once or twice lately that perhaps she wasn't young enough any more to get away with that sort of attitude – it seemed that in every interview she gave to the media, her indifference to her personal appearance was mentioned, never mind what she actually said, but she was impatient with the idea of making herself over. It was what she was, not how she looked, that mattered to Maggie. Although once . . .

Well. It hadn't always been so.

Jamie Conolly settled back in the Club class section seat of the 747 from New York into Heathrow and opened the complimentary copy of yesterday's *Times*, flipping straight to the sports pages to see how they were doing at Wimbledon. It had poured down for two days, he read, to the unprecedented extent where all play had been abandoned.

He closed the newspaper, having no further interest in what *The Times* had to say to him. He rarely bothered to read any newspaper, in fact. Catching up on the news via the TV or news flashes on the radio was enough for him, since what was happening in the world was less important than what was happening to Jamie Conolly.

He stretched out elegantly, enjoying the generous amount of leg-room. Not as good as First Class, this, but better than steerage. He couldn't have afforded First, nor even Club, come to that, but the plane wasn't full and his ticket had been upgraded. His friends would have said that just about summed up Jamie Conolly. Lucky Jim. Never troubling himself overmuch about anything – or anyone – but landing on his feet, someone always making out for him. The luck of the devil. Actually, he wasn't unlike his father in that way, with the exception that Hugh had at least never been afraid of augmenting his good luck with hard work.

At the thought of his late father – and the provisions in his will – Jamie's handsome face darkened, and he switched off. Liz came instantly to mind, though he wished she hadn't. One of these days he was going to have to make a firm decision about her. Why the hell couldn't he have fallen in love with some long-legged Sloane beauty – preferably one with money? Liz's endowments were otherwise. Generous, sensuous, down-to-earth. But not, unfortunately, out of the top drawer, nor anywhere near it, either! His opposite in everything, yet good for him in a way that he vaguely appreciated but didn't understand, and certainly wasn't ready to acknowledge.

This was the time of day in Max Fisher's busy schedule that was delegated as his relaxation period, only his over-active brain rarely responded to such instruction. He had finished his dinner and was sitting with a book on his lap, though he wasn't reading it. He was turning over in his mind the surprising proposition regarding the takeover of Fisher-Conolly which had been put to him recently – risky and rather near the mark, but immensely profitable if it came off. But that wasn't its only appeal. The business had outlived its usefulness as far as Max was concerned: it was becoming seriously successful just as he was becoming bored with it. He needed the stimulus of something new.

He'd been contemplating changes during the last few months – ever since he'd learned of Hugh's condition, in fact – but some sense of delicacy had prevented him from implementing them before his partner actually died. It would have surprised him, however, if Hugh hadn't guessed his intentions, it would have been the natural thing to assume some changes would be necessary. Maybe that's why he'd been so keen to have Max buy him out. But he hadn't said a word about the future of the company, and so neither had Max.

Big, shambling, genial Hugh whose life had been an emotional mess, but whom women found enormously attractive, and who had left behind him fond memories and great affection. Max had many reasons to be grateful to him.

He sat looking out into his shadowed garden: still largely unrenovated because the business had come first when he bought Orbury House, then attention to the house itself, this last partly halted by Hugh's illness. Although it was distinctly chilly at the end of this dark, wet June day, now shading off into evening, the window was open to let in the intense scent of the old early rambler that was one of the few remains of the original garden. Out there, somewhere under the knee-high weeds and couch grass and the moss-cushioned paths, and the unkempt yew trees with wild, waving arms, were more roses and a flagged terrace and maybe formal parterres and God knew what else. The major restoration of the garden, a new and tempting prospect, would have to wait yet awhile, or even be abandoned now, though he'd arranged for contract gardeners to come in and make cosmetic touches in time for that salmon and strawberry thrash he'd offered to host for the local Labour party. He had no serious political affiliations but had agreed when he'd been approached and rather regretted it now, or at any rate all the ensuing upset and involvement.

He shrugged and turned without much interest back to his book. Kat had enthusiastically lent it to him, a book about a man who could talk to horses. Not his preferred reading, but he'd conscientiously worked through it and was now almost at the end. He saw where it was leading and doubted whether he could finish it. Life was never like that. Impossible sacrifices for impossible dreams.

But let her dream, he thought, while she was still young enough to have them. Wherever she was. Let her work out whatever need had driven her to desert him. He'd learned how to be patient and wait. She would come back, he had forged links between them that could never be broken.

Yet, an unusual restlessness filled him. Closing the book, he wandered over to the piano, a beautiful instrument he'd inherited from his mother. His fingers began to pick out notes here and there of the Samuel Barber sonata that had sung through his mind all that day.

He and Hugh had known each other since schooldays, for longer than Kat's entire lifetime, notwithstanding that they'd recognised each other for what they were. Being fond of anyone had so far never been allowed to impair Max's judgement. There was an objectiveness in his character that enabled him to see people insomuch as they could be useful to him, a clinical detachment which made it possible for him to stand aside and evaluate situations clearly. It was perhaps as much a part of his Austrian inheritance as his high cheekbones, the thick hair springing from his high forehead, his exceeding height. It caused him a certain amusement to know that, meeting him for the first time, people were apt to class him as a cold fish, and that further acquaintance was not inclined to temper this view. It was only to the very few who were allowed to come closer that Max ever showed anything of his true self, and then only partly.

Success had always come easily to him. He came from a family who was born to achieve it, by whatever means they set their hands to. His grandfather had come to England from Vienna in 1937, Anglicised his name by dropping the 'c' in Fischer and proceeded to make his fortune out of selling cakes, pastries and coffee, Viennese style, in a chain of immediately successful coffee shops modelled on the *Jugendstil* one designed by the great Otto Wagner for his own father in the Ringstrasse. The business continued still, now run by a cousin, and Fisher's Viennese pastries were a byword in the area for deliciousness. Not *given* away, by any means, in fact they cost a few other body parts besides an arm and a leg, but their popularity proved Grandfather Fisher's dictum that people everywhere were prepared to pay for the best.

Max had early decided that he, too, would make money – that went without saying, given his family inclinations – but God forbid it should be as a pastrycook. He couldn't envisage himself making sachertorte for the rest of his life. His quick brain gained him a history place at UCL, where he did everything but work and consequently failed to achieve a predicted First. He shrugged off the failure easily. Not hungry enough, one of his more astute and penniless friends had remarked, and perhaps that was true. He had enough inherited wealth to keep him in comfort, even luxury, for the rest of his life, without lifting a finger, although that had never stopped him from wanting more.

Since a brief, passionate and idealistic affair with one of his fellow students, he had not allowed himself to have any encumbrances, or not for long. Comparisons didn't stand up. The nearest he had come to commitment was in his devotion to music, a true Viennese family tradition. His father and grandfather had both played the violin, his mother had a sweet contralto voice. His own chosen instrument, one that gave rein to the deeper levels of his nature, was the piano, which he played well, though not well enough to take it up professionally, as he had once, briefly, hoped. He played Chopin, and Beethoven sonatas, for other people, and the wilder shores of the modern composers for his own delight.

He left the piano to switch on another lamp against the humid, overcast evening. This melancholy weather echoed the mood that had overtaken him when Hugh's condition had been diagnosed, an accidie that couldn't be shaken off ... intimations of his own mortality, perhaps, though at forty-six he assumed that to be a long way off. The two of them, he and Hugh, had been through a lot together, since the wild days at UCL. Maybe not as wild for Max as he now remembered them in retrospect. Unlike others, he had always been in control. Hugh, just before his death, had liked to talk of those days. People and events swam about in his dying consciousness and he often remembered things that Max had forgotten.

The dog, Alice, lifted her head from her paws, cocking her ears as though she heard her beloved Kat's footsteps. Max looked up, almost expecting to see her, his thoughts winging back to that late April night when she'd burst in on him from outside, running in from the dark woods with Alice bounding behind her, her hair flying, cheeks red, sparks of residual anger still in her eyes. Such lovely eyes, such a beautiful, wondrous girl. So young, so malleable. That was when he'd finally made the decision which had been hovering over him for months. His blood had moved with the old, slow, dark stirrings that were a prelude to a new adventure. A moment or two of returned doubt, then – Why not? What did convention matter? He'd never before been one to let that stand in his way.

His resolution hadn't faltered, though two months stood between that night and now.

4

Orbury House, 26th April

Hi Jools, it's me again!

Why haven't you written to me yet, telling me what you've decided to do? Remembering how you implored me to write back immediately, I can't help worrying that something awful's happened ... but heavens,

I have to stop thinking like this! You're not the sort to get yourself into real trouble. All the same, I wouldn't want to be in your shoes. Why don't you just walk out and turn up here one day, out of the blue, like you've done before? It would be the best thing you could do. Though I suppose that's an over-simplification. Meanwhile, you'll be pleased to know that I've made some decisions of my own.

I slipped out to meet Andrew last night.

I knew I could leave Dad for a while with an easy mind. Max had been in to see him in the afternoon, which had tired him out although he's always very pleased to see anyone, especially Max, who's been marvelous about visiting, despite the fact that I know he hates illness of any kind, especially when it's terminal and when what Nurse Dunston used to call 'the end' is very near.

I hate to write that down, it makes it so final, but everyone knows it won't be long now, even Dad. There's no escaping that sort of knowledge, if you're an intelligent man like my father. He's amazingly brave. I think that's because he's accepted that the time will very soon come when the pain will stop, though he doesn't say this. Whereas me – I can accept it with my mind, but not inside myself. It's so hard to watch him. Sometimes it's impossible, and I have to go out of the room in case he sees my tears and knows I'm so much less brave than he is. But I shan't cry when it's over. He won't be hurting any more then.

The new nurse the agency has sent is called Elaine. She's nicer and less bossy than Dunston, and Dad likes her, too, if only because she's better looking and has long legs, or so he says. I'm glad he's still able to joke.

She told me he would probably sleep through the night, so I phoned Andrew and arranged a meeting outside the old lodge. I told Elaine I was going out to get a breath of fresh air.

'It'll do you good, but take Alice with you,' she advised, in that sensible Scottish way she has. 'I don't think it's such a wonderful idea to wander about alone in those woods in the dark.'

I didn't point out that the grounds of Orbury are as well protected as Fort Knox – after all, if Max can't secure his premises, who can? Nor did I say that the only danger to any attacker from Alice, who is a golden retriever and lovely but very old now, would probably be from smothering with love and kisses! But I did as Elaine suggested and took the dog along, as company for me and exercise for her.

I forgot that even sweet-tempered old Alice could take objection to some people, one of whom turned out to be Rabbit. Not Andrew, who I expected to see, but Rabbit. Which made me feel very put out.

I always feel so silly calling him Rabbit, because that's just what he isn't, but I've no idea of his real name, everybody just calls him that. And it suits him, in a stupid sort of way, though I wouldn't underestimate him. I'm still not sure how far I can trust him. I have the feeling he could be very nasty if he had a mind.

Although he's paranoid about secrecy in other directions, Andrew would never use anything but his own full name. He hates it when anyone calls him Andy, or Drew. He even calls me Kathryn, like one of our teachers, though I'm sure you've never heard anyone else call me that. Dad used to call me his green-eyed Kitty-Kat when I was a baby, and Kat – or Katie to my Mum – just stuck. I don't mind Andrew using my full name though, if he wants to.

Andrew Inskip. Remember him, yonks ago, when you and I were in the sixth at the Princess Mary and he was one of the boarders at Lavenstock College? I haven't told him what a drip we thought he was in those days. Never mind how fabulous looking he was. Even then, he wasn't like the other guys, who were of one mind in chatting us up – and the rest! – or anyway made big noises that they were. I suspect they didn't actually get lucky with many, not with me and certainly not with you, I'll bet. You can be a bit high-minded at times, if you don't mind my saying so, in more ways than that. I suppose it's partly because your father's a big wheel in the police, but probably because you're just made that way! But my father likes you a lot. He thinks you help to keep me on the straight and narrow. Which is ironic, considering . . .

I've never been able to figure out why Andrew was in with that crowd at his school, seeing how apart he always seemed, and how uptight he was when we spoke to him. I know some of the girls thought he was most likely gay or something, but having met him again quite by chance at the gym last year, I can vouch for it that he certainly isn't! All right, I know! But he is different, nowadays, he really has changed in lots of ways, and I did think, for a while . . . until quite recently, in fact, when he began to seem so – well, unsatisfactory, I suppose.

There's no easy way to let someone know you just don't fancy them any more, although I think maybe he's guessed already. It's hard to say, with Andrew, he's so secretive, but sometimes I catch him looking at me, and in view of how I've changed, I feel like a heel.

I was thinking about all this and not very happy about the prospect of telling him as I let myself out of the gates and stood waiting on the roadside by the lodge. I waited for about five minutes, and the first indication I had that anyone was there was when Alice set up a low growl, deep in her throat. This unusual sound made me jump and I nearly cried out. I put a hand out and whispered 'Steady, old girl', which is how Max calms her, but when I touched the back of her neck, I actually felt her risen hackles.

'Who's there?' I couldn't see who it was at first, only a shadow under the trees, but I somehow knew it wasn't Andrew.

Rabbit must have parked his motorbike quite a long way off. He came out of the darkness and I took a backward step. I wondered how long it was since he'd had a bath. Alice growled again and I said, 'Friend, Alice,' but I doubt if she got the message. I had her on a short lead and I could feel her vibrating against my leg.

'What you got that dog with you for?' Rabbit asked, in the fake-Cockney he thinks neccesary to identify himself with the ~~prolat~~ proles. It annoys me, because when he forgets, his normal accent is pure Home Counties. It's very condesending. I once told him that and it didn't go down very well!

I've never enquired into his origins. We've none of us asked about where we came from, though one or two of us already knew each other, and they must all by now be aware of who I am.

Rabbit is big, bearded and burly. He's a few years older than Andrew. From something he let slip once, I think he and Mary might have met at university, which means he must be more intelligent than he lets on – though not as bright as Mary, who's writing a book and is one of those clever types who make you feel so thick. She's very intense, even more so than Andrew. I wouldn't like to get on the wrong side of her, either. She has a very sharp tongue and I don't think she forgives easily. I saw her storing up that remark of mine about Rabbit's accent. Although she doesn't care how she looks and wears grungy clothes, she's really prissy about other things, and I still can't actually get my head round the fact that she can fancy Rabbit but maybe he has hidden qualities!

He was still going on about Alice, who was sniffing around him with great suspicion. I told him that she was only trying to make friends, but this was spoilt when she gave another growl on hearing her name, which made him back away. 'Where's Andrew?' I asked.

I was very dissapointed that he'd sent Rabbit, of all people, and especially that he hadn't bothered to tell me he couldn't come himself.

'_Some_ of us have things to do,' Rabbit answered pointedly. 'How long you going to be here?' he added, accusingly, as if I'd chosen to spend time at a health farm. If he'd seen me without my bulky anorak concealing the weight I've lost recently, he'd probably be convinced I had.

I don't feel like eating much these days. Sorrow for Dad and being in love is a great appetite reducer. All the same, I know that food is there any time if I want it, which doesn't happen at Belmont Avenue. When you're living off the Social and have other priorities, like Rabbit has for running his beloved motorbike, money for food is short, so I'd brought supplies with me – some boiled ham, cheese, plus bread and fruit cake, chocolate and a few bananas. It had seemed quite a lot to me when I picked it up, but as he snatched my offerings, I thought guiltily that I should have brought more. There wasn't going to be much left for anyone else the way he was tearing the foil off and cramming chocolate into his mouth.

'Here, what's this place?' he demanded through a mouthful of fruit and nut, jerking his head towards the lodge. I was reminded of that night when we'd turned off Sphagetti Junction in Birmingham in search of food, when he'd bought three deep-fried battered Mars bars from a chippie (I kid you not!) and gobbled them up one after the other. It was so _gross_. I felt sick all over again at the memory.

'This? It's just the old lodge,' I told him, with a sinking sensation in my stomach that I hoped wasn't a premonition.

'Nobody lives here, then?'

'Not now. There's no electricity and no water and the floorboards are rotten. No facilities of any kind.'

'No inside bog, you mean? That wouldn't bother us none. There's a roof, at least.'

'It leaks. Buckets. The whole place is due to be pulled down.'

'Then nobody'd bother us if we decided to use it.'

It came to me then just how much I was going off all this lark. Perhaps I had been for a long time, only I hadn't admitted it to myself until the other day. Jamie had noticed. It's what's called growing up, he said, *in your case long delayed.* I'd ignored the brotherly insult, you know what Jamie is. Not exactly what you'd call mature himself, either, but he can be quite perceptive at times.

'Well, come on, what you want, then?' Rabbit asked grumpily. 'I have to get back.'

'Oh, it's nothing. It was just that I wanted to talk to Andrew.' I had to, if I was being fair to him, though that wasn't any of Rabbit's business, as I told him pretty sharply when he tried to press me.

'You mean to tell me you've had me coming out all this way for nothing, wasting petrol?' he asked coldly, in his normal accent, forgetting the common touch.

I wasn't going to take that from him, and I was equally rude. 'I wouldn't have bothered coming all the way through the woods myself, either, if I'd know it was only you I was going to see!'

'Well, stuff you!'

'And it's been nice meeting you, too, Roger Rabbit! And next time you come near me, have a bath first.'

Alice sensed my fury and saw him on his way with a dash after him, pulling me along behind her like a water skier for a few yards until I could stop her. She's old but she has the right instincts, that dog. But as I hurried back up to the house, I thought I might be sorry later on that I'd lost my temper with Rabbit.

I soon forgot him, though. It was a cool, windy night with the soft scents of spring all around and I let Alice off the lead to snuffle about in the undergrowth, among the bluebells. Then, as we left the trees, I saw the lighted windows of the house, and Max bending over the table, working on some papers. I felt a sudden rush of happiness and I began to run, with old Alice bounding at my side as though she were still a puppy.

Maybe things will turn out all right, after all.

Luv,

5

Saturday morning saw Maggie in Lavenstock, settling her
mother comfortably before going out, with the curtains drawn
across the window to keep the room cool, the cushions plumped
up in Nora's favourite armchair and a cup of tea and two Mr
Kipling cakes on a plate on the table in front of her. Another
thing Stephanie would disapprove of! Shop-bought cakes (unless
they were the expensive kind, from Fisher's) were common, but
Nora loved these, and Maggie had slipped out earlier and
bought her a box from Patel's, on the corner.

'Do you want the telly on, Mum, the tennis?' she asked,
although she knew the answer would be yes. Even so, she
couldn't let herself simply switch on and plonk her mother in
front of the set without so much as a by-your-leave, though that
was what Nora expected and even liked these days – cricket,
Morse, EastEnders, Delia, Open University, it was all one to her,
unlike the days when she'd enjoyed nothing better than a quiet
read with a good Joanna Trollope. But Maggie refused not to let
Nora have the dignity of choosing to have the set on or off.

She bent down to kiss her, took the frail hand and put it
momentarily to her cheek, and was rewarded with a smile of
extraordinary beauty, recalling the Nora of old, a pretty auburn-
haired woman with a great zest for life. How thin the hand was,
how light and insubstantial . . . 'Steph's here,' she said, hearing
the back door open and close. 'You'll be all right now, m'duck,
till I get back.'

'She needn't have bothered herself,' Nora said, rather tartly.
'I'm perfectly all right on my own.'

At the moment she was. Lucid and in control of herself, all
her wits about her, merely a frail old woman who couldn't get
about as easily as she used to. But who knew how long this state
of affairs would last? Within minutes, she might not even
remember she'd ever had a daughter, never mind that she'd just
been there with her, Maggie thought, closing the door behind

her after handing over to Stephanie and going to get her little Fiat Uno out of the lock-up behind the terraced house. Until recently, Nora had been rational enough for most of the time, but her condition had deteriorated during the past year and now she couldn't be left alone. The last time that had occurred, she'd turned the gas tap full on to make herself a cup of tea, wandered away to fill the kettle and forgot it. Later, she remembered what she'd been doing and was just about to strike a match when Stephanie, coming over from Pedley Wood on one of her duty visits, entered the kitchen and only just saved her mother-in-law from being blown to Kingdom Come.

During the week she had a series of officially approved 'carers', and today Stephanie had promised to spend the afternoon with Nora, albeit with her usual air of martyrdom. You don't know what it's like, was her (mostly) unspoken comment, left with all the responsibility of looking after Mother while you pursue your interesting career in London and only have to put up with her at weekends, and even then with excuses for getting out. She ignored the fact that Maggie came up to the constituency to work; a different slant was put on things, however, when she was able to say, 'My sister-in-law, Maggie Vye, our MP, you know.'

But that was Stephanie all over, Maggie thought wryly as she drove upwards through the cramped, familiar streets of Holden Hill, past the old Odeon, and Stanley Street Mixed Infants where she'd first learned to read and write. The school was now a community centre, and the Odeon a bingo hall.

The light engineering firm where Maggie's brother, Brian, was MD was up there on the right, wedged, like so many other small businesses around here, between houses and shops and the high-rise flats that perched up on the hill and ruined the skyline. Brian had done all right for himself, he was a good husband and saw to it his wife had all she could reasonably have wanted in the way of material comforts, but that wasn't good enough. It irked Stephanie that, out of the family, it had been Maggie who'd been the one to achieve fame. And since she had, it was beyond Stephanie's comprehension why she should still choose to stay at the cramped little house in Danvers Street when she came back to Lavenstock at the weekends. She herself wouldn't have lived in Holden Hill for a pension. Their big house out at Pedley Wood was a long way from all this: a far cry from the nineteenth-century sloping terraces of workmen's cottages, hugger-mugger with between-the-wars pebble-dash semis, high-rise flats and new bungalow developments. None of them far from the corner shops and the chain works and glassworks, and the old steel rolling mill where their father had been a foreman. Hints had lately been slipped into the conversation about getting rid of the Danvers Street house and the proceeds being used to pay for putting Nora into a home.

But Maggie would no more have dreamed of staying else-where than Danvers Street, where she and Brian had been born, than she would of selling it over her mother's head. Though the time was fast approaching when Nora could no longer live alone, she reminded herself with a sinking heart – and there was no way she could look after her mother properly in London. And that being so, she couldn't reasonably expect the same of Brian and Stephanie. She was already very conscious that they bore the largest part of the burden. But Nora would hate the thought of a home, almost as much as she hated – when she was conscious of it – the idea of being a burden.

As Maggie drew up at the traffic lights by the glassworks, ready to turn left over the canal, she noticed that, although it was barely quarter to twelve, a queue was already forming outside the fish and chip shop on the corner of Mailer Street. It would be nice to think they were all wanting to get the midday meal over early and hie themselves down to Austen Hay Park where she was to present the prizes at the fête, but the best Maggie hoped for was that a decent crowd would turn up, despite the murky residue of last week's relentless rain.

In view of the role she was to play at the fête, she'd taken trouble with her hair and chosen her clothes carefully, a deep jade green, short-sleeved suit that was becoming, far from new, but comfortable and so plainly cut that it could offend no one. Her last appearance in the press had been a report of a hard-hitting and pertinent speech on air pollution that she'd made, but a leading Conservative Sunday had glossed over the content and made some snide comment on the unevenness of the hem-line of the Member for Lavenstock East and the lack of fashion consciousness in Labour women in general, Cherie Blair excepted.

Maggie was so busy with her thoughts that she scarcely noticed she'd lost the traffic at last. It always came to her with a small shock of surprise how quickly the grime and dirt were left behind. Clear of Holden Hill, this was another country. Blessed quiet, red earth and sandstone rocks rolling away into woodland either side as the road climbed one hill after another towards the summit. It was still possible to get pleasure from driving, here. Maggie wound the window down to let in the fresh air and sat back more comfortably. A car was hopeless in London, and unnecessary. There, she did her bit for the environment by relying on London transport – taxis when she was feeling flush – while keeping her car here. A drive out into the country, and a short walk, was her one indulgence during a busy weekend, one that buoyed her up for the next week; today she was combining it with a visit to a constituent who lived on the edge of Freyning Wood. This extensive stretch of woodland was the only one now left of the three great medieval woods which together had once formed an ancient royal hunting forest. Deer still roamed freely here: beautiful fallow deer with their flattened antlers and reddish spotted coats; roe deer, small and graceful; and the odd-shaped little muntjac with its hoarse bark.

She pulled off the road and parked just below the crown of the hill, put on the light waterproof jacket she kept in the car and slipped into her flat shoes, determined on her usual walk, though it was miserable sort of weather, humid, overcast, unable to make up its mind whether to rain or not. She walked for about twenty minutes to the vantage point over the valley, meeting no one except noisy jays and wood pigeons which clattered away at her approach, and a small herd of greyish-brown deer who watched her warily from a distance. There were posters here, too, stuck to the trees, the same sort which decorated all the lamp-posts in Holden Hill, advising No New Road, and similar slogans.

When she reached the crown of the hill, overlooking the valley below, she perched on an outcropping of rock, pulling a bag of Maltesers from her pocket by way of lunch and looking down into the valley where this proposed new road, plans for which had just been announced, connecting two motorways and linking up with the Lavenstock bypass, was to be gouged out of the red sandstone. The silent, sunless day added to the sense of things passing beyond redemption. We won't try to comprehend what we're doing, ever, she thought sadly, we never learn. Once, the desecrated land she had left behind in Holden Hill had been like this, a rolling countryside of coppices and dells, with the river winding below, a natural habitat for its teeming wildlife. The spoliation of that land, too, had been gradual, not understood. The rich coal seams beneath its surface had been both its prosperity and its undoing, leaving behind an unending legacy of dirt and dinginess. Not for nothing was it named the Black Country.

Unthinkable that this rich, rural beauty in front of her could be so despoiled, for it was only another kind of desecration, this road that was to alleviate the congestion in the town centre and destroy another small part of the environment. Work hadn't yet begun on it, it was still only a proposal that might, or might not, go ahead, yet already the forces of opposition were mustering. The Greens were against it, as were those concerned with flora and fauna, and those whose protest against anything innovatory was automatic. She was in two minds about it herself, the part of her that loved the forest wholeheartedly agreeing with them, while knowing it was not politically expedient at the moment to say so.

Not for the first time, Maggie cursed the ambiguities of her beloved career. Never a doubt about it did she have, but many reservations. She'd taken a well-defined route into politics. Bred into her by her father, a fierce little immigrant Welshman who'd come from a family of steel-workers in the Rhondda to work in the foundry here, an active trade-unionist who took after Lloyd George in looks and Nye Bevan in politics. He'd worked on both his children since their birth, but it was Maggie who inherited his socialist principles and his passionate nature, listened to and absorbed the folk-history of deprivation and exploitation in the Welsh valleys; slogged to get into university ... more politics there ... a job teaching social sciences at Birmingham University ... Labour Party Association activist, Lavenstock town councillor ... then, when the opportunity arose, into Parliament.

41

She looked at her watch, winkled out the last Malteser, screwed up the empty bag and put it in her pocket. Her appointment was with one of the anti-roaders before she went to pick up Rollo and then on to the fête. In view of the constituent's address, she brushed the jade green linen skirt, hoped she hadn't picked up any stains and looked carefully for any flake of chocolate that might melt and reveal itself later.

You came upon Little Freyning unexpectedly, a slight hollow in the steeply sloping woods that surrounded it. It was considered a very desirable place to live, a hotchpotch of houses of various ages and styles that had grown up harmoniously together, clustered around a church, a pub, a shop and a duckpond. Mostly cottages, but there was also a crescent of council houses and a spattering of larger houses, with some extremely des. res. built on the periphery of the village, off the narrow road which Maggie now took.

The one she was headed for turned out to be the sort of residence she'd expected, a sizeable white house, calling itself Prettymans and nestling against the background of the forest. The main gate was shut, so Maggie left the Fiat pulled well into the roadside verge and let herself through the wicket at the side. She walked to the house up a winding drive, through a sweet and lovely garden. Then, rounding the last bend before the house, she came suddenly face to face with a tall, weatherbeaten, elderly woman who had on a wide-brimmed straw hat, a khaki divided skirt and check shirt and was holding a gun up to her shoulder, pointing straight at Maggie.

'Right, I'll get you, you bugger!' the woman's voice rang out.

Startled, Maggie had a momentary sense of having strayed on to the set of an old B movie western and being confronted with a doughty frontierswoman, except that the scenery was all wrong: the damply serene English garden, the table with the furled sun umbrella on the lawn, the old woman speaking in the commanding, ringing tones of the British Raj. She called out sharply, 'Mrs Farley-Flint, it's me, Maggie Vye. I think you're expecting me.'

'Oh,' said Zena Farley-Flint, pulling her spectacles out of her skirt pocket, putting them on and peering through them. 'Oh Lor', I'm sorry! Thought you were one of those bloody little muntjacs. Been eating the roses, every damned one. I've been keeping an eye out for 'em all morning. I swear I'll kill the next little bugger that gets in.'

Not if you can't see better than to mistake a two-legged human being in jade green for a deer, thought Maggie. But she took a careful look at what she saw was an air rifle and was relieved to see that it was no longer aimed at her.

'Well, come in, have a cup of coffee, too miserable to sit out here, afraid. Better still, how about a scotch, eh?' Raising her voice as Maggie followed her through the front door, she screeched over the sound of TV tennis, 'Maggie Vye's here, Horace! She needs a scotch, I damn near killed her.'

She showed Maggie into a chintzy, wildly untidy, dusty room with big windows, smelling of dog and looking out on to a further stretch of garden, so neat that even a blade of grass bending the wrong way would have looked out of place. An old man, equally as tall as Mrs Farley-Flint, followed them in after a short interval, walking with slow, shuffling steps, a rattling tray with glasses, a bottle of whisky and a jug of water balanced precariously in his hands. Behind him waddled a chocolate brown spaniel, so old and fat it could hardly walk either. 'Scotch, did you say, my dear?' His china teeth slipped and rattled nearly as much as the glasses on the tray.

Maggie, who wasn't enamoured of whisky, and especially at this time of day, dutifully sipped a dram of The Macallan from a smeary glass, not daring to imagine what chaos she might cause if she asked for coffee after all. But she'd drunk worse in the interests of good constituency relations, and had been allowed to have this one well-diluted after she'd mentioned she was driving. Mrs Farley-Flint sat opposite, drinking hers neat, her thin, stick-like bare legs in raggy old canvas plimsolls thrust out before her, delivering a diatribe against the deer who ate the roses, badgers who dug up the lawn, squirrels who stripped the bark off the trees and the rabbits who ate everything. Maggie smiled and nodded sympathetically. She saw she had the wrong impression of country life. The dangers of living in London and daily facing muggers and rapists and the hell of Oxford Street were, it seemed, as the cankers of a calm world and a long peace, compared to this. She could see it was going to be some while before they actually got around to the purpose of her visit. By this time, Horace appeared to be asleep in his chair, the old dog ditto at his feet.

Maggie coughed and herself made the opening: 'Why did you write to me, Mrs Farley-Flint?'

'Ha, my letter, yes. What are you proposing to do about it?'

'Mrs Farley – '

'Oh, Zena, for God's sake! The other's too much of a mouthful by half. Had to put up with it ever since I took old Horace here on ... Why did I write? you ask. Didn't I make it plain enough?'

'I'm sorry, I meant, what do you think I can do about your problem, exactly?'

'You *are* our MP, on this select committee thing for the environment, aren't you?'

Maggie sighed. She needn't have bothered to come here in person. She could have sent one of those standard replies ... 'Thank you for your letter. Your comments have been noted,' and left it at that. But that was never her style.

'All right,' her hostess said, 'I know what you're going to say. That damned road won't be here for years, but that won't do, y'know. *Now's* the time we need to take action, before it's a *fait accompli*. Riding roughshod over public opinion – the only bit of decent countryside for miles, and they want to ruin it with their noise and pollution, it won't do! And what about all the wildlife?' she demanded suddenly, showing a hitherto unrevealed concern for nature's creatures. 'You know that damned road's going to pass within two hundred yards of this house?'

Two hundred yards of forest trees. The road wouldn't be seen from here. Doubtful if it would be even heard. 'I understand how you feel about that,' Maggie said, mentally sighing again, coming to what she now saw was the nub of the problem. 'I suppose you're worried about falling property values.'

'Of course I'm worried, but me and old Horace here, can't be that long before we drop off the twig, won't matter all that much to us, in the long run. It's more the principle of the thing. And it's not only my problem, is it? It's everyone's, or should be.

44

Cities gobbling up the countryside. What I want to know is, what are you proposing to do about it?'

Maggie saw she'd been doing the old girl an injustice. It was plain to see that Zena Farley-Flint was sincerely concerned and, if not one of the most active of the leading spirits in the campaign against the new road, at least one of its most militant. She was eighty if she was a day, which still made her, by Maggie's rapid calculations, too young by half to have been a suffragette, but she wouldn't have been surprised.

All the usual people were grouping their resources, Zena went on, getting their acts together, raising petitions – those who were dedicated to getting their way by peaceful means at any rate – she averred scornfully. Friends of the Earth, RSPB, Group Six, World Wide Fund for Nature, Greenpeace –

'Group Six?' Maggie intervened sharply.

'Namby-pambies, all of 'em. Too pussy-footed by half,' declared the lady, lumping all the protesters together and dismissing them. This was not at all, it seemed, her idea of how the campaign against the new road should be conducted. Herself, she was all for making a human chain across the path of the bulldozers when they arrived, as they undoubtedly would if the new road was given the go-ahead. 'Reason I asked you here,' she went on, growing ever more heated, 'you're something to do with the Environment – in a unique position – I want your categoric assurance that Something Will Be Done to stop it.'

'Now then, Zena,' intervened Horace mildly, opening a pair of clear, bright blue eyes. 'Over the top, again, over the top!'

And, amazingly, Zena Farley-Flint blushed and took the rebuke on the chin. The tough, brown, wrinkled face turned an unbecoming shade of puce, then the blush receded.

'Her father was Russian, you know,' Horace added, as if this explained everything.

His wife sighed and said, surprisingly, showing her old yellow teeth in a smile, 'He's right, I shouldn't get myself so worked up. Blood pressure, too high as it is.'

'These protesters, this Group Six,' Maggie said. 'Tell me what you know about them.'

6

Orbury House, 3rd May

Hi again, Jools!

Thanks for letting me have your new address right away. I'm really
glad you've made your mind up what to do at last, and left, that you
haven't let your emotions influence you – though I'm a fine one to talk,
you'll say! I wish we could meet, though I shouldn't be much use in
cheering you up.

I'm afraid Dad is very much worse. I wish I were the sort of strong
character who could cope with this awful feeling of watching and
waiting and not being able to do anything to help, but I'm not. I feel
so helpless. Writing to you will at least give me something to think
about apart from that – and this other thing which I can't stop thinking
about.

Something incredible's happened. It's shattered everything I'd come
to feel certain about during the last few months. My opinion of myself
has taken a nosedive. How can I be like this? Never staying constant
to one thing? Why am I so easily swayed, so faithless?

It's funny how a chance meeting can change your life. I once thought
it was meeting Andrew again that had changed mine, and of course it
did, in a way. Before that, I'd simply done what I wanted to do,
without thinking about it, and I have to say I was happy enough. But
after meeting him, and what has followed, I don't suppose I shall ever
be the same again.

It was through Andrew that I was introduced to the other people in
his group. Group Six, they called themselves, simply because there were
six of them – apart from those who appear when they've nothing better
to do, the hangers-on, I call them. I suppose I ought to have realised
that the group was never entirely going to accept me when they didn't
attempt to change the name to Group Seven. Of course, that could get
ridiculous, having to change the name every time anyone joined, but
this isn't likely. Andrew wants to keep the group small, as it is now,
he says it's safer that way. They voted for me to be a member, but I'm

46

under no illusions. I know I was only included because it was Andrew who wanted me in.

Perhaps they were right to be suspicous of me. Somehow I can't summon up the enthusiasm the rest of them have for all these protests. It was fun at first, and the danger was exiting, so different from anything I'd ever done before, but after a while (after I spent the night in a police cell in Swindon and came up before the beak the next day, to be truthfull!) I decided that not all these protests were for me. If that's how you feel, OK. Trouble is, I don't. I can't be angry about *everything*, which is what the group seems to be most of the time. I mean, I don't mind going on demos about experiments on animals or about big food chains exploiting the third world but I can't get worked up about out of town shopping centres or motorways that are going to bypass busy towns, or about lunchtime abortions . . . after all, a bypass helps take the congestion and pollution away from town centres and if you accept abortion in principal, the time it takes doesn't really matter! And nothing at all could ever make me lie down in front of a lorry taking sheep to France, or live in an underground tunnel! Or chain myself to a tree if it comes to that. What I'm trying to say is, I think, that I don't see protesting as a way of life, like Rabbit and Mary do, for instance.

They sense I'm lukewarm, Mary especially. I know that from the way she looks at me, like a mouse inspecting a piece of suspect cheese. They don't take me along with them on the really dangerous protests, which I only guess about by putting two and two together, like the time when they all dissapeared for three nights and that big lab up north was set on fire and the animals freed. Even Andrew doesn't tell me everything – perhaps especially Andrew. He's very aware of security and plays his cards very close to his chest.

I finally told him that it wasn't on between us any more. He just gave me one of his looks and said well, nobody owns anyone else, after which he's gone on as though nothing ever happened between us, which is quite extrordinary when you think about it. You know the look I mean. He can stare at you without blinking for ages, which is very unnerving. Something to do with that pale skin of his and his light blue eyes, that makes him look like one of those blind-looking marble statues the Romans had, or was it the Greeks. But then he'll smile, when you least expect it. He has a lovely smile.

I often think that in spite of having been so close to him, I don't know Andrew at all, or what makes him tick. Actually, I shouldn't think anyone does, really. He goes to a lot of trouble to give the impression of being cool, but in actual fact, he's the most fired-up person I know. It's a sort of rebellion, I suppose. His parents were travel writers, too busy exploring way out corners of the world and then getting books and articles about their travels published (aimed, Andrew says, at bored rich people who've already been everywhere and want somewhere new to go) to have any time for him. He was sent to board at Lavenstock College when he was seven and sometimes even spent his holidays at school. Their excuse was that the places they went to were remote and could be dangerous, and they were right, of course, because they were both killed in that earthquake somewhere – Peru, I think it was. Ocasionally, if his holidays came at the right time, they would take him with them but he always knew he was an encumberance.

Well, I can truthfully say that I was never made to feel like that by my parents, not even by Mum, who must have found caring for Jamie and me a heavy burden. It's caused her to grow a hard shell, unlike Dad, and once when we were having an argument about me wanting some new clothes she said she couldn't afford and I thought she could, I said it was a pity she wasn't more like Dad, more generous.

'That's easy enough when you're too imature to face up to your responsibilities,' she replied, very sharp, in that tart way she has, and when I thought about it, I felt mean and small for having critisized. But although I can see in a way what she means about Dad, she's always underestimated him. It's being generous in a different way, deep down, that really matters.

For instance, on election night, when our MP, Maggie Vye, the one Dad used to know years ago, got in again with such a huge majority, we were watching her on TV and listening to people sing her praises and hearing her promises, which I have to say sounded genuine, not the usual pie in the sky. He said, 'Oh Maggie! Still the same old Maggie!' He looked amused, but also tender and somehow sad. 'She always was a great idealist.'

'She's a politican. She'll say anything that'll get her into power,' I reminded him, which was cynical but how I feel.

'Not her, not Maggie! Never!'

I shrugged but I felt him watching me while he sipped at the nightly tot of whisky he isn't allowed but which Max and I think he should have since he enjoys it so much and Elaine shuts her eyes to. 'She was once very like you, you know. Not in looks, and perhaps not in temperament. But you have the same sort of spirit. You try and be like her, Kat, true to yourself, and you won't go far wrong.'

This sort of embarassing stuff isn't a bit like Dad, but the amazing thing was I think he really meant it. If only he knew! What I'm really like, I mean.

I tried to laugh it off. 'You're not serious! I'd never make a politician, not in a thousand years!'

He smiled at that and let the subject drop and we watched further antics about the election. Later that evening, when he was ready to be settled for the night, he took my hands and said, 'How far can I trust you?'

'Dad!'

'I'm, sorry, I should have said, How far did I <u>ought</u> to trust you – for your own good? Kat, will you do something for me – after I'm gone?'

It was the first time he'd ever mentioned dying, in so many words. I could only nod.

But he didn't tell me what he meant. His pills were working and he was slipping off into the past again. Something had stirred him up, making him say things he normally wouldn't dream of. There was a lot of stuff about what a rotten husband and father he'd been, and his mind was still on Maggie Vye. He said soberly, just before he fell asleep, 'She's doing a good job, what does anything else matter?' That's what I mean about generosity of spirit . . .

I'm sorry, I can't write any more. Later.

Luv,

7

'That letter,' Rollo said, as he and Maggie were having a cup of tea before going on to the fête.

It wasn't Mrs Farley-Flint's letter he was referring to, but the other he'd forwarded to Maggie in London. 'Don't get worked up about it,' he went on. 'No one's going to take any notice of such rubbish, I'm sure.'

You were sure enough that they would when you sent it on to me, Maggie thought. Otherwise you wouldn't have bothered. 'I've ridden out worse than this, I suppose,' she said. But she wondered if she had. It had felt like a load of bricks descending on her, attempting to crush her spirit, if not her body. And in spite of her doughty words, she knew they were both deceiving themselves, and Rollo's next words showed he did actually feel the same.

'If it does come out, though, there'll be a hoo-ha,' he warned, 'whichever way you look at it. If you deny it, everyone will say there's no smoke without fire – if you admit it, you'll lose credibility. I'm afraid, Maggie dear,' he finished sadly, 'you haven't got a lot of option but to agree to what these cretins want.'

He was a large teddy bear of a man, with big, dark brown eyes, curly brown hair and an olive skin. Rollo, the chocolate-covered toffee with the soft centre, someone without much insight and a juvenile sense of humour had once called him to Maggie's face, and received a dusty answer. His kind expression, his malleable features and ears that stuck out endearingly, his worried frown, might make him appear so, but they belied his capabilities, his unswerving loyalties. His wife was an independent woman, following her own career as a physiotherapist, and her own inclinations, and didn't seem interested in him now that their children had grown up and moved away from home, so his whole life was devoted to Maggie and the party.

'There's nothing to admit, Rollo!'

'Of course not, angel.'

'Well, nothing that's done anybody any harm.'

'Right, but the voters might not look at it like that. They'll hate it, their Maggie turning out to be . . .' His inventiveness failed him, or his courage.

'Rollo, are you on my side, or not?'

'Need you ask that?' He looked stricken.

'I'm sorry, of course I didn't need to! We'll ride it out,' she repeated, with more conviction. She could, she was sure she could. All the same, events were getting too close for comfort.

He laid his hand over hers, large, soft but capable, and oddly comforting. She let it stay for a moment before gently withdrawing her own. He sighed and didn't attempt to renew the contact. One time, years ago, after they'd both had a little more to drink one night than they should have, things had progressed further, but in the morning, she'd let him know that it had been – not exactly a mistake, but an indiscretion that was best forgotten. Knowing Maggie, he hadn't persisted – but occasionally, when he sensed her defences were down, he made another bid.

Not now, however, when she was on the warpath. He could see it in the set of her chin, the determination that blazed from her eyes, the familiar way she impatiently tucked the thick fair hair, now greying a little, behind her ears in the gesture he loved. The stance that the voters saw when she was on the hustings, up against it. 'They're not bloody well going to get me down – they can do their damnedest!' she declared.

Which they probably would, thought Rollo. Although they didn't – hopefully – know that what they had discovered was only the half of it. 'Good girl,' he said softly, then added, 'Don't worry. Leave it to me, I'll think of something.'

She hoped he wasn't going to act rashly, as he sometimes unfortunately did, out of mistaken kindness. 'Rollo – ' she began, then stopped. He looked up inquiringly, hopefully, smiling encouragingly. 'Thank you,' she said simply.

He turned away, disappointed as usual. It had been too much to hope that she was going to say more, that thanks would be expressed more tangibly. That was the cross he'd learned to bear. He had loved her, like a faithful dog, from the first moment of their meeting, and always would.

As fêtes go, Lavenstock's turned out to be a huge success, with no more trouble from a handful of rowdy teenagers than was usual on the Saturday nights when Lavenstock United lost their home game, and with an unprecedented sum being raised for various charities.

At one point, at precisely the time Maggie Vye was due to present a satisfactorily sizeable cheque to the local hospice to be exact, proceedings had looked as if they might be disrupted by a group of demonstrators converging on the platform, carrying anti-road banners, chanting slogans advising those who hadn't already made up their mind to join in the protest *now*. But what might have spoiled an otherwise successful day was nipped in the bud due to the vigilance of the police, aided by those who weren't going to have the *entente cordiale* of the past fortnight messed up at this stage. Even more to the point, nobody was going to be told what to do by a bunch of lefties. Especially since the proposed road might never happen.

Insults were hurled from either side as the protesters who refused to disperse were hauled away.

'It'll be too bloody late when they bring the bulldozers in!' shouted one skinny young woman in combat boots as she was dragged away into a police van by a hefty uniformed constable.

'Ostriches!' yelled her companion, a neatly dressed housewife who'd lost one of her court shoes in the mêlée. A policewoman threw it into the van behind her. The doors closed on half a dozen more screaming, unrepentant demonstrators and the van drove away. The great demonstration was over. The fête proceeded to its final conclusion with no more trouble.

'It's been a long time, Maggie, how long? Far too long, but never mind, you're here now.' The light flashed ruby reflections from his glass of red wine as he raised it.

It was the next day, Sunday, and Maggie had come to lunch with Max Fisher. She had telephoned him and he had asked her

to have lunch with him and she had said yes, though not sure
whether this was a wise move. His charm, which was considerable when he wished to exert it, had already won her over,
however. He had not altered, substantially, from the days when
they'd been students together. He might still have been the
young Max who had towered over them all, literally and figura-
tively, a god, the Sun in Splendour, though none of them had
thought of it like that then, or would have said it if they had.

'Of course, I'll have the garden tarted up before this shindig
of yours,' he'd said, showing her around Orbury House before
they ate, explaining what had already been done to make it
habitable, why some things were still to be finished: the necessary wait until exactly the right wallpaper could be found, or
the correct chair which would fill that gap, until the restorer
could come to repair the cornice where the damp had got in
when the house was unoccupied for so long. They returned to
the finished, opulently furnished part of the house. 'It's all
genuine Georgian. Very nice – don't you think?'

'Very nice.'

Georgian, indeed. It was evident he was still the same perfec-
tionist who'd cultivated an outrageous, stylish and idiosyncratic
undergraduate eccentricity, his clothes tailored and his hair cut
in town, concocting exquisite little meals, plus the correct wine.
Trying to give the impression he'd been born into the wrong
century. An aesthete, amongst the general miasma of smelly
Afghan sheepskin coats, torn jeans, uncombed, uncut and sometimes unwashed hair, the baked beans, beer and dope of their
contemporaries. Well, for one thing, unlike the rest of them, Max
had been well-heeled enough to be able to do it, though he'd
never admitted he had enough. Money then, and perhaps now,
was his god. But she had been taken in, infatuated by it all: she,
Maggie, the sensible, pragmatic socialist, swept away on a tide
of sex and luxury.

In the end, the price had been too high. Carefree and liberated
as she was, she did not want to be owned, she had plans for her
own career and Max was possessive. They'd quarrelled about it
and she'd stormed out, in one of her famous but short-lived
tempers. It might have blown over had she not gone immediately – and ultimately disastrously – straight into the arms of

someone else, and spent a subsequently much regretted time kicking over the traces.

After that, they had consigned each other to the past, she and Max, until now, and she was relieved to find there was no awkwardness between them, no desire on the part of either of them to dwell on what had gone.

The obvious eccentricities of his college days were no longer needed as a statement. He was wearing casual trousers and a sweater over his open-necked shirt, though the trousers were superbly cut and the sweater was cashmere and his authority was apparent. Maggie was glad, despite herself, that she'd worn the jade green suit again when he complimented her on it. Max had always had impeccable manners and the ability to imbue one with what they now called the feel-good factor. She wondered if he remembered how he'd tried to change her, to make her more svelte, slimmer, tame her rough hair ... The old intimacy, once sharpened by sexual tension, could never be forgotten, but he seemed to have forgiven her, which surprised her: he had never been a forgiving man.

They talked of how their lives had changed and what they knew of other members of their particular set as they ate pheasant and drank a bottle of fine Margaux, followed by fruit and cheese. They spoke, carefully, of Hugh Conolly's last illness, because this was marshy ground, and of his beautiful daughter, whom Max had apparently taken a shine to, but who had taken herself off after her father's death. 'Do you regret not being married, Maggie?' he asked suddenly.

'No,' she answered, honestly, meeting his eyes, expecting him to follow this up. But he merely offered cheese, remarking on the ripeness of the Stilton, to indicate the subject was simply of peripheral interest. 'I've had my career,' she added, cutting herself a generous portion. Marriage was something she didn't want to talk about, either, any more than she was yet ready to broach what she had come here to discuss. 'What brought you back to Lavenstock?' she temporised. 'I've never left, in a sense, but I wouldn't have thought it your scene at all.'

'I met up with Hugh again, he was wanting to start up one of his enterprises and needed capital. He'd found this house, far too big for what was needed, but I liked the idea of using it partly as offices, partly as somewhere to live. I was willing to help him, but under my own terms, none of his hare-brained set-ups – you know the sort of things he used to get up to.'

The sort of things they all used to get up to lay in the silence between them. 'We were all hare-brained, all except you, Max. '

'Oh, I don't know. There were things . . . '

Yes. But you never did anything without full knowledge of the consequences, she thought. You were manipulative and what we did must have seemed childish and immature to you.

'I'm grateful you found time to come and see me, Maggie. You have a busy schedule,' he said, looking at his watch under cover of pouring the last of the wine.

'I must go soon.'

'Not just yet. I've a tiresome appointment later, but there's still plenty of time.'

He was really asking her why she'd come, why she'd telephoned, ostensibly to thank him for his offer to throw open his grounds for the forthcoming fund-raising event, but what he really must have guessed to be something else. She couldn't put it off any longer.

'Something's happened that I think you should know about.'

He leaned back expansively, twiddling the stem of his wineglass. He drained it. 'Coffee? My housekeeper makes excellent coffee.'

She did indeed. Just as she cooked pheasant to perfection, kept a well-run house. She wouldn't have been employed by Max if she hadn't. 'Oh dear,' he said when Maggie had finished explaining. 'Oh dear oh dear. Why now?'

His eyes darkened in the way that was peculiar to him, as he listened. He smiled. 'Well, we shall just have to do something about it, won't we?'

After Maggie had gone, Max went through into the rooms lately occupied by Hugh and his daughter. All traces of the impedimenta of illness had been removed from the room in which Hugh had died, but Kat's bedroom was just as she'd left it. The wardrobe still held some of her clothes, bottles and jars littered the top of the dressing-table, but the little desk in front of the window was bare of everything, even the photo of himself which she'd insisted on keeping there.

His hand hovered over the drawers, and withdrew. Not from any sense of delicacy – he had no scruples on that score – but because when she came back, he wouldn't like her to know that anything had been disturbed.

But after a moment he pulled out the centre drawer and there it was: the book he'd given her – leatherbound, tooled in gold with her initials, expensive, Max-like, in which he'd encouraged her to write some sort of diary, something of what she felt and thought. It might give him a clue as to where she'd gone, what had happened in those last days to make her leave, without a word. He burned to know.

He opened the book at random. The large, round, schoolgirlish hand stared back at him, accusingly. For a while, the words registered nothing. Then he went over to the window and seated himself in the armchair.

The entry he was looking at was dated 2nd June.

I've just finished writing to Jools, he read. *I told her about everything that's happened recently, which is why I'm going to have to leave here. I wanted to talk to her about Dad, but I found it impossible, except to say that he'd died. I can write about it here, though, in my Diary where no one, not even Jools, will ever see it . . .*

8

24 Belmont Avenue, 2nd June

Hi Jools,

It's two weeks since Dad died. I promised myself I wouldn't cry, and I haven't. It's over, and I'm glad, but I can't write about it yet.

Please note my new address, changed by reason of two things, one of which I mentioned in my last letter. Yes, you did warn me, and I took no notice, but even you couldn't have known . . . Utter misery.

First, I met a dark angel. Truly! Then I left Orbury House –

56

although one wasn't dependant on the other. Or was it? Am I fooling myself?

I'm now staying with Andrew. Not with Mum, where I'd like to be. I haven't seen her all that much, lately – I couldn't, without telling her about my future, and I wanted her to get used to the idea of Dad being dead before I did that. One shock at a time's enough. I'm so glad now that I didn't, since everything's changed. I can't face her just yet, so I told her I was going to visit you in America, which is what I would have done, only you'd told me you were going to leave. I wish I could talk to you, not just write. I really, really, need to talk to someone who'd understand.

I'd nowhere to go after I left Orbury House, and precious little money, but Andrew has agreed to let me stay here indefinitely and seems pleased that I asked. Unlike Rabbit and Mary, who are pissed off with me, mainly because Andrew lets them have the middle bedroom and they don't want me here too. Margot and the twins are barely speaking to me either, for other reasons. Margot is middle-aged with two grown-up children, living with her husband in a neat detached house on a new estate. She's a real pain, she's so ernest and righteous. She gives the kitchen here a spring clean before she'll even have a cup of coffee, though she has a point there. I don't know where the twins live, Adrian and Justin, but I suspect it isn't anywhere like this, judging by the Sarb convertible they share. I don't think they've anything against me, personally, it's only that they're too thick to think for themselves, they just go along with the rest.

I've hardly any money until Dad's estate is sorted out, so I was very glad indeed, though very surprised, everything considered, when Andrew was so good about me coming here after I had to leave Orbury. After all, I was the one who ended what was going on between us.

Anyone can make a mistake, as you know only too well, but why do I make so many? I thought I knew, with absolute certainty, that I wasn't doing it again this time. Which just goes to show how wrong you can be.

It seemed to me that I was standing at a cross-roads. As Dad used to say: you can take the easy way and become boring and ordinary like everyone else and be sorry for it all your life, or choose a more difficult path and maybe find yourself sometimes up on the heights or down in the depths – but at least you'll have had fun on the way.

Max said more or less the same thing, in a different way – but I won't think about that. Let's just say I took the wrong road.

Andrew's parents left this house to him. It's a poky little semi but not bad if you can bear the scruffy decorations and the furniture which, after Orbury, is hard to take, plus the grot in the kitchen. My mum would have a ball with all the Tudor-twee, the imitation wood beams and leaded windows and plate racks and the huge, brick, mock-olden fireplace that's horrendous, really, but looks quite magical somehow when Andrew lights a coal fire in it. Andrew's mother had never bothered with the house. You can tell the sort of people his parents were, too high-minded to care about their surroundings: zillions of books but everything else dire. The walls are all greige and there's a hideous florescent lighting in the hall and kitchen and a centre globe in a paper moon shade in the sitting room. The chairs and sofa are covered in tatty, rubbed brown corduroy, the same colour as the threadbare carpet square. And all over the house, those gruesome African masks and things. Plus a lot of other old junk that no one in this family has ever thrown away. Victorian stuff belonging to people as far back as Great-great-grandfather Inskip! Which Andrew thinks is great. Funny, but I'd still rather have it than Dad's penthouse flat, with Terri's choice of furnishings.

I was still helping with work for the Group while I was at Orbury, though I'd made it plain I didn't want to be an active member any longer, so I was still seeing Andrew. He was the one who finally persuaded me that I should have to go over to Dad's and do what he'd asked of me.

The flat and all its contents will have to be sold, and I've no problem with that because there's not a single thing I'd want to keep. What it fetches – quite a lot, I should think – will be all mine, as well as the money Dad left to be shared between me and Jamie. I wish Dad hadn't done that. Or rather, I wish he'd left it so that Jamie shared the proceeds from the flat with me. I wonder if it was because he knew Jamie was too much like him, and he suspected it would run through his fingers like water? I haven't told anyone except Andrew – and Jamie, of course – but I've made my mind up that when the flat's sold, I'm going to give Jamie half. Andrew didn't say anything, except that it was my choice. The way he looked at me, I wondered just what he meant.

I had it in my mind to get a firm of house clearers to give me a price for emptying the flat and getting rid of the lot – including the droopy-drawers Austrian blinds, the chandeleer big enough for the Albert Hall, and those yukky draped muslin curtain things over the emperor-sized bed that Terri used to call a 'corona'. But before I did any clearing out, I had to find the box.

I wouldn't even have bothered with that, if Andrew hadn't insisted. I'd dismissed it as being part of Dad's state of mind before he died, but when I mentioned it to Andrew, he said I couldn't just forget about it, it wouldn't be keeping faith with Dad. He seemed to think it important, and when I thought it over, I agreed with him that perhaps it wasn't just Dad not knowing what he was saying.

For some reason, the box had prayed on his mind. All through his last days, when he wasn't sedated, he kept muttering about it. Saying that he shouldn't have kept it, telling me to get rid of it, and not to let anyone see it. The only thing was, he never told me where I could find it.

'You'll have to go and look for it,' Andrew said. 'Then you can throw it away, whatever it is. You promised.'

I suppose I had, in a way, though I doubt whether Dad had been aware of that. Anyway, Andrew shamed me into thinking that I had to brace myself and go along and search for this box, perhaps even among Terri's belongings, which I absolutely didn't want to do. I decided to leave her dressing table until last, but as it happened, I didn't need to go through her underwear or anything dire like that, for which I was truly thankful, though not as much as I might have been, once. There was a photograph of the two of them on the dressing table. He had his arm around her and they were laughing and looked happy. I stared at it for a long time and realised I was beginning to feel a bit less harshly towards Terri, ready to forgive her for her terrible taste in clothes and furnishings, even that awful mosquito netting over the bed. She had, after all, made my father happy during the last part of his life – and now that I know myself what it's like to be really and truly in love . . .

I found the box quite quickly after all. It was easy enough. She hadn't been one for keeping anything that hadn't a rightfully designated place, and Dad hadn't been one for keeping much, period. I knew I'd found the right thing when I came across an old shoebox tied round with string hidden on a high shelf in his wardrobe, under some heavy sweaters and trousers and other walking gear that he hadn't used for at least a couple of years before his illness, not to my knowledge.

'Well,' Andrew said, 'aren't you going to open it?'

'No, I'm just going to throw it away, like he wanted. It's nothing to do with me.'

'How do you know?'

Well, of course, I didn't, and I didn't _want_ to know, but Andrew's insistance was too much for me, though _I_ think he'd intended all along that I should open it. After a bit, I agreed to do so and found it full of nothing more than ancient photos, most of them taken in Dad's youth, a lot of them when he was at UCL, with people I'd never seen before. I hardly recognised Dad with his hair all long and wavy. There was one where a group of them were larking about on a punt somewhere and another hilarious one when they were all dressed to the nines, the girls with big doe-eyes and amazing hairstyles and white boots, and the men with sharp shoulders and long pointed collars and flares. The photos were all shoved into the box any old how and when I'd been through half of them I decided that sifting through the rest would be a waste of time. Something in those old snaps must have made Dad feel guilty, but they were meaningless to anyone else now, after all this time.

'Hang on, what's that?' Andrew said as I was putting them back before closing the lid. He reached out and lifted the spool of film I hadn't noticed beneath the bottom layer of photos.

Well, that was it. When we got back here, Andrew dug out an old projector of his father's from the attic and insisted on playing it through. I wish now with all my heart and mind and soul that he hadn't. It's weird enough seeing photos of your parents and their friends when they were your age, looking smooth-faced and young, and knowing one day you'll be like they are now, with wrinkles and everything, never mind viewing what was on that film.

And that, of course, was when it all started.

I could sense the thoughts racing through Andrew's mind, and I knew he was going to make use of it. 'We can have it transferred to video,' he said, in a quick, exited voice, quite unlike himself. I was quite amazed, because Andrew is usually narrow-minded and disapproving, would you believe, about that sort of thing. But he's totally single-minded once he gets an idea into his head. All the rest of them thought the idea was brilliant, too. Except me. Everyone would see

*that wretched film, it would become public property, and I just
simply could not bear that. It wasn't what Dad had intended, and I
wouldn't agree. That's why they're not speaking to me.*

*Oh God, I do wish you were here. I don't know what I'm doing.
When I made myself go back to Orbury to pick up a few clothes and
things, anything, it didn't matter what, I left all sorts of things
behind that I ought to have taken, including the only thing that
really matters to me – though it can't be of interest to anyone else –
my Diary.*

Luv,

9

Although he was still a young man – if he'd ever been young,
that is, which some people had reason to doubt – Jonathan
Gould took a lot of pride in keeping up the old-fashioned
standards of Freyning Manor, a small, privately owned country
house hotel standing in grounds of outstanding beauty. As
manager, he made comfort his prime consideration – ensuring
spotless cleanliness, that his beds were well sprung, the heating
efficient, the food beyond reproach. He had his own quarters
and all his personal needs were looked after by his staff, as if he
were indeed the squire he sometimes imagined himself to be. He
would have thoroughly enjoyed the life, had it not been for the
guests.

Unpredictable people, guests. Like children, needing constant
supervision. Otherwise, they created havoc, just one damn thing
after another. Endlessly locking themselves out of their bedrooms, then taking their keys with them when they departed;
leaving personal belongings behind which had to be posted on,
or valuables scattered around to tempt the cleaning staff; smoking where they shouldn't and setting off fire alarms, burning

61

holes in carpets and furniture and, occasionally, the sheets. Scalding themselves with hot coffee. Inconsiderately slipping in the bath and breaking their arms. Even leaving without paying their bills. The list was endless.

But until now no one had ever gone so far as to get themselves murdered in his hotel.

She lay sprawled across the bed in Derwent, the room with the french windows opening on to a balcony, one slim bare brown leg dangling, a blonde in scanty silk underwear, most of it covered in blood. She might have been posing for the lurid cover of a cheap thriller. Except that she wasn't going to get up and walk away when the cameraman had finished.

The police photographer moved around the bed for another shot.

Oh, the bed! moaned Gould silently, almost wringing his plump hands, averting his pained eyes from the mutilated body, an outrageous intrusion into the plushy room. Not quite their best one, but all of their rooms were individually – not to say expensively – designer-luxurious. Not numbered one to twelve, but each one named after a river. Derwent here had been done out in blue, white and yellow, everything toning. Blue flowered spread, a yellow and white striped sofa with a row of scatter cushions. Grey-blue carpet, an arrangement of yellow roses in the fireplace, draped and tied-back curtains, a blue, buttoned armchair. His eyes swivelled back to the bed, trying his best not to notice the pervading odour of death that overwhelmed even the Summer Scents pot-pourri in the Wedgwood bowl, heartily regretting by now the unwise decision to finish his dinner with Chef's Death by Chocolate pudding. The bed would never be fit for use again. And possibly the carpet, too. A complete redecoration job would be needed on the walls. He closed his eyes, calculating the expense he would have to account for to the owner.

'When did she check in?' asked the CID sergeant, a big, morose-looking man with a strong Liverpool accent, Carmody by name, when they were back in his office, leaving the white-overalled forensic team to continue their grisly business.

'Today. She rang to book an overnight stay.' Gould uneasily twitched a stem in the vase of Bourbon roses on his desk, and added testily, as if the sergeant were implying everything was his fault, 'She really didn't look that sort, at all.'

'Oh? What sort's that?' asked Carmody. He might look like a basset hound, with his long, mournful face and sad eyes, but these last could sharpen with sudden interest, as Gould now saw.

'What I meant was . . . the sort to get herself into that position. I mean, you know . . .

'You mean a tart that's got what she deserved?'

'Well, I wouldn't put it exactly like that!' Gould flushed. 'We don't allow that sort of carry-on here – not if we know about it, that is. But it does look, doesn't it . . .?'

The sergeant didn't answer that, but asked if he could see the register. The manager produced it and opened it at the day's date, pointing to the name written in a clear, upright, rounded hand. For a long time Carmody stared at it. When he raised his head, Gould saw that he looked sadder than ever, the lines running from nose to chin had deepened, his mouth drooped at the corners. He unwedged himself from the velvet chair, uncoiling his length abruptly, thanked the portly young manager for his time and said he'd be back.

Gould speculated, as he stood by the window and watched the sergeant sprint across the car-park and pick up his telephone, as to what it was that had galvanised Carmody into action. He bent over the register again and, brushing aside a fallen pink rose petal, ran his plump, manicured finger down the list of names.

Julia Mayo, said the signature, which meant nothing at all to him.

Nightmares were not always lingering remnants of past horrors and bad experiences, fiends of the night. Sometimes they could presage unspeakable terrors still to come, as yet only grasped on the edge of consciousness. Sometimes they *were* the present: waking nightmares. Mayo was an expert on those. When his wife had died and he'd been left with the sole and terrifying responsibility for bringing up a young girl, he'd been tormented by doubts and fears and the worst imaginings of someone who was in a unique position to know just what could befall the innocent and unprotected. He'd done his best to give Julie guidelines to live by without robbing her of her self-confidence or sounding pompous or foolishly over-protective, hidden his worries and tried to take comfort in the sure knowledge of her basic common sense. Not long ago, he had stood over the murdered body of an innocent sixteen-year-old girl and sorrowed at the randomness of inflicted evil and pain and thanked God that he'd escaped the grief that child's parents were going to have to endure.

He stood now by the bed, grey-faced, and looked at the fair hair spread over the pillow and words could not describe the torrent of emotion he felt. Fingers were squeezing his heart. He breathed with difficulty.

Turning his back abruptly on the stifling, frilly, over-furnished room he walked heavily downstairs and outside.

The west-facing gardens of Freyning Manor were one of its major attractions: a gracious terrace outside the french windows with steps leading down to rose gardens, a wide grass path between twin herbaceous borders, parkland beyond. The day had been grey and heavy, and now the shrubs and trees stood motionless, limned against a darkening sky. As he stood there, a stag with proud, branching antlers appeared in a gap between the trees in the park and paused for a moment. With a look over its shoulder, it moved gracefully away and a troop of following does leaped on delicate hooves after him, one after the other, across the gap.

She had danced so lightly through life, and now she, too, was gone.

A slight cough behind him announced Carmody, looking as though he wished he were anywhere else. 'Sir, I – sir, I just wanted to say . . . how sorry we all are.'

Mayo looked at the sergeant's troubled, concerned face. A face that had seen it all and could still be shocked. The face of a family man with three grown-up children, a boy and two girls. A man who realised that fate was not discriminating, that this could happen to anyone.

Mayo, not a demonstrative man, uncharacteristically laid his hand on the sergeant's arm. 'It's all right, Ted.' Any emotion – anger, embarrassment – always brought out his northern persona. 'It's all right, lad. That girl in there isn't Julie.'

But it wasn't all right. Despite the mutilation of her face, he knew with dull certainty who she was.

'She's Kat – or Katie – Conolly. Her mother owns the flower shop in Bressingham Street – Orlando's, it's called.' The relief that she was not Julie had overwhelmed him almost as much as if it had been, the joy of it welling up inside him and making him ashamed. He said brusquely, 'I'll tell her mother myself.'

He owed that at least to Diane Conolly, if not to his own Julie. The girls had been at school together, boon companions, best friends, closer than some sisters, living in each other's pockets, sleeping over at each other's houses, keeping up the friendship even after school when their ways had parted, when Julie had left for catering college and Kat had ... done what? Nothing much, that he could remember, except perhaps float around pretending to help her mother in the shop. Enjoying life to the full, no thought for tomorrow. Plenty of time.

She'd had a wonderfully attractive personality, lively and fun to be with. He could see why she'd been so popular, why Julie had liked to be with her, why he'd liked her so much himself, despite misgivings about certain aspects of the friendship. For he'd always thought Kat immature, and undeniably spoilt – by divorced parents competing for her favours, by a lazy but charming nature which invariably got her what she wanted for the price of a winning smile ...

The girls had been superficially alike in outward appearance – fair-haired, tall, slim, but there the resemblance ended. Julie came of good Yorkshire stock and, he'd always reassured himself, was basically level-headed. A lovely girl but not, even he had to admit, in the same class for looks as Kat, who'd been nothing less than stunning, with a dazzling smile – and those eyes! They'd been her best feature, an unusual luminous dark green, almost olive, with lashes long and thick as a deer's. She'd had, for want of a better expression, star quality. Bright and shiny, new-minted.

The girls' ways had parted after school but Mayo knew she and Julie had kept in contact, wrote constantly and that they'd met whenever Julie returned home. He was also in a position to know more than he'd ever revealed to Julie about Kat – about the mad escapades in that sporty white car with the souped-up engine which her father had given her for her eighteenth birthday, and the reckless way she drove it, attracting wolf whistles and envy from the opposite sex and parking tickets, fines, licence endorsements from the police. He'd heard about suspect, late-night parties. And the way she'd been running around with various wild young men ever since she was sixteen. Life was a joke she refused to take seriously.

What part of all that had led to this?

There were other questions burning deeper into his brain, such as what the hell was going on with his own daughter? Like why had the room been booked in Julie's name, and where was she now? The gnawing worry took hold of his guts again.

And running alongside was the question of his own position in all this. One thing at least was clear: there was no way that he'd be welcomed anywhere near the investigation. Personal involvement could not be allowed to prejudice the outcome of an inquiry. He would have liked to believe that his senior officers had enough faith in his moral probity to be sure this would never happen, but his own opinions didn't enter into it. The top brass would be sympathetic, no doubt, but it wouldn't alter the case. Every police authority had become sensitive – sometimes unduly so – to the issue of police accountability; the public wanted to be heard, they had a right to it, no cover-ups. He'd backed this attitude too often to play it down now.

He realised Carmody was still waiting, warily alert for his reactions. Apprehensive, too, for some reason, like a bad-news messenger waiting to be shot. 'Who found her?' he asked.

'One of the maids. She'd ordered a light supper in her room – Caesar salad with chicken. When she didn't answer the door, the girl thought she was probably in the bathroom, so she used her pass key to get into the room.'

'That was when?'

'She'd ordered the meal for seven. Doc Ison's already been and certified death. He thinks she couldn't have been dead much before then. Inspector Moon's on her way. So's the Prof. Talk of the devil.'

A familiar, dark red vintage Rover turned into the drive and drew up in front of the house, with the Home Office pathologist in the driving seat. Mayo blinked as Professor Timpson-Ludgate emerged from the car. It took a moment or two for it to register that it really was T-L, another to realise this was because, since Mayo had last seen him, he'd lost what at first glance appeared to be half his weight. Good God! He really had gone on that diet he'd always preached to other people. He was almost unrecognisable. No doubt he was a healthier man, but in the process he'd lost his sleek air of well-being, of being highly satisfied with the world in general and himself in particular. He'd need to replenish his wardrobe, his jacket hung from his shoulders like a sale garment on a hanger. Timpson-Ludgate without his avoirdupois wasn't right, somehow. It made Mayo uneasy, reinforced the feeling of everything falling apart.

Abruptly, he said to Carmody, 'Let me see what he has to say, then I'll be off.' He repeated, 'And I'll let Mrs Conolly know, myself.' Which in both cases was certainly going further than he ought, and caused a momentary flicker on the sergeant's impassive face at Mayo letting himself in for a task usually reserved for a WPC, but what the heck? He could allow himself a lapse of protocol. He didn't have much time before his bowing out of the case became inevitable, and there were a lot of things he needed to know, fast. 'Inspector Moon's on her way? Good. You wait until she gets here, Ted.' He added heavily, 'She'll be in charge of the case, at least *pro tem*.'

Abigail Moon had been as far engrossed in painting her bathroom door as she was ever likely to be in any such utterly mind-numbing occupation when the summons came. She'd been determined to finish the job before getting herself a bite to eat. Muttering imprecations on all telephones, she squeezed past the stepladder, knowing that sure as hell was hot this would be a call-out and she'd have to leave the door half-finished. She absolutely hated painting, and it was Sod's law that whenever she finally psyched herself up to get down to tackling some, she'd be interrupted. And while anything that took her away from a paint pot was welcome, it was frustrating to know that the door would now be ruined. All that wasted effort for nothing. You couldn't ever carry on after it had dried without the join being obvious – she couldn't, anyway.

And to cap it all, she wasn't sure about the colour she'd picked for the walls. 'Sunkissed' it had said on the chart, but against the white door it looked more like a severe case of over-exposure at Benidorm. Was it better to respond to a challenge and fail, or play boring safe and paint everything magnolia?

She'd been right about the call-out, anyway. And just as she put the phone down it rang again. Mayo this time, already out at the scene. She listened carefully to what he had to say, then got a move on.

As she drove out of the lane, she tooted and waved to the elderly look-alike married couple who lived in the bungalow at the end, letting them know who was passing. Their unlovely pet, the black hound from hell, set up a frenzied barking just the same. She'd grown to love the Fossdykes dearly – dog excepted – but lived in hopes that one day she might escape their assiduous booking in and out, while at the same time admitting there was no chance. Anyway, mostly she was grateful for their watchful presence in this back of beyond where she'd chosen to live. It was their self-appointed mission in life to watch over her, Olive donating ambrosial home-made loaves whenever she made a batch of bread, Jack pointing out when the guttering needed repairing and giving a hand at tree-lopping. He'd have jumped at the chance of painting her bathroom for her, if she'd let him, but the painting had been a kind of displacement activity, ostensibly to prevent her from dwelling on what had lately become – not exactly a problem, but a preoccupation, something that niggled more or less constantly at the back of her mind.

Ben Appleyard, newspaperman, the man in her life. Ex-editor of the local paper, thriller writer, now on assignment in the Middle East.

Rain spattered the windscreen and her stomach grumbled, reminding her of her missed supper. She should have grabbed a banana, the ultimate convenience food. The good idea of always keeping an emergency bar of chocolate in the glove compartment remained just that, an idea that always got eaten before the emergency occurred. She looked anyway, but found it empty.

Although the village of Little Freyning was only three or four miles out of Lavenstock, it was on the other side of the town, and she'd decided on the long way round as being quicker in the end. Anything was faster than stop start through the traffic-clogged centre of the town, Sunday evening not excepted, with families returning from a day out in the country. You could die waiting to get out on to the bypass.

The road she'd taken circled the hill that rose behind the cottage; making a left turn, she had a view of it in her rear-view mirror.

The first postcard she'd had from Ben had said, *When are we going to climb that hill together?* Ben was great on postcards, poor on letters. A few words scribbled on the back of a view from wherever he was at the moment was the most she ever got. And unsatisfactory messages on her answerphone, because she was never in when he called. What had once been a successful combination of two disparate and demanding careers didn't seem to be standing the test of separation. They'd never lived in each other's pockets, but now that she *knew* he was further away, she missed him too much for her own peace of mind. Someone had warned her, when she first got to know Ben, that she should grab him and hold on to him, otherwise she'd lose him: but that sort of attitude had never been an option, with either of them.

When he'd been struggling with his second novel, a follow-up to his first successfully rated political thriller, he'd found it impossible to write about something he hadn't experienced first hand. Or so he'd said. In the end, since his current book was set in Israel, he'd managed to wangle a short-term contract as Middle East correspondent for a national Sunday. Which had meant giving up the editorship of the *Advertiser*. She'd been doubtful, not only about the wisdom, but about the ethics of what he was doing, until she'd read his sympathetic reports of what was really going on out there. That was the real Ben, and she had to be satisfied with that. Reports of how he was, how his book was progressing, evidently didn't fit on to the back of a postcard.

Maybe it had been a mistake to come this way. She'd calculated fifteen or twenty minutes would get her to Freyning Manor, but she hadn't counted on the labyrinthine nature of the lanes as she approached the forest and Little Freyning, nor the leisurely-strolling herd of cows on their way to be milked, which effectively blocked one narrow lane for a hundred yards from field to farm entrance. 'Come on, come on!' She batted the steering wheel, moved into first gear, did calming breathing exercises, followed the bony rumps and the swaying udders and prayed for patience.

The light was fading as she eventually emerged from the lane and came to the road running through the deep woods, and she kept a cautious eye out for deer. Visitors from the town came out for afternoon rides hoping to see them, oohing and ahing when they did. Beautiful as the forest itself was, it would be less attractive without them, but the police had reason to regard them otherwise, when they leapt across the roads without warning, causing accidents, sometimes serious. As had the residents of Little Freyning, who regularly missed winning the competition for the best-kept village in the county, on account of their marauding habits.

The journey had taken thirty-five minutes, if the clock on the dash, as she eventually turned into the hotel driveway, was to be believed. She found the hotel at the end of a long drive through parkland, with enticing vistas that delighted the gardener in her. The hotel, when she reached it, appeared to be smaller than she'd imagined, a discreet conversion from a Victorian country house, whose size, Abigail was willing to bet, was in inversion to its prices, judging by the cars parked on the gravelled car-park at the side. Not a model less than R reg, except for a stately fawn and black vintage Bentley. By comparison, the cluster of police cars drawn up in a knot to one side only lacked price-stickers on their windscreens to be mistaken for a used-car lot. Her middle-aged Beetle, which as usual needed cleaning, didn't improve matters. She left it next to Carmody's five-year-old Escort and hurried to the porch.

10

When he arrived at Orlando's, the flower shop in Bressingham Street, Mayo was invited into the flat above the closed shop, where Diane Conolly had been watching television while waiting for her evening meal to cook. An appetising odour of onions, tomatoes and browning cheese permeated through to the living area, suggesting something Italian: lasagne perhaps, or pizza.

In the small, attractively furnished sitting-room the TV set was tuned to the highlights of the week from Wimbledon. Diane, he recalled, had been a tennis player in her youth, up to county standards if he remembered aright, and still played competitively in local tournaments. That was why her face was familiar to him, in the one-remove way newspaper photos project; though they'd known of each other through their respective daughters, they'd never actually met. He could see that Kat's looks hadn't come to her through her mother. Diane could never have been a beauty, and by now, in her mid-forties, she presented the slightly hard face of a woman who'd had to make her own way in the world, with a bitter twist to her lips which said that life hadn't come up to her expectations. He guessed she was used to hard knocks but that wouldn't make it any easier for her to accept what he had to tell her. When he did, she didn't throw hysterics, or even burst into tears, but her face drained of colour and when she spoke her voice sounded dry and husky, as though she'd shrivelled inside.

She'd turned the TV sound down before answering her door but hadn't turned it off, and she now stared blankly at the flickering screen where Rusedski and Philippoussis were attempting to annihilate each other with services like weapons of mass destruction, in front of an enthusiastic crowd which was making the most of an unexpected break in the weather, and determinedly ignoring the threat of further disruption to play. Diane stared at them unseeingly, her fingers picking at a loose thread in the stitching of her skirt. She looked up at Mayo and, helpless before the pain in her eyes, he suggested the usual panacea, a cup of tea, trite, but invariably helpful.

She insisted on making it herself, obviously feeling the need to occupy her hands with mundane tasks while her mind tried to encompass the enormity of what she'd been told. He went into the kitchen with her. Her hands were steady as she switched off the oven – there'd be no question of eating, not for now – warmed the pot, measured in three heaped caddyspoons of tea and poured boiling water over them, but the mugs rattled on their hooks as she reached them down. They sat at the kitchen table to drink the bracing liquid.

'Is there anyone you'd like to have with you? A friend, or a relative?'

He had the impression she was about to say yes, she would, but then changed her mind. 'I'll be all right. I'll get through.'

'I can get a policewoman to stay with you. You shouldn't be alone.'

'Jamie,' she said. 'He'll come. Later, when I've had a chance . . .'

He remembered then that there was a son, a brother who'd also have to be told. 'It'll be a question of someone taking a look at Kat, as well,' he told her gently.

Diane drew in her breath. 'Identifying her, you mean? Yes, yes, of course.' She hesitated, then came to a decision. 'Jamie'll take this badly – much better if I did that. No – it's all right, I can cope.'

He studied her for a moment or two, then nodded, sure she could. 'As you wish. I'll send someone tomorrow to go with you. But meanwhile, would you like me to get hold of your son?'

She shook her head and wrapped her hands round the mug of hot tea, as if seeking comfort from its warmth. Someone had had the mugs personalised, and they were obviously in daily use. The gold lettering of the name on the one she was drinking from was only just recognisable as 'Kat' by now, though the smiling Cheshire-cat face with exaggeratedly long whiskers on the opposite side had fared better. His own mug read, 'Diane' and the design was of crossed tennis racquets.

'You've enough with telling Julie,' she said in answer to his question, drawing from another level of her conscious mind, above that which was trying to suppress unacceptable pain. 'It'll go hard with her, poor girl. Still in America, is she?'

He nodded. It was easier not to explain. He couldn't bring himself to tell her, not yet, of Julie's apparent connection with the affair. If there was anything, she'd learn, soon enough. It was a fact he was finding it hard enough to come to terms with, himself, amongst other things.

He pushed his chair back after he'd finished his tea. He didn't like the idea of leaving her alone, but he could see her too taut composure beginning to waver, sense the need to be alone to do her grieving in private. 'What about her father?' he asked. 'If you can give me his address, I can at least see he's told.'

There was a moment of silence while she stared into her tea. 'He's dead. Didn't you know?'

Dead? 'I'm so sorry, no, I hadn't heard.'

'He had a bad car accident that killed his – his wife, and badly damaged him. But that wasn't what he died of. They found out he had cancer as well. Awful, that, isn't it? And Hugh, of all people. You didn't somehow think...' Her lips pressed hard together. 'He died last month. Katie went to look after him and nursed him until the end. Surprised everyone, though it shouldn't have. She was absolutely devoted to her father, you know, it was that Terri she couldn't stand.'

Terri was the new wife, she explained, who'd been much younger than Hugh Conolly, only a few years older than Kat herself. Her dislike of this Terri was undisguised, her tone speaking volumes, and maybe it was that which released the words that were now tumbling out. 'Katie thought she'd married Hugh for his money, we all did. But if so ... well, if she hadn't been killed first, she'd have got a shock when he died. He always gave the impression of having plenty, but he never could handle money, not really. I'll say this in his favour, though – when he knew he was dying he sold out his half of the business to Max, and used most of what he got for that to pay his debts off. And this place – the flower shop – he owned it, you know, and he made it over to me in his will, which was more than I

73

ever expected. More than I deserve, some might say, seeing that I threw him out.' An unreadable expression that might have been regret crossed her face.

'What about Kat? Didn't she inherit anything from her father?'

'Katie was provided for, yes. *Katie.* Kat was her father's name for her. I never called her that, though her friends did – they have these daft names, don't they? Like your daughter, Jools. Yes, he left her a bit. I expect it'll go to Jamie, now.' She stared out of the window with an unseeing frown.

'When did you last see her, Diane?'

'Six weeks since, maybe two months, though she'd phone me, of course, couple of times a week, maybe.'

'She hasn't been living with you, then?'

'Not since she first went to Orbury House.'

He hadn't really thought she would still have been living at home. It was in the nature of things for children to fly the nest as early as they could – college, their own flat, anything for independence. 'When Hugh died, she moved out and went to stay with a friend, somewhere in the Saltcote End area, I think it was. I didn't know a lot about her private life – do any of us parents?' she asked, setting up an echo in his mind. She suddenly did a double take, as if what he'd told her was all at once catching up with her. 'What was she doing, staying in that hotel? I didn't even know she was back in England!'

'Back from where?'

She stared at him. 'Why, she went out to the States to stay with your Julie after Hugh died. Didn't Julie tell you?'

He was beginning to think there might be rather a lot of things Julie hadn't told him.

Abigail ran up the wide stone steps at Freyning Manor, and found the big front door of the hotel wide open to a pine-panelled, encaustic-tiled hallway with stained-glass windows and pictures in ornate frames on the stairs. No one was around, except the uniformed constable on guard before the dining-room door, from whence came the rich aroma of haute cuisine. Abigail's stomach growled again. To her left was a gothic arch, through which could be glimpsed armchairs covered in tapestry or plush. Embroidered screens for privacy. Crimson and green silk-shaded lamps stood on tables beside the chairs, long windows were curtained in heavily embossed velvet, with draped and fringed pelmets and matching tie-backs. One or two genuinely antique pieces of furniture, tasteful arrangements of flowers everywhere. A Victorian country house pastiche, the effect so unstudied you could tell how much thought had gone into it.

'They're all upstairs, ma'am,' Spellman told her. 'The SOCOs and Sergeant Carmody. The others are interviewing the guests in the dining-room.'

'Thanks, Andy.'

There was nothing so vulgar as a reception desk, only a heavy polished table with bulbous legs on which reposed a tall vase full of pampas grass and peacock feathers, and a chair behind it; this might, or might not, be where you signed the register. She ignored the discreet bell and walked up the wide staircase, where the expected sounds of police activity directed her to the crime scene.

Ted Carmody was waiting for her at the top of the stairs, looking like a long stick of Blackpool rock in the transparent plastic that clothed him from head to foot. His face, doleful and long as the Mersey Tunnel, was creased into lines of concern. His brow was furrowed like sand when the tide has gone out. 'Jeez, this is a facer,' he greeted her. 'He'll have my guts for garters.'

Abigail had followed the sergeant's line of thinking too long not to know who was meant by 'he' and to guess just how poor old Carmody was feeling. Chastened. Furious with himself.

'So what? You've made a right pig's ear of it, but he doesn't bite, you know that. OK, OK, he might chew you up and spit you out in little pieces, but he doesn't bear a grudge. Could have been worse.'

'Oh, right. Like his daughter *really* lying in there.'

But Christ, if only he, Carmody, hadn't been so gobsmacked by seeing the name Julia Mayo in the register that he'd jumped in with both feet, and for the first – and if he'd any sense, the *only* time – in his career, bypassed routine procedures and, out of mistaken sympathy with Mayo, informed him first. But how in hell, Carmody asked himself, was he to have known she wasn't who she'd declared herself to be? He'd never seen the superintendent's daughter.

Quite so. There could, conceivably, be other Julia Mayos.

'Hey, come on! You weren't to have known. And he'd have had to identify her sooner or later. He's probably never given it a thought.'

Carmody threw his inspector a soulful, disbelieving look, then gave himself a shake and a resigned shrug, not unlike a bloodhound being forgiven for losing the trail. The idea of suicide was shelved. 'OK, I'll learn to live with it. What's done's done, as the bishop said to the actress . . . See you got around to that painting after all.'

She raised her eyebrows. 'How come?'

'Either the painting, or you've had a shock that's turned your hair white overnight. '

A quick glance in the darkening glass of a nearby window as she scrambled into her protective clothing revealed her coppery hair delicately frosted with white, where she must have brushed it against the wet paint. Blast. Probably left several strands of her crowning glory adhering to the paint as well. Hopes of retrieving the bathroom door received their final death knell. 'People pay an arm and a leg for this at Comb and Scissors, maybe I should stay with it,' she wondered aloud, squinting at the effect, snapping on thin latex gloves. 'Well, what have we got? Put me in the picture before I have a look.'

Carmody obliged with his usual laconic conciseness. It didn't take him long. She gave him a quick glance when he'd finished. 'Ted, you know what this means?'

'The super won't be i/c the case . . . more or less told me as much himself before he left. This one's yours, now, petal. Should be, anyway.'

'Who're you kidding? With someone of his rank involved? And he *is* involved, if his daughter and the victim were as intimate as all that. She may have used Julie's name without her permission – but not necessarily.'

What Carmody didn't know yet, and what she didn't feel obliged to tell him until she'd spoken further with Mayo, was that he'd told her when he rang that Julie's whereabouts were, at the moment, uncertain to say the least. So however it had been, and with the inquiry scarcely begun, what the areas as yet unexplored might reveal didn't bear thinking about. She was confident she could have handled the investigation herself, no problem, but that wouldn't be an issue, either. 'They'll bring in somebody higher up from outside,' she affirmed with gloomy resignation.

Although maybe . . . a gleam of hope stirred . . . maybe they just wouldn't at that. Maybe . . . Like heck they would! Dream on, Abigail.

Anyway, who wanted to be responsible for an investigation that was so close to home, involving your immediate senior? Nobody with any sense. Better to be a dogsbody, not to have to make decisions about where to poke your nose, just do as you were told. No hassle . . .

She said, brisk as a breeze, 'That doesn't mean we don't carry on as per usual routine, until we know to the contrary.'

Carmody, who had two clever daughters of his own, not much younger than she was, and was never a great talker anyway, knew when to keep his mouth shut. He nodded agreement. They had a good working relationship. After twenty-six years in the service, the sergeant had no further ambitions for himself. He accepted her seniority with equanimity. Though that didn't mean he wouldn't let her know if he thought she was making a cobblers of something his wider experience told him was wrong, nor that she wouldn't take it as given. An unspoken agreement they'd both had reason to be grateful for, more than once.

'Funny she should come here for the night – alone – when she's a local lass, local to Lavenstock, anyway,' he commented, cocking a cynical eyebrow. 'A bit of how's your father with one of the other guests? Would explain why she signed in under another name. Not a thing you want to advertise.'

True, Abigail acknowledged. 'We'll get the guest-list from the manager – Gould, did you say? We need to check all of them, staff as well. We shall want their rooms searched too, and their belongings – from what you tell me, whoever did this is likely to have blood all over him. Make that a priority.'

77

'I've got it lined up, after they've finished checking the non-residents, those who were just dining here.'

'Good.' She thought for a moment. 'We're not going to be able to do much more than that tonight ... but meanwhile, we'd better try to fix up some room or other we can use for a bit. We'll have a briefing first thing tomorrow morning at Milford Road. Timpson-Ludgate arrived yet?'

'You just missed him. Man in a hurry, as usual, but he's agreed to do the PM a.s.a.p. The SOCOs are still here and the manager's wanting to know when the body will be taken away, so that he can keep his guests out of the way. He's wetting his knickers at all this upset.'

'One of life's little difficulties he'll just have to put up with. He's lucky this room's where it is.'

It was likely that the SOCOs would be here for some time yet. When a few hairs could yield enough DNA to convict a murderer, it was of paramount importance that the room would be minutely gone through, combed for the slightest traces of forensic evidence. With Dexter, the SOCO man in charge, it surely would be.

Derwent, where the crime had occurred, was situated at the end of a short corridor that turned a right angle, thus virtually cutting it off from the main building. Providential for all concerned – sealing the room off and giving the police elbow room to work should cause the minimum of inconvenience to the rest of the hotel. Providential for the murderer, too, unfortunately – its situation being such that any sounds made during the murder were unlikely to have penetrated to the other rooms.

'The guests'll hardly know we're here.'

Carmody rolled his eyes. 'I don't somehow think our friend believed me when I told him that same thing.'

She pulled on the plastic overshoes and drew the hood up over the offending hair. 'Presumably the Prof's left you with some information?'

'Much as he could at this stage. Her throat's been cut, likely by someone right-handed, carotid arteries severed, which was probably what killed her, though there's other cuts. She's undressed but doesn't seem to have been sexually assaulted.'

Abigail couldn't postpone it any longer, the moment when she must confront the body. She breathed in and entered the room, redolent with the scent of smotheringly sweet pot-pourri mingling with the overriding, metallic smell of fresh blood. A slight odour of cooking food added another nauseous dimension.

Three men were already in there – Napier, the police photographer; Dexter, the ex-police sergeant turned scenes of crime man, and a technician whom Abigail didn't know. With Carmody bringing up the rear, the small space had suddenly become seriously overcrowded. Dexter stopped what he was doing, but Abigail motioned them all to carry on as best they could and moved nearer the bed. Dexter, taciturn as ever, nodded and went on adhesive-taping the door frame of the french window for hairs or fibres.

Abigail's first reaction when she brought her gaze round to the body was, as usual, one of anger. And outrage. That anyone felt they had a right to think they could get away with doing this to another human being – in this case a woman, always, by definition, more vulnerable than a man, and if that sentiment was sexist, too bad. It wasn't by any means the first time she'd seen a mutilated corpse, it wouldn't be the last, and some of them had been worse than this, but she always felt the same. It was only a body, she told herself. The spirit had gone, leaving nothing but a shell. But there was a constriction in her throat as she looked at what remained of Kathryn Conolly.

It had been what the media were wont to call 'a frenzied attack', which meant that she'd had her throat cut, and been slashed repeatedly, mostly on her face. She had bled copiously. Her smooth skin was criss-crossed with slashes crusted with blood, her throat gaped like a wide, smiling mouth. She was on her back, lying sideways across the bed, facing the door. One slender arm was outflung, her legs disposed in a way that was almost elegant. The fingers of the other hand were stiffly clenched in cadaveric spasm round a handful of silken, quilted bedspread. Her designer underwear – bra and bikini briefs – had once been emerald green satin, but was now darkened with drying blood, and the high-heeled strappy sandals were of soft, dark blue leather. A short-sleeved, button-through dress in some thin material, patterned in dark blues and greens, lay tossed across the buttoned back of the sofa. Her toenails had been varnished green to match her fingernails. Outsize green and lapis-lazuli blue titanium ear-rings dangled from her ears. A kingfisher corpse. She might have been beautiful, once. It was hard to tell.

In the confined space of what was not a large room, the blood was everywhere. Soaked into the bedspread and the padded headboard, pooled on to the carpet. The long, central mirror on the heavy, mahogany Victorian wardrobe was sprayed with a pattern of diagonal slashes, and the pattern on the wallpaper had gathered an added dimension of crimson spots, reaching as high as the egg-and-dart moulding on the heavy picture rail.

Abigail closed her eyes briefly and forced the nausea down before she eventually turned away from the bloody bed. 'You've finished with her, Bob?' she asked Napier. The photographer nodded. 'Have her taken away,' she said softly. A few minutes later, the body of Kathryn Conolly, zipped into a body bag, her head and hands encased in plastic, had gone.

Dexter took the opportunity to say into the silence which followed, 'He likely came in this way, ma'am – we've found footwear prints, too big to be hers, still damp. We can lift them, no problem.'

She skirted the marked area and peered out of the window. There seemed little point to the wrought-iron metal table and two matching chairs set out on the small balcony outside, except as a gesture, since the lovely view of the hotel grounds was confined to the front; here at the back, the room looked out on to nothing but an upward slope of rough grass, pitted with rabbit holes. Two shallow steps led down from the balcony on to a flat-roofed extension. It looked new, and a cowboy job to boot: the bitumen was buckled in places and pitted with small pools of residual rain here and there.

The smell of the cooking which had infiltrated the bedroom drifted up more strongly from below, and steam was issuing from a ventilator. 'This extension's the kitchen, I take it?'

Dexter said, 'Yes, and there's a water butt in the yard directly below, with a fallpipe emptying into it. Anybody reasonably athletic could've got on to the roof via that. It'd be a doddle.'

'So it would. Straight across the roof and in here.'

Such an entry suggested an opportunist attack, someone discovering an easy method of access to one of the hotel rooms, surprising a guest when she was semi-clothed. Well, it was possible. A demand for money, a mindless attack on her when she refused, a loss of control resulting in her being finished off in a panic. But – those slashes to her face!

Abigail considered this for a while, looking back at the bed. Half-dressed the victim might have been, yet there was no suggestion of attempted rape. There was a dent in the pillows, and the bedspread, which had been left as undisturbed as possible after cutting around the piece of it still clutched in the victim's hand, was all ruckled up as though she'd been lying down on top of the bedclothes, resting or asleep, then dragged across it. If she'd struggled, the attacker could have been scratched by those long green fingernails, and with luck the post-mortem might reveal traces of skin underneath them. With more luck they might find someone whose skin matched. Which called for a lot of something not too often in evidence in a murder case.

She didn't think much of the idea of an opportunist burglar, though. Surely anyone bent on such nefarious activity would have more oil in their lamp than to break into a lighted hotel bedroom at that time of day, when its occupants were quite likely to be there, getting ready for dinner?

'I'm more likely to go for the notion of somebody having a room key, or her having let them in,' she remarked. 'She was expecting room service.' But not in her underwear.

Dexter nodded. 'The door lock hasn't been tampered with.'

Abigail's gaze went searchingly past the cluttered opulence of the room. Everything a guest might conceivably need, from writing paper and a book of stamps,' tissues, spare toothbrushes and a comb, to sheaves of magazines, a bowlful of cellophane-wrapped boiled sweets, a dish of chocolates and a well-filled basket of fruit. 'Where's her suitcase, her bag or whatever? I don't see one.'

She'd noticed a flimsy robe hanging behind the bathroom door, but there was no nightdress. Maybe Kat was one of those who slept *au naturel*. Not in Chanel No.5, à la Marilyn Monroe, but in Paloma Picasso, a large black flask of which stood on the dressing-table, together with a powder compact and a few other oddments of a personal nature that seemed unlikely to have been provided by the management. No nightdress, then, and neither were there clothes of any kind in the wardrobe or the drawers, not even a change of underwear. And the tiny, soft blue and green leather shoulder bag on the dressing-table wasn't big enough to hold even the scantiest of underwear, not to mention the expensive cosmetics, lotions and powders scattered around the bathroom. It gaped open, and it was plain to see there was no room for even a wallet, merely a change purse, a comb and a crumpled tissue.

'How did she intend paying her bill? And she must've had some luggage with her.'

'Yeah. She did.' Carmody consulted his notes. 'Small, black Louis Veeton suitcase, the manager says. No call for a receptionist or a porter, small place like this, and he checked her in himself and showed her to her room, carried the bag up for her.'

Abigail could imagine it. Men falling over themselves to carry her bags, even small ones. A girl like that – the long legs, the see-through dress, the long flaxen hair, it stacked.

'Is her car still around?'

'She didn't drive herself here – she was dropped off by a young feller driving a white Sierra Cosworth, again according to Gould. But the super seemed to think that'd be her own car, the one her dad gave her for her eighteenth,' Carmody added, rolling his eyes heavenwards at the thought of such a motor, let alone for a daughter.

Abigail made a mental note to talk to the manager next. If he was observant and sharp enough to recognise things like Louis Vuitton luggage and Sierra Cosworths, he might have noticed other things that could be important.

'Any sign of the weapon?'

'Still searching. Something like a short-bladed knife it would've been, very sharp, the Prof thinks. The kitchen staff have checked to see if there's something of the sort missing but they say not. Seems the killer came equipped.'

'Here we are, then!' announced Dexter triumphantly at that moment. But it wasn't the weapon he'd found. He was pointing to a cupboard underneath the TV set, inside which a small safe was discreetly hidden, of the type found sometimes in hotel

82

bedrooms, with a combination chosen by the guest and known only to him or her. 'Knew there'd be one somewhere.'

'Let's have a decko,' Carmody said. 'Can't see her using it to stash her clean undies, but her cheque book, credit cards, whatever might be there.'

'It's locked and no way of getting into it without knowing the combination.'

'Never mind, I'll get the manager to open it. I'm on my way down to see him,' Abigail told Dexter.

'Try her birth date,' Gould said wearily, when asked about the combination lock on the safe. 'They all think that's a brilliant idea. Or her phone number.'

'We could if we knew either. Don't you have a master-key?'

'That would defeat the object, wouldn't it?'

Without comment at what he thought was an asinine arrangement Carmody, with exaggerated Liverpudlian offhandedness, said, 'Thar'll be no problem, break it open.'

Gould flushed, hesitated, then reached into a drawer. 'There's no need for that. We do have a key, as a matter of fact – for emergencies only, you understand – one has to be so careful . . .'

'Thank you,' Abigail said, contemplating the sleek, well-fed, anything-to-avoid-trouble countenance before her.

While Carmody took the key and went back upstairs with it, she questioned Gould further. Although he could describe the victim's luggage and her car, he was curiously blank about the young man who'd driven it, other than that he was wearing a baseball hat and sun-glasses.

'OK. Did Miss Conolly by any chance ask for any particular room when she booked?'

'Not in so many words, but I told her that was the only one I had available when she rang. I explained, as I always do to our guests, that Derwent was rather more economical because it's over the kitchen . . . They're usually quite amenable if they're not left to find that out for themselves.'

So she'd known beforehand which room she would occupy, which presupposed someone else could have known it, too – especially if she *had* booked into the hotel for an illicit assignation. Someone who'd visited her in her room, someone she knew well enough to entertain half-dressed.

It didn't account for the footprint.

'What about keys, Mr Gould?'

He explained which of the staff held keys.

'And what about the guests' own keys? When they're out, and so on?'

'In the drawer of the reception desk.' She took this to mean the table in the hall. 'It's locked by whichever member of staff puts them in,' he said defensively, obviously realising the inadequacy of his security.

She merely nodded. The sort of security that was par for the course, only reviewed when things went wrong. The sort of place where anybody could walk in or out without being noticed.

11

It was DC Farrar who'd made the connection between the murdered girl, Kat Conolly, and the young man who was working in the kitchens.

'Also named Conolly, ma'am. Jamie Conolly. She was his sister. He didn't volunteer the information, but when I saw the surname, I thought there might be a connection.'

'Good thinking,' Abigail said.

The irony was wasted on him. He smiled modestly, while still managing to look like a Keen Young Policeman, which was exactly what he was: bright, eager to catch the eye of anyone higher up, a DC who'd passed his sergeant's exams and was desperate to find a posting, if anyone would have him. He hadn't succeeded so far, mostly due to an attitude problem which he but not others totally failed to recognise.

Yet Abigail always felt constrained to praise Farrar more than was necessary, simply because his bumptiousness constantly irritated her. Plus the fact that he was nearly always right – which undoubtedly made him an asset to the department. Or would have done if he occasionally forgot to remind everyone of this.

'All right. Let's have Conolly in and see what he's got to say for himself.'

With grudging reluctance, Gould had temporarily given up his office to the police for the questioning of his guests, since the only other room available was a bedroom, presently in the throes of redecoration. So far the results of the questioning hadn't been helpful. The sedate clientele seemed unexceptional: the three American ladies, using the hotel as a base for touring the Cotswolds and attending several Shakespeare performances at Stratford-upon-Avon, using the rooms called Trent, Severn and Medway, had heard nothing. They'd returned late from a Sunday afternoon conducted tour of Stratford and were in too much of a rush getting ready for dinner to notice external noises. The two middle-aged married couples making up a golf foursome for the weekend – rooms Aire and Clyde – had gone down early and were having pre-dinner drinks in the lounge. Another couple who, despite the fact that neither would see seventy again, bashfully confessed they were on their honeymoon, were listening to the news and weather forecast in the Thames suite. Humber, Tyne and Tweed, respectively occupied by a brother and sister and her female friend, were at the opposite end of the building, as was Avon, occupied by the only guest staying at Freyning Manor alone.

None of them had seen Kat Conolly. She'd been shown straight to her room on arrival, and stayed there. Nor had anyone heard screams or the sounds of a struggle, this almost certainly due to the room's position along the corridor and over the kitchen.

They'd all been spoken to, and all seemed unlikely suspects, with the possible exception of the lone man in Avon. William Turville, it appeared, was a representative for a firm of wine importers, who'd come to the hotel to do business with the manager and stayed the night, apparently a regular occurrence. His was the Bentley outside. Abigail decided she was in the wrong job if the wine trade could afford to run Bentleys for their reps, until she discovered he was a director of the firm, combining business with pleasure. He was unpromising as a suspect, a

gnome of a man, an elderly Big Ears with a small pot-belly ...
all of which proved nothing: he was also, presumably, well
heeled and able to pay for favours bestowed, and could easily
have arranged with Kat for her to be there that night. Such
accommodations weren't unknown. He had allegedly been sitting in the lounge at the presumed time when she had been
killed, though the two golfing couples having a drink there
claimed not to have seen him. This, he said, was because the
Knole chair he was sitting in was at an angle to the seats they'd
occupied and the high, roped-together sides of the chair hid him
from the rest of the room. It was possibly true; such a small man
could easily have disappeared into the depths of a chair like
that. And it was hard to envisage him as a desperate killer. He'd
asked to see a doctor, saying he wasn't feeling well. The local
doctor had been summoned and was on his way.

As Jamie Conolly came into the room, his head bowed in
sorrow, Abigail immediately sensed a strong resemblance
between the slimly built, good-looking young Adonis before her
and his dead sister, the difference being that he was as dark as
she had been fair. The same thickly lashed eyes watched her
warily, only his were a smoky blue, not that unusual olive – an
unexpected juxtaposition: you would have thought it would
have been the other way round, hers the blue eyes and his the
dark. He'd changed from his working garb and was dressed in
a manner reminiscent of a Regency buck: light trousers tucked
into long polished boots and, despite the warmth of the evening,
a waisted velvet jacket and a lightweight cream polo-neck. He
disposed himself in the chair with a grace that had been suggested in the girl, even in death, accepting Abigail's condolences
gravely.

She began by asking him why he hadn't come forward straight
away when he'd learned that the guest who'd been killed was
his sister.

'I was much too upset. I knew you'd want to question me and
I wanted time to get myself together, you know?' He achieved a
wan but attractive smile. Even in such harrowing circumstances,
Abigail felt he was consciously exerting his charm, but he was
indeed very pale, and no doubt upset, too.

'Why was your sister staying in the hotel?'

'I don't *know*, it was news to me that she *was* here, I'm only kitchen staff, you know,' he said with a moue, 'we don't mingle with the guests.'

Abigail thought he was possibly the most elegant kitchen worker even Freyning Manor had ever employed. 'How long have you worked here?'

'Three days.'

'Your regular line of work, is it?'

'God no, it's only a temporary thing,' he exclaimed, eager to explain. 'Do I look like a kitchen boy? I'm a group leader with a travel firm – I speak several languages and I'm able to go where and when the fancy takes me.'

'Sounds good – so what brought you to work here?'

He shrugged and stubbed out his half-smoked cigarette in the ashtray. 'I've a friend who also works for the agency – and, well, we had a bit of a falling out, and I thought we'd be better not seeing each other for a few weeks, till he came round.'

She favoured him with a look. Evidently, it sounded pretty lame to him, too. He shrugged and laid one shining black leather boot on one exquisite, fawn-clad knee, and smiled at her. 'I've done it before, worked here, I mean. Ever since I first took it as a vacation job in the school holidays.'

'All right. Let's talk about tonight ... what were you doing in the half-hour up to seven o'clock?'

'Seven? Is that the time she was – oh God!' His jaw clenched. Tears sprang to his eyes. He put a hand across them. She waited until he'd got a hold on himself, which took but a few minutes. 'Where was I before seven?' he repeated her question, dashing the last of the tears manfully away. 'In the kitchen with the rest of the staff, of course. Dinner starts early, from seven thirty, so we were working flat out at that time. Non-residents come in for dinner too, you know.'

'You didn't go out at all?'

'Not a chance, not with Helga's beady eye on us. She keeps us all with our noses to the grindstone, like a female sergeant major, she is.'

Helga was the capable young Scandinavian in charge of the kitchen, someone who was increasing the hotel's reputation for good food, a formidable presence in a long white overall and apron, her hair scraped back under a white cloth severely pinned around her head. Very role-conscious, very responsible.

'But she says you did go out at one point.' Abigail didn't add that Helga had been unable to remember exactly when she'd looked round for Jamie and found him not there.

His self-assurance was shaken, but just for a moment. 'Well, maybe I did, now I come to think of it, but only for a minute or two. For a – a breath of fresh air. Well, a ciggie, to be honest.'

Or to shin up the drainpipe by way of the water butt to the room occupied by his sister, armed with a knife? Under the effete exterior was a lithe and fit body, no doubt capable of such a manoeuvre. He'd been back in the kitchen within a few minutes, according to Helga, but for all the horrific injuries inflicted on the dead girl, a few minutes was all it would have taken.

'Is that right? OK, then how do you account for the bloodstains? You know why we've taken your clothing away? For forensic tests?'

His air of injured innocence dropped away like a caterpillar shedding its skin. He looked sharp and angry. 'God, this is pathetic! They had bloodstains on them because I'd been preparing some calves' liver, not because I'd just been stabbing my sister! I told you so, told that big Scouse bloke of yours, anyway. Ever tried to prepare liver *without* bloodying your hands? I must've wiped them on my apron, it's a habit you get into.'

'No, I haven't, but never mind that,' Abigail said shortly. Appreciation of good food was, she acknowledged, one of the finer pleasures of life, but liver – calves' liver in particular – was not within the range of things she wished to know about. Nor were unsavoury, behind the scenes glimpses of the habits of staff in kitchens where food was prepared for public consumption.

It took a stretch of the imagination to envisage this young exquisite in a bloodstained apron and kitchen fatigues, his fingers dappled with blood . . . 'What's that Band Aid on the back of your hand for?'

'I cut it. Blame that on the blasted liver, as well! The knife slipped.'

He looked suddenly as queasy as she herself felt. As well he might, if he'd come back to a job like slicing liver, after stabbing his sister. Or had he cut himself during the attack? If it was a wound sustained while cutting up the meat, it was in an odd place. There might equally be scratches made by Kat's fingernails under the plaster – or even a self-inflicted cut to cover up. 'There'll be a doctor on the premises shortly, I'd like him to look at it,' she said.

'I've no objections.'

His confidence quickly disappeared when she changed the subject. 'What sort of relationship did you and your sister have?'

'Better than most brothers and sisters, as far as I can see.' He blinked, and she saw his eyes were again bright with unshed tears. This time, a tight white line had appeared around his mouth. 'I need a smoke.'

She nodded and watched, fascinated, as he extracted a cigarette from a flat gold case taken from the inside pocket of his jacket. She hadn't ever seen anyone use such an object, apart from Noel Coward in old films. He lit it with a matching lighter, dragging the smoke deep into his lungs. 'She was older than me, not much, and we were always close. She was a sweet kid, ask anybody. A bit feather-headed, but what does that matter? She used to stand up for me against my father. She could twist him round her little finger.'

'*Against* your father? Didn't you get on with him?'

'Not like she did,' he said shortly.

Abigail made a mental note that this might be a profitable sideline to pursue, later. 'Where did she work?'

'She didn't, not recently. She wasn't trained for anything. She used to help my mother in her flower shop occasionally, and sometimes she worked for my father and his partner. But then he got ill – Dad, I mean – and she spent her time looking after him. After he died, she went to live with her boyfriend. I don't think she'd been working since then – unless she did anything for Max – you could ask him.'

Considering what sort of clothes, make-up, luggage she had, the car she ran, that was fairly astonishing. Unless she'd found someone or something to support such expensive tastes. Tastes which her brother evidently shared: his cream polo-neck was silk, his boots looked to have a pedigree, the plum-coloured velvet jacket had surely been tailored for him; he sported a gold nugget on a leather thong, an affectation she particularly loathed in a man. He accepted her scrutiny as though he was used to it and was enjoying it, then after a while glanced at the slim gold watch on his wrist, the price of which could have kept a family for a month. 'I don't want to rush you, but I have to go to my mother. She's alone.' His voice had taken on belated urgency.

'You can be on your way in a few minutes, this won't take much longer.' Abigail looked back at her notes. 'Max, you said. Who's that?'

'Max Fisher, my father's partner. Fisher-Conolly Security Systems, that's their firm.'

She made another note of the address. Orbury House, interested to see that it was just the other side of Freyning village. 'And her boyfriend – who is he?'

'He's called Andrew, that's all I know. I've never met him. He sounds a right berk to tell you the truth. Why she was going to marry him beats me.' And no, he didn't know where he lived, but he had a telephone number – though he'd need to look it up.

'Do it before you go and let me have it. They were going to be married, you say?'

'That's what she told me, last time I saw her.'

'Which was?'

'Weeks ago, actually. After the funeral – my father's.'

'Are you quite sure of that?'

'That's what I said, didn't I?'

She looked at him steadily, and then said suddenly, 'I presume you know your sister's friend, Julie Mayo?'

'Jools?' He blinked at the change of subject. Startled, yes, and also wary. 'Sure I know her. Haven't set eyes on her for yonks, though. I think she's in Australia or somewhere.'

'You've heard that Kat booked in here under her name? Any idea why she should do that?'

He raised one eyebrow, for all the world like Cary Grant in black and white, not easy to achieve without a lot of practice in front of a mirror. 'Oh, I shouldn't read anything into that, if I were you. It's something they used to do, use each other's names, borrow each other's clothes . . .'

'Did they? Why?'

'For the hell of it, I guess. See what it felt like to be somebody else, like she was sometimes Katie, sometimes Kat. Or just to muddy the waters. Put unwanted boyfriends off the trail, that sort of thing, I dunno.'

'Or like using Julie's name because she was out of the country and Kat didn't want what she was doing here traced back to herself?'

'If you say so.'

She looked at him steadily. 'So, it's a coincidence you coming to work here – taking a temporary job – where your sister's been murdered? A coincidence that you knew where her room was?'

'What are you talking about, know where her room was? I told you, I didn't even know she was here! I didn't kill her, either! I'd as soon kill myself as Kat! Why should *anyone* want to – Kat, of all people?'

It was, she thought, the first time he'd showed genuine emotion.

Carmody put his head round the door as this outburst finished. 'Oh, sorry, I'll come back.'

'No, come in, Ted, I've finished with Mr Conolly, for the time being. You can go now, but we shall need to see you again,' she told Jamie, who did not look overwhelmed with joy at the prospect and rose to depart with alacrity. The door closed behind him with a definite thud.

'Mr Phoney-Baloney,' said Abigail, who had picked up a low tolerance threshold for pseuds, working under Mayo. 'I can't wait to face him with that footprint.'

'If it's his.'

'You bet it is, I've a hunch about it. What've you got there, Ted?'

Carmody held out one of the plastic evidence bags he was grasping. 'We found her notecase in the safe. It doesn't give us much to go on – about fifty pounds in notes, a Visa card, health club membership card, and her driving licence.'

'Nothing else?'

'I was just coming to that.' He produced the other bag and when she looked closer she saw it held a video cassette. 'Labelled *Goldilocks and the Three Bears.*' His eyebrows climbed.

'Goldilocks?'

'Yeah. But not for the kiddiewinks, I'll bet – or anything to leave lying around, neither. All tucked up in the safe it was. In case somebody came looking for it, like. So maybe somebody did, and got mad when she refused to give it up?'

Abigail looked at the cassette, speculating. *Goldilocks!* Strewth. 'So what exactly was our Miss Conolly up to, Ted? She hadn't apparently worked much, according to her brother, but she managed to satisfy some fairly expensive tastes. Though we might give her the benefit of the doubt and put that down to Daddy forking out – it seems he thought a lot of her. Still, no point in speculating, until we've run this through.'

What Jamie Conolly had said about his sister didn't stack with the sort who'd be involved in pornographic films, but apparent innocence was no guarantee. Death might leave tangible clues to enable reasonable deductions to be made about a dead person's mode of life but it left no indication as to what that person's essential nature had been – whether they'd been kind or cruel, generous or grasping, warm or cold-hearted, or whether they'd had a sense of humour, none of those things. Tomorrow they'd begin to try and find out. She rubbed her eyes and tried to relax her shoulders. Tomorrow. Today had been long enough, and it wasn't finished yet.

'I think we've just about wound it up here for tonight. Go home and get yourself some sleep, Ted. I'll be on my way myself after I've been down to the station.'

Mayo was still there when she arrived at Milford Road. He hadn't let the grass grow under his feet since he'd left Carmody at Freyning Manor. He was looking grim.

'Sit down, and let's get this sorted,' he said, before she had a chance to speak. 'I've just seen Sheering.'

Sheering was the ACC (Crime). That he was still here, at this hour, said something, and after a glance at Mayo's face, Abigail didn't need a crystal ball to know what it was.

'I've filled him in on the necessary details,' Mayo went on, 'told him Kat was staying at the hotel under my daughter's name, that they were great friends and that now Julie's apparently disappeared.'

'You still haven't been able to contact her, then?'

'I've tried to get in touch with her at her last known address in Texas and they say she left for England three weeks ago.'

He gave no sign of how much this bothered him as he told her what had happened. It had been around two o'clock on the Bay of Mexico when the courteous female American voice at the seafood restaurant in Galveston had answered the telephone. 'How may I help you?'

Not perhaps the best time to ring a restaurant, when the place might still be full of customers, and he'd made his apologies, which had been graciously accepted when the woman learned the reason for his call. 'Mr Mayo, I have to tell you Julie left here three weeks ago, safe and well. Didn't she let you know she was coming home? Well, I guess she was in a hurry. I drove her into Houston myself to get the flight home. OK, not directly, I guess, she was going via New York.' She pronounced it veea.

'And you are Miss . . .?'

'Ms. Dana Mazucelli. I manage this restaurant for Tony.'

'Pardon me, but who is Tony?'

'Tony Caravello.' There was a pause, as if the woman, three thousand miles away at the other side of the world, was calculating how much she ought to tell Mayo of things he obviously wasn't aware of. 'Julie's friend,' she came up with at last. 'The owner of Shrimp and Shell.'

'Perhaps I'd better speak to him.'

But Tony Caravello was not available – on vacation, touring in Morocco, with no way of getting hold of him. Mayo spent a few more minutes in conversation with the lady, during which he learned nothing that was new to him, apart from the fact that Dana Mazucelli stated categorically that neither anyone named Kat Conolly, nor any other British person, had ever visited Julie. 'We were all truly sorry when she decided to leave us so suddenly, though I guess that doesn't signify when you're homesick as she was. We've always prided ourselves on our standards, but I have to say the cooking here surely improved while she was with us. And it was a pleasure to know her.'

Like any parent, he was not displeased with this unsolicited testimonial to his daughter, but he'd sensed that spending any longer on this transatlantic call would be futile and unproductive, until he'd sorted a few facts out and perhaps needed more information. He'd have been prepared to take the next plane out of Heathrow for Houston if he'd thought it would achieve anything, but meanwhile, he had the basic piece of information he needed, that Julie had left Texas for England. He hadn't allowed himself to believe that she might not still be in England. Or that, once in New York, she could have taken a plane to anywhere in the world, Morocco included, to be with this Caravello character.

But whatever he felt about that, he wasn't letting it show, as he said to Abigail, 'I've also seen Kat's mother, and she seemed to think Kat's been out there with Julie, but the person I spoke to had never heard of her. I doubt whether she ever actually left England. I have an address where she was staying after her father died.'

He handed Abigail a sheet of paper with an address and phone number in Saltcote End, a nondescript area stretching outwards from the town centre. There was also a phone number. It was the one Jamie Conolly had given her before he'd left Freyning Manor to go to his mother, the number of Kat's boyfriend, Andrew, whose surname he'd suddenly remembered. Inskip, it was.

'Sheering knows all this,' Mayo went on.

'What did he say?'

Mayo half smiled. He'd chosen to ask for compassionate leave before it was thrust upon him and had seen the relief appear on Sheering's big, craggy face as he did so.

'He said, "That's right. You take a holiday, old son, until all this has blown over. You're due some time off, anyway, all the hours you've been putting in."' He'd caught the ACC's unctuous tones so perfectly Abigail might have laughed, had he not looked so bleak. 'In other words – "Bugger off and leave us to it – you're off the case, Mayo."' He rubbed his hand across his face. 'He wants to see you, Abigail. I don't know how he's decided to tackle this.'

'Maybe it won't be such a bad idea, a holiday. Away from here, at least.'

'I know. The situation's untenable. Truth be known, there's no way I could conduct an unbiased inquiry – no way I'd want to try. I'm better away from it. And besides – ' He stopped himself, then said, 'Look, there are things I need to know – '

'Just because Katie Conolly used her name,' Abigail interrupted, 'it doesn't mean your Julie had anything to do with this. You're not going to try and sort it out on your own, are you?' she added in some alarm, thinking that would be just the way Mayo *would* react to a situation like this.

'No, but I'm bloody well going to find Julie, and I want to be armed with all the facts. And at the same time . . .' He left that hanging on the air, gazing with consuming interest at the map of Lavenstock spread across the wall opposite his desk, letting her make what she would of his silence: *At the same time, there's no reason why I shouldn't be kept informed of what's happening.*

She told him everything they had, so far, up to and including the finding of the cassette in the safe. 'For the moment, Jamie Conolly has to be a prime suspect, though he's pretty cool – what we don't have on him is a motive – unless something turns up on that tape.'

'I can suggest a possible line on one. Not overwhelming, but possible.' He told her what Diane Conolly had said about Hugh Conolly's will.

'Then Kat wasn't short of money.'

'Depends on how much Daddy left them. According to Diane he sold his business partnership to pay off a load of debts, so possibly there wasn't much left. What Kat inherited from her dad had to go to Jamie if anything happened to her, and vice versa. It's a motive, compounded perhaps by jealousy. And I had a feeling, just a suspicion, that Diane wasn't perhaps being as co-operative as she might've been.'

'Hostile?'

'Not at all – she talked freely enough, but she was holding back on something, or telling me only what she thought I should know. I'd suggest you try and find out what it is. Maybe she'll be more forthcoming with another woman. Wouldn't bank on it, though, I doubt Diane's the confiding sort. And I could be wrong about her holding back, maybe she just wasn't totally in control of herself at the time. She's just lost her daughter, after all . . . and incidentally, she doesn't like the name Kat, maybe because it was her dad's name for her. She calls her Katie.'

He stood up, a big, robust man, just a little of his forthright energy worn off, the edge of his authoritative certainty blunted. She was sorry for more reasons than one that he wouldn't be working on the case. She'd rather work with him than anyone else, and she liked him as an individual, as well. She might have fancied him, in fact, if he hadn't already been spoken for by one of her best friends. Nothing out of the ordinary in the way of looks, an anonymous type, you might think, until you met that air of authority and decision. A sure aphrodisiac, they said. Hmm. She looked away, embarrassed at her own thoughts.

'Just one thing.' He suddenly sounded immeasurably tired. 'If anything on that tape involves Julie – you'll let me know, hmm?'

'Of course I will. '

'Thanks.' He walked to the door, then turned back and said, 'And there's another thing to consider, isn't there?'

Of course he hadn't overlooked it. Neither had she. The possibility that Kathryn Conolly had been killed in mistake for Julie Mayo.

'That's why I've got to find her,' he said before closing the door.

She waited until he'd had time to get clear of the building, then she went to tidy up, combing the front of her hair forwards so that she could hide as much as possible of the offending paint streak before she went upstairs. The attempt wasn't a success, but what the heck? The state of her hair wasn't going to affect what Sheering had to say to her.

'I have, of course, every faith in your abilities, don't get me wrong. Your track record has always been excellent, and in other circumstances I wouldn't hesitate, but this is – I don't have to tell you – a very sensitive case.'

'Yes, sir.'

'More coffee, Inspector?' Sheering lifted his coffee pot, smiled his handsome, confident smile. Not a bad sort, really, if you disregarded the pomposity, which he apparently thought was indispensable to maintaining his position, like real coffee and smart cafetières to make it in.

'Thank you, sir, I'm fine.'

Abigail indicated her cup, still almost full. For some reason she was finding it difficult to get the coffee down, while she waited for what was to come. *Sensitive.* Ironic that the first time Mayo wasn't in overall charge of one of their cases, she wasn't to have the chance of conducting the investigation herself because it was *sensitive.* Someone else was going to take over. The point was, who? Someone she hoped would be easy to work with, though coping with awkward-squad members wasn't any problem, routine if you worked in CID. Unless –

'. . . someone from outside,' Sheering was saying. '. . . lucky to get anyone so quickly . . . detective superintendents aren't hanging about on trees . . . happy to say Hurstfield Division's been able to oblige. On a dual function basis, but it's the best they can do.'

'Yes, sir.' Abigail forced down a mouthful of now cold coffee, then wished she hadn't. It was quite on the cards that she might be sick. Glenda Nightingale. The worst had actually happened. Hell's teeth.

'You've no objection to working under a woman, I take it?' Sheering's voice was sharp.

'On the contrary, sir. That would be against my principles, wouldn't it?' She forced a smile. *Any woman on earth but Nightingale! What had she done to deserve this?*

'Well, that's good,' Sheering said. 'Because I realise some of the men may not be quite as enlightened as you women, waving your equal opportunities banner.' He smiled benignly while Abigail bit her tongue in an effort not to gnash her teeth. 'Superintendent Nightingale is one of the best. But remember, she's new to this area, to the people she'll be working with, so give her all the help you can. You have your loyalties, I realise that, but I know I can rely on you not to let them interfere.'

He was no fool, Sheering. Aware that Mayo commanded a lot of respect, that there wasn't a man or woman on the strength who wouldn't sympathise with his present predicament or who wanted to be involved in intrusions into his private life. But it had to be done. Sheering knew someone like Nightingale would have no scruples if events turned awkward and although he,

97

like anyone who hadn't been on the moon for the last five years or so, must be aware of Nightingale's low position in the popularity ratings, he was pledged to give her his support.

Nightingale, my God, thought Abigail. Her reputation had spread even from the neighbouring division. How she'd ever reached Superintendent was a mystery to most people who met her. Simply by walking on the faces of those she'd trampled underfoot, it was popularly supposed. With spikes on her size nine regulation shoes, and her twelve stones of too, too solid flesh. She was generally regarded as a dyke, but Abigail doubted if that was true. It was questionable whether anyone of either gender would fancy her.

But...

There were other stories she'd heard about Glenda Nightingale: over-promotion due to several lucky breaks and a Chief Constable who was anxious not to be accused of sexual discrimination. An unwillingness to stick her neck out. Things like that. But obviously, a big capacity for hard work – she was going to row this inquiry in with her other duties at Hurstfield, Sheering had said. With one hand tied behind her back, no doubt. And with a detective inspector to do the leg work, it wouldn't be her fault if she didn't have this sewn up before you could say easy peasy.

Abigail's spirits were low as she drove home very late that night under scudding highwayman clouds and rain slashing intermittently on the windscreen. It wasn't a night to spend alone, but Ben was in Israel and there hadn't been a postcard from him for over a week. Not even a scrambled message on her answering machine.

12

Glenda Nightingale was evidently intending to start as she meant to continue, blowing into the department briefing the next morning like a Force 10 gale for which there'd been no storm cones hoisted.

Word had got around about Mayo; the news had run through the ranks quicker than salmonella and speculation had been rife ever since as to who was to head this investigation. Abigail had been running as hot favourite, but this was more a vote of confidence in her than in any real belief that it would happen. The odds had dropped dramatically when Nightingale was seen to breeze into the station just before half-past seven that morning.

She was a big woman – not over-tall, but strong and well upholstered and wide-seated, like a sturdily built Georgian wing chair. Brassy hair, cut punishingly short at the back, a tailored no-nonsense suit, sensible shoes, a regular ballbreaker. She came into the CID room accompanied by Sheering, a big man himself, a handsome ex-rugby player with intimidating shoulders and beetle brows. Beside her, he appeared a veritable pussycat.

'Morning, everyone,' Sheering said, politely pulling out a chair for her, which she ignored, preferring to perch her rump on a desk to one side. Sheering pretended not to notice this, cleared his throat and began. 'If some of you haven't already heard all the details of this distressing case, you'll be familiarised with them shortly, and you'll understand why Superintendent Mayo felt he could not participate, that he couldn't give of himself, fully and undivided.'

Abigail looked at her shoes. There he went again. Why couldn't he talk normally? Sheering always loved the sound of his own voice and never just talked when he could make a speech, though he'd no need. He'd been an ordinary copper on the beat himself once, and had come up through the ranks through his own ability, gaining a lot of respect for it on the way. People would listen, and with more attention, if he didn't lay it on so thick, but he could never seem to believe this.

'In the circumstances, we're lucky to have the services of Superintendent Nightingale here, who needs no introduction,' he intoned, in the manner of a Women's Institute president welcoming a speaker, and similarly went on to introduce her for several minutes, listing what he called her formidable qualifications, while Nightingale fixed several unfortunates, disposed in various relaxed attitudes around the room, with her crocodile smile. Most of them shifted uneasily, even if they'd nothing to be uneasy about. Those who hadn't met her had heard of how she liked to be thought of as one of the lads, a rumour to make her more distrusted than ever. You could never be sure with women like that. It would be a brave man who dared to call her 'Flossie' to her face, her nickname at Hurstfield.

'I know every one of you will give her all the support you can,' Sheering concluded, after more in the same vein. 'If everyone pulls their weight, I'm sure this case will work out satisfactorily for all concerned. Now, Superintendent, may I leave the rest with you?'

He looked at his watch, emphasising what a busy man he was, and beat a strategic retreat.

Nightingale waited until the door had closed behind him and then eyed the troops. 'Right, I know how you all feel about me being here, but we're stuck with one another, so you'll just have to put up with me for as long as it takes. As Senior Investigating Officer, I shall be responsible for tactics and strategy, Inspector Moon will be working with me and Inspector Atkins will manage the incident room. OK?'

She smiled again.

There were sidelong looks in her direction, a few raised eyebrows, one or two uncertain grins. Unsure of what was expected of them. It hadn't occurred to anyone that this assignment might be something Nightingale herself hadn't wanted, and her virtual admission was unsettling. A right bitch they could have coped with, but nobody was sure how to take all this frankness and bonhomie. A woman may smile, and smile, and be a villain.

George Atkins, having already encountered Nightingale, responded ponderously from his seat at the back of the room. His retirement loomed, this could well be his last major case, and what Milford Road station was going to do without his encyclopedic knowledge of all things criminal, and what he was going to do without Milford Road, was anybody's guess. As it was, he was well content with this admin role assigned to him.

Abigail introduced the rest of the fifteen-strong team, additional manpower culled from various sources. The regular CID – Farrar, who, despite his K. Y. Detective look, sitting up as though he had a poker rammed down his jacket, came in for a sharp, scrutinising glance that took everything in, from his tasselled shoes and his light grey suit to his floral tie; big Pete Deeley, amiable, reliable and immutable as the Rock of Gibraltar; Jenny Platt, who was capable besides being decorative, and fast becoming the biggest asset the department had, though she was at present sitting apprehensively close up front, near to Abigail, in silent affirmation of a united sisterhood ... Abigail went on round the room, naming names, knowing Nightingale hadn't a chance of remembering them all, though the way she was nodding as if she would, it was probably safer not to bet on it.

'Right, now pay attention, everybody,' Abigail said, when she'd finished the introductions, 'while I put those of you who weren't there last night into the picture.' As briefly as she could, she gave the substance of what had transpired so far. 'If you've studied this lot – ' she indicated the charts, plans and photos pinned up on the wall – 'you'll have seen how easy access is to that room, so we can't rule out an opportunist thief. And we do have evidence that someone came in through the french window, possibly armed with the short, sharp knife that appears to have been the murder weapon. So, say she refuses to hand over her money or whatever, he loses his temper, kills her and exits the same way as he came in. Her overnight bag – and the weapon – are missing. That's one possibility. Another likely supposition at this point is that she was there specifically to meet someone – maybe to do with the video that was found in the safe. Anyone could have slipped up to her room without being seen, security's poor and it seems likely she herself let her attacker in. Possibly he was interrupted by room service. The medical evidence suggests she hadn't been dead long when she was found. It may have been someone from outside, but we also need to check up on all the names on the list of non-residential diners, as well as the residents ... You've all seen this video?'

There were nods and one or two ho-ho responses, but mostly, they looked bored. The film had failed to titillate those who'd seen the run-through, they'd seen the same subject matter countless times before, and far better presented. Certainly more explicit. So what? It was tame stuff, by today's standards. Laughable, even. In black and white, with jerky, amateurish camerawork, an old 8 mm film transferred to video. Not to mention the farcical teddy bear masks worn by the two male characters. The simulated sex and all that heavy breathing.

Abigail's own reaction to it had been anything but amusement. A young woman had died, needlessly and in terror, the life in front of her snuffed out – for *this*? This dirty little perversion, without even any pretensions to art or entertainment? So old-fashioned it seemed unlikely it had been intended as part of some sexual shenanigans in that hotel room. But which someone had needed to get hold of so desperately that they were prepared to kill, brutally and without mercy? That they hadn't succeeded in their objective made it no less appalling.

As usual, it was Farrar who came up with the first question. Still sore from losing face by having had to let Dustin Small go for lack of any evidence that would pin him to the electrical warehouse job, he was anxious to make up for it. 'If he went so far as to kill for the video, why leave without it?'

'The safe was pretty well hidden, inside a cupboard. Anybody could've missed it – the SOCOs took it for a minibar at first. He may even have been interrupted by room service, and hid in the bathroom perhaps, slipping out while the maid went down the back stairs for help. Whoever did it must have had blood all over him, the towels in the bathroom were damp, and they're testing the drains for blood. I should remind you again that we have a possible suspect for the person who made the footprints – her brother, who happened to be working in the hotel kitchens, just below the room. He denies it, of course, and until we have a lab result we don't know for certain the footprint's his. But don't forget, he also has a possible motive.'

'I'd like to see another run-through of that vid, ma'am,' Farrar said, ignoring the ribald comments on this request equably enough, even managing a grin at his own expense. A sense of humour, or even common sense asserting itself, at last? 'It's just that I've got a feeling about it. I mean,' he continued gamely in the face of more sniggers, 'there's something about it that rings bells . . .'

'You recognised one of the – actors, for want of a better word?'

'Might have been that, but I'm not sure *what* it was, exactly.'

'Well, fine if you did, Keith – ' whatever else, she respected his acuity – 'but remember how old it is. The women's clothes –

when they had any on – and the hairstyles, are a dead giveaway. Plus its poor quality. Made years ago, early 1970s latest, Napier thinks.' Bob Napier was not only the official police photographer, but also an enthusiastic amateur film-maker, and his off-the-cuff opinion was probably as good as any they'd get from the lab. 'So, that's what we have so far.'

She handed back to Nightingale. Despite only having confronted the case half an hour before, with no time to do more than skim through what reports had already been handed in, the woman had familiarised herself instantly with everything that mattered. In a few minutes, the team, having received a clear indication of how the investigation was to be tackled and having had their individual tasks delegated, had dispersed. Apart from directing that the main thrust of the inquiry was to be concentrated on the video, she had made it abundantly clear that she was going to tackle this unwelcome assignment in her own highly individual fashion: that is, although she said she'd be working closely with Abigail, being here as often as she could, she wasn't going to interfere overmuch. A watching brief, was how she phrased it. Which was fine by Abigail, except that any kudos flying around after a successful outcome didn't seem likely to land on her own shoulders. But she was already resigned to that. It was no more than she'd expected.

Orlando's was considered to be Lavenstock's classiest florist. The sort of place you thought of if you needed top quality flowers for weddings, receptions, or special anniversaries. Funeral wreaths – which you didn't expect to last – you could buy cheaper at The Flower Basket, and colourful bunches for hospital visits at Sid's greengrocers or down the market. Here at Orlando's, there were never any tin buckets of flowers outside, no bunches of garishly mixed blooms and pots of African violets for Mother's Day wilting on the pavement. Instead were a blue and white striped and scalloped canopy over the front, the name in gold letters across the window and two bay trees in tubs either side of a door with the Interflora sign on it, today wide open to the already warm morning.

It wouldn't have been surprising to find the shop closed,

considering. But orders had to be fulfilled, deliveries accepted, Abigail supposed. A young assistant came forward, wiping her hands on her overall. She'd been occupied at a long table at the back of the shop, with what appeared to be a beautifully arranged bridal bouquet in shades of peach and cream that echoed several smaller table decorations standing by, already completed. A pale, ginger-haired girl with a puffiness around her eyes that showed she'd been crying, a slightly buck-toothed smile and her name embroidered over the top pocket of her overall: Amber.

'Can I help you?' she asked in a tiny voice scarcely above a whisper.

Abigail produced her identification. 'I'm here to see Mrs Conolly.'

The girl gave a little gasp of alarm, and her eyes widened as she read the card, as if a woman police inspector were another species. 'Well, she's upstairs, but I don't know – I mean, she's not seeing anybody, in the circs, and she's already . . .' she stammered in a frightened sort of way.

'She's expecting me.'

'Oh, well, in that case. I'd better – give her a buzz and tell her you're here.'

Leaving Abigail at the front of the shop, she went to a white intercom telephone on the table where she'd been working, pressed a button. A whispered, one-sided conversation ensued, while Abigail was left amongst the display surrounding her, most of which, as a gardener, she didn't rate too highly. Too artificial-looking, too contrived, against nature. Chrysanthemums in June, hydrangeas in March, daffodils for Christmas. Containers of flowers, stiff, exotic, brilliant, expensive and perfect, almost extinguished those of the paler, more delicate, home-grown varieties. The air felt damp and green but the individual flower scents mingled homogeneously together until they almost cancelled each other out in one overall, all-purpose perfume that smelled like funerals. She picked up an innocuous-looking parlour palm from the huge array of lush pot plants ranged down one side of the shop to look at the price, and when she saw what it cost, nearly dropped it.

'You can go up that way, it's not locked,' Amber breathed,

104

coming back to where Abigail was hastily replacing the palm. She indicated a door in the corner. Abigail caught the heavenly scent of freesias as she passed the arranging table, the only individually identifiable scent in the shop.

The police would need a photo, Mayo had told Diane, and she'd been shuffling through what few she had: she'd never been a great one for keeping them, seeing no reason to dwell on what was past. Eventually she found one which was a good likeness, though there never had been a photo that had showed Katie as she'd really been. Perhaps that was why she'd never kept many – it was one reason, anyway.

The intercom buzzed and Amber told her the policewoman was here. She told the girl to send her up and waited for her visitor's head and then the rest of her to appear, like a bus conductor emerging on to the top deck. Friends visiting for the first time were more than likely to shout, 'Any more fares, please?' but it was a joke worn thin by now. An open stairhead like that took up less room, and Diane was glad of anything that gave the feeling of more living space in this tiny flat.

That sounded ungracious, when she felt anything but ungracious about her good luck in having such a place. Small it might have seemed, cramped even, when both children were still at home, but now it was more than adequate for her own needs, and she'd found a lot of enjoyment making it into an attractive, cosy home, discovering a liking for home-making she would never have expected in herself. She'd decorated it in shades of green, from lime to olive, with pretty curtains and matching slipcovers which Katie had helped her to choose.

She waited, feeling disconnected and unfocused. She should have been downstairs, in the shop. There was that big order for the mayor's daughter's wedding tomorrow and a masonic function that evening . . . But Amber was a wonder as far as flower-arranging went, and her mum had promised to come in and give a hand this afternoon, as she often did when they were extra busy. Anyway, even the shop, normally all-important, didn't seem to matter, not really. The day had lost all semblance of normality after that visit to the mortuary with the sympathetic young policewoman who said her name was Jenny and who'd offered to stay with her afterwards. But Diane had needed, as in every crisis in her life, to be alone, at least for a while. Even though she knew that if she let herself think about how Katie had looked she'd start having nightmares – though they'd done their best to clean her up. And now there was this other policewoman to face, who would ask her more questions about Katie . . .

The door at the bottom of the stairs opened and a voice called, 'Mrs Conolly?'

The inspector introduced herself as Abigail Moon, and extended a cool hand with a firm grip. Diane liked the look of her, shiny bronze hair and a clear complexion, and the way she expressed sympathy without sounding either perfunctory or over-effusive.

'I know you told Jenny you didn't mind answering some questions, but they'll keep, if you've changed your mind, if you don't feel up to it.'

'Katie's been murdered,' Diane answered flatly. 'It won't help you to get whoever was sick enough to do that to her if I don't, will it? Though I'm not sure what use I can be. What is it you want to know?'

She was relieved to find that she was able to sound so well in command of herself, though she moved stiffly, her fit, athletic body feeling like an old woman's. The ravages of last night's tears had been camouflaged with discreet make-up and she'd chosen the outfit she was wearing with care: in the mirror this morning she'd seen that the pallor beneath her tan had made her look old and yellow but at least the cream silk top and navy skirt didn't make her look worse, and she'd made herself up with more than usual care. She'd draped a light scarf around her neck, in an attempt to soften a jawline that she knew was always too tense; nothing could conceal the bruised look under her eyes and the lines around her mouth. She was looking her age, and was well aware of it, but nevertheless she intended to face the world with her defences up.

'Is your son here?' the inspector was asking.

Diane shook her head. Jamie had gone out, announcing his intention of going across to the travel agent's, something about seeing if they had some work for him, and to tell the truth she'd been glad to see him go. His intention in coming over last night, she supposed, had been that he should play the role of loving son and comfort his mother, but it didn't seem to have worked that way. Jamie's ideas rarely did. Jamie, her boy. Always her boy, just as Katie had always been Hugh's girl. And both of them a disappointment, one way or another. Well, Diane had never let that get her down. It was all part of the constant battle that life had been.

She shivered, hugging herself, though she was too hot, rather than cold. This room, being just under the eaves, could become unbearably stuffy, and they were forecasting a spell of scorching weather. 'How about some tea, coffee, before we start?' she asked. 'I could do with something myself. I can't seem to satisfy this thirst I've got, somehow.'

'Coffee would be very welcome, thank you.'

'Instant all right?'

'Fine. Black, please, no sugar.'

'I'll just move these then.' Diane began to shuffle the pile of assorted clutter which she'd tipped from the large, battered leather handbag where she'd kept what photos she had, now standing empty on the floor. 'I suppose I should've had all these sorted years ago, into proper albums, but somehow I've never bothered. I'm not sentimental about things like that. Here's the photo Mr Mayo said you wanted. It's a good likeness, except for the hair. One of the phases she went through.'

The lovely thick, smooth fair hair that Abigail had seen last night spread out over the bed and clotted with blood at Freyning Manor Hotel was, in the photo, untidily frizzed out in a fringe at the front and caught up anyhow at the back. But even the hairstyle couldn't hide what a lovely young woman she'd been. An open, uncomplicated face. Beautiful eyes, a smile with a hint of mischief.

'You won't want to be bothered with the rest,' Diane said, pushing the clutter on the coffee table to one side. 'Most of them are rubbish, should've been chucked away long since. Now's the time to bin the lot and make a bit of room.'

'Leave them and let me look at them while you make the coffee.'

107

Diane shrugged, evidently not caring one way or another, and went into the kitchen, leaving Abigail sitting on the sofa, shuffling through the photos: Jamie and Kat, taken alone or together, baby snapshots, gap-toothed junior school photographs. The snaps became more self-conscious and fewer as the children grew into adolescence. Only in the earlier ones did either parent occasionally appear, holding a baby, say, but nowhere was there a family group. It made Abigail wonder how many years Diane had been on her own, how long since she and Hugh Conolly split up.

She studied his face. Good-looking, he'd been that all right, evidently the one from whom the family looks had descended. For quite a while she looked at one taken at the seaside, with Hugh, a big, clumsy-looking type with a gentle smile, hunkered down, holding a two-year-old Katie between his knees to face the camera. After the lack of interest Diane had claimed in the photos she had no compunction in slipping it into her pocket. She didn't want Diane to know, not yet anyway, that she was interested in her former husband.

Diane brought in two mugs of strong, hot coffee. 'Let's get this over.'

'When you're ready.'

'I have to sometime, don't I? Whether I'm ready or not.' She was prickly, not an easy person. She'd brought a Safeway's carrier in with her and swept everything off the coffee table into it, after which she went to sit at the other end of the sofa, tucking her bare legs sideways beneath her. She had good legs, slim and brown, and a taut, athletic figure – stringy might be more truthful, if less kind – and a skin which all that tennis playing had exposed too much to the sun.

'Well, what I have to ask may distress you, personal questions that might seem irrelevant, though I assure you they're not – you see, we have to try to build up a picture to get some insight into what might have led to this.'

Diane's voice hardened. 'I know what you mean – and I know what you might turn up about Katie. You always think, don't you, when a person's been murdered, well, there has to be a reason, and I admit it, Katie was a bit – wild, I suppose you'd call it, a while back, but she wasn't what you might think . . .'

She paused to take a sip of coffee. 'I can truthfully say that she was lovely, not just to look at, though she was that, right from a baby, but a lovely person. D'you know what I mean?'

Abigail thought of the video in the hotel safe, and its implications. Blackmail was not lovely. But she nodded, and Diane said suddenly, 'I'm glad he's dead, her dad, I mean. I'm glad he never had to face this. I don't really think he could have borne it. He used to say to me, when she was growing into her teens, " 'She's going to be a heart-breaker. I hope it won't be her dad's heart she breaks." '

'Katie was very fond of her father as well, I gather?'

'They adored each other.' Abigail guessed that was an extravagant expression for Diane but now it was used without exaggeration, matter-of-factly. 'Never a cross word – oh, except sometimes he used to go on at her because she didn't make the best of her abilities – she was quite clever, you know, only she was a bit lazy, all her school reports said so. Hugh wanted her to apply herself and get into university, but she only laughed and said she'd had enough of school, and he let her be – not like Jamie.'

'Fathers and sons often don't hit it off.' Abigail was remembering what Jamie Conolly had said about not always getting on with his father.

'You're right. Even when Jamie did work hard it wasn't ever good enough for Hugh. I think he saw himself in Jamie, you know, and wanted better things. But it got so's Jamie just didn't bother.' She laughed with a brittle sound. 'I've no fear for him though. He's my son, he'll manage for himself. He'll get through.'

Abigail, thinking of her interview with him, and the vibrations it had set up, couldn't help but agree.

Hugh Conolly, though. What sort of man had he been, this ex-husband, first for him to set his ex-wife up in the shop, and then to leave it to her, as she'd told Mayo he had? Well, generous, obviously, and not one to bear a grudge. Communication between them evidently hadn't been severed, despite the divorce, and he'd thought enough about Diane to leave her sufficiently provided for. The shop appeared to be prospering and well looked after, like this room here – flower-filled, as was to be expected, and with the unmistakable signs of a very recent redecoration, the whiff of new paint and wallpaper, the new-carpet smell still apparent. A larger than life TV dominated one corner of the room. Indeed, the situation seemed to be that sort where the couple were on such good terms one wondered why they'd ever bothered to go through the trauma of separation and divorce at all.

'How long had you been divorced?'

'Eleven years, when he died.'

'He'd remarried?'

'Quite recently. She wasn't the one that caused us to split, though, the other woman. It was other *women*, in the plural! I think Hugh was one of those men who can't really help it, but I got so I couldn't stand it. In the end I told him he'd have to go, it wasn't fair to me. After all I'd done for him.'

Abigail often thought this was one of the saddest phrases in the English language ... as though what you did for other people was only done in the expectation of getting something back.

'What can you tell me about Katie's boyfriend, Andrew Inskip?'

'I can't tell you anything. I've never met him.'

'But weren't they were going to be married?'

'*Married*? Katie?' She laughed. 'If they were that's the first I've heard of it.'

'When I spoke to Jamie last night, he seemed to think so.'

She was silenced by that. She picked up her coffee mug and, finding it empty, put it down again, running her tongue round her dry lips. She sounded sharp when she eventually spoke. 'It's news to me. I didn't know he was anyone special – just the current boyfriend, I thought. One of – well, she had a lot of boyfriends, I suppose, though I never knew many of them.' She stared into space, contemplating the closed book of her daughter's life. Eventually, however, she said, 'But now I think about it, I had the feeling sometimes lately that there might have been someone special. Once or twice, she seemed to be on the point of mentioning it, but changed her mind. I didn't press her. You know what girls are, they'll tell you when they're ready.'

'They don't want to be pushed into getting serious too soon, to commit themselves. '

'Yes,' Diane said, 'that might have been it.'

13

Much earlier that same morning, Alex Jones had been sitting on the padded seat in the bay window, with her long legs drawn up to her chin. Her dark, almost black hair fell forward as she flicked through the sample book of furnishing fabric swatches propped up next to her. Moses was heavy against her leg. The best time of the day, not yet eight o'clock and the sun warm on her back. Summer was on its way at last, with a heatwave imminent, they said, and Alex wanted to believe it, feeling there surely couldn't be any more rain left in the sky. For the moment it was luxury to sit here, blinking like Moses in the warmth. She wiggled her bare toes sensuously and watched the changing reflections play over them from the small panes of stained glass at the top of each of the big sash windows. The coloured light bounced off her feet on to the floorboards, bare now that Miss Vickers's Wilton had been taken up. She languidly turned one of the samples over with her big toe and absently assessed the potential of the next one in relation to the room. No vibrations. Nothing there that was going to bring this pleasant, but still rather undistinguished room to life.

Miss Vickers had been apologetic about not leaving the carpet. 'I'm very fond of it, and it still has years of life in it, so I've decided to take it with me. The price of new ones!' she'd tutted. 'Bob Sullivan says he can make this fit in the bungalow, and I've no doubt he'll do it very well. He's made a good job of laying those tiles for me in the new kitchen. New floor covering's going to run you in for a lot of expense though, I'm afraid.'

'Bob's good at most things,' Alex said cautiously, wishing Freda hadn't succumbed to his blarney. He was a local self-employed handyman whom Alex and her sister used occasionally. He could do most things if he set his mind to it, and if he thought there was enough in it for him, but he had to be watched. He preferred back-pocket money to invoices and receipts, which would almost certainly conflict with Miss Vickers's headmistressy honesty. Alex made a mental note to have a stern word with him.

As for the old carpet, she was secretly very pleased indeed not to be lumbered with it. Though a new one would make a big hole in their budget, the insipid pale gold wasn't a colour she could see herself living comfortably with, and wouldn't at all go with what she'd had in mind for this room. On the other hand, had Miss Vickers thrown it in as part of the sale of the house, she wouldn't have felt justified in buying a new one, and had envisaged having to put up with it far into the foreseeable future, simply because it was too good to throw out.

Leaning back against the white-painted inside shutters, she pushed the sample book away. It was clear none of them would do for the sort of effect she wanted. Vibrant Pre-Raphaelite colours that would bring out the room's character and glow in the evening lamplight. A piano, she thought, that would please Mayo. She already had her eye on an Edwardian walnut upright, complete with its original sconces, coming on sale next week. And that embroidered silk scarf which Lois had picked up last month to drape across its top. Bookshelves . . . lamps with deep fringes, she thought through half-closed eyes . . . and perhaps, in the alcove, that drawing in sepia pastels she'd done of Julie, the last time she'd been home.

Mayo had kept the phone red hot yesterday, ringing to any imaginable place where Julie might be, his face growing grim as one after the other her friends informed him that they'd had no recent contact with her. But at least he'd been able, by bulldozing his way through, and using police channels, to establish that she had indeed landed in Britain three weeks ago.

So why hadn't she let them know she was here?

Alex tried not to let him see that she was worried, too. She had a rather different view of Julie than her father did. They'd always got on extremely well together. Julie had been eleven years old when her mother, Lynne, Alex's friend, had died. Without attempting to take Lynne's place, she'd been available when Julie needed advice, support, a shoulder to cry on. More like an elder sister, really. But Alex knew Julie to be a strong-minded and independent young woman and she'd no doubt that if she'd got herself involved in this business with Kat Conolly, it had been her own decision to do so. Just as it had been her decision to spend the last few years hopping from place to place, much to her father's disquiet. But Alex had lately thought she might be starting to regret certain aspects of her nomadic existence. It wasn't getting her anywhere and Julie, as she grew older, like Alex herself, had begun to emerge as one who liked her life to be well defined. Though Alex hadn't said anything to Mayo, she'd recognised a touch of what she could only call panic in Julie's recent letters home.

She could hear him moving about upstairs, which meant he'd finished his shower after returning from his walk. One of his seriously long hikes that had stopped Alex from offering to go along with him for company. She wasn't up to his punishing pace for one thing, her long legs and her tough ex-police-woman's stamina notwithstanding, but even if she had been, she wouldn't have offered to go with him today. Walks like this meant he wanted to be alone, to think. It seemed to help him to stride along for mile after mile, when he had pressing problems to mull over. The night she'd lost the baby he'd walked for fifteen miles, though she'd only found that out later.

She began to gather together the wallpaper and carpet samples, yawning. He'd been thrashing around and muttering most of the night, and Alex had finally given up her own attempt to sleep, got up and made herself a cup of tea. After that it hadn't seemed worth going back to bed. Mayo had wakened at five, and announced that some stiff exercise was what he needed, and had set off immediately, before the day, as was forecast, became too unbearably hot.

Her own disturbed night was making itself felt. She was reluctant to move, the warmth more conducive to sleep than to constructive thought. She could feel herself dozing off, and in that moment of clarity before sleep comes, she had a thought that woke her up with a jump and precipitated Moses on to the floor.

113

Mayo was taking bacon, eggs and sausage from the fridge when she went into the upstairs kitchen. 'Like me to do you some as well?' he asked.

'Had my breakfast earlier, thanks.' A piece of toast, another cup of strong tea. Mayo hadn't eaten before setting out, and he was obviously ravenous, but a fry-up wasn't her idea of the best way to start the day. She brewed coffee while he cooked, and they sat at the kitchen table as he made inroads into the food.

'That's better,' he said, accepting a large, wide Continental cup of steaming coffee from her.

'Gil, I've had an idea. About Julie. Maybe not a very good one, but . . .'

'Any would be welcome.'

'Do you remember Marie-Solange?'

He thought for a few seconds. 'The French girl? The one Julie stayed with in Dijon, married that John whatshisname . . . the one who was at catering college with Julie? The one,' he said, pointing, 'who's the rightful owner of that damn bird over there?'

'That's right. And didn't Julie say something about them coming back to England, that they were thinking of starting up a restaurant?'

'They all dream of starting up restaurants, love, her college mates – that's what they were trained for.'

'It was somewhere on the south coast, wasn't it?' she persisted.

He pushed his plate away and she picked it up, with his knife and fork, and put them into the dishwasher. When she came back to the table, he said, 'Forget it. Do you realise what the odds are – even if I could find him – of his knowing anything at all of Julie's whereabouts?'

'They were very good friends.'

'So much so that I've no idea what his last name was.'

'Smith,' Alex said. 'I remember it. John Smith.'

'That's helpful. There can't be many John Smiths on the south coast. His mother may as well have called him X.'

They were both silent, contemplating the task of finding a John Smith who (possibly) ran a restaurant, anywhere on the south coast of England. How many miles from Dover to Land's End? How many cafés and restaurants?

'It's on the tip of my tongue,' she said. 'It'll come to me. But wouldn't one of her other friends be likely to know where we could find him?'

Any of those she'd been at Loughborough with, he said dourly, all of whom he'd already tried.

'There's Marie-Solange's parents, they'd know.'

Tracing the parents of a Marie-Solange, whose surname they didn't know, and whose address they knew only as Dijon, made looking for John Smith seem like child's play.

'That's not one of your better ideas, my love.'

'Glenda thinks we should have another go at Jamie Conolly,' a shirt-sleeved Carmody informed Abigail, looking up from the report he was laboriously pecking out. She'd just got back from her meeting with Diane Conolly and gone into the busy, noisy incident room in search of someone to take with her when she went along to see Andrew Inskip. 'She favours the tactful approach, so it has to be me.'

'Not if it means me being lumbered with Scotty, it doesn't!'

'No chance of that, the idle bugger's disappeared again.'

'Where's George?'

'Gone for a smoke.'

It was late in the day, just when his retirement was imminent, for Atkins to be getting the message that his pungent brand of tobacco wasn't everyone's favourite idea, but who was grumbling? Abigail went to look at the allocations list he'd pinned to the wall.

Most of the team were out gathering information. She cast around among the variously employed personnel left behind, wondering whether to take Jenny off what she was doing, which happened to be the chasing up for questioning of the non-residential diners who'd given their names at Freyning Manor, most of whom didn't, for various reasons, want to be chased. Abigail sometimes thought ninety per cent of the population was up to something it shouldn't be, while the other ten per cent wished it was.

Barry Scott appeared at that moment, his absence explained by the double sausage sarnie, well laced with fried onions, he was eating out of a paper bag. Abigail suddenly rebelled against the smell of that little lot in the car, on top of Scotty. Having been made very much aware by his colleagues in CID, none of whom were backwards in coming forwards on such matters, that he had an undesirable personal problem, DC Scott had taken to dousing himself in the sort of cologne and aftershave you could smell a mile off, so that the CID room smelled like a bordello when he was around. No. Not my car, as well, Abigail resolved. She turned to Carmody.

'I want you with me when I see the boyfriend, Ted. Jamie Conolly will keep.' Carmody would be a bonus, though anyone, really, was better than the competing odours of fried sausage and onion, plus Scotty's Eau de Cover-Up. 'And you, Barry, set yourself on to helping Jenny.'

Scotty looked so surprised and grateful for not having to bestir himself out of the office that he roused himself enough to offer to get Jenny a coffee from the machine. Abigail left with Carmody, refusing to meet Jenny's reproachful glance.

At Belmont Avenue, in what had been Kat's bedroom, Mary Somers was throwing clothes on to the bed, looking disparagingly at the pretty suits, dresses and shoes which had been discreetly hidden in the wardrobe, tossing them indiscriminately on top of the tatty assortment of jeans and T-shirts, heavy boots and combat jackets Kat had worn in an attempt to project her image of solidarity with the rest of the group. Not very successfully, thought Mary Somers, viciously tipping the contents of a dressing-table drawer anyhow into a black plastic bin liner. As the nail varnish bottles clattered in with the lipsticks, the jars and tubes of this lotion and that cream, Mary's thin lips pressed together in satisfaction. But after a moment's hesitation, she reached back into the bag and brought out a crystal flask of Dolce Vita. A sniff, a couple of quick squirts on the wrists, another hesitation.

Down below, a car drew up in the street outside, and a moment later the bell rang. Mary glanced out of the window, then slid the Dior bottle into her pocket and left the room.

*

116

Carmody rang the bell, while Abigail stood back to inspect the row of very small pre-war semis, the outward appearance of which gave every indication of the accommodation within. Three bed, two recep., kitchen and bathroom, that's what they'd be. No garages. Cars lining the road. Houses like these, which had been all she could afford when she was house-hunting, were the reason Abigail had ended up in her own out-of-the-way cottage, cheap not only because it was out of the way but because it had been near derelict when she bought it. Even in that state, it had seemed better than these cramped, faceless Identikit houses, and still did, though number twenty-four possessed a certain individuality by virtue of its uncared-for look, the dingy curtains dragged across scruffy windows. And the tiny front garden which, unlike the neatly flowering plots of every other tidy little house in the street, had been converted into hard standing on which was propped a motorbike leaking oil.

A big, bearded figure answered the door. He was probably in his late twenties. A collarless, greyish white shirt worn outside his jeans hung over what might be the beginnings of a belly. He had small dark eyes which slid over her with a darting glance, and a luxuriant fall of none too clean wavy dark hair. A few years ago, there'd been a Greek singer with a high voice, who looked so like the man in front of her that Abigail almost expected him to break into a soprano rendering of some Hellenic folksong.

'Andrew Inskip?'

'Who wants him?'

Never take anything on face value. His voice was deep, with no falsetto overtones. His eyes were sharp, too, and calculating, his movements far from the effeminate Greek's. Not fat, either, just heavily built, Abigail saw now, strongly muscled most likely, underneath that shirt . . .

She produced identification. He glanced at it, eyed them both suspiciously, weighing them up, assessing. 'Hang on, I'll get him.'

He turned away, pushing the door to, and since it appeared quite likely that they were to be left on the doorstep, Carmody stopped it with the flat of his hand and walked inside. The young man didn't look round, but left them standing in the passageway at the bottom of the stairs. Minutes passed. Nothing to do but inspect their surroundings. Scruffy and neglected, the air smelling of old chip-fat, stale cigarette smoke and the residue of illegal substances. A tatty stair carpet with dustballs in the corner of the treads. Floorboards that might once have been polished but no longer were, a line of dust and fluff outlining the worn strip of coconut matting that led along the hallway from the front door. Several old cardboard boxes thrown into one corner and an overburdened coat rack with a pile of scruffy shoes and boots beneath. Dingy walls weathered to the colour of tired old string and a plate-rack sporting what appeared to be a collection of dustily forgotten native artefacts. African, Aztec, Greek were just some of the ones Abigail could recognise. Not an uplifting ambience.

The bearded man had gone through what was evidently the kitchen door, letting himself in and the sound of a washing machine on its last legs out, over and above Celine Dion passionately asserting that her heart would go on. Carmody jerked his head towards the door of the front room, which was ajar. Abigail pushed it further open and saw that the room appeared to be equipped as some sort of office, stuffed with electronic equipment: computer keyboards and monitors, printers, a fax machine, plus a row of mundane grey metal filing cabinets and shelves stacked with old-fashioned box files and folders spilling off the shelves.

She'd pulled the door back to its original position before the kitchen door opened again, and the man who'd admitted them returned with another, shorter man, who stepped forward and immediately closed the door into the front room completely.

Andrew Inskip was of medium height, slightly built, his blond hair neatly cut. He was pale and had a full, sensuous mouth. Large, light-coloured eyes. A closed, self-sufficient face. He waited for one of them to begin, with the sort of cool, disconcerting, slightly insolent stare designed to make other people feel uncomfortable, and shifty when they fail to meet it. Inviting them to state their business, though he must have known what it was about and might have been expected to make the first move.

Abigail ordered herself not to be annoyed and explained why

118

they were here. She told him bluntly how Kat had been murdered and saw his jaw muscles tighten, though all he said was, 'We heard about it. On the local radio.'

'I'd like to say how sorry I am, Mr Inskip – you and she were close, I understand.'

'You could say that,' intervened the bearded one, grinning, exploring the inside of one ear with the finger of a grubby hand. He had very shiny red lips and very white teeth between his beard and moustache. Abigail found him no less repellent than she had at first sight.

Inskip said, without looking at him, 'All right, Rabbit. Make us some tea, will you?' It wasn't couched in any way as an order, but the other nodded and turned away to obey as though it was.

'Don't bother, thanks, we've just had some,' Abigail lied.

The big man shrugged and went back into the kitchen. A woman spoke to him above the music and he answered with a laugh.

'What did you call him?' Carmody asked, as Inskip led them into the back room of the house, a living-room overlooking a small, wildly overgrown garden.

'Rabbit. His name's John Rabbett, e double t, but he'd rather have Rabbit than Bunny.'

'He live here as well?'

Andrew Inskip regarded the sergeant for what seemed a long time before he chose to answer. 'Sure. There's room, though it isn't a very big house, as you can see. My parents bought it, years ago.'

The rest of the house would be like this room, poky. Adequate, but made even smaller by having panels formed by imitation oak beams, between which the walls were roughcast plaster, once white, perhaps, but now time-darkened to the same dirty string colour as the walls in the hall. It was that style of interior decoration popular in the second and third decades of the century, in imitation of lath and plaster, employed to achieve the 'quaint' atmosphere of a Tudor cottage. The overlarge brick fireplace which dominated one wall seemed to be part of the same design. Another plate-rack ran round the room, burdened with a further haphazard collection of strange objects; otherwise no attempt had been made at decoration, other than the one redeeming feature, the well-stacked bookshelves which filled one wall.

Abigail began by establishing that Kat had left the house at around three on the previous afternoon, which would indicate she'd gone straight to Freyning Manor. 'Did she tell you she was going there, Mr Inskip?'

He replied with a shrug that she hadn't, he'd no idea that was where she was headed.

'How was she dressed?'

'Dressed? The usual – jeans, T-shirt, I suppose. Trainers. No jacket – it was warm for that yesterday.'

'She had a bag with her?'

'Can't say I noticed.'

'When she didn't arrive home, weren't you worried?'

'Not particularly. She didn't have to account to me for her every movement.'

Considering they were about to be married, all of this was detachment to a remarkable degree. It was cool not to show involvement, not to be possessive, but what was going on behind those intent eyes? Abigail was rather disconcerted by suddenly thinking it might be amusement. 'How long have you known each other?' she asked abruptly.

'Since we were at school.'

'She went to the Princess Mary – that's girls only.'

'Sure. I was at Lavenstock College.'

Abigail remembered, from her own sixth form days at the Princess Mary, the ferment caused in the female breast by the college boys – most of whom, it had to be said, came from a very different background from Andrew Inskip's. It might be only a minor public school, but its reputation was high, and the fees didn't come cheap. You heard of parents who beggared themselves to send their children to the 'right' schools, and if this applied to Inskip's, you had to wonder if they had their priorities right. Then suddenly she thought, *Inskip!* and her mind leaped, by association, via the artefacts on the plate-racks in this room and the hall, to the row of books on her own father's bookshelves. Books he never tired of reading and rereading.

Her eyes sought, and found, a similar set on one of the shelves here. 'Are your parents Peter and Lavinia Inskip?'

'Were,' he said, bored with a question he must have been asked a thousand times.

She remembered, then, too late. 'I'm so sorry, I'd forgotten – '

He shrugged. 'It was a long time ago.' Not so long, she thought. Four or five years, if that, when they'd been so spectacularly killed in a disastrous Central American earthquake that had made world news. Belatedly, as if he felt explanations for his indifference should be forthcoming, he added, 'They were never here much – too busy writing books to encourage the affluent traveller.'

And in a way, it did explain. She saw how it had probably been: this little house, bought perhaps with love when they were young, first married, and thereafter regarded simply as a base before they were off on their travels again – kept on for convenience, though doubtless they could have afforded better, had they wanted it. Seen only as somewhere to park the artefacts they collected, somewhere to make plans to get away again as soon as possible. What about their son? How far had he figured in such a lifestyle?

'We've been given to understand you use the house as the headquarters of a group calling themselves Group Six, that right?' Carmody, who'd been doing his homework, was asking.

Something at last flickered in the pale blue eyes. 'If we aspired to anything so grand as a headquarters, yes,' he shrugged. But the implication of importance behind the word 'headquarters' had evidently pleased him, if the mention of the group's existence had not.

'What sort of a group are you?' Carmody asked.

'If you've been told about us, you must know that.'

'I wouldn't be asking if I did, lad.'

'We're a protest group.'

'Protesting against what?'

'Against anything we see as injustice, or exploitation, or which is ruining our planet – and believe me, you haven't far to look for that! We're not passive, we don't just talk about these things, we're willing to actively demonstrate our support for any cause

121

that opposes injustice.' A touch of colour appeared on his high cheekbones, a gleam of fanaticism lit his cold eyes. He sounded like a double-glazing salesman.

'Oh, right. You make the numbers up, like?' Carmody said.

Inskip looked at him with dislike. 'We're not Rent-a-Mob, if that's what you're implying! We're not hired to do what we do!' He'd let his anger show and he went to lean against the window sill and folded his arms across his chest as if to contain it.

'How do you finance yourselves, then?'

He was calmer now. 'I've a private income, my parents left me enough to live on. For quite a while, if I'm not rash.'

The door opened and Rabbit came in, a couple of doughnuts in one fist, a mug in the other, followed by a small, thin, bespectacled young woman bearing two more mugs. Abigail felt she'd seen her somewhere before but couldn't pin down where. She gave one of the mugs to Inskip and settled down on the floor next to where Rabbit had parked himself. He immediately began to wolf down the doughnuts and they both leaned their backs against the sofa, showing every intention of staying.

'This was private,' Carmody said, as a matter of principle, not because it was.

'You mean somebody's succeeded in murdering our Kathryn, and you don't want to question us, then?' the girl asked, in a quick, sarcastic voice.

Abigail flicked a signal at Carmody and turned to her. 'You are?'

'Mary Somers.'

'Yes, we do want to talk to you. Kat was very brutally murdered and we're going to find out who did it.' Weren't any of them sad about their friend? 'You didn't approve of her, seemingly.'

The girl laughed shortly. 'Approve? That's beside the point. She wasn't my type and we never had much to do with one another.'

She had a small, peevish, intelligent face. Her mouse-brown hair was pushed behind her ears and the strong lenses of her spectacles enlarged her eyes, giving her the appearance of a lemur or some other night-time creature. Putting her at about twenty-six, probably even a little older, Abigail suddenly remembered: she'd been one of the demonstrators pulled in at the fête last Saturday.

You could tell a lot about a person from the way they spoke: from this Mary's voice, quick, educated, yet with strong Welsh overtones, as much as from the mangled Cockney Rabbit employed. It was patently obvious that the two young women had been as different as chalk and cheese, but Abigail asked the question anyway. 'What do you mean, she wasn't your type?'

Mary Somers made an impatient gesture, pushing her spectacles up the bridge of her nose. 'Frankly, she bored me. I've never found it easy to communicate with someone who can't understand anything not in words of one syllable, someone whose horizons are limited by clothes and make-up and hairstyles.' By that criterion, Abigail thought with amusement, Mary Somers considered her own horizons to be admirably wide.

'Oh, come on, love! Don't spoil your case by over-exaggerating,' Inskip intervened neutrally, but warningly it seemed to Abigail.

'Two syllables, then.' The way she said it, it sounded as though she didn't much like Inskip, either.

But Inskip smiled. Another studied, insolent smile. Very full of himself, Inskip, but underneath, not a lot to write home about, Abigail suspected, this leader of theirs. She was surprised at someone like Mary Somers swallowing it – but that sort always had their reasons.

She was wearing a baggy-necked, once-black T-shirt, now washed out into an indeterminate shade of dark grey, with sleeves down to her fingertips, a long, skinny brown wool skirt, heavy boots. Her body profile could have been lined up with a ruler and her hair could have done with a wash. Yet she smelled spicy and sophisticated. 'The truth is,' she announced suddenly and savagely, 'Kat Conolly got on my nerves, why beat about the bush? Acting as if she were slumming it, living here, gracing us with her presence. Doing us all a favour by coming along with us to the demos. I knew she'd soon tire of it, and she did. She was – well, she was just so *silly*.'

Contradiction came from an unexpected quarter. Until now, the one they called Rabbit had been too busy eating to contribute to the exchange. 'You underestimate her, Mary.' Spite robbed the words of any palliative intention. 'Not silly. Like dangerous, know what I mean?'

'Dangerous?' Abigail wondered at the measure of ill-will in Rabbit's voice. 'In what way was she dangerous?'

He thought about it, his tongue licking a smear of jam from his upper lip. More had fallen on to his shirt. Sugary crumbs nestled in his beard. 'She didn't do what you'd expect of her,' he said at last.

'Well, she was a woman, wasn't she?' Inskip put in with a stiff smile, as though he wasn't habituated to making jokes, perhaps steering them away from something too uncomfortably near the truth. 'Poor Kat, she was never really committed, as we are.'

'Did any of you drive her to Freyning Manor on Sunday afternoon?'

'I don't drive,' said Inskip. 'On principle.' Simultaneously Rabbit chipped in, 'Wot, me? In that precious motor? No way!' Mary Somers simply rolled her eyes.

Abigail looked at them. She hadn't mentioned that Kat had been driven to Freyning Manor in her own car. 'I'd like you to tell me where you all were on Sunday afternoon.'

'Sunbathing, all of us,' the young woman answered quickly. 'On the lawn.' She pointed to the scrubby area of uncut grass outside the windows, the size of a large tablecloth, studded with daisies and dandelions. 'Listening to the radio. One of the neighbours will confirm that. He complained we were playing it too loud, which of course we weren't. What it is, he just objects to nude sunbathing – though the only possible way he can see us is from his bathroom window – standing on the loo seat at that.'

'Bit on the cool side for sunbathing, wasn't it, Sunday?' Carmody put in.

'Fresh air bathing, then. You get used to it.'

Abigail had some sympathy with the neighbour. She preferred not to think of Rabbit – or Mary Somers, come to that – in the altogether. It was an alibi – but only of sorts: the neighbour couldn't have been standing on the lavatory seat, doing his Peeping Tom act, all afternoon.

'All right, then, let me ask you about a video that was found in Kat's possession.'

It was too much to have believed that they would admit to knowing anything about it, and they didn't. They were all, in their different ways, accomplished liars, parrying police questions was meat and drink to them, and if they'd had anything to do with it, it was the one question they'd have been prepared for. But it had been worth a try.

She stood up and said to Inskip, 'Will you show us the room Kat used?'

Should she have said 'your room', the room they'd shared? He had, after all, been her boyfriend, it would have been what she expected, and as if he sensed her unspoken question, he said, abruptly, 'We didn't share a room, not any more. We did once, for a short while, but not lately.'

'Weren't you going to be married?'

'Not that I've ever heard of.'

'She was engaged to someone.'

There was a silence, then a short, hard laugh from Mary Somers who said, 'Married, was it? Then I should try the glamorous Luke. If she was inclined to marry anyone, it would be Luke Raeburn.'

Inskip's eyes swivelled towards her.

'Tell me about him,' Abigail said, looking at Inskip.

After a moment, he took his gaze off Mary, then shrugged. 'Not much to tell. Kat brought him along here one day and he seemed very interested in what we were doing, so – '

'Since he's not short of dosh, he was allowed to become one of us,' Rabbit intervened with a malicious glance at Inskip.

Inskip gave no indication that he'd noticed this, and Mary Somers added bitchily, 'And doubtless why our Kathryn had latched on to him – for the same reason.'

'Where can we find him?'

'He comes and goes,' Inskip said, absently. 'He's often abroad. He works in that travel agency down Sheep Street, I forget what it's called.'

'Palgrave's Travel,' said Mary Somers.

Abigail, sensing undercurrents, searched Inskip's face for any signs of jealousy in his words or expression, but found none. His face remained as shuttered and controlled as it had been all along. Whatever emotion was behind it, it was hard to say.

125

'Look,' he said at last, 'it wasn't serious between us any more, at any rate I wasn't suicidal when she called it off. She wasn't living here at the time, she was still looking after her father, over at Orbury House. It was only after he died that she came and asked if she could stay here again for a while. Why not?'

He smiled unexpectedly, differently. A smile that had charm, making her wonder if she might possibly have been wrong, if he wasn't simply uncertain of himself. Driven by his principles to run this group, in so far as it had any structure, seeing in it a role for himself? Elevating its woolly aims and ideals, giving him a reconstructed view of himself? He seemed to her to be the only one of the three with any real sense of commitment.

But could he really be as detached as he appeared, about Kat? Even if the relationship had been a casual, no-strings affair?

'Why did she leave Orbury House and come back here?'

'She didn't say. Except that she was short of ready cash. Until her father's estate was settled, I suppose.'

'OK. Let's have a look at her room, then.'

It was the smallest of the three bedrooms, not much more than a boxroom, the one in such a house generally given to the youngest child, and, like a child's bedroom, it had three or four stuffed animals on the pillows, an old teddy bear, a black plush cat with one ear missing, a frog and a Friendly Lion. 'She was a Leo,' Inskip said.

And a bit of a chameleon, Abigail decided as she looked at the strange variety of clothes thrown into a heap on the bed.

'Go ahead. There isn't room for three of us in here, I'll wait downstairs.'

The clothes were mostly drab, in dingy blacks and greys . . . T-shirts, rubbed old sweaters, clumpy shoes and boots, thick socks, the sort of apparel Mary Somers favoured. But there were also a few things in expensive, outrageous styles and lovely materials, more like the type of thing she'd been wearing when she died. Abigail tried to imagine Kat sashaying forth from this house in any of these last, and failed. Pre-Belmont Avenue clothes, she guessed, perhaps kept as insurance, in case her idealistic period didn't last. The lingerie which was tossed in and amongst, she was interested to note, was all of it, without exception, luxurious – but then, it wasn't necessary to make a statement with something not normally on public display.

'Somebody lost no time. Looks like they couldn't wait to get rid,' Carmody said, raising his eyebrows in disapproval at what looked like a clearance sale.

There was indeed something needless and shocking about the speed and the contemptuous way Kat's clothes had been thrown out, and the rest of her things tipped into a black plastic bag, ready for the dustbin. Abigail sniffed. Expensive French scent lingered in the room, scent recently smelled, a spicy fragrance that wasn't the Paloma Picasso Kat had with her in the hotel. Nor did it tie in with any of the scent bottles in the plastic bag, either.

'Mary Somers,' she said eventually.

'Huh?'

'This scent you can smell in here . . . Mary Somers was wearing it.'

So, despite her disregard for appearances, she was no different after all from most other women when it came down to the small frivolities of life, much as she'd sneered at Kat. Perhaps illogically, it confirmed Abigail's suspicion as to just how far she really was committed to this protest group, and why. She said as much to Carmody, that maybe Mary Somers had taken up an attitude some time since which she found herself unable or unwilling to renounce. He looked more than a mite sceptical.

The claustrophobic little room appeared to have no more to tell them. Abigail had had enough of it, anyway. 'What about this lock-up, then, where she kept her car?'

The white Sierra Cosworth was there, in one of the row of garages round the back of the houses. Abigail walked around it while Carmody rang and arranged for it to be taken away, then came back and stood admiring its pristine whiteness, its fancy, spanking clean alloy wheels, looking as if he would like to stroke it. It would be towed away and gone over minutely for any traces, not only of Kat, which would be expected, but of the man who had driven her to Freyning Manor, but it was doubtful if there would be anything useful to be gained from it. Whoever had driven it in there had cleaned it within an inch of its life.

'And never mind what they say, I'll bet it was one of them,' Abigail said. 'Or one of the other members of this so-called Group Six.' They had the names of these other people: Adrian and Justin Moore, twins who worked in their father's radio and television business, Margot Lloyd, a housewife. Occasional supporters, such as a minicab driver called Chaz Dawson, a PE teacher by the name of Daniel Eustace. They'd all have to be interviewed and would doubtless give away as little as the case-hardened trio they'd just spoken to. But Abigail was as convinced of their guilt as she'd ever been about anything. 'They're lying through their teeth when they say they know nothing about that video. They knew why Kat was at Freyning Manor, why she had it. I think it was to blackmail someone who was featured in it – for money, maybe, for one of their causes, whatever. We need to take another close look at it and find out who that was.'

'Kind of difficult to spot, half of 'em wearing teddy bear masks.'

'How true. And if we're right, it knocks out any motive for any of this lot having murdered her. Not much point, really.'

'Not to get hold of the video, anyway.'

'You shouldn't have said that, about Kat being dangerous. You could see it giving that detective woman ideas,' Mary Somers scolded John Rabbett in the privacy of their bedroom.

'I only said the truth. We should never have trusted her.'

'We can all be wise after the event. But there was never any point to the whole idea in the first place, it was never going to succeed. I said so at the time.'

'But you went along with it. '

'Rabbit,' Mary said, as if speaking to a child, looking up into the bearded face looming over her, the animal heat and smell of his body radiating out towards her, 'there are things one has to go along with. We need to keep a roof over our heads till I've finished my book, for one thing, and don't you ever forget that.'

'I have my eye on somewhere else we could go, at a pinch. Not exactly the Ritz, but there'd be no rent to pay.'

'A squat, I suppose. God, Rabbit, sometimes you're pathetic!'

'Come here and I'll show you who's pathetic,' said Rabbit, who didn't like unpleasant truths, and whose ideas tended in one direction.

'This isn't the time. I've work to do.'

'Bugger that.' He pulled her towards him, removing her glasses and almost extinguishing her skinny form in his bearlike embrace. 'You smell yummy. I could eat you, Honey Bun,' he said, licking his red lips.

The bed creaked on its ancient springs as they bounced down on to it. And the manuscript of what was going to be the definitive novel of the twentieth century by Mary Somers, BA (Exeter), and bring them their fortune, lay untouched on the rickety table under the window. As it had lain, distressingly, for several weeks, perhaps even months, now.

14

'Right bunch of layabouts, that's what that little lot are! Private incomes! Piss idle, more like it, none of 'em ever done a day's work in their lives.' Carmody, whose whole *raison d'être* was based on the belief that necessity provided a strong incentive to work and thus to a long and happy life, continued in like manner as they drove away. He didn't appear to notice that no comment was forthcoming from his inspector. She was deeply absorbed in another train of thought, rerunning the mental tape of the last half-hour and thinking about Luke Raeburn and the possible connection Palgrave's travel agency might provide with Jamie Conolly.

Ungratefully, Abigail cursed the sun that was making up for lost time by pouring into the car, which did not have the benefit of air-conditioning. The windscreen acted like a burning glass on her bare arms. Sweat stuck her thighs and her back to the seat. Her hair clung damply all over her head and to the back of her neck and the draught from the open windows churned the air around like thick soup, doing nothing to help what must now be a non-existent hairstyle. She would really have to do something about the white paint streak. She was fed up with boring jokes about paint stripper and turps and blow lamps, despite having tweaked out a few of the whitened strands, which she'd hopefully imagined made it look a little better. She pulled the sun visor down and looked at her reflection in the mirror on the front, hastily put it back and looked at her watch. Her usual *maison de coiffeur* wasn't far away, on the edge of this same Saltcote End area, in one of the back streets only a few steps away from Milford Road nick, which they were fast approaching. 'Drop me here, Ted, and go and get yourself some lunch. I've a bit of business to see to.'

She hurried round the corner, wondering if she wasn't mad. Tantamount to voluntary euthanasia, this was, putting yourself under a blow-drier in this weather.

It seemed that someone else might have been wiser than she. 'I've just had a cancelled appointment, I can do you in five minutes,' Nigel said, holding up a mirror for a boiled-looking but apparently satisfied customer to see the result, and shooting up his eyebrows as if Abigail's hair was an emergency necessitating quick action. 'If you can manage it.'

'I can if I miss out on lunch.'

'No problem. Joanne'll fetch you a sandwich from next door after she's washed you, won't you, Joanne? I can recommend the bacon rolls.'

A bacon roll wasn't on, not today, not even one of the ambrosial ones from Sandra's Sarnie. It made Abigail sweat even more just to think about it. 'No thanks, just one of your ice-cold Cokes.'

Joanne, a dark-skinned teenager with a big smile and a hairstyle wonderful to behold, and skilful fingers that massaged and soothed as she washed and lathered, presently took money from the till and directed herself hopefully towards the Coke machine while Abigail submitted to Nigel's ministrations.

He was a big, rugby-playing fellow who'd inherited his mother's modest hairdressing shop and made it into one of the most sought-after establishments in Lavenstock: it had turned out that when it came to manipulating comb and scissors he was an undiscovered genius. The salon was still situated in the same back-street premises where it had started, a smart manoeuvre, since the rents in the town centre were escalating to unapproach-able levels and small businesses were closing down faster than branch libraries. The downmarket area wasn't reflected in his prices. His wife, Adrienne, a sprite of a woman with X-ray eyes, manned the cash desk and telephone and saw that no extras were missed, not even a squirt of hairspray.

Nigel didn't really care to talk much while he worked, unless you were into rugby, but he'd learned that most of his clients did, so after tut-tutting at the paint streak which yes, he *might* be able to do something with, he made the usual opening gambit: 'Got any holiday booked for this year?'

Possibly the only person in Lavenstock who hadn't, Abigail said no, not yet, but had he? South of France, said Nigel, he and Adrienne were going to try there this year, Palgrave's had a very good offer on. Last year they'd spent a fortune and been to India with Cook's and a right rip-off that had been, all steamy heat and beggars in the streets, a rotten hotel and Delhi belly. You never got that with Palgrave's. 'Not cheap, mind, but you get what you pay for. Bend your head forward a bit so's I can get at your neck.'

'It sounds as though you've used them before?'

'Yes, and wouldn't go again with anyone else, not after last year. They'll book you in with all the usual tour operators if you want, but their own are by far the best. Arrange them theirselves, see? So if anything goes wrong, you know where to go to complain. Not that it ever does, they never let you down. You should try them.'

'I might go along when you've finished doing your worst with me.'

Nigel looked pained until he saw she was smiling.

'You won't regret it,' he assured her, referring either to her hair or to her holiday, she wasn't sure which, plugging in the drier and thus putting an end to effective conversation.

Sipping the satisfactorily icy Coke which Joanne had managed to wrest from the machine at the back of the shop, which sometimes worked and sometimes didn't, Abigail reflected while her hair was being dried that since Palgrave's was only five minutes' walk away, it made good sense to call in on her way back to the station. Only it wouldn't be to book a holiday. It would be interesting to discover whether Luke Raeburn was the friend Jamie Conolly had alleged he'd had the falling out with. Thinking about it while Nigel shaped and moulded her damp hair with his usual magic helped to take her mind off what the operation was costing.

But when she looked in the mirror after he'd finished, she didn't begrudge a penny. Trite but true, Nigel was right, you got what you paid for. Her white streak had disappeared without the aid of paint remover, or without looking scalped. She added an extra generous tip to the bill, always a bit chancy when the boss was also the staff. Adrienne showed no offence, however, as she tucked it into the cash register. 'Oh, and the Coke,' she reminded Abigail. Money was money, however it was come by. Another little bit towards the South of France.

The smiling, smartly dressed woman at Palgrave's informed Abigail that Mr Raeburn wasn't available just now, and no, he wouldn't be available any time today, he was in fact in Italy, but she could help with any queries Abigail might have.

She smiled when Abigail said it was Mr Raeburn himself she wanted to see, but it was a smile grown a little thinner, her slightly weary tone suggesting that she was used to young women preferring to be attended to by a handsome young man rather than herself, though Abigail thought it might also work the other way round with male customers, decorative as she was. She had plum-coloured hair which she wore in a Dutch girl bob, the fringe calculated to miss her eyelashes by a millimetre, dead white skin, blood red lips and nails, long silver ear-rings that matched the big brooch on her long, scarlet, sleeveless tunic and a knuckle-duster silver ring on her right forefinger. She also had on a long, narrow black skirt that hinted at difficulties when it came to sitting down. Abigail resisted smoothing down her own denim skirt and despite herself was glad she hadn't come in thirty minutes earlier, before she'd had her hair done.

'There's nothing Mr Raeburn can tell you that I can't,' the woman observed, a shade more acid entering her tone. 'I'm Jenna Palgrave, the owner here.'

'It's a personal matter, Miss Palgrave.'

'Ms.' Seeing the opportunity of business departing, the other woman's lips tightened. 'He'll be back tomorrow.'

'I'll come back then.' Abigail got half-way to the door, then turned round. 'On second thoughts, perhaps I can have a chat with you first.' She produced her warrant card and watched the eyelashes on the big brown eyes disappear into the fringe.

'You'd better come into my office.' Ms Palgrave led the way into the back, changing the sign on the outside door to 'Closed' before she did so, into a room that was tiny, but as well ordered as she was herself, and cooled by a small but very efficient portable fan. 'He hasn't got himself into any kind of trouble, has he?' she asked, perching herself on the very edge of a stool and twisting her legs sideways. So that was how it was done.

'Have you reason to think he might have?'

'He wouldn't be working for us if I thought that! No, it was just, the police . . . and well, he does go abroad a lot.'

Her mind had obviously flown straight to drugs. 'Nothing of that sort, as far as I know,' Abigail reassured her. And hope, she added to herself. 'What sort of job does Mr Raeburn have with you?'

Her long red nails tapped the desk, her mouth was a luscious red fruit. The long split in her skirt revealed slender, black-clad legs, ending in heeled, lace-up ankle boots in fine leather that any Victorian governess would have been proud to wear. 'He's one of our group leaders. Rather more than that, really – ' She broke off, without explaining what she meant.

'How long has he worked for you?'

'Oh, six, seven months, I suppose. I took him on when – ' Again she stopped, but resumed almost immediately, 'I'd better explain that I have an invalid husband. When we started the business, I was the one who used to go abroad looking for suitable places, while Gordon kept things going at this end, but he can't work any more and I can't leave him.'

'And that was why you took Luke Raeburn on?'

'Yes. I didn't want to, I didn't want anyone. I was terrified of leaving that sort of thing to anyone else, our reputation stands or falls by the quality of what we offer our customers. We started this business ten years ago and it was tough, and then, just when things began to fall into place, Gordon was diagnosed . . . well. Never mind that. Worse happens at sea.'

Although she'd seemed young at first appearance, with her slim figure and quick movements, Jenna Palgrave could be seen, on closer acquaintance, to be no spring chicken. There were lines at the corners of her eyes, the make-up was laid on with a heavy hand.

'It can't be easy,' Abigail sympathised, 'when you're competing against some of the big operators.'

'We try to score by offering a more personal service than they do. What we do is, we offer the usual beach holidays, of course, but we also organise tours with emphasis on cultural activities – visiting museums, looking at art and architecture, listening to music, that sort of thing, mostly in France and Italy but all over Europe and occasionally in America as well. We try to cater for a discriminating class of person. You can understand how anxious I was, but I didn't have a lot of choice except to take someone else on, and I have to say, I've had no regrets. Who better than Luke, with his background?'

'Which is?'

'He has an art history degree, he's worked on conservation projects all over Europe, especially in Italy. Plus, he's half-Italian, so language is no problem. And he has a nose for sniffing out just the sort of cultural activities which will appeal to our clients.' She frowned. 'What sort of bother is he in?'

'None at all, that I know of. It's just that he appears to have been a friend of Kathryn Conolly – Jamie's sister,' she added, drawing a bow at a venture and being rewarded by Jenna Palgrave's instant response.

'Poor Jamie! And poor Kat, of course, though I only met her once. Beautiful girl.'

'Jamie works for you as well, doesn't he?'

'Has done for three or four years, at a guess, though he's not exactly an employee. He works as a freelance, whenever we have something suitable we offer it to him, and it's up to him whether he takes the opportunity.' A certain dryness had entered her tone. 'He's a bit choosy, our Jamie – but very popular with our customers, as you might imagine. He's just conducted a very

134

successful tour in America. Actually, it was he who suggested Luke.'

'Yet they haven't been the best of friends recently?' Abigail queried, glad to have her suppositions confirmed.

'Haven't they? That's news to me! They were certainly chummy enough on Saturday morning.'

'You saw them together then?'

'For a few minutes – Luke was off to Italy, and they had a quick coffee together, but it was me Jamie had really come to see. I'd offered him the chance to accompany a group to the Loire valley next month. The girl who was to have led the party for us has taken it into her head to have a baby and she's finding the early months by no means the easy ride she'd imagined. Don't know what these silly girls expect if they will go in for babies,' she said impatiently. 'The next thing to cross off their list of things to be acquired, I suppose.' Ms Palgrave was plainly not a mother. 'Anyway, travel's out of the question for her at the moment. So I was very glad when Jamie agreed to do it.'

'What can you tell me about his private life – Luke Raeburn's, I mean? Friends? Girlfriends?'

'I don't suppose someone like Luke is short of them, but I've never seen him with any girls – until Kat came in with Jamie one day when Luke was here, that is. And then it was only what I guessed – no, to be honest, it was more than guessing, you can always tell, can't you? She was on Cloud Nine.'

Stars in their eyes, no one else in the room except them, Abigail could imagine.

'Other than that,' Jenna Palgrave shrugged, 'I can only say that his private life is his own.'

Sensing this was the end of any useful information she might have to give, Abigail thanked her and took her leave. 'I don't suppose I shall have to trouble you any further. Let me have Luke's address if you will and we'll see him at home before he leaves for work. What time do you open in the morning?'

'Half-past nine. You'll be popular, going to see him before then! He's not one who's at his best, first thing.'

That was the idea. Nothing like catching 'em just out of bed, when they were only half awake, before their first fix of caffeine. This was a Mayo dictum, one that worked, as often as not, one of the many she'd come to believe in, almost without knowing she'd done so. But he wasn't a bad role model to follow, she thought with a smile, which faded as she debated, making her way back to Milford Road, what measure of success he was likely to have in getting to grips with the problem of finding his daughter.

'Kidderminster!' Alex announced suddenly, next morning, pausing on her way out to work. 'That's it, I'm sure of it!'

'Kidderminster?' Mayo, glasses perched on the end of his nose, peered at the almost reassembled mechanism of Gerald Vickers's bracket clock, which he'd decided to take to pieces because he was still at a dead end in his determination to find Julie and for the moment he couldn't think what the hell else to do. Except tinker with a clock, an occupation that more often than not got his mind working in tune with the mechanism.

He'd rung every conceivable friend, relative, or place where she might have hung out and come up with precisely nothing. The only person who might have known, he strongly suspected, was dead, lying in the mortuary. The idea that followed, the memory of Julie's name in the hotel register, he was doing his level best not to think about.

He poked around for a part of the clock mechanism that had apparently been spirited away, God alone knew where. 'Has anybody touched this table?'

'Nobody, as you well know,' Alex replied, 'would have the temerity to approach that table when you're working on it. And since there are only two of us living here, and it wasn't me, you probably ought to get your glasses changed. Did you hear what I said about Kidderminster?'

'There's a balance-wheel missing.' Mayo continued to search. Kidderminster? It seemed unlikely. 'It was Dover last night,' he remarked, not too impressed with this new insight. 'You were dead sure that was where they were opening that restaurant.'

'That was an association of ideas with the Dover sole.'

They'd been eating out. 'Fish, I think,' she'd mused, scanning the menu as if that wasn't what she invariably ordered. Fish was

136

one of her favourite dishes, but she saved it for when she could have it without the smell all over the flat.

'I was mistaken.'

'You might be mistaken about Kidderminster.'

'No, I *know* that's it. I was just thinking how right that carpet we've chosen for the downstairs sitting-room is, and about ordering it today – and there it was, Kidderminster. I knew it would come back to me.'

Amazement at female logic had long since been replaced by respect for their intuition in Mayo's mind. How it worked, he didn't know, it defied all the laws of probability, but work it sometimes did. Not always, but quite often. Even for someone as cool and sensible as his finicky, neat and rational Alex. But why Kidderminster and carpets should be any more certain than Dover and Dover sole escaped him. 'Bit of a long shot, isn't it?'

'It's worth a try, surely,' she said, glancing at her watch and picking up her handbag.

'You just can't bear to see me at a loose end.'

She returned his grin. 'True.' But not because she thought him idle. Not a word that featured in any vocabulary applicable to Mayo. It was – partly, at least – because she knew only too well what it felt like to be suddenly cut off from work that had absorbed you totally and utterly. Twice it had happened to her – firstly when she'd been injured in the line of duty, beginning a lengthy convalescence which had started a long period of self-doubt about her chosen profession. And secondly, when she'd lost the baby.

In some strange way, coping with that had redefined her view of herself. She'd been through a period of self-pity, then she'd found herself possessed of a ferocious energy that sometimes she didn't know what to do with. After which, she'd begun to get on with her life, even convincing herself of the positive advantages of not being pregnant at her age – though accepting the fact of non-motherhood was harder to endure. Accepting what you can't change is a difficult lesson to learn.

'I'm sure I'm right, that's where John Smith came from originally. I think. Somewhere near there, anyway.'

'He did?'

Oh well, that was more like it. Mayo took off the spectacles that Alex said made him look like an old Swiss watchmaker and felt suddenly hopeful. Alex had only met John Smith briefly – as, indeed, he himself had – on his way, with the French girl, Marie-Solange, to say goodbye to the parrot which had once been his, and to pick Julie up on the first stage of her Round the World in Eighty Years. But she might well be right.

'I'd love to come with you, only I've an appointment I can't put off,' she remarked wistfully. An opportunity had presented itself not too long ago for her to get back into investigative work – not back into the police, that was a period of her life that was definitely over, but into private inquiry work. She'd very nearly taken it, but subsequent events had made it radically impossible. Sometimes she regretted that. Quite often, she envied Abigail Moon. But she and Lois were working on a commission to decorate a set of prestige offices, and the client was being difficult, wanting it to look like a TV set for *Dallas* on a budget for *Coronation Street*, and Alex had decided the time had come for plain speaking. She was quite looking forward to it.

'Kidderminster's not far,' she said briskly. 'It'll be easier tracing a John Smith in Kidderminster than along all those miles of south coast. There can't be all that many French restaurants there – all that many restaurants at all if it comes to that.'

So, here he was, on his way to Kidderminster, after taking the precaution of making a few preliminary inquiries, but still not at all sanguine about the outcome. Alex had convinced him that anything, however, was worth a try. Anything to break the deadlock he'd found himself in.

Mid-week, he'd thought to miss the scrum of traffic which at weekends left behind the Black Country for the delights of the Severn valley, heading west with all the enthusiasm of Gold Rush pioneers. But it was the holiday season and, trundling along behind the seventh caravan he'd encountered, Mayo reflected that he might conceivably have arrived more quickly had he boarded a narrowboat in Lavenstock and let it carry him down the canal which flowed through the town centre. Thankfully, he spotted his turn-off point.

Kidderminster, a town synonymous with carpet manufacture. He'd heard about cheap imports, a slump in the industry, and imagined a ghost town, the clack of looms and factory hooters silenced. What he found was a pleasant little Worcestershire town, not exactly thrusting towards the next millennium, but busy enough without being overcrowded, due to what there was of interest being sealed off within the confines of the ring road, which travellers were not inclined to broach.

He spent some time walking around the town amongst the shoppers, having taken advantage of parking free in the local police station car-park. Within five minutes, following directions, he'd found what he sought.

The desk sergeant, like desk sergeants everywhere, had known immediately where Le Bistro was. If unimaginatively named, it was apparently gaining a reputation, said to be very popular. John Smith was the chef and Marie-Solange the businesswoman, as befitted a Frenchwoman. The bistro had been open for lunch and, as he ought to have foreseen, was now closed for the afternoon. He went back to the nick and inquired where the owners lived. The sergeant, only too happy to be of help to a senior officer, even one from another division, found out within a matter of minutes.

Clark Road turned out to be one of the roads off the hill that sloped up from the valley, and number four a detached Victorian redbrick villa of pretensions its size didn't warrant, much decorated with mullioned windows and high gables and curlicued trim. It was converted into flats, much like his own house had been. J & M.-S Smith, according to the card beside the bell-push, occupied the ground floor. Sounds of juvenile roars and protests could be heard as he pushed the bell.

A harassed young man opened the door, holding in his arms a squirming, yelling, miniature baseball player in navy and red striped T-shirt, jeans and a peaked denim sun-hat. The few-months-old baby was fighting ineffectually with the hat, trying to pull it off, but at the sight of Mayo standing on the step, the roars abruptly stopped, the fat tears sliding down his cheeks were arrested and he gazed with disconcerting solemnity at this new apparition within his small world.

'Come through into the garden,' John Smith invited, their

recognition mutual after Mayo had introduced himself. 'We can't talk in here and it's Quentin's time to be outside for some fresh air. He's not allowed out in this sun without some covering on his head,' he added in explanation as his offspring began a renewed and vociferous attack on his headgear. 'I expect he'll get used to his new hat, but just now he hates it.'

As well he might, thought Mayo, following John Smith down the hallway and through the room behind, charting a pathway through baby bouncers and packs of disposable nappies, a high chair, a car seat and a baby buggy. He didn't remember Julie demanding so much paraphernalia and attention, not to mention such an outlandish wardrobe, but maybe he'd simply forgotten.

Out in the garden, Quentin wriggled about on his father's lap, red-faced and grizzling, wrenching off the hat every time it was placed on his head and dashing it to the ground.

'Sorry his mum's not here, she's out shopping,' the beleaguered John Smith apologised above the roars. 'She's much better with Q than I am.'

Mayo was not at his best with babies, either. He thought they should be born at four years old. Realising that conversation was going to be impossible, in a highly untypical and what he was soon to discover was an exceedingly rash gesture, he picked the hat up and perched it on his own head, pulling a funny face for the baby's amusement. This turned out to be a mistake of serious proportions, for Quentin appreciatively doubled up with laughter, snatched the hat off and demanded a repeat performance, plus encore after encore, as if Mayo were Pavarotti.

Mayo felt that the resultant interview with John Smith could not go on record as being one of his finest, but it didn't really matter, he assured himself as he extricated his car and began the return journey, since the young man had had virtually nothing to tell him.

Quentin, exhausted by his endeavours, had eventually fallen suddenly and heavily asleep in his father's arms, the picture of sweet innocence, while Mayo related everything to John Smith.

They sat in garden chairs under the one apple tree, and John stroked his sleeping baby's damp hair and told Mayo that he and Marie-Solange had heard nothing from Julie since last Christmas, when she'd sent them a card and a letter from Texas.

'I won't hide it from you, Mr Mayo. I haven't kept Jools's letter, but we both thought she sounded worried, unhappy, I don't know. Something. Not like Jools, anyway.'

The irritating nickname didn't get on his nerves, as it usually did. Julie's friend looked so young, so earnest, brown-haired, brown-eyed, serious. He'd only entered Mayo's life briefly, once before, and Mayo could smile now to think of the ogre he'd conjured up before he met him. A bearded student weirdie, he'd imagined, a long-haired, pot-smoking, work-shy rebel, getting up to God knows what with Julie when they roamed in tandem round the world, learning about Life. Until he'd arrived on the doorstep, a conventional and polite young man, complete with a French fiancée and a parrot they couldn't take with them on their travels . . .

The baby having fallen asleep on his lap and not wanting to disturb him, he'd requested Mayo to forage in the kitchen for a couple of beers. Unharassed and relaxed at last, he proved to have an unexpected gift for telling a funny story. Mayo saw a different aspect of Julie's character as he was regaled with various exploits which were entirely new to him.

'She'd never have done anything you need worry about, though, no way. She couldn't have. People don't act so far out of character,' John Smith asserted.

That wasn't necessarily – or even generally – true, in Mayo's experience. Actions that at first seemed atypical often turned out to be the essential characteristics of the people concerned.

'She's pretty tough, you know.'

'Wilful, you mean.' Mayo smiled, thinking of various child-hood incidents.

'Besides,' John went on, 'if anyone would have got up to anything dodgy, it'd be Kat, not Jools.'

Mayo was surprised. 'You knew her, then?'

They'd met, once, he said, on that brief stopover in Laven-stock, but he remembered hearing her name constantly from Julie. He couldn't add anything to that. He promised to try and think up a few more people who might be able to give a lead on where Julie was. Neither was hopeful as they eventually parted.

No more wild-goose chases, Mayo thought as he drove home. He'd achieved nothing, but on the other hand, he wasn't sorry he'd come. Part of every investigation was the process of elimination.

He hadn't mentioned Bert, either, as he'd fully intended, to his rightful owner. John Smith seemed to have forgotten that he'd ever owned such a thing as a parrot, and Mayo told himself that the young man had enough preoccupations in his life without having Bert dumped on him. He knew he was kidding himself. The truth was, life would lose much of its rich pattern without the colourful old bird. Who was he going to lose his temper with, if he couldn't shout at Bert?

15

Back again the next day to Saltcote End, the area behind which stretched the architectural desert numbering Belmont Avenue among its treasures – this time to Cross Street, to see Luke Raeburn before he set out for work. Miraculously finding a tree-shaded parking space within walking distance of where she wanted to go, Abigail thought maybe the same sort of luck would be with her for the rest of the day.

It was the sort of wonderful summer morning that made you think like that, bright and clear, long shadows sloping across the pavements, trees casting dappled shade. An old lady sang to herself and pranced along as happily as did her chihuahua on the end of its leash. A greengrocer, whistling, arranged oranges in glowing piles on a trestle covered with fake grass outside his shop and called out to Abigail. 'How's this weather suit you, then, m'duck?'

No doubt about it, sunshine brought out the best in people, but the morning was already hotting up, and tempers would likely rise with the thermometer, and patience begin to fray. Perhaps the British were temperamentally, in the end, more suited to the dismal weather which normally passed as summer.

Hidden behind the town centre, overshadowed by Lavenstock's ultimate shopping experience – the pleasure domes of the new precinct – Cross Street emerged. As much of a far cry from the precinct as it was from its neighbour on the other side, where the network of narrow, ancient streets sloping up from the river was an inconvenience put up with in deference to the trade it brought in: a lot of people liked shopping there more than anywhere, they liked the ambience and the personal service and the out of the ordinary merchandise, never mind the higher prices. No one, on the other hand, could have enjoyed shopping in Cross Street.

It was a pre-war development of the worst kind, a depressing 1930s parade, its name revealing what seemed to be its prime purpose: merely to serve as a connection between two other streets. An upper storey of flats decorated with mock-Tudor gabling surmounted the shops, which faced the yard of a disused church on the opposite side, a desolate, overgrown place of fallen tombstones and untended graves. Several squares of baked earth set at regular intervals amongst the paving in front of the shops bore witness to what had once been a row of urban trees, now desecrated by vandals, the sole survivor drooping to one side, as if ashamed of itself for being alive. Two sets of empty premises, the rest with a desperate air of hanging on. Abigail's feeling of well-being in the bright morning took a nosedive as she regarded the rest – a newsagent-cum-general stores, an ironmonger, a seedy-looking dentist's with a dubious net café-curtain stretched across the dirty plate glass. *Aargh!* She'd sooner have all her teeth fall out. There was a shoe repairer, also selling plastic handbags and umbrellas, plus Fryer Tuck's chip shop with its lingering smell and its accompanying take-away detritus punctuating the end of the row. Abigail found Luke Raeburn's flat to be the one over Sew and Sew: dress materials, knitting wools and archaic haberdashery of the sort which lent a whole new meaning to the word. This sort of accommodation didn't seem to be that of a man with money to throw around, as the occupants of Belmont Avenue had suggested of Luke Raeburn.

He came to the door bearing the blank expression of the not long awakened, but he was dressed and, presumably, ready for work, although a roll-neck black jersey, black jeans and black leather bomber jacket scarcely chimed with the elegance of Palgrave's and its owner. His appearance provided another reversal of the mental picture she'd had of him. First, at Belmont

Avenue, a picture of some sort of Flash Harry, splashing his money and his favours around. Jenna Palgrave's description of what he'd previously done for a living had transmuted this to a serious-minded, responsible academic type. She reminded herself that Jenna Palgrave had told her he was not at his best in the mornings as he blinked and waved her to a black vinyl chair, folded himself into its companion, slid his length as far down as he could get, and waited, yawning. Ms Palgrave, it seemed, was not given to overstatements.

Apart from the two chairs, there was nothing else at all in the white-walled room except a cheap, low table with a glass top, containing a single ashtray. Not an ornament or a cushion, plain blinds instead of curtains, not a book or a picture. And this for an art conservationist. The pale, sanded floorboards were bare, innocent of rugs. The minimalist style of interior decoration, fashionable among the over-precious, necessitated by the rather poor. Ten minutes into his company, however, Abigail decided that in Luke Raeburn's case, it was neither: his surroundings, she guessed, were a matter of indifference to him. These were the basics that had come with the flat and he hadn't bothered to augment them. But now, in the first moment of meeting him, the extent of this had yet to be revealed – though indifference of another kind was immediately apparent.

'Kat?' he repeated casually, when she'd told him her business. 'Nice kid, she was. I was sorry to hear – '

Nice kid? Sorry to hear? Not shocked, or even appalled. Nor devastated, the in-word to describe every emotion from missing a bus to seeing your house going up in smoke, or just being knocked sideways by the latest TV heart-throb. Only sorry – about the murder of someone you were going to marry? She put that to him, watched his face change. From amazement to wariness to what could have been real anger.

'Oh God, is that what she was saying – we were going to be married?'

'It wasn't true, then?'

'You can't be serious!'

She was getting rather tired of hearing this in relation to Kat's matrimonial intentions. 'Why do you think she said it, then?'

'Christ, I don't know! OK, then, OK, I can make a stab at it.'

He pulled a cigarette pack from his pocket, offered it, pulled one out and lit it for himself when the offer was declined. 'Look, she was a great kid, as I said, but no way were we an item. This is embarrassing, but the truth is, she – well, she had the hots for me. But – *marrying* me? You sure?'

'Her brother seemed to think so.'

'Jamie? You've got me confused, why should he say that?'

'Presumably because Kat told him.' Although, to be precise, Jamie had thought the one she was going to marry had been Andrew Inskip. It was those at Belmont Avenue who'd thought it would be Luke Raeburn.

Someone had got their lines of communication tangled. Or else Kat was a romancer. Or else Inskip, or Luke Raeburn, had been stringing her along.

He was the type to appeal to women. Some women, she amended. Tall, broad-shouldered, slim-hipped, sensuous lips and high cheekbones. Dark curls. Such dark, Italian eyes. Devastating, if you must. Yet he had a taut, held-in look, something cold at the centre. Possibly frightening, even. Exciting, but cruel, with a suggestion of animality. Oh yes, there was a type of woman who did go along with this. She'd seen more than enough of it when she'd worked on the Domestic Violence Unit. Battered wives and partners who inexplicably went back for more.

'How long have you known her?'

'Not long. I met her through Jamie. He introduced us and we hit it off straight away. She wasn't the world's greatest brain, but fun, you know? And a cracker to look at, I have to say that, and at first – well, I may have given out the wrong signals, because frankly, she seemed to think I was just waiting for her to fall into my arms. And she was very willing, believe me. Too willing, know what I mean?' He took another deep drag. The stream of nicotine into his system had brought him awake and banished any disinclination to talk, it seemed. 'But no way did I want to get involved to the extent she did – and she made it pretty obvious she thought I was the best thing since the microchip. I damn sure didn't give her any encouragement as far as that goes – certainly no ideas about getting married!'

Oh, he really loved himself! Arrogant assumptions like this

were what made the feminists want to draw out the long knives, and Abigail could go along with that, but behind it all, she sensed the protestations were self-justification. He'd probably led Kat on until the poor kid didn't know where she was, and knew it.

'So,' she repeated, 'You last saw her . . . ?'

'Friday night, for a pub meal. We drove out to the White Boar at Over Kennet.'

'In her car?'

'That fancy Sierra Cosworth? No way! She wouldn't let any-one drive that, but in any case, I don't like being driven by anyone else, especially after they've had a few drinks.' And no, she hadn't said anything, had given no indication of what she was about to do the next day, and he certainly hadn't driven her out to Freyning Manor, was baffled by why she should have taken a room there. He also stated categorically that he knew nothing about the video found in the bedroom safe. He was so emphatic Abigail wondered if she imagined the leap of aware-ness in his dark eyes at the mention of it.

'OK. Let's talk about Group Six.'

'Oh, them!'

'That sounds very dismissive. Why's that? You joined them, after all. And gave them money, I understand.' And where this kind of money came from was another thing that interested Abigail. Not from his job with Palgrave's Travel Agency, surely?

'I didn't join them, just contributed a bit towards their funds,' he corrected. 'Anything that'll give the Establishment a bit of aggro has my support. Sorry, shouldn't have said that, should I, you being part of it? But that was before I found out they were just a bunch of amateurs. Inskip, he's . . .'

'He's what?'

'Oh, I don't know. Too bloody full of himself, for one thing, the Inscrutable Enigma image, or at any rate that's what he'd like to put out. But there's nothing to him, he's all wind and puff, and he knows it at bottom and he's afraid someone will find him out so he has to make big noises. He'd like to make big gestures, too, but he hasn't got the balls. One day he'll do something stupid, just to convince himself and other people.'

146

Well.

There was a silence while he put out his cigarette, lit another one immediately. Abigail had the impression that he feared – not having said too much about Andrew Inskip, most of which might be perceptively near the mark, it seemed to her – but that he might have given too much of himself away while doing so.

'Thank you for your help,' she said fifteen minutes later closing her notebook. He'd answered the rest of her questions with the ease and readiness of someone whose every statement can be proved: provided details of his trip to Italy and the business he'd conducted there, spoken openly of his friendship with Jamie Conolly, telling her how they'd met: in Amalfi, when an elderly man in Jamie's group, disdaining to use the lift, had had a heart attack on the steps leading up to the converted monastery where the party were staying. Luke had been on the spot and helped to get him to hospital. Afterwards the two young men had had a drink together, a friendship had formed which eventually led to Luke joining Palgrave's.

'My father was English, but he died when I was very young and meeting Jamie made me realise I hadn't spent nearly enough time over here,' he said, smoothly, as if the explanation had been given many times before – though apart from his eyes, there was very little to show his Italian heritage and upbringing, nothing in his mannerisms, or his speech, to show he wasn't wholly British. 'I shan't be here much longer, though, I'm beginning to feel homesick.'

She quizzed him about the quarrel with Jamie. Hardly a quarrel, he corrected with a smile, just a few words, but nothing heavy, a personal matter, soon over, sorted out as soon as it began. Over Jamie's choice of girlfriend, as a matter of fact. 'That's what Jamie's doing, working at Freyning Manor, chasing a woman . . .' He eyed Abigail speculatively. 'You don't know about that? Big trouble there, all right, though he wouldn't admit that when I told him . . . but I apologised later. None of my damn business, after all.'

'Mr Conolly should have told us that,' Abigail said severely. 'Not that it materially alters his case.'

'His case?' he repeated, very quickly picking her up on that.

'You don't mean he's under suspicion for his sister's murder? Are you serious? We are talking about the same person, Jamie? You're not even at first base there! He hasn't got the bottle – or he'd be too frightened of messing his beautiful clothes up! Anyway, Kat could do no wrong in his eyes.'

And what about you? Abigail thought. She wouldn't have been averse to pinning this one on to him. In fact, she found the prospect singularly tempting because she did not like this young man at all, distrusted everything he said and was aware of the dangers of this. But he had his alibi, he was air miles away in Rome when Kat had been killed. Or so he said. And so it could almost certainly be proved. And as yet, no motive, though motive was an elusive concept at the best of times.

'One last question, Mr Raeburn. What had Kat been doing with herself since her father died, by way of work, I mean?'

'What did she ever do?' he asked. And then, with a sudden curious blankness in his expression, 'After her father died, she sometimes worked for Max Fisher. Why don't you ask him?'

As she stood up to leave, she was faced with the outlook over the now disused graveyard. What must it feel like, when the only view from your window was row upon row of graves, the last resting places of those long dead? It was a place of dereliction, frequent haunt of dossers and druggies, sad no-hopers who were regularly picked up by the police, a continuing stream of degradation. Fallen lives. Fallen tombstones, old graves, the cemetery long since full, but graves, nonetheless. Some of them with morbid Victorian stone effigies and white memorial headstones. Marble angels and monuments with bas-relief carving. That barren view, the bare solitude within the flat; it could give one nightmares, or ideas. How did he live here, this young man with such a high opinion of himself? Did he feel he needed nothing more but himself and this morbid view?

These were only some of the question marks against Luke Raeburn, Abigail felt, promising herself that she'd be back. Somewhere along the line he was lying, and she wanted to know why.

16

It was a delicate subject of a highly intimate nature, not for the ears of their coarser companions. 'And so I said to her, "Don't think I'm going through all that bloody rigmarole again, because I'm not. You'll just have to accept it. You're not the only one in the history of the universe who can't have a baby." '

'Keith, it's a hard thing for a woman to accept,' Jenny said.

'Is that right?' Farrar responded heatedly. 'How does she think I feel? Makes it worse that there's no reason – none at all, except that she tries too hard. '

'There's ways round it.'

'Adoption? Forget it! They all want to keep their kids now, so's to get a council house, or else they won't allow them to be born at all. As for any other way – uh-oh, no way, not me!'

This was not a Farrar everyone saw – as dumb and obstinate and macho as the rest of them. And strangely enough, Jenny liked him better for it. She was smiling sympathetically at him as the door opened.

Which was the first thing Abigail saw when she popped her head into the CID room. Keith Farrar perched on the edge of Jenny Platt's desk, and Jenny smiling up at him. They were unusually alone in there for the time being, technology humming all around them, and maybe this was why he'd chosen this moment to bend Jenny's ear further with tales of domestic dissension, which Abigail knew he regularly did, and suspected he was doing now.

Something wrong with that today, however. There was a definite feeling of having interrupted something, which sharpened her senses. It seemed more like Jenny was lending a willing ear than having it bent. Enjoying the intimacy, what was more. God, surely she couldn't be such a fool? She had twice as much about her as Farrar, for all his sharp wits, and she wasn't short of menfriends. Outside the department – inside too, if she'd been willing and hadn't had more common sense.

As soon as they saw her, Farrar reached out for the papers on the desk in front of Jenny and began busily scanning them, while Jenny said, 'We've completed the check-ups on all those dining at Freyning Manor, ma'am, all of them except for – '

'That's it,' Farrar interrupted suddenly, his finger pointing to a name on the list. 'I mean, that's her – the woman in the video! I knew there was something. Seen her photo in the paper, dozens of times, that's what it was. She's older of course, and her hair was long then, and not greying like it is now, but it's Maggie Vye, I'd bet my next week's overtime on it.'

'Our MP? You're sure?' Startled, Abigail tried to envisage Maggie Vye as Goldilocks, equipped with long, blonde hair, but that took more imaginative effort than she was capable of.

Backtracking, because he never liked to be put in a position where he couldn't withdraw, if necessary, Farrar said, 'I never did get to see that run-through of the video again, but I will now, though I don't *think* there's much room for doubt.'

'And she *was* at Freyning Manor that night? Having dinner with . . .' Abigail picked up the list. 'Rollo Forbes – who's he?'

'Her party agent,' Jenny said.

'Who's down to interview them?'

'I am.'

'Leave that to me, Jenny. Meanwhile, let's have another look at that video.'

Abigail's door was pushed open and Nightingale's head thrust around it. 'My office,' she barked decisively, like an irascible senior officer in a TV cop series.

Abigail rolled her eyes heavenwards, capped her pen and followed the heavy footsteps up the stairs.

'What progress?' Nightingale demanded, as soon as she put a foot in the door. 'I'd like to have my powder dry before facing the vultures.'

Oh God, yes, the vultures, the rat-pack, the ladies and gentlemen of the fourth estate, Abigail had nearly forgotten them. The journalists and photographers, the TV cameras, even now gathering downstairs for the announced media opportunity.

'Sit down, Moon.'

Accustomed to Christian names and much less abruptness than this from Mayo, Abigail looked round for a seat, found a chair against the wall.

'There've been some developments,' she said, as she brought it forward. 'We should be able to come up with a firm line of inquiry soon, given a fair wind and bit of luck.'

'Luck,' said Nightingale, 'has nothing to do with it.'

She sounded exactly like Mayo.

Not that she was like Mayo in many other ways that Abigail could see, except perhaps in her capacity for keeping at it. She was wearing a track between here and her office in Hurstfield in an endeavour to keep both jobs on the ball. Give her her due, so far she was managing to cope with the day-to-day administration as well as keeping abreast of the murder investigation. Seeing to it that there could be no complaints levelled at her for the way she was running this operation, she was playing it entirely by the book – directing strategy, keeping her finger on the pulse . . . delegating, letting others do the leg work, naturally. But her heart obviously wasn't in it. It was clear that the brunt of the inquiry was to rest on Abigail's shoulders while Nightingale, though ultimately taking overall responsibility – and, hopefully, the stick if things went wrong – played a supporting, advisory role. Certainly not the hands-on approach favoured by Mayo. The King is dead, long live the Queen.

She'd had Mayo's desk moved so that she now sat with her back to the window and the view of the ugly, smoke-blackened brick Town Hall it was Mayo's prerogative to hate, together with its rows of urban pigeons who occupied every one of its Victorian parapets, window ledges, alcoves and orifices. The light now fell on the face of the person sitting opposite Nightingale. 'No reason why I have to look at piles of pigeon-shit all day,' she said forthrightly, disconcerting Abigail, whose thoughts must have been more apparent than she knew.

She pushed her chair back and lit a cigarette. The ashtray was already full, the air blue with smoke. Mayo would have a fit to find his office reeking of old fag ash when he returned.

I must stop thinking like this, Abigail told herself, the woman's only doing her job. And an unpopular one at that. Standing in for anyone was no picnic. Then suddenly Nightingale smiled and picked up the case file from the desk. 'OK, then, where are we?'

She should smile like that more often, Abigail thought, recovering from it – a natural smile, not her get-the-missionaries one. She wasn't wearing any make-up, but even beneath the tobacco smoke Abigail recognised her scent: Calèche. Sharp, citrusy, delicious. She had a good skin, too, though not for long, the way she smoked. Pity about the hairstyle.

'I gather Mrs Conolly was told on Sunday night,' she remarked.

'Mr Mayo knew the girl personally – and it was before he was officially off the case – ' Abigail stopped abruptly. That sounded very like making excuses, and she was damned if she was going to make them, especially when there was no reason to be defensive. She added briskly that she herself had also seen Diane Conolly.

Watching her wryly, the superintendent said suddenly, 'Look, I've met Gil Mayo several times, and if I've read him aright, he's not going to sit around on his backside letting all this go on without him. Well, that's his problem, and while I won't officially support him, I'm not going to make waves about him interfering. I can see this is a special case.'

'I don't think – '

Glenda ignored the interruption, sitting foursquare in her chair, legs inelegantly apart, feet planted on the floor. 'But special or not, my reputation's at stake, as well, and I've no intention of letting personalities affect the outcome of this case, please understand that, Moon.'

The two women took each other's measure. Do I actually *prefer* working for a man, rather than a woman? Abigail asked herself. And if so, what does that say about me? No, she decided, it didn't depend on gender, but rather on whether the woman was Nightingale and the man, Mayo. She took a deep breath and bent over her file. Briefly, she explained about Farrar spotting the resemblance to Maggie Vye in the video. After they'd seen the run-through together once more, she'd had to agree that Farrar was right, as usual. She'd wanted to see it herself again, for a different reason. To compare it with the photo she'd purloined from Diane Conolly and check if one of the male actors in that film was, as she'd half speculated he might be, Hugh Conolly. There was something, regardless of the ludicrous teddy bear mask ... but, looking at the film again, she still hadn't been sure. But if he was, it answered the question of how Inskip's group had got hold of the film. Ten to one Kat had found it among her father's effects when he'd died. *If* . . .

However, whether there was doubt about Hugh Conolly or not, there wasn't much doubt, once you'd had it pointed out, that the young woman playing Goldilocks was a much younger and very much slimmer version of the respected Maggie Vye, MP. And even in black and white, allowing for the poor quality of the film, it could be seen that Maggie, in her younger days, had been well worth looking at.

'Maggie Vye. Well.' Glenda's mouth set in a thin line. 'We could have done without this! Bloody media will be on to it like wasps round a jam sandwich at a picnic.'

'This Group Six reckon they've never heard of that video, but I reckon they're lying. And now that we've identified Maggie Vye as being the star of the show, as you might say, it seems likely they were using it as blackmail. Trying to force her politically in some way, to trade in the video for promises. She's something in the Environment department, and the group's allegedly involved in the protest against this proposed new motorway bypass.'

'Blackmailing someone over juvenile high jinks with a camera? Well, I suppose it's possible. Half-baked, but possible.'

'They're a half-baked crowd. On the periphery of everything, I gather.'

'I wouldn't put much past politicians – but cutting the girl's throat just to get a dirty video back! That's a bit OTT, especially for someone like Maggie Vye. She's reckoned to be straight as a die.'

'And therefore might do a lot to protect her reputation?' Abigail shook her head. 'Maybe, but for what it's worth, I can't see that happening, either. And the motive's screwy. For one thing, blackmailing someone like her wouldn't get them far. She hasn't got anywhere near enough clout to stop that road going ahead, so it would be pretty pointless. Anyone who didn't have a few slates short of the full roof would know that. On the other hand ...'

'On the other hand, what?'

'She's not without influence altogether – she'd be a good one to have on their side, arguing their case. Also – it doesn't take a genius to work out that there's bound to be more than one copy of the video, ready to turn up elsewhere if she didn't immediately agree to what they wanted.'

'And with this government being so touchy about that sort of thing – determined their members should appear whiter than white? Mm, I don't know. They might be prepared to overlook a marital infidelity or two in a valued cabinet minister. But Maggie Vye's not that indispensable.'

'This sort of sleaze'd put paid to her long-term career prospects at any rate – and her constituents are going to like it even less.' Abigail stared out of the window. 'Have you seen the PM report yet?'

'Not yet.' Nightingale ground her cigarette in the ashtray and immediately lit another, and began riffling through the formidable stack of papers in front of her. 'It's here somewhere, when I can find it. What does it say?'

Abigail had been quite happy, for any reason you might like to think of, to let Carmody attend the post-mortem while she was interviewing Luke Raeburn. There had been no surprises. Kathryn Conolly had bled to death when the carotid arteries had been severed. The incised wounds to her face, inflicted after death, were caused by the same weapon – a thin, exceedingly sharp-bladed instrument. A knife honed to the thinness of a razor blade, Timpson-Ludgate had suggested. 'There was no evidence of a struggle, no defence wounds on her hands suggesting she'd tried to grab the knife. She apparently didn't scratch the assailant, there was no skin tissue under her nails.' She paused. 'The Prof doesn't rule out the possibility of her killing being sexually motivated. That mutilation of her face. Psychopathic, maybe.'

Nightingale drew in smoke, blew it out, looked at Abigail through narrowed eyes. 'Let's not get into that sort of speculation, shall we? Not yet, anyway. Not when we have this very good line to be working on.'

What did that mean? That it would lead into another dimension entirely, sure. It would mean turning the investigation on its head, which Glenda Nightingale patently didn't want. What she wanted was this wrapped up, quick – but even at the risk of the killer never being found? An easy ride was one thing, this was something else!

Abigail breathed deep, to stop herself saying what she thought, and turned to what was a safer subject – for the moment. The team had worked damned hard, trying to build up a picture of Kat's life during the two weeks prior to her death, and they'd now got together a thick file. She'd brought it in with her and flicked through the pages. 'We've traced her movements back from the time she went to live at Belmont Avenue, but it's given us very little at all that's useful to work on.' Nothing to indicate anything during that time which might have caused her murder, no one new in her life . . . they were still ferreting about, sifting carefully through statements. Boring, mundane work, but finding out as much about her background as they could was vital, as in all cases of murder by person or persons unknown.

'She seems to have spent most of her time these last few weeks either working out at the health club or mooching about, reading, watching TV. One of the attendants at the gym did say that she hadn't seemed her usual sunny self lately, a bit depressed, but that's all.'

When she'd heard that, somewhere in Abigail's mind had been conjured up a dispiriting picture which kept running round like a continuous movie reel, provoking stirrings of pity: who wouldn't have been depressed in Kat's situation? Her father's death and then – what must her reactions have been to that sordid video – viewing it and suspecting (or worse, knowing) that her father was one of the main actors? Any daughter would have found that difficult, if not impossible, to handle. Then why – why on earth – had she allowed herself to be involved in its exploitation? Acting as a go-between?

'So far she's a bit of an enigma,' she said, 'played her cards pretty close to her chest as far as her mother was concerned. Her brother – her friends, too, come to that – if they know anything, aren't saying. We've spoken to nearly all the names her mother gave us, and she seems to have been well liked for the most part, a nice enough girl, if a bit superficial at times.' Fun was a word which had cropped up time and again. 'She seems to have messed around since she left school, not doing anything much.'

At an age when most of her contemporaries took jobs or began preparing for some sort of career – or even travelled the world, from continent to continent, as in the case of Julie Mayo – Kat Conolly had apparently been content to stay in this small town. A backwater was how a lot of young people saw it, how Abigail herself had seen it in her own youth, half as big as Highgate cemetery and twice as dead. Yet this young woman with so much potential had chosen to lead an aimless existence here, at least until nursing her father during his last illness had injected it with some sort of purpose.

'What do you make of this business of the victim using the name of Gil Mayo's daughter?' Nightingale asked suddenly. 'Do you believe all that guff her brother suggested, about swapping names? Is Julia Mayo that sort of young woman?'

Anybody was capable of doing daft things when they were young – and not so young, either, Abigail thought, depressingly reminded of several of her own indiscretions. 'I don't really know. I've never actually met her.'

During all the time she'd been working with Mayo, his daughter had been living abroad. Abigail had seen photos of her and knew that she was tall, slim, fair, attractive and with an outgoing smile – but what did a photo tell you? It said nothing about the inner person, whether Julie was a chip off the old block, i.e. sensible enough not to have got herself into trouble, or if she was the type to kick over the traces and land herself in bad company. God forbid into the same situation as her friend, Kat Conolly. It was vital that she was traced, but nothing had been heard of her since her arrival at Heathrow. She could be anywhere. Thoughtless little madam, not even letting her father know where she was!

The idea of Kat Conolly, murdered in mistake for Julie Mayo, was something Abigail had been trying, if not very successfully, to avoid thinking about.

156

17

'What would you like? Nothing more than a bag of crisps and a G & T for me, alas!' Nan Randall gave a huge, regretful sigh from the considerable depths of her magnificent bosom. 'I'm on a diet. But please, you have what you want.'

'Same for me, thanks,' Abigail said. 'Any flavour but salt and vinegar.'

Nan, the senior reporter on the *Lavenstock Advertiser* who had been made editor after Ben had left, had asked Abigail if she could spare the time for a pub lunch after the scrum of the press conference was over. What did she want? Media interest in the murder was hotting up. Among the press pack had been a good sprinkling of reporters from several nationals, as well as from the regional TV and local radio stations. Somehow they'd got wind of a possible protest involvement in this provincial murder and had their noses to the ground. All had now departed, not satisfied but appeased for the time being with the judicious information they'd been fed, and Nan and Abigail had repaired to the Saracen's Head, where they'd claimed a quiet corner, made cool and comfortable by the air-conditioning.

Nan came back with two bags of plain crisps, two gins and a bottle of slimline tonic. 'Are you going to tell me you've some inside information?' Abigail asked, fishing out the lemon, which she'd forgotten to say she didn't want, out of her gin. 'Is that why you asked me over here?'

She'd been surprised to see Nan at the conference as well as the young cub from the *Advertiser* who was now dignified with the name of crime reporter. At one time it had been Nan who'd done this job, as well as covering every other main story, and she and Abigail had constantly bumped up against each other, but since she'd stepped into the editor's position they'd scarcely met.

'Wish I had. No, I just wanted an angle on something I might use later. Kat Conolly was living with young Inskip, wasn't she, Andrew Inskip?'

She considered asking Nan how she knew this, but such questions were pointless. How did any newspaperman or woman ever get to know anything? They had minds that stored information like computers, gigabyte memories.

'She was living in the same house, if that's what you mean. Nan, I can't talk about the case,' she said, surprised at Nan, who knew the score and was savvy enough not to overstep the mark.

'Perish the thought! But I met his parents. Did features on them once or twice, being local celebrities. The son's very like his father.'

'In looks, you mean?'

'Well, he may be, as far as I know, I've never seen him, it's his politics I'm interested in. I might be able to do something on that line, later. Socially concerned, both.'

'That's right? I thought the books were written for, quote, affluent travellers. His son's words.'

'Oh, that's underestimating them. You've never read any?'

Abigail shook her head. She'd been meaning to pop over to the village where her parents lived and borrow one from her father's bookshelf, but there hadn't been time to do that, much less the opportunity to read it.

'You should. He did the pictures, she wrote the text. The pictures alone are a vivid commentary on the social conditions they encountered. A very good read, stimulating. Talking of writers, I've had a letter from Ben.'

'Oh, good,' Abigail said, biting her tongue in an effort not to say sharply, that was more than she had.

Nan screwed up the empty crisp bag, looked at it in sorrow and finally said, 'That was good to neither man nor beast. I'm for a ploughman's, how about you?'

'Well . . . they do a lovely bacon, lettuce and tomato sandwich here.'

'That's my girl.' Nan heaved her twelve stones out of her seat and went to the bar to order, announcing when she came back, 'I've asked for coffee as well. There's some scrummy apple pie if you want it.'

'No thanks, I've to work this afternoon!'

158

'I thought you'd have the strength of mind to refuse, but I've ordered for me. To hell with the diet! As from now, I've decided we're all as God made us.' She sighed. 'Until I look in the mirror, that is, and decide he must've been having an off-day when he made me.'

She had a rich, throaty laugh and her size had never hidden the fact that she was also a very attractive, very sexy lady. Known as Randy Nan in her younger days, and perhaps still was. A good sport, a respected and hard-working journalist who had married the rich, older man who was the proprietor of the still privately owned *Advertiser*. Ben had always had a very soft spot for her, and vice versa. It was Nan who'd told Abigail to grab Ben and hold on to him. What did she want? Abigail again asked herself, a little ashamed of her suspicions, but not very. You got used to it in this job, being wary of everyone, even your friends.

'I may be resigning the editorship,' Nan said as she mopped up the remaining chutney with wholemeal bread, and ate the last morsel of cheese. 'I'm long overdue to spend more time with my family, as the politicians say. You look surprised.'

'I was under the impression you regarded the job as a feather in your cap.'

'Only because it struck a blow for us women. Come on, Abigail, you know it was only offered because of who I was, and I only took it because I knew it was temporary.'

'And here was I, thinking you'd been hankering after it for years.'

'*Moi?* Well, in that case I could've had it if I'd wanted it, couldn't I, my old man being who he is? I have to tell you it suited me very well to be ace reporter with no responsibilities. But I liked working with Ben as editor and when he left I decided I'd rather do the job myself than work under anyone else.'

Abigail stared at her, doing a double take. 'What did you mean, temporary?'

'I knew he'd be back, my love. I've just been keeping his seat warm.'

This took the biscuit. 'He – he's coming back? To his old job?' She hated to hear herself stuttering, but she couldn't help it.

159

'Sooner or later he will.'

'I don't believe I'm hearing this! First he chucks in a perfectly good job here, and manages immediately to get himself contracted to a big national. He wangles the very assignment he wants . . . and then . . .' She stopped.

'That's Ben, love, isn't it? Charm will get him anywhere. Plus a fair complement of brains.'

'Has he told you he wants his job back?'

'Not in so many words, not yet, but I can read between the lines. Why else do you think he writes to me?'

I don't want to know, Abigail thought. Or maybe I do. Ben is devious, no one can deny that. He knows who his friends are, when to pull strings, he has his ear to the ground – plus any other old cliché you may come up with.

'I read his first book,' Nan went on, 'and I think he's got a great future. Trouble with Ben is, things have always come too easily to him. He couldn't believe it when he found he was having such difficulty with his second. So he convinced himself it was because he wasn't there, on the spot. Now he realises it isn't. Writing a book like that's just damned hard slog wherever you are.'

'I see. So now he's gathered enough background he's prepared to jack it in,' Abigail said coldly. 'What's he going to do for his *next* book?'

'Well, there's plenty places and events he *has* experienced. He'll have to dig into his memory.'

Before editing the *Advertiser* – waste of a good man, in the eyes of many of his colleagues – Ben had been foreign correspondent in more places in the world than Abigail knew existed. But he'd had his reasons for wanting to edit a small town weekly: the wherewithal to live on, and enough time to write his thrillers. Until he'd become restless.

'All right, he knows now he made a mistake,' Nan said. 'He wouldn't listen to me at the time, when I told him he had just the right mix – a day job and writing in his spare time.'

'So, now he's missing all the thrills and excitement of editing the *Lavenstock Advertiser* . . . oh God, sorry, Nan, I didn't mean –'

160

Nan laughed. 'It isn't the paper he misses, for God's sake, it's you!'

'Funny way of showing it.'

'He wouldn't be a man if he hadn't, m'duck. He hasn't spelt it out,' Nan said, tucking into deep dish apple pie over which had been poured a generous dollop of thick cream, 'but he's worried about how you might take it.'

'Oh, wonderful! He expects to come home and find me waiting to throw myself into his arms when he can't be bothered to write me more than a postcard!' But it was pique talking. Pique at Nan knowing more about Ben and his intentions than she did, warring with the warm and wonderful feeling that he might be coming home, soon. And not altogether liking the feeling of knowing that when he did, she would just be there, waiting. Was she all that different from those battered wives she'd been thinking about earlier? Only in degree.

Waiting for Jamie Conolly to be brought in for interview, Ted Carmody shuffled through the papers contained in the stiff manila envelope sent in from the lab, until he found the report he wanted. His reading of it, with his usual thoroughness, lifted the natural lugubriousness of his expression into a small grimace of satisfaction.

Jamie entered in the company of DC Tiplady, a study in contrasts, Tip stocky and stolid, Jamie bringing a whiff of *jeunesse dorée* into the drab pedestrian surroundings of the interview room, though dressed with a slightly less studied elegance than before. Another pair of light, beautifully fitting slacks this time, a dark blue, fashionably crumpled silk shirt, sleeves rolled to just below the elbow. Still the slim watch on his wrist, the lump of gold hung around his neck. Carmody was not impressed. He preferred his own shirts well ironed, trousers that were just trousers and nothing that he was ever likely to wear having a designer's name emblazoned upon it.

Jamie's cocksure certainty vanished when confronted with the incontrovertible evidence that the footprints in his murdered sister's bedroom had been made by his trainers. Blustering at first, he demanded to know if there were any forensic results from his clothing, and smiled triumphantly when he learned that nothing positive had been found there.

'You can grin – but you're not off the hook yet, son. The blood – apart from the calves' blood – was Group 0. Pity you and your sister had the same group. We haven't got the DNA results yet.' In the face of Carmody's mournful-visaged, nasal Scouse presentation of this fact, Jamie suddenly looked less certain.

The cut on his hand had proved inconclusive. Medical opinion was that it could just as easily have been sustained from a sharp knife in the kitchen as from whatever might turn out to be the murder weapon. Neither did it appear to conceal any scratches made by the victim, and in any case there had been no traces of the killer's skin tissue underneath Kat's long fingernails. But Carmody didn't feel obliged to tell Jamie that at this stage. 'You were in that room, no question, so why don't you admit it and save us all time?'

There was a long pause while they listened to the distant ring of telephones and Tip shifted his weight on the chair.

'What if I said I was there, then?' Jamie said finally.

'What if you did?'

'It's not how you think.'

It never was. Carmody sighed. 'Let's be having it then, Jamie. Right from the start.'

'She was already dead when I got there,' Jamie said, apparently unaware of any risibility in the statement, his face taking on a greenish, waxy tinge as memory compelled him to relive the scene in the bedroom.

'That's not the beginning. Like why did you go into her room at all? Just in case you've forgotten, I'll remind you that you told us you didn't know she was staying in the hotel.'

'Yes, well, I didn't know, not until a couple of hours before, anyway. And I didn't know it was her, even then. I thought it was Jools – Julie Mayo. She – when I was arriving for work, I'd passed Kat's car belting down the drive with some bloke or other at the wheel, and then I saw the back of her – what I *thought* was her – going in by the front door. She must've lent her car to somebody, I thought, and then I thought no way, she was so bloody possessive about that car it wasn't true, wouldn't even let me drive it.' He paused fractionally, a look of pure envy crossing his face. 'So I sneaked a look at the visitors' book and lo and behold! Jools, registered in Derwent! What the hell's going on? I asked myself. So – as soon as I could, I went to find out, slipped out of the kitchen and into her room via the flat roof and – and there . . . well, there she was. Kat, not Jools . . . and that's God's honest truth.'

Truth was an ambivalent concept from those appearing in this room, sitting on that side of the table. Dependent upon circumstances, or what was in it for them. Men found with a knife in their fist and a corpse at their feet and its blood on their hands would deny they'd ever touched the body; doped to the eyeballs, others would swear they didn't know how the wrap of heroin and the tackle had got into their pockets.

The room was warm, and Jamie Conolly was sweating freely, spoiling that beautiful shirt, no doubt. 'So then what did you do?' Carmody pressed on.

'I got out, quick, so fast I nearly fell into the blasted water butt. I was shaking like a leaf, I tell you, when I got back, it's a wonder I didn't cut my hand off, never mind just nick it! She was my sister, for God's sake!'

'She was, son. Your sister, lying there, cut about. So why didn't you raise the alarm, get help, like?'

'She was dead, wasn't she? I'm not like you lot, used to seeing dead bodies every day, but even I could see there was nothing anybody could do for her!'

Carmody looked at him sorrowfully. 'All right, we'll leave that for a minute. Let's talk about why you happened to be there, working at the hotel. Far cry from your usual occupation, isn't it?'

'I've worked there on and off, on a casual basis, ever since I took a holiday job there when I was still at school. They're always short-handed. Welcome anybody who knows the ropes a bit.'

'That doesn't answer my question. I asked you why.'

Slight discomfiture, Carmody noted, followed by bravado, a shrug, and finally, a man-to-man smile. 'Well, you'd better

163

believe I don't do it for the money! There's a girl,' he admitted. 'Works there, in the hotel.' Another shrug of the elegant shoulders. *And if you don't believe me, tough.* 'You know.'

'What's her name?'

'Liz Westerby.'

Carmody assimilated this, looking at Jamie and speculating. 'She's the maid who took the supper tray in and discovered the body?' Jamie nodded. 'You found it necessary to work there to have it off with her?'

Jamie looked pained at the crudity. 'Makes it easier to see each other, that's all. I take her home, put her bike in the back of the car, after we've finished work.'

'Shall I tell you something, flower? I don't believe you.'

'Ask her, then!'

'Oh, I can believe that about – who is it? Liz, yeah. What I find hard to swallow is all this crap about your sister. How are your finances? Not in good odour, are they?'

'What the hell do you mean, my finances?'

'What I mean, sunshine, is that you stand to gain by your sister's death, don't you?'

'*You* know what? I think you're sick.'

The local Labour party had its headquarters in a utilitarian building on Victoria Road. Formerly the double-fronted brick house of a long-dead mayor of Lavenstock, it was now tightly sandwiched between the Bradford & Bingley and a dress shop for the larger woman, its two storeys dwarfed by the new high-rise offices which stuck up behind it.

Victoria Road was a main thoroughfare, so Carmody swung out of the traffic stream and parked in front of the tower block in one of the empty spaces marked 'Reserved for ECW staff'. Most of them, by this time in the early evening, had gone home already. Lucky devils.

The windows of the stuffy room where Maggie Vye received them were wide open and hot, dusty air, heavily laced with exhaust fumes, belched in from the slowly grinding cars and buses outside, stop-starting at the traffic lights further along.

Rollo Forbes had met Maggie off the train and they'd come straight here. Now, she pushed away the half-eaten sandwiches which had come with the tea she'd plumped for instead of the drink he'd offered her after one look at her tense face. She offered her visitors a cup and when they declined, refilled her own, drinking it thirstily.

'Perhaps you'd start by telling us why you were dining at Freyning Manor on Sunday evening, Miss Vye?' Carmody began, while Abigail shifted to get comfortable on the moulded plastic chair, angling it better so that she wasn't directly facing the manically grinning portrait of the prime minister and his wife.

It was Rollo Forbes who answered the question, unexpectedly acerbic. 'For the same reason as everyone else there, I imagine! They have a reputation for excellent food.'

Abigail looked at the big, cuddly-looking man with the curly brown hair and was aware of something unexpectedly compelling in the big brown eyes.

'Fair enough,' Carmody acknowledged with a grin. 'Did either of you know the girl who was murdered?'

'No.'

A quick, deep-throated denial from Forbes, a slower shake of the head from Maggie.

Abigail said, 'Well, we have to tell you that a video was found in her room. An old 8 mm film to be more exact, transferred on to video. We've reason to believe that one of the people featured in the film was you, Miss Vye. Can you offer an explanation as to why it should've been there?'

Maggie tipped the teapot over her cup, but it was empty. The lid rattled slightly as she put it down. She looked up at Abigail and, though she seemed greatly troubled, met her gaze candidly. 'I've been afraid you might have found that. I knew it had to be connected with that poor girl's murder. I can see I'd better explain.'

With Rollo Forbes's eyes watchfully upon her, her hands clasped tightly together, in a few crisp and obviously well-rehearsed words, Maggie told them about the letter she'd received, which had informed her that some wacky group calling

165

itself Group Six held a video-copy of an amateur film she'd taken part in many years ago, and were threatening to make it public if she didn't comply with their requests.

'Nasty,' Abigail commented.

'Nasty? That's mild to describe what I felt about the letter when I read it! I was devastated – but not so much that I'd be willing to promise whatever they wanted to get my hands on the thing. Their demands weren't only outrageous, but ludicrous. In return for the film, I was apparently expected to promise opposition to the proposals for the new road. I agreed to meet one of them briefly at Freyning Manor, though I'd no intention of promising any such thing. I imagined if they're so naïve as to believe I would do as they wanted, getting the video from them should pose no problem. I don't react kindly to threats.'

'So what happened?'

'I did as instructed, went to that little annexe off the bar, really nothing more than a corner, just three or four chairs, but it's shielded from the rest of the bar. It's not much used this time of year – too dark and dismal, I imagine, people much prefer to sit on the terrace outside the bar, or in the conservatory if it's raining. One or two people did look in but they moved away. I waited for half an hour and when no one came I gave it up and we went to the bar for another drink. Rollo had insisted on being there as well and I think whoever it was might have suspected someone was with me.'

'They couldn't have, love.' Rollo explained to the others, 'I was sitting facing the window in one of those big chairs they have all over the place, the ones with the high sides. I was well hidden.'

'Perhaps.' Maggie smiled at him. 'Anyway, just then a policeman came in and herded everyone into the dining-room, where we learned what had happened.' Her face looked suddenly drawn and tight. 'How – how *unbelievable* it all is.'

The threats themselves didn't seem to have upset her overmuch. She probably thought she could have faced it out, even had the contents of the video been made public, and maybe that was so. It would hardly constitute a major scandal, barely register on the Richter scale of today's improprieties. All the same, it was decidedly unpleasant and had the capacity to damage her and her reputation to the point where she *ought* to have been bothered by it, Abigail thought.

It seemed to be upsetting her much less than the murder of Kathryn Conolly – though Abigail wondered if she wasn't overestimating this distress. Looking at the shadows like bruises under the other woman's eyes, however, listening to what she was saying, she believed not. 'When I heard the name of the girl who'd been murdered, I knew she had to be connected with this group. Somehow, I'd imagined them sending a man, I never thought it would be a woman. And for it to be Hugh's daughter, my God!'

Better to deal with, a man, Abigail could understand that, from Maggie Vye's point of view. She faced male adversaries across the floor of the House every day and no one appeared to enjoy the challenge more than she did. Used to hard exchanges, she must have been fairly confident of getting hold of the video without compromising herself.

'What I'm most curious about,' Maggie went on, 'was why they chose to do it that way. Handing it over in that open fashion?'

'It puzzles me, too,' Abigail said. She looked at Carmody. Then at her notes. ' "Hugh's daughter", you said. *Did* you know her, then?'

'Not really. I – I saw her when she was a tiny baby.' She added after a pause, 'I never met her again – but what sort of person could she have been? I *mean* – that film? I thought it had been destroyed. It must have come from Hugh himself, of course, who else? Things turn up after people die, no cause of shame to them any more, only bother to the living. But for his daughter to *use* it . . .'

There was no doubt her distress was genuine now, not a politician's crocodile tears. Masculine watch on her wrist, thick, ashy blonde hair tending to fall in an untidy wing over her eye, a cotton two-piece whose only virtue was serviceability, utilitarian specs doing nothing for those rather lovely eyes, which one maybe wouldn't have noticed but for seeing her on that video . . .

'I think it would be useful if you told us how that film came about,' Abigail said.

She caught her breath. 'Yes. Yes, I suppose I'd better.'

A heavy lorry shifted gears and ground up the hill to the traffic lights. Air brakes hissed. Maggie glanced at Rollo Forbes and received an encouraging nod, then looked down at her hands for a while, gathering her thoughts before she spoke. They'd been students, she began eventually, the film had been made when they were all at university together. 'Never mind why we did it, that won't excuse it, except that we were hard up as hell . . . why shouldn't we be paid to do something we did for free all the time? Yes, yes, that's deplorable, but that was how we all liked to talk then. Except that it wasn't for real, in the film. It didn't work out the way we thought, needless to say, the whole thing fell flat, the idea was better than the reality. Like all Hugh's schemes. A giggle, we'd thought, but then it became embarrassing all of a sudden. I don't have to tell you what a terrible film it was. It was supposed to have been what they call a pilot, and if it had been any good, Hugh knew someone who'd get it – and maybe more like it – produced professionally. What a hope.'

'Who were they? The actors? Yourself and Hugh Conolly, and who else?'

'Hugh didn't take part! Goodness, no. He wasn't actually involved in any way, apart from the idea, which was typical of Hugh.' So Kat had, at any rate, been spared that, Abigail thought. 'He was just acting as a sort of agent between us and the man who was going to distribute it. Some person he'd met up with, somewhere.'

A man called Greg Eastwood had played Baby Bear, she said, colouring deeply at the embarrassing triteness of it all. 'But he won't be any use to you, you'd better forget him.'

'Why's that?'

'I tried to get in touch with him when I got the letter and I was told he's no longer in England. He's become an Amaravati Buddhist, of all things! About a year ago, he went to stay at their headquarters in Thailand.'

'He's still there?' Carmody broke in, making notes, having trouble with Amaravati.

'As far as I know.'

'And the other woman? Who was she?' he asked.

A pause. 'Gabriella, her name was. Gabriella Fonseca. She came from Siena. She was over here on a business studies course but I don't believe she ever finished it. She went home and I lost touch with her.'

There was that in her tone which suggested reservations.

'And what about the second man?'

Maggie hesitated. She glanced quickly at Rollo Forbes. 'I don't think I can tell you that,' she said firmly after a moment.

'Maggie, my love – ' began Rollo.

'No, Rollo.'

Startling at first they'd been, these endearments, coming from this reserved, mild-looking man. Something between the two of them? Abigail had wondered, until she'd realised the soft little words were a mannerism, a habit, more like using a familiar pet name. Maggie seemed hardly to hear them.

'No, I mean it. We all do things when we're young that we're sorry for later. *Very* sorry for, in this case.' She avoided Rollo's eye. She'd grown exceedingly pale. 'Oh God, what made Hugh *keep* that thing? No one else would have! I'd forgotten it.'

Though that wasn't exactly true, she thought, even as she spoke. Just tidied away into a locked compartment of her mind, that was all, because it had seemed futile to dwell on it. On what was, after all, only a moment of madness in the span of time. Incredible how we thought, acted then. The permissive society, a phrase new-coined for then. Freedom, liberation, social revolution. Over the top, anything goes, if you can think of it, do it. We believed ourselves so sophisticated when all we were was naïve, dangerously so, not knowing what we were setting in train. And now we deplore the lack of morality we helped to start. Maggie gave herself a mental shake, having long since abandoned trying to link events to cause and effect, and came back to hear the inspector saying:

'There'll be copies, you realise that.'

Oh God, yes. Copies. Not the end of it, then. She'd known it, of course. She looked down at her hands, away from the face of the inspector, carefully uncommitted, and the pessimistic sergeant's less so, a man who'd probably voted for her and was now wondering whether he'd done right. An indication of what would have happened if this story had ever been made public.

Most of her constituents would feel the same. Never mind that they'd voted Labour, many of them were conservatives with a small 'c'.

The Great British Public would shrug off almost any peccadillo in their leaders nowadays. Corruption, a secret mistress. A child born out of wedlock. People forgave more easily – or more likely, cared less – now than they used to. Or because too many were in the same boat – there but for the grace of God. But this . . . They watched sexual antics and innuendo on the television every night, but it was less acceptable when it concerned their elected representatives at Westminster. They wouldn't be shocked, but they might be disgusted – and that would be nothing to what she felt herself but that was, as they said, her problem. She might manage to avoid being compelled to resign immediately, which would force a by-election, but she could be deselected at the next election. Either way it could put paid to her career prospects.

But what did that matter, compared to the young life of Kathryn Conolly being snuffed out?

'Do you mind?' Suddenly, she was finding it difficult to breathe, pushing her chair back. The room was all at once unbearably hot and oppressive, the sticky vinyl beneath her thighs insupportable. A clammy sweat came over her. 'I need some air.'

She hurried to the door, white as milk, Rollo one step behind her. 'Stay here, Maggie. Let me get you something.' But she waved him away.

'No, I don't want anyone, I'll be back in a minute.'

'Was it something we said?' Carmody asked Rollo Forbes as her quick footsteps retreated down the corridor.

Rollo was silent, looking from one to the other, debating whether to enlighten them. 'She's upset,' he said at last, sitting down heavily. 'It's her daughter, you see.'

'What's the matter with her daughter?'

He stared at them, then shook his head and explained slowly. 'She's upset like that because Kathryn Conolly was her daughter. Hers and Hugh Conolly's.'

Both police officers were old hands at concealing shock and surprise. 'Go on, Mr Forbes,' Carmody said.

170

Rollo shook his head, refusing to elaborate. He looked sorry he'd spoken, apprehensive, like a schoolboy who's sneaked on one of his classmates and didn't want to face the music. 'I think she'd better tell you herself,' he said evasively.

They sat in silence until Maggie came back, carrying a paper cup of water. Looking even more nervous, Rollo spoke to her in a low voice, saying something the others didn't hear. 'Oh, Rollo, you fool!' she replied, but she didn't seem angry. Sad, but possibly relieved, even. She sipped at the water and Abigail let her take her time.

'So Rollo's told you – about Kathryn. Nobody else has ever known. Hugh promised he'd never tell her she'd been adopted. That her real mother hadn't wanted her.' There was a world of self-castigation in her voice. 'I hope he never did. It was a very brief affair I had with him, on the rebound from someone else, and I was appalled to find myself pregnant. Young and selfish too, horrified at what it would do to my career. There wasn't the same outlook on single motherhood in those days. Abortion? Out of the question. I'm anti-abortion not because it suits my political corner but because I believe absolutely that no one has a right to terminate a human life. I didn't love Hugh. He offered to marry me but marriage between us would have been a disaster, and anyway, he was already planning to marry someone else. In the end, they took the baby when she was born . . .'

She looked empty, drained, while Abigail remembered, with vivid clarity, the bitterness in Diane Conolly's voice and finally understood what she'd meant when she'd said, '*After all I've done for him.*'

She saw now, too, why Maggie hadn't simply ignored the threats from Group Six, as Maggie said, 'I couldn't be sure how much this Group Six knew, you see . . . oh God, I just hope she didn't ever know that I was her mother.'

'You think Forbes was the second man?' Carmody asked, manoeuvring the car into position for rejoining the traffic on the main road.

'I suppose he could have been. I wonder how long they've

171

known each other? He knew all about the baby, and he's devoted to Maggie, looks like his life's work is protecting her. '

'Not to mention himself. His own interests are pretty bound up with hers. But would he kill the girl, to get at the video?' He shook his head. 'That wouldn't have done him much good with our Maggie.'

'It's too much of a stretch, anyway. How would he know she was staying in the hotel, for a start, or if he did, which room to go to? And he was questioned immediately after, remember. Granted some of our lot can be pretty thick at times, but even they wouldn't miss someone covered in blood when they were questioning them. There's something else wrong though here, Ted.'

'About Maggie Vye? Or Rollo Forbes?'

'Maybe neither. But I don't know, I need to think about it.'

Carmody knew that faraway look. The one that appeared when his wife, Maureen, got it into her head the spare room needed repapering. Or when Vicky, his youngest, needed more funds out of him. Or when Abigail was on to something . . .

He stole a glance at her absorbed profile and saw that pushing his own ideas would at that moment be *de trop*, and probably biased, anyway. He'd started off wrong-footed with this case and there wasn't much he'd liked about it since. The premature and beastly ending of a young life always upset his usual stoicism. Moreover, he preferred Mayo in charge, he could be an unreasonable bastard if you didn't toe the line, but at least you always knew where you were with him. And he thought Abigail Moon should have been given at least half a chance to show what stuff she was made of, instead of bloody Flossie Nightingale.

He looked at the clock as he drove towards Milford Road and hoped that Maureen wouldn't have used the hot weather as an excuse for yet another unimaginative salad for his evening meal.

18

The music played on while his beer went flat and the rest of the bread and cheese was left untouched. The last notes finished and Mayo sat back with his eyes closed in the silence, letting the splendid, sweeping chords echo and reverberate in his mind. He thought about it – Dvorak's Cello Concerto – comparing it with Elgar's, which an eminent and otherwise intelligent professor of his acquaintance had recently described to him as a 'limp, broken-backed piece'. He resolved to play the Elgar again to see if there was any possible justification for that sort of heresy; certainly he hadn't cared for it quite so much the last time he'd heard it, but had put that down to the new and abysmal recording he'd mistakenly acquired.

It was all relative. Response triggered by emotion. Emotion triggered by memory. Thought and action dependent upon time and place, one piece of information leading logically to the next. Or so it should . . .

All he had to do was find his own daughter, for God's sake, and he hadn't a clue. Literally not even one small clue, which was all he needed to lead him off. And all the while these crucial first days were fast closing in. Days when vital evidence became gradually obscured, dissolved and disseminated by the passage of time. Spurred on by this sense of urgency, he'd spent hour after disappointing hour on the telephone, making inquiries which came to nothing, finding it impossible to accept what he'd told other people often enough when a loved one had disappeared into thin air: if anyone was determined to disappear, they could. His logical thought was impeded, however hard he tried, by the block of his terror for her safety, by the wild possibilities that were surrounding her in his mind.

He had his own methods of being kept informed of what was going on, and from what he was hearing, the rest of the investigation wasn't progressing anywhere near fast enough: he suppressed the thought that it bloody well would've been if he'd been in charge, there on the spot, getting things moving.

Two and a half days away from the office and he was already climbing up the wall. Keeping his emotions in check was harder work than working, when he was always in a rush, too much to do, the next thing on top of him before he'd finished the first. Which was, admit it, how he liked it. He hated being in the doldrums, personally or on a case. There were, after all, dammit, plenty more crimes to be solved, plus all the administrative detail that was part of his life nowadays. To hell with that. It didn't even begin to be a realistic proposition. How could he control a team of detectives and not be part of the major incident that was dominating every minute of their working lives at the moment? But what next, faced with a brick wall?

He was beginning to have some inkling of how George Atkins was feeling in the face of his imminent retirement. He had a choice between cleaning out the parrot's cage and watching the tennis. Any more of this and he'd be attempting the crossword puzzle.

Gerald Vickers's Edwardian walnut clock struck the half-hour. He looked at his watch and checked the correct time as eleven minutes past. Even the damn clock was frustrating him; it had been given a balance-wheel transplant from an alien source in place of the one which had disappeared, and was now showing rejection symptoms. Why this should be so remained a mystery, the new one was exactly the same in every respect. He readjusted the clock to the correct time, thought about coffee. In the end, in a mood of masochism, he decided he might as well, while he cogitated his next move, face up to the parrot's cage. Further down than this you couldn't get.

He'd just relined the cage with clean newspaper and was about to screw up the old when the doorbell rang. At the same moment, he glimpsed some foreign body amongst the unsavoury debris he was about to dispose of.

Leaving everything where it was, he went downstairs to find Abigail standing on the doorstep.

'You look chuffed!' she remarked, following him upstairs, with an enthusiastic 'Yes, please', to his offer of coffee. Her eyes asked a question which she didn't voice, no doubt assuming he'd tell her if there was any news.

174

'I've just recovered stolen goods,' he answered, smiling and not attempting to interpret a private joke. Resisting the desire to offer riveting explanations of how the missing balance-wheel had come to be in the bottom of the parrot's cage, all of which would involve explaining Alex's misplaced sympathy with Bert, her ideas on freedom and caged birds, and could only involve the subject of his own infra dig activities.

She raised her eyebrows but made no comment as she followed him into the kitchen. 'I was on my way to see Max Fisher and I thought you might like an update,' she offered as an explanation for her presence. 'And I'd like your advice.'

'Anything new come up, then?'

Pulling a stool out, she perched on it, and told him about the new developments regarding the video, and sketched a picture of the members of Group Six and the house at Belmont Avenue where Kat had been living. 'There's a theory been put forward that they may have kidnapped Julie because you're her father and she knows too much about their activities.' She laughed. 'Guess who?'

'Deeley, for a pound!'

A useful lad, Deeley, when things got tough on a Saturday night at the Punch Bowl, a bit slow on the uptake sometimes. But as Mayo filled the kettle and reached for the coffee grinder, he tried not to remember how many times the big feller's apparently naïve theories had turned out to be right. 'This'll take a few minutes. Or – ' he peered at the label on the jar of instant granules 'would you prefer something full-bodied, bold and adventurous?'

'The way I feel, that's the one I need.'

Munching on a chocolate biscuit while he made the instant coffee, she gazed out through the window at the tops of the trees in the garden below. On the few previous occasions when she'd been here she'd liked it, upstairs in this hilltop house, among the clouds, with a view from the sitting-room window over the spreading town. Self-contained and cosy, this flat. Mayo and Alex might conceivably, she thought, find themselves rattling around a tad too much when they were occupying the whole house, but that was their business.

Relaxed in T-shirt and cotton slacks, his usually disciplined hair ruffled where he'd run his hands through it, he looked years younger, and despite the tiredness in his face, somehow vulnerable. She sometimes envied men, unburdened with this feminine urge to comfort and the knowledge that it might so easily be misconstrued. How much easier a male slap on the back, a wry joke.

'What do *you* think?' he asked, handing her a mug of coffee.

'It's no more way out than Maggie Vye having killed Kathryn Conolly to get hold of the video.' Than *anyone* having killed her for that, she thought. And anything was less disturbing than the darker thoughts which must inevitably be present in his mind, which she'd come intending to discuss with him and now thought better of. With his daughter still missing, reminders of a possible psychopathic killer on the loose he could do without. She drank some coffee. 'This group,' she said. 'Is it possible Julie could have been involved with them, too?'

He wished he hadn't been so impatient over the coffee. This instant wouldn't do anything for anybody. 'Anything's *possible*.'

Like many young people – more than were given credit for it – Julie had always been idealistic, feeling passionately about many issues. In her teens, she'd joined in more demos than he could remember, she'd turned vegetarian, even to the point where she couldn't bear to cook meat – fish, she didn't object to – and had given up a career previously dedicated to it. That was the old Julie. He didn't think she'd changed that much, but over the past two days he'd faced several hard truths, one of them being that her independence had always held a core of secrecy. He'd never known quite what she was thinking or feeling. For instance, why hadn't she told him when she was leaving America? Or contacted him when she'd heard about Katie's murder? He couldn't envisage any circumstances in which she wouldn't immediately have telephoned him if she'd heard about that – or any that he wanted to envisage. She would surely have wanted to know all the details – unless, of course, she knew already. But that possibility was one so unthinkable that he shut it completely out of his mind.

Expecting someone from the police, Max had chosen to see them in his own quarters, leaving his business commitments to them-

176

selves: separated by the hall and staircase, Fisher-Conolly Securities occupied its own wing. The hum of computers, the clatter of printers, fax machines, telephones, the subdued buzz of voices (especially the female variety with its essential penetration), the whole caboodle of a busy enterprise was left in its own world on the other side of the wall. Another universe that, but still his, very much his, a world of success, anything less unthinkable, piling money that he didn't need on to more money, as it had always been.

The need to move on again was becoming stronger: the success of his enterprise no longer gave him – what was the word? – a buzz. Sell out, start again. Fresh fields, new pastures, new experiences to stimulate a jaded appetite. Nothing to keep him here now, not really. Maybe, came the thought, before the implication caught in his gullet – a new woman to go with it, not demanding and certainly not permanent. That was a lesson learned long ago, and should never have been forgotten. A temporary lapse.

He'd finish the garden and the house first, here at Orbury, though. He'd pretty well decided to get those two interior decorating women in to help with the rest of the house, though he wouldn't necessarily take all their advice, good as they were. He was always his own best adviser, an instinct for knowing what was the right thing was a gift he'd been born with.

He walked to the desk and found the letter he wanted, reread it with care, avoiding thinking about the sensation it evoked, winced at the price quoted, but knew he'd accept: he had never been one to quibble unnecessarily, and he respected people who patently knew their own worth.

She was red-headed, the police inspector, a rich bronze that caught and reflected the sunshine. He knew an expensive haircut when he saw one, and approved. Of the good skirt and the stone-coloured silk shirt, too, that said she didn't have to be a frump because she was a police officer. And she moved well, a quick stride that reminded him of other women with warm, impulsive natures. Maggie Vye, for instance . . . and Kat.

Impossible to believe she wouldn't ever come into the room

again with her light, dancing step. No warm hug, feeling momentarily the slenderness of her body in his arms, no more watching her watching him while he played to her. His Galatea, gone for ever. His eyes closed against the sunlight which she had once brought into his life.

Abigail saw the briefest of brief closing of the eyes, glimpsed something not understood in the narrow, ascetic face, instantly smoothed over as he smiled in welcome. A tall man with flecks of grey in his brown hair, he must be at least in his mid-forties, though if she hadn't known she might have given him ten years less than that. Brilliant intelligence in a pair of light blue eyes. A man who could attract – or annihilate – with a look at twenty paces, the sort of look she'd run a mile from if it were directed at her for either reason. He had a tan, possibly sun-lamp origi-nated. Despite the warmth of the day he was dressed conven-tionally in a sober business outfit and yet ... The suit suggested – though only suggested – a certain exaggeration in cut, the perfectly matched tie was of a Beau Brummell elegance with just a hint of flamboyance.

Like his clothes, the beautiful drawing-room he showed her into hovered just on the edge of affectation, every table and chair in period, fabulous in their perfection against pale green walls. Most of the furniture looked worthy of a place in a museum, as though sitting on it or putting it to any kind of use would be a sacrilege. Two long, gilt-framed mirrors in the alcoves of the fireplace reflected disconcerting images of herself and her host, who was regarding her amazement with an amused look as he gestured towards a pair of tall, mahogany connecting doors that led through into another room, presumably his study. She was relieved to find here ordinary, comfortable chairs and a sofa across which sprawled a golden retriever of venerable age. A bank of bookshelves, a desk, a beautiful modern grand piano and a soft, furry rug completed the furnishings.

'All right, Alice,' Fisher said, laying a hand on the dog's head as she lifted it expectantly. The dog trembled and sank back. 'Excuse her being there. I spoil her disgracefully, and she takes advantage, but she's very old, and she misses Kat,' he explained, leading seamlessly into the reason for her visit.

He had coffee ready, keeping hot, and went across the room to pour it from the machine, leaving the papers he'd been occupied with on the table between them. Abigail, expert in reading upside down, saw the letter on top was a photocopy, black and white, and the gist of it had registered in a glance before he turned back with the cups in his hand.

He swept the papers away with strong, thin fingers and pushed a cup of coffee in front of her so rich, dark, smooth and excellent she was instantly reminded of the origins he'd obviously travelled a long way from. Crass to mention them, even to remember that all this elegance was due at least in part to the start they'd given him. The very subject she was here to question him about seemed an intrusion.

But she'd grown adept at ignoring such subtleties and at coming quickly to the point. 'Can we talk about Kat?'

'I presume that's what you're here for, but I don't know how much help I can be. Her father came here terminally ill and she came with him. She left shortly after he died and I never saw her again after that.'

'I suppose there was no point in her staying here any longer – after her father died.'

A quick anger, for some reason directed against her, leapt like a flame in his eyes. Trying to assess what it meant, she kept silent and he said, abruptly, 'That's a long way from the truth. She knew she was more than welcome to stay here as long as she wished.'

The dog stirred. Abigail picked up her coffee and sipped. 'I looked on her as a daughter,' he went on more calmly. 'I believe it was reciprocated – why not? Does that surprise you?'

It did and it didn't. He wasn't anyone's idea of a father-figure, but you had to remember that Kat had been young, perhaps immature. 'It doesn't matter whether I'm surprised or not. It isn't part of my job to comment. But why did she leave, Mr Fisher?'

'I don't know. She went suddenly, without even telling me where she was going. That did hurt me a little.' Which she saw immediately was an understatement. It had hurt deeply, she guessed, though maybe it was his ego that had mainly suffered. 'I've thought and puzzled over it, and come to the conclusion that she suddenly couldn't bear to stay in the house where her father had died. But she would have come back, I know she would. I was prepared to wait until she did.'

'Did she ever mention Group Six to you?'

'Group Six? Who are they?'

'Friends she went to stay with.' Abigail thought she could be forgiven for stretching the truth. One of them, at least, had been more than a friend, once. 'They're a self-styled protest group who were into a spot of blackmail. Using a suggestive video, in return for certain promises. Kat came into possession of the video,' she said, stretching it further with a possibility that was almost a certainty. 'She was going to hand it over but she was murdered before she could do so.'

'Blackmail? Dirty videos? Kat? This I don't believe!'

'It was found in the safe in her hotel bedroom. To be precise, it was a video made from an old film. Indiscreet, made years ago when the participants were young, at college. We think Kat may have discovered it among her father's possessions after he died.'

'Oh God. We're talking about the video that was being used to blackmail Maggie Vye? She was here to lunch the other day and she told me some crazy group had got hold of it. But Kat, a party to that sort of trick?' He shook his head in disbelief.

Smooth. He couldn't be sure Maggie wouldn't have told the police he knew about the blackmail, so he'd pre-empted it. A little late, however, after his earlier protestations of ignorance about the group, and the film. 'I suppose Miss Vye warned you about it because you might be the next victim?'

'Ah.'

'Seeing you were also in the film?'

It was a long shot which had found its mark. He pulled a wry face, but made no attempt to deny it. 'Hm, yes, I'm very much afraid that I was. Juvenile indiscretions ... typical of Hugh to keep the thing, probably forgot it was there. His affairs were always chaotic.'

'When you heard about the threat to expose Miss Vye, didn't it suggest a reason to you for Kat's departure?'

'Why should it? I didn't know she'd found the film.'

'I think you might have put two and two together.'

Seeing the film, Kat must have suspected, at least, that he was one of the participants. His height, for one thing. And if she'd swum with him in that pool, that glimpse of blue water Abigail had glimpsed in an adjacent building as she'd approached the front door ... Oh yes, she'd have recognised him all right. A terrific shock, it must have been, father-figure or not. Briefly, Abigail wondered about that. 'May I see her room?'

'Of course, but you won't find anything there. It's been cleared out – her mother came and removed all her possessions.'

'Her mother?'

'Diane,' he said, answering the question that had sprung into her mind as to which mother he'd meant. Did he, in fact, know that Maggie was her natural mother? 'Badgering me with questions and insinuations about her daughter that didn't seem to have bothered her when Kat was alive.' His lips compressed together so that there was a tight white line around them. 'Come along, I'll take you to her room,' he said, getting to his feet, suddenly suave and smiling again.

Nothing much tangible remained of Kat in the pretty, spacious room she'd occupied, few clothes, or possessions of any kind, yet her shadow was here, as it had not been at Belmont Avenue. It hovered in the corners, trying to tell her something. Fanciful, but that was how she felt.

Mayo felt better for having talked to Abigail as he drove out to Over Kennet to hand over the clock, now reunited with its own balance-wheel and hopefully returned to permanent good health.

Gerald Vickers was a retired tax inspector, a widower who had come back, after his wife had died, to share with his sister the house they'd been born in. Before his stroke he'd been a man with wide-ranging interests, a sharp and analytical mind and an astringent sense of humour. Mayo found him being settled into his chair with a jigsaw puzzle by his sister. 'It passes the time,' he remarked wryly. Mayo sympathised and contemplated asking if he'd any he'd be prepared to lend out.

'Let me show you around,' Freda Vickers said, 'before you two start gossiping.' She was as pleased with her new bungalow as a child with a new toy, taking him on a tour which took all of ten minutes, demonstrating the latest gadgets with which the kitchen and bathroom had been fitted, the view from the bedroom window and the small patio and easily managed garden. Though newly built, the plaster scarcely dry, the bungalow had already assumed the character of its owners: the sideboard stood in the same relation to the windows as it had at Chestnut Avenue, the same ornaments in identical positions on it, their easy chairs faced each other across the fireplace as before, standing on that pale gold carpet which Bob Sullivan had successfully fitted; there were the gold-framed watercolours and the Dresden shepherdesses, the line of elephants on the mantelpiece. It must have made the transition from the home in which they'd both been born much easier.

The old man was a great reader with an inexhaustible appetite for new books, anything from biographies to crime. Mayo had brought him the new Peter Lovesey, which his sister Prue had given him for Christmas. Because he was a detective, people always assumed he liked to read crime novels, and sometimes he did, but not often. He generally found the detective-hero too damned know-it-all. He liked Diamond, though.

Gerald's stroke had left him looking transparent and thin, and he tired easily, but between his sister and the day nurse who came in for an hour each day, he was pulling through. He offered many thanks for the book, and was obviously delighted that Mayo had been able to get his favourite timepiece going again. Like Mayo, he couldn't abide a clock that had stopped, and he'd missed its friendly tick.

'Coffee?' Freda Vickers said, as Mayo was putting the clock into place, setting it going.

'Er, tea, perhaps, if it's not too much trouble? Too much caffeine, I'm afraid.'

'Oh, how wise! We all drink too much coffee, don't we? We

never used to, I think we got the habit from across the water,' said Miss Vickers disapprovingly, as if everything bad came from abroad, and then produced tea strong enough to stand the spoon in upright, its caffeine content roughly one hundred per cent more than the liquid she called coffee.

The nurse arrived at that moment, a tall, calm Scottish woman, youngish and with a good-humoured face. Gerald, his beautiful manners not impaired by his stroke, introduced them: 'Nurse Gillespie, this is Superintendent Mayo, a very good friend. He's the head of Lavenstock CID.'

'I hope you find who killed that poor girl.' She seemed to think he was in charge of the investigation into the Freyning Manor murder and he saw no reason to go into complicated explanations in order to disabuse her of the notion. 'Who could have done such a thing to such a lovely young woman as Kat?' she asked.

Mayo was instantly alert. 'Did you know her, then?'

'Oh, I did. I nursed her father through his last illness and I got to know her quite well during the time I was there, at Orbury House. She coped wonderfully. Relatives often go to pieces, you know, but not Kat, for all she was so – well, for all this attitude she had . . . you know what I mean, a lot of young people have it. Pretending not to take anything seriously.'

Elaine Gillespie could not have been much over thirty-five, but she spoke as though Kat's generation was as far removed from hers as she was from Queen Victoria's. But then, she appeared to be a serious-minded young woman, and she was, after all, a Scot.

'And yet she wasn't like that, you know, not really. She confessed to me once that she wanted to be a writer. I don't know how far she meant that, but she was always scribbling away in that notebook of hers. I daresay you've come across it.'

'If we have, I don't think I've seen it,' he replied ambiguously.

'You'd know if you had. It was beautiful, leatherbound. Mr Fisher gave it to her and she used it as a sort of diary, I think, though she was a bit secretive about it. You must have known her well – wasn't she a friend of your daughter's?'

'Yes, she was. Did she speak about Julie?'

'Jools, she called her,' said Elaine Gillespie. 'Goodness, yes, she talked about her all the time. One of the last things I did before the job finished was to post a letter to her.'

'I don't suppose,' Mayo said, very quietly, because he thought by the sound of the blood thundering in his ears that if he didn't Nurse Gillespie might well have another stroke patient to deal with, 'you happened to notice the address it was sent to?'

She looked disapproving at the very thought that she might pry into the destination of other people's mail. 'Only that it was Scotland, nothing else. I happened to see that just as I was putting it into the box. Well, I would notice that, wouldn't I?'

After driving from Orbury House, Abigail stopped the car and found a parking space at the top of Butter Lane, on the off-chance that her friend Alex Jones might be there, at Interiors. She found her at the back of the shop, drinking coffee with her sister, eating pastries from Fisher's, a coincidence if ever there was one, should you believe in such. Two elegant, dark-haired women, with a fleeting, superficial facial resemblance, but ending there: Lois, thin and mercurial, with the sparkling brilliance of cut glass, jangly ear-rings and a bracelet to match. Personality overriding her lack of size. Having snatched, with both red-nailed hands, at her sister's quiet taste, her unerring eye for what was genuine and lasting, she had prevailed upon her to join her in her already established business, combined it with her own creative inspiration and made the whole thing work. Filling a gap in the market which Lavenstock hadn't known existed until Interiors was launched upon it.

Abigail eased her way through the exotic richness spilling over at the front of the shop, between the stands of wallpaper books and rolls of furnishing fabrics jostling modern and antique pieces of furniture. Swathes of rich, stained-glass-coloured old silk and velvet lay side by side with currently fashionable jujube-coloured cottons, lemon and lime and orange. She was greeted with cries of delight, accepted more coffee and said, with a gesture towards the box in which the pastries had come, elegantly gold on white, 'Funny, I've just been talking to Max Fisher.'

'Oh, he's got nothing to do with them now, hasn't for years! It's a cousin who runs the business now. He's into other things,' Lois said, showing the quick awareness of circumstances whenever there was a man concerned.

'The hotel business, for instance?'

'You mean Freyning Manor? Where the murder was? Yes, he owns that, didn't you know?' Belatedly remembering the unhappy connections with Julie Mayo, impulsive, unthinking Lois was – not embarrassed, never that – but sorry she'd mentioned it, seeking for escape and finding it in the entrance of a customer, going forward to greet her with a quick 'Excuse me,' leaving the other two to their coffee.

Alex and Abigail retreated with their mugs behind a Chinese screen strategically placed to hide part of the overflowing stock which was crammed into a corner by a side window. The sunlight filtered through, like a Dutch interior.

Alex stood, leaning folded arms on a golden laburnum-wood chest, while Abigail perched on a stool and stroked the fine, soft velvet of an antelope-toned sofa cushion smudged with plum-colour, tracing the elegant pattern drawn on it in grey. Next to it, for matching, lay a swatch of heavier velvet, the glowing shade of a ripe aubergine. Sensuous fabrics, soft cushions, thick rugs, dazzling accessories . . . an unbelievably far cry from the harsh realities of life in the police. Alex could hardly have found a greater contrast if she had tried. It had to have been deliberate, she must have consciously chosen such a conspicuously different career change.

Inevitably, Alex immediately asked Abigail if any news had come in of Julie, sighing at the answer, thinking of Mayo. 'God knows where she is. Gil won't admit it but he's worried that her disappearance is sinister . . . what am I saying, for heaven's sake, *worried*? He's nearly demented about it! But he'll never believe she had anything to do with Kat's murder until he hears it from her own lips.'

'Apart from Kat using her name, there's nothing to indicate there is, Alex.'

'I know. But Julie not writing for so long is worrying on its own account.'

'Tell me about Max Fisher.'

185

'Max Fisher?' Alex screwed up her face in an attempt to recall. 'Not sure I know much about him. Lois is the one you should be asking.'

'I saw a copy of one of your estimates on his desk this morning – an estimate for work at Freyning Manor.'

'That's possible. We deal with Jonathan Gould – the manager – but I expect he has to refer ultimate decisions to the owner. We're decorating a bedroom at the moment, and we've been asked to quote for redecorating this other one – Derwent, they call it, where the murder happened.' She pulled down her mouth. 'Gould hasn't lost much time over that, has he?'

'So it's Max Fisher who owns Freyning Manor? Sole owner?'

'So I believe. What's the connection?'

'Maybe none – but too many coincidences have me a bit edgy. Kat Conolly's father and Max Fisher were business partners until shortly before Hugh Conolly died. Plus, she was murdered in the hotel Fisher owns, and her brother – still a prime suspect – was working there that night, and actually went into her room and claims he found her dead there.'

'Lordy, lordy!'

'Look who's here!' The door was being held open for the departing customer by Mayo, who came in as though the devil were at his heels.

19

Alex drove him to Crewe, where he picked up the midnight sleeper and slept through the night. While he'd been packing, she'd arranged for a hire car to be ready for him at Fort William. Easier, in the end, than flying and driving from Glasgow.

Scotland! He'd known with absolute certainty that he'd found Julie, immediately Elaine Gillespie uttered the word. Moreover, exactly where in the thousands of square miles, the highlands and islands that comprised Scotland, she would be, though Elaine Gillespie hadn't been able to be more specific. Only the name 'Scotland' had leaped out at her as she was pushing the letter through the postbox mouth. It was so obvious, he cursed himself for not having thought about it before.

He'd made a telephone call before setting out, just to reassure himself that he was right – although, if he hadn't been able to get through, he'd still have come. He was so certain.

He picked up the hire car at Fort William mid-morning, emerging off the train rested, breakfasted and freshly shaved, and began negotiating the streets of the small, familiar town, thronged with backpackers and climbers and hikers in boots and anoraks, bright as tropical birds in their multicoloured Dayglo sportswear. Being Scotland, the weather was not tropical, but at least it wasn't raining. He drove through Corpach, taking what the tourist guides called 'the Road to the Isles', settling down, feeling tension slide from him like oil. He'd been coming this way, on and off, for more than thirty years, firstly with his parents, later with Lynne and Julie, when the road had still, in some places, been single track, but the wonderful sensation of freedom, of everything being left behind, of a new, untouched world ahead, never failed him. Forty-odd miles lay ahead of him still, though the road had now been widened and made safer, passages blasted through the rocks, losing much of its charm in the process but doubtless a boon to the inhabitants. Ben Nevis was a perfect snow-crowned peak in his rear-view mirror. Either side were the hills, grey-green, craggy, not yet purple with heather as they would be later, high and getting higher, many of which he had walked, often with Julie accompanying him. The road ran alongside the lochs, still and glassy, with tiny islets mirroring stands of Scots pine on to the surface. Romantic, Landseer, Monarch of the Glen stuff. Glenfinnan, more romance, forever associated with Charles Edward Stuart, Bonnie Prince Charlie. The first magical view of Skye, Eigg and Rhum, the chain of blue islands across the water. Ahead lay Arisaig, Morar and Mallaig, the end of the road and the Skye ferry, but before that, he made a left turn at Loch Ailort on to the Moidart peninsula, wary of sheep who regarded the road as their right of way, only passing the occasional vehicle, the roads becoming progressively less navigable until the last one climbed to a cluster of small houses and outbuildings, and petered out altogether at a rusty iron gate.

He parked the car off the road in the usual spot, knocked on the door of a lonely, white-painted house, all that remained of a once-thriving community. Below was a small rocky cove where three crofts, two of them derelict and one with smoke coming from the chimney, hugged the shoreline. He breathed in the atmosphere. Silent but for a tardy cuckoo sending its monotonous note across the moor, and incredibly lovely, smelling of peat, washed with light, his own special little bit of God's heaven.

One question, the question of why Julie hadn't contacted him immediately about Kat's death, had been answered as soon as he knew she was here: the murder of a young woman in a hotel bedroom hadn't at first been enough to make more than a few lines in any of the national papers – *The Times*, for instance, had given it an inch in their News in Brief column, under 'Woman Murdered in Hotel'. No regular newspapers, TV or radio was part of the charm of this place, with national papers bought only occasionally, on weekly trips for groceries.

As he waited for an answer to his knock, he noticed the dark red Nissan, sleek and incongruous, which was parked along the further side of the house. Calum's car. But it was Margaret McDonald who opened the door. Late fifties, small and dark, energetic, swathed in cardigans and a wrap-around pinafore. 'It's so good to see you. Come away in, now, and I'll wet the tea.'

He knew her well enough to know that the formalities could not be dispensed with before he descended into the cove to see Julie. He wasn't averse to being fortified by warm drop-scones and tea, hot, strong and tasting of the peat through which the water had filtered, but he began to see that there was something else on her mind as they exchanged pleasantries and she passed on bits of local gossip. She'd never been one for getting straight to the point, but he saw why she'd been more than usually rambling when she said, at last, 'I'm afraid she knows – Julie, I mean. I am so sorry, but Calum took the newspapers across to her when he arrived this morning, and there she saw it.'

The papers, yes, anything up to a week old. News about Kat would have percolated. 'We didn't know there was anything like that in them,' Margaret went on, softly distressed, 'and wouldn't have known she'd anything to do with the girl if we had. Poor child. Calum is with her now.'

That was something. A dependable type, Calum, thirty years old, six foot two and broadly built, with a mountain-climber's toughness, a doctor's watchful expression and capable hands, and the Western Highlander's soft sibilant music in his voice. Calum drove out to see his widowed mother as often as he could from Fort William, where he ran a busy general practice and was, in his spare time, a member of the mountain rescue services. He'd taught Julie to climb, and to sail the dinghy, she'd known him since she was a child. A comforting shoulder to cry on, but Mayo wished he himself had got there first. He blamed himself for not warning Margaret McDonald when he'd telephoned, for not envisaging a situation where Julie might find out about her friend by seeing it in the press.

'You'll need the boots, just,' Mrs McDonald warned him as he thanked her for the tea and stood up. He took her advice and laced on his boots, though there'd been no rain for three weeks. It was good advice. As he made his way across the rocky terrain that stretched down to the cove and the croft with the dinghy moored at the shallow edges of the water, the bog between the rock squelched under his feet at every step. The sea was calm and glassy, the silence complete, save for the small plash of the wavelets on the silver sand, like an afterthought, and the gurgle of the thin narrow stream of peaty water trickling over the wet black rocks from the lochan above, the occasional bleat of a lamb calling for its mother. On the shore, sandpipers ducked and dipped, and a solitary black-backed gull flew in low and wheeled up to the hills. Despite the houses on the bluff behind him, it felt lonely, sad as it never had before, redolent of harsh memories of the Highland clearances that had deported this tight little community to the far corners of the world and left their homes to rot.

She'd seen him coming across the rocks and came to the door of the croft, where she stood waiting for him. When he got within fifty yards she began to run. Sheep kept the grass surrounding the cottage cropped as smooth as a bowling green, but the bright cascade of water spilling down the hill broadened out as it spread over the rocks to join the sea and came between them. She slipped and slid in her hurry on the wet boulders, but managed to keep her balance as she crossed to where he waited for her.

Five hundred miles south, DC Keith Farrar was once more interviewing Dustin Small – whom he was still pursuing for his part in the electrical warehouse thefts – this time on account of a telephone call from Dustin, offering to trade information about the murder at Freyning Manor. 'What's in it for me if I tell you?' Dustin asked, once he was seated at the table opposite Farrar and DC Tiplady.

Farrar looked at him.

'I've been thinking. You get off of my back about them vids and stuff and I'll tell you something I saw on that Sunday night.'

'Forget about the deals. Just tell us what you saw.'

'That ain't fair – '

He got no further. Farrar, who for some time had had enough of playing cat and mouse with Dustin, leaned across the table and took hold of a fistful of pristine white shirt, dragging Dustin to his feet. His chair clattered to the floor behind him. 'You gonna tell me, Small, or what?'

'Let me bloody go!'

'No deals, mate. But you tell me what you know and we'll see what happens.'

'Orright, orright, keep yer 'air on!' Dustin smoothed his shirt down with hands on which a lot of gold gleamed against his dark skin. He had a gold filling in one of his very white teeth, too.

He had, it appeared, just heard an appeal on local radio for information regarding the murder at Freyning Manor. His natural inclination being to avoid trouble, he'd hesitated, but he had felt himself morally bound to come forward . . .

'Spare us, Dustin!' The only person likely to have felt Dustin was morally bound to do anything would be his wife. Charmian was black, too, a lovely-looking woman and intelligent with it, who was trying desperately to bring up their two kids with some decency, in spite of Dustin. She had Farrar's sympathy. 'What were you doing out there?'

'Jogging,' Dustin said, daring Farrar to disbelieve. 'Me and my mate was driving out, looking for somewhere to do some running. He's in training, see, but running round Austen Hay Park's no good. Every dog in the bloody neighbourhood joins in. So we decided to find somewhere quiet.'

A likely story. Especially in view of the large and expensive properties in the area of Little Freyning. It opened up interesting possibilities, though breaking and entering wasn't normally Dustin's bag and his mind did not incline towards the innovatory.

'What it was, we'd just run over this deer, see,' Dustin was explaining in an aggrieved tone. 'One minute we was driving along, mebbe a bit fast like, but not all that fast, and the next there's all these bloody deers jumping across the road. Didn't stand a chance, we didn't. We coulda been killed! But it was that deer what copped it. Dead as mutton.'

'Dear dear,' said Farrar, pleased at his own wit. 'So what did you do? Report it to the game warden?' It was a question which expected the answer no, and he got it.

Dustin looked shifty. 'Nah. It was dead, wasn't it? My mate says he knows where he can get rid of a bit of good venison. Never cared much for it, meself. Dry, not like a good T-bone steak. But any road, we humped it into the – into the boot of my car, and took it to this 'ere guy he knows.'

Farrar looked at him with a jaundiced eye. 'Got your car outside, Dustin?'

'No, I walked here. What's that got to do with it?'

'You walked because your car's in dock, I suppose?'

'In dock?' Dustin looked genuinely puzzled. 'I walked 'ere because I'm meeting me mate in the Anchor and I don't drive after I've had a drink,' he said virtuously.

'Very commendable. Big deer, was it? That one you ran into?'

'It wasn't no Bambi, I can tell you that! Antlers like this.' Dustin stretched his arms as wide as they would go and then, belatedly, realised where the questioning was heading. ''Ere, what you want to know that for?'

'Ever seen a motor that's hit a deer that size, Dustin?' Farrar shook his head. 'You wouldn't be driving that heap of yours anywhere but the knacker's yard if you had run into it, mate. Come on, let's be having it, no more fairy stories.'

It wasn't going to be as easy as that but in the end, bit by bit, the story came out. Poaching, of course, that was it. Driving there in his mate's pick-up. But they hadn't got any, honest, Dustin insisted, except the one they'd run into. Farrar chose to believe him. They'd just been in the middle of trying to haul it into the back of the pick-up, Dustin went on, when this car came along. The pick-up was blocking the road and this bloke got out to see what was up. When he saw what was happening he'd offered to help them. 'There was blood and guts and all else besides but he didn't seem to mind getting hisself messed up – he just laughed and said it didn't matter so much as getting the road clear. I'll tell you this – he was in a bostin' hurry.'

'Time?'

'Sevenish, give or take ten minutes.'

'What was he like, this chap?'

Dustin shrugged. 'Tallish. Spoke posh.'

'Wearing?'

'Jeans, one of them sleeveless denim jackets, trainers.'

'How old?'

Dustin looked vague. He hadn't noticed. All they'd been wanting was to get the hell out of it. Then he brightened. He'd noticed the car, though. A red Montego, M reg.

Inside the croft, Mayo took his boots off and put them in the cupboard by the door where Julie's gear already hung, an old habit automatically assumed, and walked in his stockinged feet to the chair he'd always liked best. Nothing had changed since the last time he was here. When they'd first come to this lonely place for a walking holiday, he and Lynne and Julie had stayed at the house with Mrs McDonald and young Calum, but in later years, after Calum had fixed the croft up for his mother to rent out, they had taken that whenever they had come to stay.

There was a living-room with cooking facilities, a sink, and a huge fireplace that burned driftwood. A bedroom, and a small, primitive bathroom which had been added on to the back. A sofa-bed in the living-room which he would sleep on that night.

And now, another cup of tea in his hand, which he hadn't the heart to refuse. Plus sandwiches. Typical Julie sandwiches, nothing so simple as cheese and pickle, or good old corned beef. Where in God's name had she got hold of fresh rolls and salad, pastrami, especially for him red onions, plus all the ingredients for making a wonderful salad dressing? This far out from civilisation, where gourmet meals were necessarily limited to what could be held in the store cupboard? Calum, of course, was the answer, arriving this morning from the big metropolis of Fort William. At one time, at about ten years old, Julie had trailed at his heels, obeying his commands like a faithful little dog, while he, in his lordly adolescent way, had tolerated her. As she grew older, the roles had subtly become reversed, a relationship which, he suspected, still held good.

He sipped his tea and looked at his daughter over the rim of his mug.

She looked superb – fit and well and suntanned, her hair bleached even fairer by the Texas sun. But she'd been crying when she came to meet him across the rocks. Calum had followed her outside then disappeared towards the shore with a wave of his hand. The tears had left her dewy-eyed; she was young enough for them to have enhanced, rather than diminished, her appearance. It wasn't sorrow which made her look, in some way he couldn't define, subtly older.

On the way here he'd debated how much to tell her and decided to play it by ear. By now, she knew he'd been searching for her, that he'd rung Galveston, and how he'd eventually discovered where she was. 'I'd sooner you hadn't found out about Kat in the way you did, love,' he'd given as his reasons, not going into detail as to why he'd needed to speak to her so urgently, though they would have to talk about that, soon.

She spiked his guns by saying, 'Dad – I don't want to know any more than I've read about – about Kat, not yet. Please not. Not until I've had time to get more used to it. There's something I want to tell you first.'

He gave her a straight look but she avoided his eye. 'What's been going on, Julie? What's been happening to you, over there in Texas?'

'Come on, get your boots on again and we'll walk up the hill. Tell you as we go.'

OK, if she found it easier that way.

But it wasn't until they'd made the climb to the hidden lochan on the top of the hill, and were getting their breath back on a rocky outcrop by the water, that she began. 'This won't take long. It's a story you've heard a million times, I guess.'

That meant a man, which Alex had divined all along. He wasn't sure he wanted to know, but he said nothing, let her make her own pace.

'What did Dana tell you when you spoke to her?' she asked.

'Only that you'd left in a hurry, that she was sorry to see you go. You made a hit there, she liked you.'

'I liked her, too. She's nice. And – and Tony?'

'She mentioned him. He wasn't there.'

There was a breeze up here that rippled the surface of the water, bent the reeds fringing the edges of the lochan and blew through the cotton grass. The sky was immense, cloudless, blue. She followed the progress of a peregrine falcon freewheeling down to the water on the thermals from the high hill beyond and soaring up in one graceful curve. Her fingers pulled out tufts of the short, nibbled grass. 'Tony. Yes, well. It's – the usual tacky story, a great love affair, then I found out lots of things, one of them being he was married.'

Yes, he'd heard it a million times. It didn't prevent primitive urges from surfacing, mainly the desire to kick the lowlife who'd done this to his daughter right in several places where it most hurt, preferably permanently. Frustration, as well. Knowing that this was your child whom you could no longer protect, reassure her that it was just a nasty old nightmare, go back to sleep, darling, everything will be all right in the morning. Or did this sort of frustration come from knowing you'd no power, any longer, to stop them doing whatever they wanted, to stop them hurting themselves?

'I was really pissed off with him,' she was saying, self-absorbed, forgetting his dislike of her using coarse language, 'not for being married, they'd been separated for years – but because he just hadn't bothered to *tell* me.' She pulled out more grass, furiously.

'Leave some for the sheep,' he said.

She managed a smile but went on as though she hadn't heard him. 'But I guess that wasn't what it was all about – not entirely.

If I'd found out earlier, I don't think it would have mattered – when it was still wonderful. With hindsight I know I ought to have seen how crummy the whole set-up was, but it was ... exhilarating, I suppose, non-stop pleasure, wall-to-wall excitement, going places, doing different things, dining out, parties, him buying me expensive presents ... As it was – I should have known, he must have thought me so naïve – well, OK, so I *was*. Or maybe I was shutting my eyes to what I'd rather not see. It worried me right from the start that he seemed to do hardly any work. He used to tease me about puritan ethics, but I enjoyed doing my stint in the kitchen. He owns the restaurant, you know, that's how I met him, when I got the job there, though it was only a sideline for him – Dana and I ran it mostly, plus a couple of waiters. He was supposed to be a Mexican goods importer, but I saw precious few signs of it. Yet he was never short of cash – just the opposite. Absolutely money no object, he spent it like it was water. He told me his father was rich, made him an allowance, but he didn't act as though he was used to money – you know what I mean, Dad? He bought expensive things, then treated them like dirt. He wanted new things, all the time, new cars, new clothes for me. New women, I shouldn't wonder.'

More grass was sacrificed. 'I didn't like his friends. And then I found out where the money was coming from.'

'Drugs?'

She nodded. Her eyes were huge. 'Obvious, really, wasn't it? Everything fell into place. By then, that kind of lifestyle had begun to get on my nerves, we'd started quarrelling and I was looking at things without my rose-tinted specs. I realised I needed to get my head together, decide where I stood.' She looked down at her nails. They were a mess. She'd never bitten her nails before. 'I'd – I'm being honest with you, Dad ... I'd even delivered packages for him. God, I must have been so *dumb!*'

He told himself to take it easy. One thing at a time. Let her talk.

'You know how we used to come here when I was little – you and me, and Mum, before she got too ill? I remembered how you used to say it put everything in perspective. Thinking about it, back there in Texas, it seemed the answer, so right. Everything so *clean* . . . and quiet.'

'Why didn't you let me know?'

'It sounds crazy now, but Dad, I was so frightened! Tony and his brother . . . He has this awful brother, and I'd heard what happened to people who . . . I thought they might find out where I was. He knew you were a policeman, you see.'

He stretched his hand out and covered hers to stop its nervous plucking at the grass. He was surprised how steady his own was, when he was filled with such a boiling rage. 'That's one thing you needn't worry about any more. I'll take care of that.'

There was a long silence.

'They've been wonderful to me, Mrs Mac, and Calum.' A faint colour touched her cheeks. 'I think I'll stay here for a while, try and find some sort of job, I don't think I can go back home just yet, not now. I – I should've helped Kat more – I was so full of my own problems, thought they were worse than hers – but they couldn't have been, could they?'

She hadn't been very sensible – all right, she'd been downright stupid – but we've all been that in our time. He said, 'She used your name when she registered at Freyning Manor. Any idea why?'

'Oh, we did that all the time! A bit of a giggle.' She stared at him, comprehension dawning. 'So *that's* why you came all this way to tell me, in person, when you could have telephoned. You thought I'd something to do with it.'

He didn't even think of asking her now if she had.

'I could have rung, but I wanted to tell you myself,' he said, which was true. And to see your initial reactions, he thought, which was even truer. He'd been too late on both counts but he was still glad he'd come.

She squeezed his hand and they walked back in silence, Indian file, along the narrow path through the tussocky grass and springy heather. When they reached the shore and were walking side by side on the firm sand towards the cottage, she said, 'So much is chance, whether you make it or not, isn't it?' She shouldn't even be *thinking* like that, at her age, life in front of her. 'But why, Dad? Why Kat?'

He thought it was the eternal question, the one he'd never

been able to answer. But it might have been meant literally, and he gave her a literal answer. 'She seems to have been hanging around with some odd characters.'

'She always did, you know. Men. She wasn't a good judge of men. She kept sending me letters.'

'Letters? What did they say?'

'I think you'd better have a look at them.'

'You've actually still got them?' he asked, thanking heaven in amazement for this wonderful, sensible, intelligent child he'd been blessed with.

'I stuffed them in the pocket of my writing case. You know, Mum's.' Yes, he knew the tan suede wallet she meant. He'd bought it for Lynne himself, had had her gold monogram tooled on it, gilt which had long since worn off, the suede now shiny. 'I always throw letters away, after I've written back. I didn't with these, because she kept writing about so many different people, and if I didn't remember who they were, I could look back and see who she meant.'

'All of her letters?' he asked, hardly able to believe in such luck.

'Most of them, anyway. I'll get them and you can read them, keep them, too. I really couldn't bear ever to read them again.'

20

'He's a pain,' Liz Westerby stated forthrightly. 'A right pain, that Jamie. If I've told him once it's all done with, I've told him a hundred times. Can't understand why he won't take no for an answer, I can't.'

Carmody could, in one way. Big, buxom young woman, bust and bottom as broad as her sing-song vowels. Good-natured, earthy, a generous laugh, a lot of tumbling hair streaked like a lion's mane, the top done up in a bird's nest. Make-up you could scrape off with a trowel. She'd made tea like a navvy's, strong as paint-stripper, orange-coloured and thick with sugar, lucky he liked it sweet. He could understand her being the sort of woman who could grab you, right. But in another way, Carmody was gobsmacked. The Mersey could have run dry before he'd have thought she was Jamie Conolly's type.

Out at the edge of Little Freyning village she lived, in one of twelve council houses built in a small crescent, shared with her two children and her mum, she said. Carmody wondered if Mum had been the little woman he'd seen titupping down the path on stiletto heels, short miniskirt moulded round her bum, forty-five if she was a day.

'It was all right at one time, me and Jamie,' Liz said, opening a packet of Wagon Wheels, extracting one and pushing the packet across the table. 'But it wasn't regular, see? Just when he happened to be home and fancied a bit – and that isn't no good to me. Two kids, and their dad buggered off years ago, don't know what I'd'a done without our Mum. But 'er 'asn't got a bottomless pocket and I like to pay me whack. So I told Jamie, I don't want you around no more. And neither would Jonty, if he knew.'

'Jonty?'

She gave Carmody a sideways look from under her lashes. 'Jonathan, of course, Mr Gould – who did you think?'

It hadn't been Gould, that was for sure.

'Look, you can make what judgements you like.' She was suddenly defensive. 'But I can't afford to look that kind of offer in the mouth. Mondays and Thursdays, suits us both, no harm to nobody else.'

'I'm not making judgements, petal.' Far from it. Women like her, Carmody had grown up amongst. He'd a lot of sympathy with them, left to make the best of it, never letting life get them down. He didn't blame Gould, either. But he still wondered about Jamie Conolly. If what Liz said was true, if he had the sense to fancy her, he'd more wit than Carmody had given him credit for.

'What about Sunday night? You were the one to find her, weren't you?'

'Oh, crikey, not again! I've made one statement about that already!'

'It's not about you finding her I want to ask, it's about Jamie.'

Absently, she took another Wagon Wheel. 'He can be nice,

you know, really nice.' Her eyes grew tender, reminiscent, her mouth soft. 'He reckons he wants to marry me, when he has the money, but I don't need no more problems. It's somebody to look after *me* I want, not t'other way round. He's still a little lad. He wants me and he doesn't want me, know what I mean?'

'Yeah, I do.' She'd make a man of Jamie, if he could bring himself not to be ashamed of her. Worth ten of him, she was.

At the back of the table was a pile of textbooks and a file, with Elizabeth Westerby, Biology, written on it in a large, careful hand. 'You studying for something, Liz?'

'What if I am?' She took a big swig of her tea. 'It gets you sometimes, all this,' she said with a large gesture that encompassed her cramped surroundings. 'But I don't intend to be stuck with it the rest of my life, I don't! I'm trying to get a few GCSEs for a start, and then I'll take it from there.'

'Good girl,' Carmody said and meant it, and thought he was right to mean it. Good in the ways that mattered, she'd never do anything underhand, hurt anybody intentionally, never lie seriously.

'So you didn't see Jamie on Sunday?'

'Not after he arrived – about half-three, that'd be. We said hello and that was it. We're a bit cool, just now..Later, I went out the kitchen and started to lay the tables up and that, only went back to pick up the tray when they called to say room service was ready for Derwent. I didn't see who was in the kitchen then – I just picked the tray up and went.'

'And you didn't see anyone else when you took the tray up?'

'Nobody that wasn't meant to be there. Staff and such. Mr Fisher.'

'You didn't mention seeing him in your statement.'

'I didn't mention seeing Jon – *Mr Gould* neither! He's part of the furniture, Max Fisher is, always there on the snoop, which he's a right to do, I suppose, seeing as how he owns the place. They were talking together in the doorway of that bedroom that's just being decorated when I went up. Not that it needed doing, in my humble, but still, if you're paying that amount of money to stay there, you want it nice, don't you? Anyway, Jonty came running when I dropped the tray, when I – when I, you know, found her. I don't know what happened to Fisher.'

'And Jamie was nowhere to be seen, either?'

'I've told you, *no!*'

'Sorry, love, so you have. As a matter of interest, when did you first meet him?'

'Couple of years back, when I started working there. He's done spells at the Manor ever since he was at school, whenever he wants a bit extra cash. He reckons he's hard up, but hard up's all relative, isn't it?'

They were sitting in the dining end of the all-in-one room. Small and spotless, it just about accommodated the drop-leaf dining-table and four upright chairs, a shabby three-piece suite and an old TV. Without people, it was bursting at the seams. With two small boys, plus Mum and Liz in it, they'd probably have to take turns to breathe. They could have done with a new carpet, and the curtains had shrunk. Carmody thought of Jamie's velvet jacket and handmade boots. Hard up was relative, all right.

She said, 'You're wasting your time on Jamie. He couldn't kill nobody, least of all his sister, he thought the sun shone out of her. And the way that poor kid was cut up . . .' Liz went pale under the make-up, automatically reached for the solace of another chocolate biscuit, then swallowed and changed her mind. Her voice hardened. 'Look, I'm not squeamish. My dad had a small-holding and I've wrung chickens' necks in my time, seen pigs slaughtered, but I tell you, I've had nightmares since I found her . . . whover did that was *sick*, and Jamie . . . well, he might be a pain in the you know what, but he's no pervert.'

Diane was back at work in the shop when Abigail called in.

Amber was at lunch so they'd have to talk in the shop in case there were customers, she said. So far, no one had disturbed them. A look of resignation had settled on her face when she learned that Abigail wasn't here to tell her what she wanted to hear.

'I'm sorry,' Abigail said. 'You'll be the first to know, when there's anything to tell. '

Diane was busy making a wreath, cutting heads off carnations, wiring the stems, sticking them, with bits of fern, into a frame filled with polystyrene foam. The clove scent was very strong. Suddenly, she pushed the work away, and sat down on a high stool that matched the one Abigail was perched on. 'Times like this, I wish I still smoked, though I haven't for years. What is it you want, then?'

'We've been told Katie kept a diary, but so far we haven't come across it. It might help us to find her killer if we could locate it. Max Fisher says you took all her things away from Orbury House. Was there anything of the sort amongst them?'

'There were a few books, yes, but no diary. I've never known her to keep a diary. Who says she did?'

'The nurse who looked after your husband. And Mr Fisher. Apparently he gave it to her. It was a thick book, not a pocket diary, about six by nine, something like that, bound in burgundy leather. Expensive.'

She pursed her lips. 'It would be if Max Fisher bought it.'

'Doesn't sound as though you care for him much.'

'I don't, never have, but what's my opinion matter? Hugh liked him, for some reason. They'd been friends for, oh, I don't know how long, but . . .' She picked up a pink-streaked carnation and stared at it as though memorising the formation of its crinkled petals. 'All right, no, I don't like him, I never did. I felt there was something . . . Well, I couldn't ever feel easy around him, that's all. What was he doing, giving my daughter expensive presents?'

'I don't want to distress you, Diane, but there's something I have to talk to you about. Something personal, but it may be important.'

'Go on, then.'

'Katie wasn't your natural daughter, was she?'

The extended silence was painful. It took an obvious effort for Diane to respond calmly. 'If loving and caring for her ever since she was a tiny baby makes her mine, then she *was* my daughter, in every way that matters. She was mine, all but for an accident of birth. That's what it amounts to, isn't it?'

'Yes, I think it does. Did you know who her natural mother was?'

'No! I never wanted to. I still don't,' she said, suddenly busying herself by tidying together the cut-off bits of wire and crumbs of Oasis, throwing them into a bin underneath the table. Meeting Abigail's look as she straightened up, she added, 'She was Hugh's, I knew that, and that was all that mattered. He told me before we were married that he'd got this girl into trouble. It had happened before we met. She wouldn't marry him. And she was too busy with her career to want the baby.'

The old-fashioned phrase 'getting a girl into trouble' came oddly from Diane, but it was the accusation in the last words that struck Abigail. She was pretty sure that though Diane might not know for certain who Katie's mother was, she had her suspicions.

'It was different for Hugh – he couldn't bear the thought of never knowing his own child, letting it go to some stranger. He confessed everything to me, and asked me if I would marry him and take the child, when it was born, as my own. I can see now that was a terrible thing to ask of any woman, but at the time . . .' She shrugged, hopelessly. 'I've often wondered if it would ever have come to anything more serious if that hadn't happened – me and Hugh, I mean – if I'd had more time to find out what he was really like. He was a real charmer, you know, and basically he was a good man. He just had this fatal weakness for women, I really don't think he could help it. Anyway, that's how it was, and when Katie was put into my arms, it was just as if she was my own child, and I never thought of her as any other, even when Jamie came along.'

'I should think she was proud to have you as her mother.'

Diane flushed. 'I don't know about that – I do know that I feel as though part of me's been cut away now she's gone. It's not natural, a child going before a parent.'

Abigail liked Diane, admired her, but supposing, she thought, just supposing Diane had known about the film – had seen it, when she and Hugh were still married, or perhaps he'd left it behind when he departed. It was still only guesswork that it had come into Kat's possession through her father's death, and so to Group Six. Diane had denied knowing the identity of her child's mother, but Abigail was pretty certain she knew who it was. Had she harboured thoughts against Maggie Vye, been jealous of her, suspecting that the love Hugh had lavished upon Katie had been partly because of the mother? Sent that letter ... purporting to have come from Group Six – and it had all gone wrong?

A convenient scenario, but not one Abigail could contemplate seriously.

You had to let your imagination run riot sometimes, though, and just occasionally something came of it ... take Fisher, now. What Diane had said about him. Plus what Ted Carmody had reported back after talking with Liz Westerby. What *about* Fisher? What had he been doing so conveniently at Freyning Manor?

Back in the incident room, she wanted to know what progress had been made in checking up on him.

'Yeah, he was there on Sunday, at the hotel,' Carmody said. 'No point in denying it, when there are people to prove he was. Seems he's forever popping in and out. The staff don't like it, think he's trying to catch 'em out, so they carry on as though he's not there, unless he speaks to them. Says he didn't stay to find out what all the commotion was about – he'd come over to see Gould about that bedroom that's being decorated and he'd finished what he had to say, so he just left.'

'And Gould didn't mention him being there because it wasn't in his interest to involve the owner, I suppose.' She thought for a moment. 'Orbury House isn't more than a few miles from Freyning Manor – less, if you cut through the woods. Have you shown Dustin and his mate that photo?'

'I have, but neither of them's prepared to ID him as the chap who helped them with the deer, but who would, from that?'

The photograph was a small, grainy publicity one which had been published in the *Advertiser* when Fisher-Conolly had first set up in business. Abigail wasn't sure she would have recognised Fisher from it either, without its identifying caption. 'See if we can come up with a better one from somewhere. He doesn't by any chance own a red Montego?'

'Not registered to him if he does.'

The driver of the Montego didn't have to have come from Freyning Manor, of course, though it was a road rarely used to go anywhere else, a roundabout route to anywhere, especially for one who'd confessed he was in a hurry. And he'd acted surprisingly, offering to help in the messy business of hauling the heavy deer carcass into the back of the truck, not minding if he got his clothes messed up. Perhaps, if he had been the murderer, actually *wanting* to mingle the animal's blood with other bloodstains on his clothing.

So far, apart from Jamie Conolly – and Maggie Vye – Fisher had been the only one in the hotel when Kat was murdered likely to have had some personal connection with her. But was it possible to imagine him attacking Kat with a knife? Then simply walking out and driving away before the crime was discovered? When Abigail had spoken to him, he'd shown obvious affection for Kat, so what motive could he have for killing her? To suppress the film? That damned film, it came up every which way, yet the more Abigail thought about it, the less she saw it as a viable reason for Kat's death. The fact of it suddenly surfacing hadn't seemed to worry Fisher unduly, that was certain.

She went back in her mind to her conversation with him, thinking about what had struck her then.

Assuming that neither Kat nor Jamie was lying, Kat had told her brother that she was going to be married. Not to Inskip, nor to Raeburn, if either were to be believed. But what if it had been Fisher? Marriage with him was more likely than with either of the other two. Twenty-five years older than Kat, but still a very attractive proposition. Handsome, rich, sophisticated, very much the sort to appeal to one kind of girl. *Like my own daughter*, he'd said. Hmm, she thought again.

She told Carmody what she was thinking and watched for his reactions.

'You see him as a father-figure, Ted?'

'No,' said Carmody.

Right. Fatherly was not a word that came to mind when you thought of Max Fisher.

Hugh Conolly might not have seen it that way, either, his daughter marrying one of his contemporaries – and one whose past indiscretions he must have known very well. And that, of course, would have been a reason for not announcing the marriage until he had died.

It still seemed logical to assume that the film from which the video had been made had been amongst his effects when he died. And that Kat had found it and recognised Max, which had so upset her that she had fled from his house. True, he'd been wearing a mask, but which woman wouldn't immediately recognise the body of her lover?

The possibility that this was a psychopathic killing, the mutilation of her face indicating sexual impulse turned in on itself, had never been far away. Was it possible to envisage the suave Fisher out of control, antisocial instincts to the fore, savagely wielding a knife on that beautiful young woman? Anything, as Mayo had said, was *possible*.

Whatever, they needed to focus more on Fisher.

Mayo had a compulsion about time, a need to know what hour it was at any given moment during the day, his fascination for the actual workings of timepieces being something quite different. He hardly ever needed a clock or watch to tell him where the day was at. But time lost its familiar dimension up here, when you could read a newspaper at ten o'clock at night. He sat on an outcropping of rock that formed a seat and a comfortable backrest, reading the bundle of letters while Julie cooked supper. When he'd finished he turned to the last page Kat had written:

. . . When we got back here, Andrew dug out an old projector of his father's from the attic and insisted on playing it through. I wish now with all my heart and mind and soul that he hadn't. It's weird enough seeing photos of your parents and their friends when they were your age, looking smooth-faced and young, and knowing one day you'll be like they are now, with wrinkles and everything, never mind viewing what was on that film.

And that, of course, was when it all started . . .

Julie came out, a bottle and glasses in her hand. She sat down beside him and poured Glenmorangie. 'Cheers.'

After that, they sat in silence. *That was when it all started.* But how had it gone on?

They watched a shag, or was it a cormorant, take possession

of a seaweed-covered rock that jutted out from the sea, spreading out heraldic wings. Then hunching over, brooding and motionless, head drawn back, as if listening for the movement of its prey in the water. The dying sun reflected light from its metallic green plumage. The sunsets here were spectacular, a golden cliché of every sunset ever extolled by poets. Julie touched the bundle of letters. 'Have they been any help?'

'Insight, oh yes. No evidence.'

'This might help. Sorry, I'd put it aside to answer, forgot to give it you with the others.' She took a bulky envelope from her pocket and gave it to him . . . Kat's last letter. 'This is the one that really counts, from what I remember.'

He opened it and began to read.

The shag dived, hardly disturbing the surface of the water. The fish disappeared down its gullet and it settled down to wait again.

21

24 Belmont Avenue, 12th June

Hi, Jools,

I'm so happy for you, that you eventually made it – to somewhere that sounds very nearly like Heaven! Good for the soul anyway, as you say. I long to be there with you, but I know you've gone there purely to be away from everyone. You need space, and I understand that, honestly I do, more now than I've ever done. Because I've managed to get myself into just as bad a mess as you, now, can you believe it? What have we done, both of us, to deserve this?

That's something I've been asking myself a lot lately. Everything in the world seems to have fallen apart, just when I really thought I'd got my act together this time, that I'd finally found what I wanted at last, all the things I'd been looking for, the feeling that my life was begining to go somewhere good, at last. But now I wonder if I'm the sort of person who's destined never to be satisfied with anything – or anybody, to be more presise.

Yes, I know, I'm being maddening again and I _did_ promise you . . . so, I'll try to describe how all this has happened, though I hardly know where to begin.

Luke, I suppose. Yes. That's when it all started to go wrong.

He's very tall and thin and tense, always on the move, with winged eyebrows and high cheekbones and dark hair that grows in thick, flat curls against his skull. His eyes are very dark, too – I'm never sure whether they're dark blue or dark brown, but they have sort of bluey-green lights in them when he's angry, or amused.

Well, that's what he looks like. What he is, is something else. A dark angel, as I said. If that sounds over-dramatic I'm sorry, but that's how I always think of him. You see, even though I feel this wonderful, terrible, iresistable attraction, I know there can be a darker side, that there's something destructive about him, too. That phrase, dark angel, came into my mind as soon as I saw him. His name making some association with Lucifer, the fallen angel? Some premonition of what was to come? Maybe.

I fell under his spell the moment I saw him in the Green Man, just like they fall in love in books. I know why they use the word, that was exactly how it was, as if I'd tripped and fallen. Flat on my face, winded. Yet at the same time feeling marvellous. Maybe it was a reaction, something I needed to redress the balance, to put me back on an even keel after those awful, endless months of watching Dad die. But I'm not going to dwell on that.

I was certain that Luke felt the same about me, too, though it soon became obvious he didn't, not in the same way. Sex, yes. Love, no. Perhaps it's true what they say – there's always one who loves and one who's loved. In our case, I'm afraid it _is_ true. I went on loving him, even though it turned out, when he'd learned more about me, that he had quite other interests in me, other uses for me. It never pays to be certain of anything, certainly not with Luke. Niether of us said a lot at that first meeting, apart from yes and no, while Jamie explained to me about meeting Luke in Italy, and Luke deciding to come and work in England. But it was as though a hot wire was strung between us, sending electrical impulses. At the same time instinct was warning me that this was something I should not allow to happen. There are times when instinct should not be ignored.

Luke's mother was Italian, the second Italian wife of his English father. She died when Luke was born. His father couldn't face up to the

207

responsibility of bringing up a baby alone and took off, leaving Luke to be brought up by various foster parents. That tells a lot about Luke, I think. All he has of family is a much older half-sister, by his father's first wife. Her name is Gabriella. I don't know much about her, except that she was beautiful when she was younger, and she had long hair, too, Luke told me, gathering mine up at the back as he likes to do, and holding it in his hands as if he was weighing it.

'Is that why you like me? Because I remind you of her?' I asked, feeling a little jealous.

'No! You're not in the least like her. And I forbid you ever to try to be,' he answered, scrunching up my hair in his fists and pulling it so tight it jerked my head back and brought tears to my eyes. He laughed and let it go when I cried out. 'You won't, though. I'll personally see to it that you don't.'

Of course, that made me long to know more about Gabriella, but after that I daren't ask. Luke had closed up, as he always does when he thinks he's giving too much away about himself. It's very noticeable how he steers clear of personal things. In a rare moment of confidence, he once said he was going back to Italy when he'd cleared up some private business. He didn't say what it was. And he hasn't yet said anything about taking me with him.

He's not a great talker, anyway, except when he's in the mood. He prefers deeds to words, he says, and thoughts to either. And it's true, he can sit for hours, staring into space or more usually into his glass of red wine. Not that he drinks too much, often he'll spend the whole evening over one glass of plonk, but he always has to have one handy – he'll twiddle it round on its stem, gaze into its depths as if it was a crystal ball. Smoking and smoking, one cigarette after another.

He's a good listener, though. He has the knack of being there just when I want to talk, like about my father, or Max. Especially Max. He's obsessive about him, always asking me questions, and sometimes I've wondered if he guesses there was more to our relationship than I've admitted. Although he acts so cool with me, he's terribly jealous. If I so much as look at anyone else, he sulks for days, either that or he's so fierce with his lovemaking that he hurts me.

I've tried to shut Max from my mind ever since I left Orbury, but I can't. I'm afraid of what he might do. He doesn't forget or forgive easily. I tell myself OK, I made a big mistake, but so did he . . . It doesn't help much. At times he can get very angry, and it's

208

all the more devastating because he doesn't shout or even raise his voice.

It was cowardly, running away like that, but how could I bear to see him, and speak to him, after seeing that film?

It was so bad it couldn't, to my mind, have possibly been erotic. I won't dwell on it, on what went on in the simulated sexual antics department, and as for the story, and the so-called acting! In other circumstances, I might have found it hilarious, but not as it was. I'm not a prude, heaven only knows, but when it's someone you've known, loved and respected, it's quite different. Max, of all people!

Before that, when he asked me to marry him, I was astonished. I'd always thought of him as a kind, dear friend. But he told me not to rush, to think about it long and seriously, and consider what it would mean. And that was good advise, the more I thought about it, the more advantages I saw in being married to an older man, especially to one like Max – not only the material advantages, either, though they weren't to be sneezed at. I saw nothing wrong with him being so much older than me – physically, he's still extremely attractive, very sophisticated and experienced, but also kind and knowlegable, and he simply oozes charisma. If I married him, I knew I'd have a wonderful life. Like the heroine in Rebecca, but better than that, because there'd be no ghost of Mrs de Winter to worry about. And Mrs Seddon's a duck, not a bit like that creepy Mrs Danvers. Come to think of it, he was a Max, too, wasn't he?

He bought me a ring when I agreed, a truly fabulous Art Decko style diamond with emerald and diamond shoulders, but I couldn't wear it because of keeping our engagement a secret from Dad. Max came up with some deep pschycological reasons about father figures and edipal jealousy complexes or something, which is maybe a cleverer way of saying what I was thinking, that Dad just wouldn't have liked the idea of me being married to someone of his own age, particularly as it was his old friend.

But then, even before Dad died, I met Luke, and everything changed. I don't mean I just switched off my feelings about Max, just like that, how could I? It was far more complex. I still loved him, though not in a sexual way. You might find this hard to believe, but as a matter of fact we'd never had sex, Max and I. It wasn't that either of us was averse, but we were both content to let things take their natural progression and we hadn't yet reached that stage when I met Luke.

I couldn't help what happened, but it's made me feel ashamed, as though I'm destined to go through life never feeling deeply or seriously about anyone or anything. Six months ago I felt Max was the answer. Who knows what I might feel about Luke in six months time?

They're quite alike in many ways, Luke and Max – the same tall, slim build, very similar way of walking, the same way of thinking before they speak. But Luke can be cruel, with words as well as physically. Sometimes, I think he does it deliberately to make me cry, then he can be sweet and gentle and sorry. Whereas Max is never anything but kind.

That's why seeing that ghastly film was such a shock. Once I'd seen it, I knew why Dad wanted it destroyed. What I didn't know, and couldn't begin to imagine, was why they'd ever made it. What was the point of it? How could they? And what had Dad to do with it? I thought at first – horror! – that he was the second man in the film, but no one could ever have taken that one for my big, gentle Dad.

Andrew managed to put aside any scruples he might have had about my owing anything to Dad and had gone behind my back and had the film transfered to video. When he told me what he'd done, I was furious and demanded it back, but he wasn't prepared to hand it over so easily.

'Kathryn, we've all agreed, haven't we, that we have a moral obligation to do all we can to stop that road being built?'

'Yes, but – '

'Yes, but that's the whole point, isn't it?'

Andrew can argue all night, if neccessary, and he was backed up by the others. They're all so much better at that sort of thing than me. Mary, I could see, despised my lack of what she calls intellectual stamina, and Rabbit likewise.

So in the end I said yes, all right, I would, just to shut them up.

But I didn't mean it. I'd already made up my mind what I was going to do, and it wasn't what they thought. It was important to go along with them, though, otherwise they'd never relinquish the video to me, never mind that it was mine by rights.

Andrew has it all worked out. He and I sussed out the Freyning Manor Hotel. It's a very swish place and we had a meal there in style one evening, with a walk around the grounds before we ate. Andrew made me wear dark glasses and dress down so I wouldn't be recognised when I book in under an assumed name! Naturally, I've chosen yours.

I knew you wouldn't mind. I've used it so often before, I shall be able to act naturally when anyone speaks to me. Andrew is going to send a letter to Maggie Vye, telling her to meet me in a little dark corner off the main bar, where I'll hand over the video in exchange for a written promise that she'll stop the new road.

Frankly, I think this is a grotty plan. Sometimes Andrew, who is usually clear-minded, lets his enthusiasm run away with him and comes up with suggestions that are way off the beam. How he thinks Maggie Vye, alone, can stop the plans for the road going ahead, is beyond me. Or that she would agree to it if she could.

But it doesn't really matter because I've no intention of asking her to do that. I shall meet her, as they've arranged, and I shall hand over the video, telling her where I got it from, but I shan't demand promises or anything else. It will be hers to do with as she wants.

I haven't been able to sleep much since I came to Belmont Avenue. My bed's lumpy and it's hot and stuffy in this titchy bedroom and if I draw the curtains back there's a street lamp outside that shines into my eyes. My room at Orbury was the size of all three bedrooms here put together, and I could leave the windows wide open and hear the breeze rustling the leaves on the trees outside.

I have to confess that although I despise myself for it, I miss all the ease and luxury of Orbury. I miss Alice, too, nice old dog. And, most of all, Max. I look at his beautiful ring and I know now that I shall go back to him and ask him to take me back after this is all over. I'm not sure that he will, more likely he hates me for what I've done.

Meanwhile, I think of you in your lonely cottage on the shore and I wonder if you could bear to think of me coming to join you there for a few weeks?

Luv

22

The police surgeon, Dr Henry Ison, came to the last of the letters Kat had sent to Julie, drained his coffee cup and held it out for more in response to Abigail's offer. She poured herself a refill at the same time and stood by the window in her office, drinking it, watching the doctor as he began reading again.

Late last night Mayo, having arrived back from Scotland, had dropped the whole bundle of Kat's letters at her cottage, saying no more than that he'd spoken to Sheering and would see her at the station the next morning. Confident that by then she would have read and thought about them – incidentally ensuring that she hadn't slept much after doing so.

Together, the letters provided an almost unbearable picture of what the last few weeks of Kat's life had been. It was tempting to read between the lines, to feel that Kat had had a premonition that she was rushing towards disaster. But that was looking at it with hindsight. Revealing as the letters were, in a way, they posed as many questions as they answered.

Abigail had arrived early at the station to find Mayo had already been there for an hour, back in charge, ready to blow a stiff wind through the ranks, or to kick somebody's backside. She smiled. It was nothing to worry about. It simply meant he had the bit between his teeth, the urge to get things moving. Things were back to normal.

Glenda Nightingale had probably sensed this, and welcomed his return even more. At any rate, Abigail found her getting ready to depart almost faster than decency allowed, scarcely able to hold back long enough to perform the handover, unable to hide her relief at shaking the dust of Lavenstock from her feet and getting back to whatever fish she'd been frying in Hurstfield. Apparently satisfied that she'd been able to nurse the case along without having had to make any significant personal contribution. Not for the first time, Abigail wondered about some senior officers, male or female.

Ison folded the last letter into its envelope and sat back, raising a quizzical eyebrow. He'd been called into the station to examine a suspect who was claiming amnesia after having attacked a school crossing lady for holding him up on the way to work: she'd retaliated with a sharp clout from her lollipop. The assailant didn't remember a thing about the incident, he said. The doc thought he was pulling a fast one, but couldn't ignore the fact that it might be genuine.

He said amiably, only half joking, 'Got more than I bargained for when I came in this morning, didn't I? And now I presume you want me to give you the benefit of my professional experience in exchange for the coffee?' Looking at his watch, meaning if so, please get on with it, I've more to do than spend half the morning here. Joking to cover the emotion engendered by the letters he'd just read, in view of what he'd been told about them. Face half obscured by horn-rim glasses and a large straggly moustache, resembling some small, furry animal, Ison was an overworked GP, a kindly and good-humoured man who also happened to be a particular friend of Mayo's, sharing many of his interests, predominantly that of music. His police work, though adding to the burden of his working life, occasionally brought him into contact with one of those cases which touched on his endless fascination with the complexities of the criminal mind. In this particular case, he had an added reason: he'd been called out to Freyning Manor when Kat's body was discovered, as required, to pronounce her officially dead before Timpson-Ludgate had been called in, and found her to be a young woman he'd seen through childhood coughs and sneezes, measles and mumps.

'Lord, I'm no expert,' he said when Mayo asked what he thought about the contents of the letters, the murder, 'it's a jungle, this sort of thing. You need to get yourself someone far more qualified than I am.'

'Oh, come on, Henry, we're not asking you to commit yourself to anything, just give us the benefit of your opinion.'

'Well, I saw Katie's body . . .' He paused. As a doctor, a police doctor at that, he'd necessarily grown a certain detachment, but he was only human, and the sight had sickened him. 'All right, if my opinion's all you want, I go all the way with T-L. Sexual connotations, without a doubt. You've got a psychopath here. Sexual impulse turned in on itself, maybe provoked by rage, jealousy, sexual inadequacy.'

With that now admitted, that darker motivation now on the surface, the room felt colder: they all knew that psychopath meant not mad, but totally antisocial. No sense of right or wrong, no remorse. It meant not only the inadequates who spent their lives in and out of prison because they couldn't distinguish right from wrong, but also the aggressive thugs. The serial killers.

'Or the other kind,' Ison added, 'the man who so far hasn't killed because the circumstances for committing a murder haven't previously arisen. Leading an apparently normal life, as many of them do.'

Take your pick, in fact, Abigail thought, mentally reviewing their list of apparently normal suspects: Jamie Conolly, Max Fisher, Luke Raeburn, the inmates of Belmont Avenue, the amateur members of the so-called protest group ... Old Uncle Tom Cobley and all.

'Anybody, in fact.' But in her mind, it wasn't just *anybody* ...

'Quite,' Ison agreed. 'A psychopath doesn't wear his murderous intentions on his sleeve. One of his chief characteristics is that he appears normal. Don't forget, you're looking at someone devious, plausible. His execution of this crime could be very complicated, he's probably congratulating himself on fooling you, having led you up the garden path and covered his tracks completely.'

'Not completely, they never do that. We'll just have to trip him up with his own cleverness, then,' Mayo said.

'Which he very well may have done already. That's just it, y'see. They're often too clever by half. I'll repeat, he's not mentally ill, he's entirely sane, simply totally and completely asocial. He probably believes he has a perfect right to do what he's done.' He stood up, brushed biscuit crumbs off his jacket. 'And that's all I can tell you ... amateur stuff, I'm afraid. You want any more, you'll need a specialist opinion,' he said again.

'This'll do very well to be going on with, Henry,' said Mayo.

*

And after that, within a few hours of Mayo's return, unfairly or just the devil's luck, information began to come in from all directions.

'Let me see all we have on Luke Raeburn's background,' he'd said, looking through the various files spread out all over his desk (now firmly returned to its own position). 'His sister is called Gabriella –' referring to Kat's last letter – 'and Maggie Vye says someone called Gabriella Fonseca was in that film. He may have wanted that film pretty badly – though it seems to me if he was in with Group Six, he could surely have got hold of it somehow, without resorting to murder. But it's a connection that wants looking into.'

Farrar was the one deputed to do the looking into, since a quick result was what was needed, and a quicker result than anyone had dared to hope for was what they got. Before everyone knocked off for the evening, in fact. This bloke was so bloody efficient, not to say lucky, it was a pity, really, that he hadn't achieved the promotion he so richly deserved, that would have got him out of the way and left everyone else to muddle along in their own fashion without having feelings of inferiority heaped on their shoulders.

'Guess what?' He came in, barely troubling to hide a superior smirk, seeming to have risen above his domestic problems. 'The good news is that Luke Raeburn changed his flight at the last minute. He didn't leave for Italy until Sunday evening. Plus, he drives a red, M reg Montego.'

'Does he, by God? And what time was his flight?'

'That's the bad news. Eighteen fifty-three hours.'

'Hell. On the other hand, he might – he *might* just have made it, if he drove straight to the airport. Bring him in. And have his car seen to.'

Farrar left, almost, but not quite, clicking his heels.

Then it was Deeley's turn to win the gold star, less spectacularly, but equally to the point.

Door-knocking, talking to neighbours, was an unrewarding undertaking at the best of times, unless you got lucky. When the only neighbours in question were likely to be either one or two on the elderly side of sixty, occupying the dingy flats above the row of shops, or lying dead in the cemetery opposite, it was worse than usual. The other frequenters of the cemetery, the druggies and drop-outs, were not inclined to be communicative on the subject of what they'd seen. Nevertheless, Deeley struck oil when he came to the flat above the seedy dentist's. He'd received no answers from any of the others, until this one. He kept his thumb on the bell and was just about to turn away when a crotchety old man, gnarled as a tree root, opened the door. Deeley soon learned why the other bells had been ignored: the old fellow, who gave his name as Ron Capstick, informed him with a tetchy pride that he, and the young chap that lived above the sewing shop, were now the only occupants of the flats. Most of the shops used their upper floors as storage premises. It wasn't a nice neighbourhood at night, he didn't go a bundle on it himself much, nowadays. Not a lot of people would, Deeley suspected. But, old Capstick went on contentiously, he'd lived there thirty years and he wasn't going to have the bother of moving, not for nobody he wasn't, he'd stay here till they carried him out, feet first. Deeley said, 'That's the ticket, Dad,' and accepted a cup of tea, eventually learning that Capstick hadn't seen or heard the young chap (whose name he didn't know) taking his red Montego out on Sunday afternoon. Might've been when he was having his nap. He hadn't seen him come back, neither. But just a minute, he'd heard him. Seven thirty, just as *Last of the Summer Wine* finished on the telly. Best programme of the week, that was. No violence, and the sex was all in the mind, eh?

What sex was that? Deeley wondered, thinking he must have missed something. Nibbling a chocolate Hobnob he recalled there were no garages round the back of the flats, just parking slots, none of which were at present occupied.

'Seven thirty,' Mayo repeated, when Deeley came in to report back, grinning like a fool at having gone one better than Farrar. 'When Raeburn was allegedly on his way to Italy.'

'When Raeburn actually *was*, sir. I've confirmed that he checked in at six forty-five for the eighteen fifty-three flight to Rome.'

'Well, good work, Pete. It seems as though Mr Raeburn still has some explaining to do.'

*

216

'You were originally scheduled to leave for Italy on Saturday morning. Why did you change the time of your flight to Sunday evening, Mr Raeburn?'

'I had some unexpected business to attend to here.'

'What sort of business would that be?'

He was very pale and appeared much more Italian than he had on the previous occasion when Abigail had visited him at home. In profile, he had the true Roman nose, resembling one of the emperors on an old coin, especially when he looked down it. 'Personal business. I don't have to tell you what it was,' he said coldly, living dangerously. Maybe he hadn't come up against anyone like Mayo before.

But Mayo knew what the occasion demanded. He said mildly, 'You might be glad to, when you hear what we've got to say. But let's begin with you. Tell me what you were doing in Freyning Woods at around seven o'clock on Sunday evening, will you?'

'I wasn't *in* Freyning Woods at seven o'clock on Sunday evening. At seven o'clock, I'd just boarded an aeroplane on my way to Rome.'

'What if I tell you we have a report that you were seen in the woods at that time? That you helped two men to lift a deer that had been run over into the back of a truck?'

'*A deer*? What is this? Are you putting me on?'

The reaction seemed entirely spontaneous. If he was acting, he was doing a rather better job than most of the soap opera characters on TV. But however well he acted, he could not have been in Freyning Woods at the same time as he was sitting on the eighteen fifty-three to Rome. Nor parking his car at seven thirty, as Ron Capstick had stated. But Dustin Small and his mate were unreliable witnesses, with only an approximate idea of the actual time they were dealing with the deer. And the time of Kat's death could not be pinned down to within fifteen minutes. 'How did you get to the airport?' he asked Raeburn.

'I always take a taxi – well, a minicab – when I'm flying anywhere. Costs hardly more than long-stay car-parking charges and you're not likely to arrive back and find your car vandalised or missing. I always use the same driver, name of Chaz Dawson.

He'll confirm that he picked me up just before half-past six, and I checked in fifteen minutes later.'

'Didn't leave yourself much time, did you? Eight minutes, that's tight! You'd have missed it altogether if you'd picked up any traffic.'

'Well, we didn't.'

'So it was Rome, where you were going? On Palgrave's business?'

'Sure, on Palgrave's business. They'll confirm that, too.'

Mayo let his contemplative glance rest on Raeburn as Abigail asked, 'What's your connection with Gabriella Fonseca?'

'I don't know anyone of that name,' he replied, after an almost imperceptible pause.

'You told Kat Conolly that you had a half-sister called Gabriella.'

'Kat?' He was rattled, evidently wondering how they knew that. His dark eyes flickered, lit with blue-green glints in the way Kat had described; to Abigail, they looked like the oily reflections of petrol spilt on a puddle. After a moment of throwing disdainful glances from one to the other, he decided that reasonableness was a better bet, and came down from his high horse. 'Yes, I have, just that I didn't realise you meant her. She's Gabriella Manfredo now, Fonseca was her maiden name. Can I smoke?'

Abigail pushed an ashtray across to him, let him light up. 'You didn't share the same surname?'

'Technically speaking, she isn't my half-sister. My father's first wife was much older than he was and Gabriella – her daughter – was already nearly grown up when he married her. She's nineteen years older than I am, in fact. My mother died giving birth to me, and my father promptly disowned his responsibilities and disappeared.' The years had not eased the bitterness. He drew deeply on his cigarette and, after a moment, resumed. Smoking, as before, made him freer with his words. 'I owe more than I can say to Gabriella. There was no one to look out for me after my father decamped and I was farmed out to foster parents. But as soon as she could, immediately she finished her studies, she took me in and cared for me.'

'She did a business studies course here in England, that's right?'

He nodded.

'What do you know about a film she acted in when she was over here at college?'

'Film?'

'Made in the early seventies, when she was over here.'

'Early seventies?'

'That's what we said,' Mayo said sharply and added, 'Don't try to pretend you don't understand. You're in deep enough trouble over this already, Mr Raeburn.' He turned to Jenny Platt, who was taking her own careful notes to back up the tape. 'Go and fetch it, will you, DC Platt?'

He and Abigail sat without speaking further, watching Luke, who was looking by no means as self-assured as he had been, while Jenny went out and returned with a labelled plastic evidence bag. Mayo laid it flat on the table so that its contents were clearly revealed. 'Do you recognise this?'

'Superintendent Mayo is showing the witness Exhibit 4,' intoned Abigail for the tape.

'What is it?'

'It's a razor, Mr Raeburn,' Mayo said drily. 'Of the type appropriately called cut-throat.'

The exhibit consisted of a pivoted blade which folded back into a slot in the flat, curved, ebony handle which was inlaid with mother-of-pearl. Open, the blade could swing free, and in use was held steady by means of a hook on the pivot, held between finger and thumb. A handsome, beautifully crafted piece. It would need practice and care to learn how to use it with confidence. The blade was wickedly sharp, about three inches long by three-quarters of an inch, with rounded ends. According to Timpson-Ludgate, it exactly fitted the profile of the incised wounds on the victim's body.

'You don't recognise it? We've every reason to believe this was the weapon used in the murder of Kathryn Conolly.'

Raeburn was looking at the razor with complete incomprehension. 'It's got nothing to do with me. I've never seen it before in my life.'

'How do you suggest that it was found down the side of the seat in your car, then?'

'My car?' He looked appalled. He knew now that he was, as Mayo had said, in deep trouble, but he could find nothing better to say than, 'Somebody must have put it there.'

'Indeed they must. Are you sure it wasn't you?'

'No!' This time he shouted.

'Let's go back. You nearly missed your flight by leaving so late for the airport. Was that because you drove out to Freyning Manor Hotel and killed Miss Conolly, took the short cut back through the woods and found the road blocked by a truck which had just run over a deer?'

'You're obsessed by this damned deer! I never saw *any* animals, never mind deer! '

There was a long silence.

'So you admit you were there, in Freyning Woods?'

Further silence. Jenny shifted on her chair. Mayo let the weight of his gaze rest on Raeburn. Raeburn looked at the lengthening ash on the end of his cigarette. He was sweating heavily. Even the flat black curls on his head looked damp. 'I was in Freyning Woods,' he said at last, 'but not at that time. Much earlier than you say, more like four o'clock, something like that.'

'It still sounds like too much of a coincidence to me.'

Another silence. 'I'd like to make a statement,' Luke Raeburn said, eventually.

23

'Don't ever tell me there are no coincidences in life. My job is art conservation and restoration, and before I came to England, I worked on various projects all over Italy. I'd been working in Naples and taken a weekend off in Amalfi the time I met Jamie Conolly. I've told you how we met, how we had a drink together after I helped him to get one of his group to hospital. It was then I discovered his father was in partnership with somebody called Max Fisher. That was a name I was unlikely to pass over! I daresay there might be several thousand Max Fishers but there was only one I was interested in and after talking to Jamie I discovered that was him.'

'Why were you especially interested in this Max Fisher?'

'You know already that Gabriella was at college in England. While she was there, she'd met Fisher, who'd swindled her out of a lot of money.' He mentioned the exact sum. In lire, it crossed the boundaries of probability. In pounds sterling, it still wasn't inconsiderable, even allowing for the passage of twenty-five years. 'She'd inherited money from her Fonseca grandfather, not a lot, but she had enough to lend him, short term, for some apparently infallible venture. It went wrong, and Fisher wouldn't return the loan, denied he'd ever borrowed anything from her. She couldn't take legal action against him – there was no proof, she'd simply handed him the money, trusted him. I think they were lovers at the time. And she couldn't get help from anyone at home . . . think of what Italian families are like. The Fonsecas are like that anyway, strongly religious . . . imagine having to tell them why she'd loaned Fisher the money! Even I didn't find that out until – until later. When I heard about Fisher from Jamie Conolly, I vowed I would find some way of getting it back – '

'Twenty-five years is a long time . . . your sister had apparently accepted the loss of her money. What made you think you'd any chance?'

'At the time he swindled her, she wasn't desperate for money. She had enough to get by, she had prospects. But now, things have altered. There's a child, she has a daughter who's ill and needs treatment, expensive treatment. Maybe you've heard of Total Allergy Syndrome? Mona has it, she's one of those children who are allergic to practically everything. The only way she can live is to have her food intake strictly monitored, live in a sealed environment the whole time. It's a terrible existence – for Gabriella, as well as Mona. She's passionately attached to her daughter, nothing else matters, her marriage has failed because of it, her career too. She's become embittered, lost her looks. She's anything but the beautiful, spirited person she was any more and she's spent every penny she possesses in searching for the right treatment for Mona. Quacks, faith healers, anything. Now someone in America, a reputable doctor, has come up with some form of treatment which offers hope. But she needs money, loads of it – her ex can't help, he's penniless. I'm not exactly without, myself, I earn a good salary at home in Italy, and I've offered whatever she wants, but it's nowhere near enough.'

'So you decided to take things into your own hands?'

'More or less. I applied for a year's leave of absence from my work, on personal grounds, and when it was granted I came over to England, to Lavenstock, got myself a job in the travel agency Jamie worked for. Very convenient, because I could go back and forth, and I could keep an eye on Fisher.'

'You mean you intended to threaten him?'

'I used no threat – in fact, I was very reasonable. I approached him, told him the facts and put it to him he had a moral responsibility towards Gabriella. He just wasn't interested. With all his money, his contacts, he wouldn't agree to funding the treatment of one sick little girl.'

He lit another cigarette, leaned back.

'You used Kat Conolly to get information on Fisher, didn't you, Mr Raeburn? Was it the money you wanted, or revenge?'

'I wanted to see him *pay*! Kat was living at Orbury House at the time, looking after her father, and very much in Fisher's good books.' He shrugged. 'More than that, I guess. I think he was probably sleeping with her.' Again that blue gleam in his dark eyes.

'No, he wasn't,' Abigail put in.

'How can you possibly know? Has he told you?'

No one answered, until Abigail said, 'It wasn't Max Fisher who was her lover. It was you.'

He shrugged. 'OK then, I was. Why not? I fancied her, and she was willing enough. I wasn't Fisher, a dirty old man, out to seduce her! Anyway, I liked the idea of taking her from him.'

Revenge in one way, if not another. Poor Kat!

'And then her dad died, and she came across that film. She ran away from Orbury House and went to Belmont Avenue, to Andrew Inskip.'

'Why not to you?'

222

He shrugged again. 'She'd never even stay the night with me. She said the cemetery gave her the creeps.' That was probably true, Abigail thought, remembering his empty room, his view of marble tombs and headstones and spaced-out junkies. She also thought of his cruelty, and Kat's ambivalence towards him.

'Did you know Gabriella had taken part in that film?'

He seemed to have realised the futility of continuing to deny knowledge of the video. 'Not until I saw it. And realised what the money she'd given to Fisher had been intended for. God, that made it really sick – that really turned my stomach.'

'Where did you see this film?' Abigail asked.

'At Belmont Avenue. I told them they were insane to think of using it as blackmail, way out of their depth. But Inskip had got the bit between his teeth and wouldn't take any notice.'

'You still haven't explained why you changed your flight.'

'I was going to Rome for Jenna Palgrave, and I thought I'd spend time with Gabriella as well. But there was something I wanted to do before I saw her. I changed my flight for one on the following day and tried to make another appointment to see Fisher on Sunday afternoon. He refused to see me – until I told him I knew where Kat was. That place of his, Orbury House, God, it made me sick! All that money he's churning into it – I know how much that sort of restoration swallows up – when Mona – when all that's needed is money!'

He lit another cigarette before the smoke of the last one had died away. 'There was someone with him when I got there, I think it was Maggie Vye, the MP. He made me wait nearly twenty minutes after she'd gone, then his housekeeper showed me into that place with the swimming pool in it. He was lying there beside it on a sun lounger, with a tray of drinks by his side, music playing from a stereo, like some damn movie star! I asked him again if he couldn't help Mona. And all he did was throw his hands out. He said if Gabriella wanted to write to him, he'd see what he could do. He wasn't made of money, but he'd see what contribution he could make, though he wouldn't promise anything. I saw red! I heaved the sun lounger up and tipped them both into the bloody pool. I was sorry he could swim, I'd have liked to see him drown. Childish, maybe, but I felt better. I left him to struggle to get out as best he could, drove home and took the minicab to the airport to catch my flight.'

'Never get entangled with the law, Owen,' was one of the many pieces of good advice Joseph Barford had passed on to his son, 'there's no profit in it.'

His father had long since died, but Owen still occupied the original premises in Sheep Street: J. Barford & Son, New and Used Jewellery, Established 1929. Modest and respectable, like his stock, nothing flashy or over the top, Owen Barford knew his customers and what they were prepared to pay. His wife was always nagging him to branch out, but he wasn't of an adventurous spirit. Not too expensive engagement and wedding rings, watches and gold chains, plus a selection of giftware in the form of silver-plated trays, vases and canteens of cutlery had always guaranteed Barford's a steady, if unexciting, trade and he saw no reason to change. Most of the used jewellery he dealt with was in the middling range, some of which had passed through his hands, profitably, more than once since he'd first sold it. Occasionally, he would be offered a secondhand piece of finer quality, which he would sell on, knowing its value to be above the price bracket of his normal stock. After he'd made sure of the provenance, that is. He'd always kept his nose clean where suspect goods were concerned, mainly because he was basically honest but also because he was always mindful of his father's advice. It was rare for anyone to come into his shop with anything as superior as the ring he was showing to DC Jenny Platt.

'I had my suspicions straight away when I saw this. It's worth ten or eleven thousand of anybody's money.'

'As much as that?'

'Maybe more in the right quarter. These Deco pieces are very popular just now. Not a style to my taste, but each to his own.'

Oh, I don't know, Jenny thought, gazing at the hexagonal diamond, emerald and platinum ring with diamond shoulders, I wouldn't say no. 'It's a rare old knuckle-duster,' she conceded.

'Vulgar. But the central diamond is two carat, and the calibré emeralds are Colombian,' Barford said knowledgeably, turning it so that the light caught the smaller, square-cut diamonds on the shoulders and the deep green fire of the emeralds. 'Not the sort of piece a character like that would have come by honestly, I knew that straight away. He came in just as I was about to close and I took it into the back on the pretext of asking a colleague's opinion. He couldn't have *known* it was the police station I was talking to, but he either guessed, or he panicked. When I came back, he'd gone.'

'I'll give you a receipt,' Jenny said, though it wasn't technically his to have a receipt for. 'Just in case he comes back for it,' she added with a smile. 'Meanwhile, think you can give me a description of this man?'

'I believe I should have no trouble with that,' said Owen Barford.

'Raeburn's telling the truth,' Mayo was saying. 'He's a slimy bastard, and a scumbag the way he treated Kat Conolly. But he's not lying about this, blast him, he's telling the bloody truth!'

'I know,' Abigail said. 'Bottom of the suspect list, Raeburn.'

'Jamie Conolly could also be telling the truth.'

'More than likely. The only blood on him, apart from the calves' blood, was his own. Not a spot of Kat's. No doubt that he did go into her bedroom via the balcony. He probably thought it would be amusing to give Julie – as he thought – the shock of her life, and simply walked into the situation.'

'But what about Max Fisher? What was he doing there at the hotel, just at that particular time? All right, popping up like a Jack-in-the-box was something he did, and I know what he's said, but doesn't it strike you as a sight too opportune?'

'Yes, it does.'

'His reasons are thin, to put it charitably.'

With Liz Westerby's statement in mind, Abigail had telephoned him and asked him to come into the station to make a formal statement of his movements on the day Kat met her death. He came in at lunch time, when Mayo was busy with

Sheering. As soon as he entered, he'd dug into his briefcase and brought out the leather-covered notebook he'd given to Kat and handed it over, not, however, explaining how it had come into his possession.

'When we spoke on the telephone, you asked if I had seen this. I remembered later that she'd left it behind. I don't think it will help you substantially,' he'd said, 'and I'd be pleased if I could have it back when you've finished with it.'

She'd gone through the book since, and he was quite right. Nothing but an intensely private record of someone's innermost feelings. Intensely moving, in view of what had happened to Kat, but nothing that could be construed as having any direct bearing on her murder. Except . . . yes, perhaps . . .

In return for the book, she'd spared Fisher the indignity of letting him know that she'd heard how he'd been tipped into his own swimming pool, but she could see he suspected she knew. His face had become darkly congested at the mention of Luke Raeburn, but he freely admitted their meeting, and the reason for it.

'I'll confess, I thought his story of Gabriella's sick child a pure fabrication in order to extort the money he seems to imagine I swindled out of his sister. Well, we each have our own views on what constitutes a swindle, and she was never a truthful person – but I've made inquiries, and find the story of her child's illness is basically true. I've sent a cheque. Knowing Gabriella, I wouldn't be surprised to find she tears it into shreds.'

'After Luke Raeburn left you, you drove over to Freyning Manor.'

'Yes, I – wanted to see Jonathan Gould over one or two matters.'

'Rather an odd time to choose?'

He said suddenly, 'Yes, it was. But Maggie had just told me about this absurd arrangement to hand over the video. I was out of my mind with worry about Kat's disappearance and some-thing told me I ought to be there. I did talk to Gould, and was just about to leave him and go down into the bar, with some idea of keeping an eye on what was happening, when this chambermaid started screeching like a banshee . . . Gould left me and went to see what was going on. All hell broke loose and I –

didn't see any point in hanging around. Of course, I'd no idea it was Kat . . .'

'So what do you think?' Mayo asked Abigail. 'Could he have slipped in and killed the girl, before talking to Gould? And if we're talking psychos, how do you rate him?'

'You haven't met him, seen that house, the way he lives. I think he relates to nothing except how it affects him personally. And that razor – well, it's just the sort of thing he'd own, maybe even use to shave with, I shouldn't wonder.'

'But how the hell did he get it into Raeburn's car?'

They fell silent.

It was a beautiful evening. Even the Town Hall had a certain louche grace about it, outlined blackly against a pink and turquoise sky with dark grey clouds moving like smoke across it. Abigail watched the pigeons jostling for the best positions during the coming night.

'Who did it, Abigail? You know, don't you?'

'I think I do. '

'And you're going to tell me it has nothing to do with that video – or only indirectly.'

She thought she'd known, subconsciously, all along, that the video had only been a means to an end, but her thoughts had only crystallised since the conversation with Ison, the interview with Luke Raeburn. 'I think it was used as a smokescreen for the real motive, yes, and to implicate someone else. Her attacker didn't come looking for it, he knew it was there, and deliberately left it.'

She told him what she was thinking. They tossed the idea back and forth, until finally he said, gloomily, 'It works. All we need now is the bloody proof.'

The telephone rang. She was the nearest, and picked it up. 'What? She has? OK, George. Send her up.' She put the telephone back on its rest and looked at Mayo. 'And Jenny's come in with something that might give us just that.'

24

The same dirty grey walls, the same greasy smell of frying. Andrew Inskip, slim, neat and compact in jeans and a white T-shirt that stretched across surprisingly well-developed pectorals. The taut figure of someone who worked out regularly. 'Oh, it's you again,' he said without enthusiasm when he saw Abigail at the door. His eye lit on Mayo's uncompromising gaze as Abigail introduced him and he spoke slightly more graciously, 'You'd better come in.'

Someone had been having a go at tidying up. The old cardboard boxes in the corner of the hallway had disappeared, along with most of the garments on the coat rack and the pile of footwear beneath. The floor had been swept. Several rubbish-filled black plastic dustbin bags stood about, a couple of large tea chests appeared to be full of the dusty artefacts which had previously occupied the now bare plate-rack.

'Having a spring clean, Mr Inskip?'

'I'm leaving. As soon as I can sell the house, that is.'

'What about your friends? Are they going as well?'

'They've already left.'

'A bit sudden that, isn't it? Where've they gone to?'

'Haven't a clue. They just felt it was time to move on.' He smiled his slightly diffident, disarming smile. 'I've just made some tea. Come in and have some with me.'

When they were seated in the back room, which had also benefited from the same sort of clearing out, Abigail said, 'It's John Rabbett we want to talk to.'

'Rabbit? Then you're out of luck.'

'You've really no idea where they are?'

'You might try his parents in Beaconsfield – but on second thoughts, not. He's strictly persona non grata there – on account of his lifestyle, you know. Daddy's a banker.'

'I see. Never mind, I daresay we'll manage to find him.' Abigail looked at the mug he'd handed her, which was slightly chipped, and the tea in it, which was slightly greenish, and put it on the table beside her. 'What's going to happen to Group Six when you move?'

'We've disbanded,' he replied loftily, not sounding too concerned about it. 'Or rather, I've disbanded the group. You can't run something like that if not everyone's of the same mind.'

'Dissension within the ranks?' Mayo asked.

'Something like that, I suppose. It's a case of how far you're committed, really.'

'Got cold feet when your plan went wrong, did they?'

'Which plan's that?' He was beginning to look wary.

'I'm talking about the idea you had to blackmail Maggie Vye over the proposed new road – which, incidentally, may or may not happen, I'm told.'

'I'm sorry, I don't know what you're talking about.'

'Oh, I think you do, but never mind that for the present. Plenty of time to talk about that, later. At the moment, we'd like to know what you can tell us about that ring Inspector Moon has there?'

Abigail was holding the diamond and emerald ring out on her palm. Inskip craned forward to peer at it.

'Sorry again, I can't help you there, either, that sort of thing's out of my orbit. Is it real? Looks like something out of a Christmas cracker.' He was making a joke of it, but his eyes had registered shock.

'Oh, it's real. Genuine diamonds and emeralds. You didn't know it belonged to Kat Conolly?'

'You can't be serious? That? You are, aren't you? Wow! And she told me she was hard up! How did you get hold of it?'

'John Rabbett tried to sell it earlier today. Not a good idea, as it turned out.'

'Rabbit?' He thought about that. 'Well, it's possible, I suppose, if you're sure it belonged to Kat. They – he and Mary – creamed off all her best possessions before they threw the rest away.'

'No, I don't think that's where it came from. She didn't leave it behind here. She was in fact wearing it when she checked in at Freyning Manor.'

Gould, of course, the noticer of Sierra Cosworths, Louis Vuitton luggage and expensive clothes and jewellery. 'Well, of course

I take note of such things, it's in my interests to place my guests, to know which of them to keep an eye on,' he'd replied testily, when inquiries had been made about the ring. Fair enough. In fact, he'd described it accurately over the telephone to Carmody before being shown it and asked to identify it positively. 'Everyone has their uses,' Carmody had commented, replacing the telephone. Abigail wished all witnesses were like Jonathan Gould.

'But if she was wearing the ring when – when she died,' Inskip was asking in a puzzled manner, 'how did Rabbit get hold of it?'

'Think about it.'

He was already there, and looking incredulous. Eventually he said, 'You're suggesting it was Rabbit who killed her? Rabbit? I don't believe it!'

'The person who killed her is the person who took the ring off her finger, and John Rabbett is the one who tried to sell it,' Abigail said ambiguously.

'He always was a fool.' Inskip shook his head. 'That's what I mean – he simply hasn't got the brains to do a murder like that.'

'Yes. That sort of murder takes a certain amount of intelligence to plan.'

She looked at him meaningfully, in a way he couldn't pretend to misunderstand, and the way he stared back, with that fixed, disconcerting stare, showed that he hadn't. She stared back, keeping eye contact until he broke it himself and, almost as if he couldn't help it, let his gaze wander among the piles of boxes, bags and tea chests which were standing about here, as in the hall. The room was looking very bare, denuded. Already the plate-rack had been cleared. It seemed as though he'd just begun on the books. 'Where are you thinking of going?' she asked.

'I may eventually go abroad again, back to America. I haven't made any final decision yet.'

She stood up and wandered over to where a couple of tea chests stood side by side. From one of them she idly lifted a painted African mask, an ugly thing like a gargoyle. 'Interesting, that.'

Inskip had come to stand beside her and now held his hand out for the object. 'Come over to the light and I'll show you ...'

He guided her over to the bay window and began explaining the meaning of the mask.

Mayo, too, had risen and was peering into the other chest. Inskip said, from the window, 'That's the junk box, stuff to throw away, the most interesting things are in there.' He pointed to the chest the African mask had come from. 'I'm sending the contents to a museum, in fact – I'm sure they'll be glad of them, as a collection. Take a look and you'll see what I mean.'

But Mayo was in quest of what he'd noticed resting on an old velvet cushion in what Inskip said was the junk chest – a clock, tarnished and neglected, imitation onyx, obviously not in working order, but he'd yet to discard any timepiece without first examining it. He lifted it, disentangling the cushion's fringe from where it had caught on a loose spandrel, gave it a cursory glance.

'I agree – you wouldn't want to be sending this to a museum,' he commented, putting it on the floor, looking at Abigail as he spoke.

Inskip's glance darted from one to the other, acutely aware of the sudden change in the atmosphere, a tautness and a tension extending itself between the superintendent and his inspector.

There was a frozen silence as Mayo extracted from his pocket a pair of latex gloves, pulled them on and bent over the chest again to lift out a small black suitcase which had lain beneath the cushion. He unzipped it and extracted a flat ebony case, inlaid with brass and mother-of-pearl. He opened it.

'What was it we found in that Montego, Inspector Moon?'

'A razor, with a black ebony handle.'

'Ah, yes. A cut-throat razor.'

Abigail started the tape of Andrew Inskip's interview.

The usual preliminaries: stating the identity of everyone present, the reminder that he wasn't obliged to answer any questions. Before beginning the interview, she asked once more: 'Are you absolutely sure you don't want to consult a solicitor?'

'Why should I go to the expense of a solicitor when I'm innocent?'

'Just as you wish, but I'll remind you that you are entitled to free legal advice. For the benefit of the tape, Mr Inskip shakes his head. All right, Mr Inskip, you understand we are questioning you about the murder of Kathryn Conolly at Freyning Manor Hotel on 29th June. We've made extensive inquiries which link you to the offence.'

Inskip sat back with his arms folded, as if the whole thing was a matter of indifference to him.

'We have every reason to believe you drove her to Freyning Manor that Sunday and later killed her by slitting her throat. To begin with, you were seen driving her there in her own car by the manager of the hotel, despite the fact that you told us you couldn't drive.'

'I didn't say I couldn't – I said I *didn't*, on principle.'

'That's splitting hairs. But all right, then, you pocketed your principles enough to drive her to the hotel and we have two witnesses who will identify you as the man seen driving a red Montego back through the woods later that same day. You stopped to help these men lift a deer that had been killed into the back of their truck, at approximately seven o'clock. What were you doing in the woods at that time?'

'I wasn't there. It must have been someone else who looks like me.'

Abigail raised her eyebrows. 'Their description of him tallies with you.'

She pointed to the flat black razor case which Mayo had found in the travel bag, now lying on the table, opened to reveal a velvet-lined interior, moulded to contain a matched pair of razors, one of which was missing.

'You've already identified this razor case as belonging to you, Mr Inskip.'

'It belonged to my grandfather, I believe, yes, maybe my great-grandfather, I don't know.'

'Nice little thing to have been throwing away. Collector's piece, I'd say, wouldn't you? Especially with the other razor to complete the pair. *This* razor – the one we believe to be the murder weapon. Can you explain how it came to be found in the red Montego owned by Luke Raeburn?'

'Since it's his car, I assume he put it there.'

'It was his car, but we're satisfied, from the witnesses' description, that it wasn't Mr Raeburn who was driving it. In any case, he was at Birmingham International airport at the time, which you knew because you found out from your friend Chaz Dawson – one of your group's supporters, isn't he? – that Luke Raeburn had booked his minicab to take him there. I suggest it was you who was driving the Montego – that you took it from his parking space, hot-wired it and used it for the purposes of the murder.'

'Suggest all you like – '

'Mr Inskip – Andrew – there's not a lot of point in denying your involvement in this crime. We've enough evidence to indicate otherwise. It looks bad for you, you must see that. Tell us your side of the story and it'll go better for you.'

'I object to this.'

Abigail leaned forward and looked him straight in the eye as she said, 'All right then, let's turn to something else and come to the video. What can you tell us about that?'

'What video are you talking about?'

'Now come on, Andrew, you know your protest group sent a letter to Maggie Vye, offering her a video, entitled *Goldilocks and the Three Bears*, in return for certain promises. There's no point in denying it. She has the letter to prove it, and we have letters which Kat wrote, detailing the plan.'

This was not welcome news to him and for several minutes he didn't answer, his mind working. 'All right then, I'll admit that – Kat found the film when her father died. It was creepy, but I decided to use it as leverage for support against the new road. Anyone who takes part in that sort of thing deserves so be blackmailed. It was pretty disgusting.'

'So you had a video made of it – which was later found in the safe of the bedroom where Kat was killed.'

He sat back, folding his arms. 'That doesn't mean I killed her – if I had, I'd hardly have left the vid in the safe, incriminating myself, would I?'

'Well, I think that's just what you did. Left it there deliberately, in order to incriminate someone else. Someone who featured in that video, hmm? Maggie Vye herself, maybe, who you'd made sure was in the hotel at the right time. Or Fisher. Or, more deliberately, Luke Raeburn, whose sister Gabriella was also in the film.'

'You can't prove that.'

'It was quite clever, Andrew,' she said admiringly, 'trying to suggest the video was the motive for murdering Kat, when that wasn't the real motive at all, was it?'

'Don't ask me about somebody else's motives.'

'We're talking about your motives, Andrew. She was playing fast and loose with you. She'd no right to do that, had she? And that was why you did it. It's understandable, anyone might have felt the same.'

'Not me. I told her often enough she'd a right to choose who she wanted to go with, that nobody owns anyone else.'

'That's remarkably detached. And it's not true, is it, either? You cared, you cared a lot who she went with. So much that you concocted a complicated plot to get rid of her when she showed she preferred someone else. You don't like being thwarted, do you?'

'You're not getting me like that! You can't prove anything.'

Mayo leaned forward. 'Oh yes, we can, Inskip. Forensic tests have found traces of the victim's blood in the suitcase we found at your house. This blood came from your clothes. You stuffed them into the case and used it for carrying them away in.'

'I suppose you're saying I took my clothes off and walked out of the hotel in my birthday suit?'

Mayo said steadily, 'I'm saying you wore the change of clothing Kat brought with her. A loose shirt, denims, a sleeveless denim jacket. Unisex clothes. You're slightly built, you could easily have worn her clothes.'

'I'm not saying anything more. I've told you all I have to tell you and you won't manipulate me into saying any more. You'll never pin anything on me.'

'We've already enough to send you down for a very long time. The suitcase with her blood on it, the weapon – and what about the ring? You'll be glad to know that we've now traced John Rabbett, and he admits to stealing it from your possession after you boasted that night you had something which would make a significant contribution to your group funds.'

'You've found him?'

'Yes,' Abigail said. She was inclined to agree with Inskip's assessment of Rabbit. If you break into premises owned by a security firm, you can hardly be very bright. He and Mary Somers had been apprehended while attempting to get into the empty lodge at Orbury House, which they'd intended to use for free temporary accommodation, failing Rabbit's attempt to sell the ring. Their accommodation now, for the present anyway, was here in the police cells.

'He and Mary Somers have stated that you left Belmont Avenue with Kat on the afternoon of the murder to drive her to Freyning Manor. They also say you didn't get back until going up to eight o'clock. Where had you been all that time?'

'They're wrong. I got back long before then, but I suppose they didn't see me come in. I went straight up to my room and didn't come down until supper time. I'd like some refreshment now, if it's all the same to you.'

It seemed a convenient point at which to terminate the interview, and Inskip was sent temporarily back to his cell. Sooner or later, they were bound to get an admission from him. He couldn't go on lying in the face of all the evidence to the contrary. Six hours later, they were beginning to have doubts. And then, all of a sudden, the next time he was brought into the interview room, he changed tack. He'd had time to think, to consider the alternatives. He came in, cocksure, and admitted that he'd committed the crime, but insisted that he was innocent of blame for it.

'All right, I did kill her, but she asked for it,' he said. 'I didn't have any alternative, I was provoked into it.'

If this was going to be his tack, if mitigation was what he was aiming for, they had a long way to go.

'Asked for it?' Mayo said. 'That poor girl must have been terrified! Haven't you any compunction for what you did, Inskip?'

'She wasn't frightened, not Kat! Not until I made her take her clothes off, anyway. I asked her what she was complaining about, she'd taken them off often enough before for me.'

'Did you attempt to rape her?'

'I wouldn't do that!' he declared, seemingly outraged. But the

235

wash of colour that came and went in his face told them why he hadn't. 'I only wanted that she'd be nice to me. I wouldn't have harmed her if she had been.'

'That was why you went equipped with a razor, made those elaborate plans?'

Inskip chose to ignore this. 'Throwing me over when something that suited her better came along – she'd no right to do that! She'd made promises to *me*. She deserved what she got.'

The more he spoke, the more convinced of his own rightness he became. And once having admitted it, he was anxious to explain just how clever he had been. The statement he made was a mixture of self-justification and self-aggrandisement.

'I met Kat one day last summer, at the health club. Met her again, I mean. We'd known each other during our schooldays but we hadn't seen each other since. I'd been abroad, in America mostly. I came back last year to Lavenstock to take possession of the house my parents had left me, which until then had been let as furnished accommodation, and started Group Six. While I was in the States, I'd become interested in the protest movement, and I was sure I could use my powers of leadership to start a group here. Kat claimed she wanted to be involved, and for a while she was. We were lovers and I gave her everything she wanted, including permission to go and nurse her father. She swore she'd come back after he died, and I trusted her. She used to come to Belmont Avenue occasionally to help with the Group's work, but then she said she was getting scared and didn't want to participate actively. I suppose I ought to have guessed, then. Later, she told me it wasn't on between us any longer. She pretended there was no one else, but I knew she was lying. It was that partner of her father's ... I could see her comparing what I could give her with Orbury House, never mind that he was old enough to be her father. But even that didn't last. She was a fickle bitch. Before you could blink, she was between the sheets with that friend of her brother's.'

He spent the next half-hour telling them how he'd contrived to pay her out.

'Well, now, Andrew,' Abigail said, playing up to him, 'it was pretty neat, this plan of yours, wasn't it? Just let me confirm that we've got it right. After leaving Kat at Freyning Manor, you drove her car back to Lavenstock, parked it in the all-day car-park and walked across to Luke Raeburn's flat, where you picked his car up and drove back to Freyning, leaving the Montego just outside the grounds. You knew she was going to be in the room called Derwent, so all you had to do was to walk into the hotel, just like any other guest, and up to her room. You murdered her, then changed into her spare clothes, stuffed your own into her suitcase and walked out again. That was pretty cool,' she added, playing up to him again.

'Was, wasn't it? But if you look as though you know where you're going, what you're doing, people don't as a rule question you.'

This was true, but Abigail would have given much to know what would have happened had he bumped into Jonathan Gould.

His egocentricity was enormous, his glamorous self-image not even slightly dented. 'You'd never have suspected me at all if those two men hadn't run into that deer. I'd no choice but to help them move it, they were blocking the road. You'd have thought they'd have kept quiet about it, wouldn't you, seeing it was illegal what they were doing?'

'Life's like that, Inskip. Just when you think you have it made . . . '

Mayo's irony was wasted on him. He showed no guilt, or remorse, or shame, but plenty of self-justification. 'That's what I mean,' he said, 'she shouldn't have done that to me, should she?'

Mayo decided there and then that there was nothing further to be gained from prolonging the interview, nothing but increasing sadness and disgust, the longer they were in the same room as Inskip. He terminated the interview and Inskip was taken away. Back upstairs in his own office, he opened all the windows. Hot air belched in and he breathed in the air pollution rising up from Milford Road mingled with the beery fumes from the brewery floating across the town. After the air in the room downstairs, it felt clean and wholesome.

'He's right, of course, Abigail, the chance of him coming across Dustin Small and his accident with the deer helped us nail him – but we'd have had him, sooner or later.'

'Yes, it helped, but I was uneasy with him right from the first. It wasn't natural to be so detached, pretending it didn't bother him that she'd ditched him, not when it's the murder of someone you'd once been in love with – even Luke Raeburn showed more emotion! Though of course Inskip *was* totally indifferent – he didn't give a damn that he'd just killed her. I suppose he reckoned that if he showed he was upset over her leaving him, it would indicate jealousy and therefore a motive for murdering her. But he overplayed it.'

'Jealousy? That's too human an emotion for him! And he overplayed everything – all that elaborate fantasy about the video. It wasn't enough for him to murder Kat, just because she'd thwarted him, he had to try and implicate someone else.'

'That video was a stumbling block all along. But everything else was simple enough – naïve, almost, except that it nearly came off. But it was Luke Raeburn, mentioning that he'd used Chaz Dawson's minicab, that really clinched it. The name rang a bell. We'd interviewed him as one on the periphery of Inskip's lot, and I'd just read the name again in one of Kat's letters. From then, it was simple to trace everything back.'

But weeks of work stretched before them yet, preparing a watertight case for the Crown Prosecutor, gathering together enough evidence for a realistic prosecution. This must not be allowed to slip through the net because of insufficient preparation.

'For tonight, go home and get your feet up,' Mayo said. 'Or better still, come round and take pot luck with us.'

'Thanks very much, but I owe my parents a visit.' Parents and children had been very much on her mind lately. 'Besides, we'd only chew the case over and over.'

'Some other time, then.'

It would be good, he admitted, to go home and spend the evening in the cool garden with Alex, eating a civilised meal under the trees. A bottle of wine. Waiting for the promised telephone call from Julie. Mowing the lawn.

Ah well, you couldn't have everything.

*

Three weeks later, the coffin of Nora Vye slid through the curtains at the crematorium to the accompaniment of suitable hushed music. A few minutes later, Maggie walked out with Brian – Stephanie behind them in a big, becoming hat – out into the sunlight.

The number of mourners had surprised Maggie – the older you were, the fewer the friends and relations left to see you out. But Nora had been popular and also, apart from family and close friends, a surprising number of people had turned up out of respect for Maggie.

What a different response there might have been had things not turned out differently! she had thought as the chapel choir sang 'The Day Thou Gavest', the hymn Nora had wanted but she could never trust her own voice to sing, much less now.

She hadn't expected to feel regret and remorse at her mother's funeral, but she did. She found it hard to forgive herself. For many things, but mainly for never having told Nora that she had once had a granddaughter. No use to tell herself that it might have done more harm than good, hurt her mother that she had a grandchild she would never know. But one thing she was glad about: Nora had never had the pain of knowing that her own daughter had felt unable to confide in her the greatest event in her life. Too late, Maggie had realised telling her might have eased her own pain, helped her to cope with the knowledge that she could never know the child she'd named Kathryn.

I've no one else to blame, I am what I've made of myself, she thought. I knew what I wanted and went for it. Regardless. The bottom line is that I gave away my baby. And so, she had not attended that other funeral, feeling that she owed that at least to Diane. Instead, she'd said her own prayers, her own committal here, today, and somehow she'd found a sort of peace.

'Maggie?' As the last stragglers left after making their commiserations, as Brian and his family got into their car, she turned at the familiar voice, astonished to see Max Fisher.

'I had to come, Maggie. To pay my respects.'

He'd never known Nora. But she thought that perhaps, like her, he too had come to lay someone else to rest.

'I'm going away, selling up. I might not see you for a long

time. Unless . . .?' A look she had never seen before appeared on his austere, high-cheekboned face. Appeal. And loneliness, she thought. He put his hand on her arm, looked down at her from his great height. 'We were what they now call an item, once. A good item.'

'I don't think so, Max,' she said, gently touching his cheek. 'I don't think so at all.'

She turned and walked to the car, where Rollo was patiently waiting.